Praise for Kate Flora

Death in a Funhouse Mirror

"A gripping story about people you believe in and care about. The conclusion left me shaken, but satisfied in the truth of it."

—Anne Perry

"Deft characterization, wonderfully original humor, and the in-your-face charm and chutzpah of heroine Thea Kozak. The book is terrific."

—Booklist

"Thea Kozak is a refreshingly bright, brave, and formidable new heroine."

—Maine in Print

Chosen for Death

"Thea Kozak is appealingly tough-minded....Chosen for Death is a first novel that sticks in your mind."
—Washington Post Book World

"Flora's characterization is assured and her plotting is tight and credible."

—Publishers Weekly

"A salute to Kate Flora! Her first novel has a tart, refreshing, and satisfying taste."
—Jane Langton, author of Divine Inspiration

"A red-hot start to this new series."

—Kirkus Reviews

"A page-turner....This is the start of an important new career in mystery fiction."

—Mystery Scene

Forge Books by Kate Flora

DEATH AT THE WHEEL

Kate Flora

FORGE®

A TOM DOHERTY ASSOCIATES BOOK
NEW YORK

This is a work of fiction. All the characters and events portrayed in this book are either products of the author's imagination or are used fictitiously.

DEATH AT THE WHEEL

Copyright © 1996 by Kate Clark Flora

All rights reserved, including the right to reproduce this book, or portions thereof, in any form.

A Forge Book
Published by Tom Doherty Associates, Inc.
175 Fifth Avenue
New York, NY 10010

Forge® is a registered trademark of Tom Doherty Associates, Inc.

ISBN: 0-812-56484-7
Library of Congress Card Catalog Number: 96-8906

First edition: November 1996
First mass market edition: September 1998

Printed in the United States of America

0   9   8   7   6   5   4   3   2   1

In memory of my father, Robert Louis Clark

*A time to be born, and a time to die; a time to plant, and a time to
pluck up that which is planted.*
—Ecclesiastes

May the gardens of heaven grow green

ACKNOWLEDGMENTS

Once again, thanks to my readers for the nit-picking, attention to detail and general good advice. For technical assistance, thanks to Concord Police Chief Leonard Wetherbee, to attorney and road warrior Howard Cubell, and to Donnie and Jane Prentiss, who kept trying to get me behind the wheel. For great lines and good stories, thanks to Susan Clark, Greg Englund and Sara Lloyd. And thanks also to that anonymous gentleman on the flight back from Bouchercon in Omaha who sat next to me and talked about cars and weekend racing; he inspired the story. I have been well advised, but, this being a work of fiction, I have taken geographical liberties and perhaps factual ones as well.

DEATH
AT THE
WHEEL

CHAPTER *1*

SOME DAYS IT doesn't pay to get up in the morning but usually, by the time we find that out, it's too late. So it was with me on Easter Sunday. I'd been up since the dawn. Since before dawn. My church attendance may be sporadic but I love the Sunrise Service. I'm not sure that makes me Christian. There's something deliciously pagan in celebrating the return of life to the earth; yet the words of redemption, rebirth, and renewal were etched in childhood, and they still move me.

I stood out on the back deck of my condo, drinking coffee, looking out at the sparkling ocean. The wind, after a chilly spring, was finally warm, and the perfect way to spend the rest of Easter Sunday would be to walk on the beach and then curl up with a good book. Instead, like everyone else in the Commonwealth of Massachusetts, I was going home for dinner, toting the obligatory potted plant. I hadn't realized how widespread the custom was until I came out of my condo carrying a plant and discovered all my neighbors doing the same thing. As I drove toward Route 128, half the houses I passed seemed to be disgorging residents in twos and threes and they were all carrying potted plants. It was like some new form of Invasion of the Body Snatchers—invasion of the plant-toters.

I turned on the radio, searching for something that would lighten my mood. There was no mystery about how the day would go. It was all predictable. My mother, worn out from her efforts to produce the perfect meal, wouldn't be able to control her anxiety about my unmarried, childless state. As the only one of her offspring likely to give her a grandchild, my reproductive prospects were a source of great concern. She would make what she considered exquisitely subtle inquiries about the state of my romantic life. If I allowed that things with Andre were going well, she'd be even more unhappy. My being married to or even seriously involved with a state trooper didn't conform to her upwardly mobile, country club notions of the proper consort. I rubbed my forehead, trying to press away the incipient headache that threatened whenever a family dinner was inevitable.

My mother's unspoken reproach wasn't all I had to look forward to. My brother Michael would be there, too. Michael the artist. Michael the talented. Michael the disgruntled, a man who had never gotten over his childhood habit of taking out his moods on others. And with Michael came his chronic girlfriend, Sonia, the workout queen, self-involved, petulant, and so virulent she made Michael look sweet. Sonia's conversation was salted with remarks that would give Miss Manners heart failure; remarks that challenged my self-control. Had I ever considered breast-reduction surgery and didn't I want the name of a good hairdresser? Did I know that skillful makeup would cover the circles under my eyes? Once, after staring pointedly at my skirt, she had commiserated about how difficult it is to get stains out of silk, one simply had to give up and throw things away, didn't one. It's not sisterly of me, but if they still had Roman games, I'd relish feeding Sonia to the lions. The poor beasts wouldn't get much of a snack, though. Under her layers of drapy garments, Sonia is rail thin.

In our minds, though never mentioned, would be my sister Carrie, dead a year and a half now, the victim of a brutal murder. Alive, Carrie had been the misfit, angry, challenging, and difficult, a constant thorn in my mother's side. I had loved her like a mother myself, my little adopted sister, and my sadness at her death, and my guilt that I had not done more to help her still lingered, especially there in the house where we'd all grown up.

Through it all, my father, the lawyer known for never backing down, would sit tight-lipped and silent, a row of little frown lines between his eyes, and then begin talking about some unrelated topic of interest to him. My dad is a sweetheart. When I was little, I was daddy's girl, and being a lawyer, he used to come home and pose legal riddles for me, delighting in my ability to solve them. We're not so close now, a fact that saddens me, but in my sometimes tense encounters with my mother, he's wisely chosen to take her side. I don't feel betrayed, just disappointed. I understand. I love my family but much of the time I don't like them. Families are given to us to make us appreciate the value of being grown up and on our own.

The radio announcer was going on much too long about how happy I'd be with a new mattress and a bottle of Bud Light. I had one and didn't need the other. I gave up on the radio and switched to the CD player, treating myself to some reggae, glad I hadn't been penny wise and pound foolish and had sprung for some luxury options on my car. I loved my bright red Saab. My husband David's rusty old Saab, a solid and dependable winter car, had gotten me hooked on Saabs, and when I replaced it, I got another. David was dead, a fact that still caused me pain, and partly my choice of Saab was memorial—a tribute to his taste and judgment. I loved my car phone and my sun roof and in the winter, I loved my heated seats. But it was April and Easter and after the awful winter we New Englanders had endured, it was impossible to stay grouchy on a warm, sunny day, even on the way to family dinner.

My father opened the door and I entered a hall filled with the rich smells of good cooking. He looked older and tireder and I noticed, with the jolt these observations always bring, that his hair was almost completely gray. "Theadora," he said, "Happy Easter. Your mother's in the kitchen." He held out his hand for my coat. "How's Andy?"

"Andre," I said. "He's fine. Still in one piece." He didn't like my answer any more than I'd liked the "Andy." No one who knows him calls Detective Andre Lemieux "Andy."

Mom smelled like cinnamon and yeast and her cheeks were flushed pink from bending over the stove. She straightened up and came to meet me, a regal, impressive woman, 5´10˝, ample, the impossible hair I've inherited cut short and crisp. She was wearing the apron I'd made her in eighth grade. Once it had been a sunny yellow decorated with bright red and green strawberries, chosen to match the kitchen wallpaper. Now, sixteen years later, the wallpaper was blue, the apron had faded to a dull yellowish gray, and the berries were just darker blotches, but she still wore it. After a hug, she backed up and examined me carefully. "You don't look as tired as usual," she said. "Are things quiet at work?"

"Never," I said, handing her the plant. She set it on the counter next to another, still stapled into its paper wrapper. "Open it now," I said. "I want to see if you'll like it."

She waved a hand at her steaming pots. "I'm busy. . . ."

"Open it." I hadn't tramped all over the planet in the pouring rain to have my offering ignored.

With a sigh, she peeled off the heavy lavender paper and the intoxicating scent of gardenias filled the room, beating back the ham and sweet potatoes and baking bread. She pulled it out, beaming at the glossy green leaves and the profusion of rich, creamy white flowers. "Thea! It's beautiful. How on earth did you ever find such a thing?"

"Just a good detective, I guess."

Her eyes narrowed. "You're not involved in another murder, Theadora? Tell me that you're not."

"Murdering the competition, but that's all."

"Don't even joke about it, dear. You know how it upsets me. Now come in the living room. There's someone I want you to meet." She bustled out, shedding the apron as she went.

Knowing her, I was expecting an eligible young man. She never listens when I tell her I'm not interested, that I'm already involved. She believes Mother knows best. But it wasn't a young man. It was a young woman. Sitting on the couch. Well, perching on the couch. Tiny and blonde and fragile looking. Holding a toddler on her lap with her arm around a little girl. Despite the pink Chanel suit and the expensive gold jewelry, the large diamond on her hand and her superbly cut hair, she looked like a recent refugee, washed up on the shores of my mother's living room. And even though her eyes were brown instead of blue, she looked way too much like my sister Carrie. My lost sister Carrie.

I felt a surge of something like panic. My ESP isn't finely tuned but there might have been a flashing sign over the couch saying "RUN." I didn't know what was coming but I wanted to rush out of the house, jump in my car, and drive away as fast as I could. Instead I put out a hand and went across the room to meet her.

"Thea, this is Julie Bass. Julie, my daughter, Thea Kozak."

She smiled up at me and held out her hand. "I'm so glad to finally meet you. I've heard so much about you from your mother." She had a light, breathless, little-girl voice. With my mother hovering behind me, I leaned down, took her tiny, cold hand in mine and was pulled into a maelstrom of chaos, deception, and death.

CHAPTER 2

UP CLOSE, SHE was pale and had deep purple circles under her big brown eyes. When I released her hand, it settled weakly back on her knee as though she'd used up the last of her strength. Her eyes dropped to the children beside her. "These are—"

"Julie volunteers for me at the hospital," my mother interrupted. "She's an angel. An absolute angel. The best volunteer I've ever had. And these are her daughters, Camilla and Emma." Mom is head of the hospital volunteer program, where she uses her boundless energy making things go smoothly. She could as easily have run a corporation but she doesn't believe women should take jobs outside the home. She was smiling at Julie Bass with all the approval she always withholds from me.

I felt a twinge of jealousy for the neat little woman and her perfect little children, sitting there being smiled at approvingly by my parents. Obviously, Julie was doing it right—married, fertile, and a good little doobie volunteer. Not like me, with my sixty-hour weeks and unsuitable boyfriend. The only thing miss-

ing from the little picture-perfect family was a handsome husband.

I assumed he must be hidden somewhere and looked around
for him, but the only man there was my father. His smile gone,
he was staring sadly at Julie from his chair across the room.
When I turned, I saw that Mom also had a sad look on her face.
And now that her greeting was over, Julie looked sad, too. It was
like watching a play in a foreign language that everyone else understood. I'm impatient with mysterious behavior. I like to get
to the point. Especially when I have a headache and feel jealous
and cranky. "Your husband isn't with you?" I said.

The wide brown eyes flooded with tears. "Julie's husband is
dead," my mother said, her tone an implicit criticism of my lack
of tact. "That's why I invited her. I wanted her to meet you . . . I
thought you might be able to help her, since you understand
about . . ." She hesitated, looking for words. In that fleeting moment, I was afraid she was going to say he'd been murdered and
she wanted me to look into it. My lips were already forming a
firm "no" when she explained. "Like you, Julie lost her husband
in a car accident."

I sank down on a chair, trying to keep my dismay off my face.
I'm not good at it like Andre is, but he's a cop. He can lock feelings off his face in a most infuriating way, while my feelings tend
to show unless I make a major effort. It's been three years since
my husband David went for a ride in his friend's new Camaro
and ended up wrapped around a tree, but remembering still
hurts. I never talk about it. I don't even think about it that
much. Still, sometimes, in the middle of a perfectly ordinary day,
a whiff of aftershave or the shadow of a man hurrying will remind me of him and the pain comes back like it was yesterday.

My parents were watching me expectantly, waiting for me
to use my experience and wisdom to console Julie Bass. While
I don't get any respect from them, my family persists in believ-

ing that whatever is wrong, Thea will fix it, just as they persist in believing that within the family, there's no such thing as privacy.

I swallowed hard and tried not to disappoint them. "I'm sorry," I said. "Was his death recent?"

"Last weekend."

I stared at her, astonished. Stared at them all. What could my mother have been thinking? This woman shouldn't be out in public all neatly done up in her pink suit. She should be in her bedroom in dirty jeans crying her eyes out and pounding the hell out of her pillow at the incredible unfairness of it all. No wonder she looked like that porcelain skin would shatter at the first unkind word, like she was held together only by an act of will.

"Daddy's car hit a wall and he got all burned up," Camilla said, her blue eyes wide and serious. She had strawberry blond hair and was wearing a frilly pink dress of the sort my mother used to dress me in at Easter. A pink dress, matching pink socks, and little black patent leather shoes.

"Camilla," her mother admonished, "people don't want to hear things like that."

"How awful," I said, feeling like anything I said would sound idiotic. "Do you have family around here who can help you?" As soon as I'd said it, I wished I could take it back. If she had family, what would she be doing here on a family holiday?

"Only a brother. Duncan. He's up in New Hampshire. He . . . they . . . he and his wife Brenda invited me . . . us . . . up there, but I just wasn't up to the drive." The small, whispery voice floated up and down. "I don't know . . . I don't seem to have any energy these days. . . ."

"I think you're doing well to even get out of bed. I couldn't function at all, when David . . . at first." She gave me a brief, grateful smile, which made me wonder if she'd been surrounded by buck-up-and-get-on-with-it types. Our society is so uncomfortable with grief that we're always pressuring people to get over it. Knowing how I felt, I try not to do that to people. I sorted through my experience, trying to think of something useful to say. It all seemed so obvious, so trivial. "It does get better, but it takes time. And you have to be very kind to yourself. It's so easy to think about the what ifs—what if you'd been nicer, said all the things you meant to say . . . taken that vacation he wanted. . . . There's always something to beat yourself with."

She was staring at me but she wasn't looking. "I know exactly what you mean," she said. "I just keep thinking, what if I hadn't given him that driving course as a present? Then none of this would have happened." She buried her face in her hands and started to cry. Little Camilla handed her mother a tissue.

My mother gave me a reproving look. I might not measure up to her expectations, but I was expected to have all necessary social graces including the ability to read minds. I felt my hackles rise and stifled a sharp retort. Julie Bass had enough troubles without having to listen to us snap at each other. "I've got to check the food," she said. "Tom, why don't you get these girls something to drink?" She looked anxiously toward the door. "I wonder what can be keeping Michael and Sonia?"

"They're probably sitting out in the car, fighting," I suggested.

Dad came over to Julie and leaned down over her. He was tall and had to lean a long way, looking a bit like a protective crane. "Can I get you something to drink?" he asked, his voice gentle. He was curbing his usual vigorous hospitality in the face of her fragility.

"Yes. Please. Some Scotch and water. . . ." She hesitated. "No. Wait. A glass of white wine would be nice."

"Thea?"

"White wine."

"Camilla?"

The little girl beamed up at him, pleased at being included. "If it's all right with my mother . . . Emma and I would like soda? You'd like soda, Emma, wouldn't you?" Emma just buried her head shyly in her mother's lap. "She would," Camilla said with certainty. "But just a little, because she's small."

Julie nodded her assent. When he was gone, she looked at me apologetically. "He's such a doll. Reminds me of my own father. You're awfully lucky, you know, to have a nice family. And I know I shouldn't intrude on a family occasion like this," she said. "Your mother's been so kind to me . . . to all of us . . . and I couldn't face the idea of spending the day alone. Somehow the weekend seems so long. . . ."

"For me, it was the nights."

She smiled at her daughters. "These two keep me so busy that by evening I'm exhausted."

Camilla, who had opened a book she'd brought, snapped it shut and said, "The Easter Bunny forgot to come." Her voice was filled with the tragedy of the forgotten child. Her mother immediately began maternal efforts at distraction and offered to read the book. Camilla responded but her face remained sad.

I excused myself and went into the kitchen. "How long till dinner?" I said.

"Maybe half an hour. Why?"

"Camilla says the Easter Bunny forgot her. I was wondering if I had time to run down to the store. . . ."

She was immediately part of the conspiracy. "Sure. If you hurry. And there's that huge rabbit that Todd won for Carrie. I wouldn't mind getting it out of the house. I can't believe I kept it this long. And I know I've got some nice baskets upstairs. You know . . . I don't think you need to leave the house. I've got jelly beans left over from decorating the cake and some chocolate rabbits and a couple other silly things I bought for you and Michael, which you guys don't need. Look in the bottom drawer in the study and see if there's still any of that Easter grass. . . ."

In a matter of minutes, two fairly respectable Easter baskets were assembled and filled, two stuffed bunnies in decent shape trotted out, and I was back in the living room, feeling a bit like Mary Poppins. "You know what, Camilla? I think the Easter Bunny left your baskets here," I told her. "At least, there's something that looks like Easter baskets out in the hall."

She bounced to her feet with the rubber resilience of the young and then stopped, waiting for her little sister. "Come on, Emma," she said, holding out her hand, "let's go see." Emma, tiny like her mother, but dark-haired as well as dark-eyed, crept cautiously off her mother's lap and seized her sister's hand. Together they trotted to the door and disappeared. The hall echoed with childish shouts and then they were back, clutching bunnies and baskets, their little faces shining.

Julie Bass took a drink of her wine and set it on the table with a trembling hand. "Thank you for doing that. You're so kind . . . I'm afraid I'm going to cry again," she said. "That seems to be what I do most of the time these days. You'd think after a while a person would run out of tears."

I'd said the same thing myself once, to my friend Suzanne, and I knew exactly how she felt. I sat down beside her and put an arm around her thin shoulders. She buried her face in my shoulder and cried. I rubbed her back and murmured soothing little noises, thinking about the unfairness of life. Even through the wool of her suit, I could feel her bones. She was so little she felt like she might break in my hands. Oddly, inappropriately, I wondered how any man could bring himself to make love to a woman so small and delicate. That's how we were sitting when Michael and Sonia arrived.

Michael took in Julie's tearstained face and the two little girls in Dad's lap. "What's this, sister dear?" he said. "Have you begun to take in strays?"

"Charity begins at home," I said. "This is Julie Bass. She's one of Mom's volunteers at the hospital. She's just lost her husband. Julie, my brother Michael. And Sonia."

Sonia, hanging back behind Michael, curled her lip as though she thought losing husbands was in very poor taste. She probably did think that. Generosity was not in Sonia's emotional vocabulary. She'd been remarkably cold when David died. Never called, never visited or invited me over even though they had lived quite nearby back then. She made no effort to greet Julie. Instead, she stroked her sleek hair and held her hand out in front of her as though admiring her nail polish. On the third finger of her left hand was a gorgeous emerald. Michael and Sonia had been semiengaged forever and had lived together for years, but they'd never bothered with the formality of a ring before. This was serious.

I managed to convert "Oh shit!" my first reaction, into a sisterly expression of joy. "Oh, Sonia!" I said. "Does that mean? Are you and Michael . . ."

She actually simpered. There's no other word for that twisted wriggle. "Yes. Yes we are!" she said. "Can you believe it?"

If I could believe in the IRA and the PLO, I could certainly believe in Michael and Sonia getting married. In their own perverse ways, the two of them were made for each other. "Oh, Sonia," I said. "How lovely. Are you going to do the whole formal wedding business?"

"Of course," she said, smiling down at her ring. "And I do hope you'll be one of my bridesmaids."

I tried not to grimace. Sonia's taste made my teeth hurt. I could easily imagine Grecian dresses with one breast nearly bared—quite a sight when you're well endowed—or perhaps little Christian LaCroix puffy skirted minidresses with ballet tops or some sort of tribal dress complete with turbans. "I'd be honored," I said. Even though she doesn't like Sonia, my mother would be pleased. She was very disappointed when I didn't have a big wedding.

Julie got up and came over to admire the ring. I envied her grace. If our positions had been reversed, I would have run sobbing out of the room. Mom joined us and we all stood there making pleasant small talk about weddings. The scene had all the elements of a play. But who would write it? Albee? Shaw? Molière? Perhaps Beckett. Call it *Two Widows and the Bride-to-be* or *Waiting for the Wedding*. It was definitely not Neil Simon.

I grabbed my wine and took a gulp. When I set it down, I saw Michael watching me, a knowing grin on his face. Knowing but incorrect. Michael is under the mistaken impression that I drink too much. I repressed the urge to stick out my tongue. "Congratulations, Michael. Do you have a date for the happy event?"

"Labor Day weekend," he said.

Appropriate, I thought.

"Dinner's almost ready," Mom said. "Has everyone been offered a drink? Sonia? Michael? And you've all met Julie?" We murmured our assents. "I'm afraid I don't have a high chair for Emma."

"It's all right, Mrs. McKusick," Julie said. "She can sit on my lap."

"Linda. Please. You must call me Linda."

So all of us, Mom and Dad, a.k.a. Tom and Linda McKusick, and Michael and Sonia, and me, Thea Kozak, and Julie Bass and her two sweet daughters, all sat down to Easter dinner, and it was a lovely dinner. Mom is one of the best cooks I know. Camilla ate three slices of ham, Michael took a mound of sweet potatoes big enough for a family of four, Emma sat on Dad's lap and carefully picked peas off his plate with her tiny fingers and fed them to him, occasionally eating one herself, Sonia spent the meal carefully cutting pieces of lettuce into smaller bits and even ate a tiny piece of ham—she's perfected the art of converting air into calories—and Julie Bass rearranged the food on her plate and didn't eat a bite. I was hungry and ate like a horse, all the while thinking that Scarlett O'Hara's mammy should have taken me into the kitchen and fed me beforehand so I could have made a more ladylike display.

The conversation bounced between wedding talk and attempts to make Julie feel at home. Mom sang Julie's praises. Julie responded politely with reminiscences about her own family dinners, kind comments about the food she wasn't eating, and the pleasures of happy family celebrations in general, while Sonia fretted about the difficulties of finding a caterer who could do low-fat cuisine. No one asked about my work, which I didn't mind, and the only question concerning Andre was an oblique insult from Michael about whether I'd gotten over my "men in uniform" fantasies. I said I hadn't. I didn't waste my breath explaining that detectives didn't wear uniforms.

Afterward there was a cake with seven-minute frosting, decorated with jelly beans, as well as a more adult Key lime tart. We got through dinner cheerfully enough, but when we sat in the living room for coffee, Julie Bass's quiet sadness filled the room until conversation was impossible. As before, she and Camilla sat on the wide sofa with its cheerful chintz covers, looking lost and forlorn, and Julie seemed too worn out to keep up a social facade any longer.

Only Emma was unaffected. She'd fallen in love with my father and was sitting in his lap looking at a book. Dad is one of those men born to be a grandfather. Too bad neither of his own children were obliging him.

Ever a workaholic, I could practically feel the clock ticking as I imagined the mountain of stuff that was waiting for me at home. Finally, I just had to go. I quickly said and did all the right things, kissed everyone good-bye, and let Dad help me into my coat. Julie Bass followed me to the door, held out her little hand, and, when I took it, clung to me like a trusting child.

"Could I call you sometime?" she said. "It might help to . . . to talk with someone who understands."

"Of course. Anytime. And I do mean anytime. Midnight. Four A.M. Whenever. Sometimes it helps just to know there's someone you can call." I wrote my home number on it and gave her my card.

"You're so kind," she said. "I'm glad your mother invited me." I left her standing there, staring after me like an abandoned puppy watching its owner walk away, sad-eyed, innocent, and trusting.

I meant to go home, take my walk, and immerse myself in work, and that's what I tried to do. The walk on the beach part went okay, but when I got back to my desk, spread out my papers, and tried to make sense of the garbled materials the admissions director of Laidlaw School had sent me, I kept seeing Julie Bass's face. Wishing, though I knew better, that there was something I could do to make things easier for her, to ease the blow and shorten the period of mourning. She seemed so lost and helpless. So wounded. So stunned by the unexpected blow life had dealt her.

We were in a busy phase at work, trying to finish projects for schools that wanted them before the end of the academic year in order to do some strategic planning before their faculties left for the summer. I didn't have time for maidens in distress and other good works, no matter how great the need. If that was heartless, so be it. Irritated, I grabbed a yellow pad and started making notes.

The papers were such a muddle it was no wonder Laidlaw was having admissions problems. The admissions director, a cheerful, ruddy-cheeked old boy who'd gone to Laidlaw, worked for Laidlaw for forty years, and would willingly lay down his life for the place, was still back in the last century. The last straw was his avuncular habit, anathema in this age of sexual harassment, of patting young boys on the rump, a habit that he had carried over, without any thought of the consequences, to the young girls that Laidlaw was now admitting. Parents had been complaining and poor Mr. Cosgrove, bless his doddering old heart, didn't have a clue what the fuss was about.

The headmaster did, of course, but he suffered from another disability that runs rampant in independent schools—indecisiveness. He didn't want to do anything to hurt Cosgrove's feelings, like reprimand him or fire him, and Cosgrove was immune to remedies more subtle. It was ironic, really, that they'd decided to hire me to handle the problem, because they were paying me to tell them what they already knew—"Tell Cosgrove to shape up immediately or you're going to have a lawsuit on your hands too hot to handle"—and furthermore, I was going to follow it up by saying they needed to revamp their entire admissions system and begin looking for a competent new assistant director who could help them ease Cosgrove out the door.

Harsh, perhaps, but sometimes that's what EDGE, the consulting group I run with my friend Suzanne Merritt, is hired for—to provide people with paper spines when they lack backbones of their own. I worked efficiently for a couple hours, reading, analyzing, making notes, but then my eyes began to glaze over. I'm only thirty but sometimes I think old age is creeping up on me. I used to be able to work so hard.

As the lovely April day sank gradually into purple night, I couldn't keep my eyes on the papers. Forlorn images of Julie Bass were back, intruding between my eyes and the page. Something about her brought out my protective instincts. She seemed so alone and so utterly beaten down by her situation. I'd only known her a few hours, and I'm not a soft touch, so I wondered what it was about her that got to me like that. And as I sat and stared at the pages, I realized what it was.

Carrie. My lost sister. I always thought of her like that. Lost was a description that had fit Carrie. That sense of not belonging was what had sent her searching for her birth parents and now she was lost forever. Murdered. Viciously. There was no nice way of saying it. She had had that same waiflike quality. A tiny blonde in the midst of a family of dark giants, my adopted sister Carrie had, from the moment my parents brought her home, been able to twist me around her finger. I'd spent twenty-one years running interference for her and being her second mother. Not always consistently. I hadn't been there to keep her from getting killed. But I'd been there to find her killer. It was the only thing I could do for her.

I was annoyed with my mother for inviting Julie Bass and expecting me to help her. When someone's loss is as new as Julie's, there isn't much you can do, except make tea and soup, hand out tissues, and reassure them that it's okay to feel sad. These things take time. But I understood why she'd done it—because like me, when she looked at Julie, she saw Carrie. And like me, she was still trying to do the right things, still trying to fix what couldn't be fixed. Conditioned by Carrie, we saw Julie broken down on the highway of life, and we had to stop and help.

CHAPTER 3

MONDAY MORNING. BANE of the working world. I was up at the crap of dawn, bright-eyed and bushy-tailed, ready to go out and look for nuts. Actually, I prefer to avoid nuts, at least of the human variety and I prefer rising closer to noon, which is why the phrase "crap of dawn," gleaned from a friend's young son, has always delighted me. The reason I was up and alert and raring to go so early on a Monday morning was that I'd had a wake-up call around six, and much as I hate the phone—Alexander Graham Bell is not among my heroes, even if he was a brilliant inventor and champion of the deaf—an early-morning call is difficult to ignore. So were the caller and the subject of the call. The caller was my mother, her voice shrill with anxiety; the subject, Julie Bass.

Her voice had come bursting out of the phone into my still somnolent ear. "Thea? Are you awake? A terrible thing has happened. . . ." I almost didn't hear what the terrible thing was, for at her words, my mind had raced immediately to which family member was dead or dying. I forced my attention back just as she concluded, ". . . and now they say that her husband's death is considered a homicide."

"Run that by me again," I said.

She sighed. "Thea, I wish you'd pay attention. . . ."

"Mom, I was asleep."

"I said the police came to see Julie Bass last night. They've determined that the car her husband was driving was tampered with and his death is now considered a homicide."

I didn't bother to ask why she was telling me this. Mom believes that bad news is to be shared. She also believes that if something is important to her, it is important to the people around her. Besides, willingly or not, I was now a fully inducted member of the Julie Bass fan club. I muttered all the right things. How horrible. As if the poor girl needed anything more to worry about. Did the police have any ideas? That I would call Julie later. That got her off the phone. I would have rolled over then and gone back to sleep, but I wasn't sleepy anymore and according to the Thea Kozak book of rules, if I'm not asleep, I go to work.

Actually, driving to work at 6:30 is better than going at 8:30 when the roads are clogged with cars. The morning was cool and sunny and invigorating. Crocuses, and in the warm spots, daffodils were blooming. The bright gold of emerging forsythia softened the brown of mostly leafless trees. Sometimes I wonder how I can live in a place where the trees are bare a full six months of the year, but if I went somewhere else, I'd miss the seasons. I like the rhythm of the year, the changes. Fall is my favorite time, but spring is a close second.

I was at my desk with an oversized coffee and a sack of doughnuts shortly after seven. When I can detach myself from the arms of Morpheus, I enjoy coming in early. The best part of the day is the quiet time before the phones start to ring, before crises come humming over the wire with the regularity of cars off an assembly line. I often feel like a firefighter. The phone rings and I spring into action, putting out fires on campuses everywhere. Then my shift is over and the phone stops ringing and quiet settles. And then I can get to work.

By 8:30 the private school day gets under way, so I had about an hour. I got out my yellow pad, sharpened a stack of pencils, and started writing. I'd covered about five pages when the phone rang. Someone's day was getting under way early, like mine.

I could have let the machine get it, but I didn't. My cheery hello met a hesitant silence, followed by a tentative woman's voice. "Thea? Thea Kozak?" I admitted that's who I was. "This is Julie Bass. I . . . uh . . . it's been a bad . . . uh . . . I've had some news . . . bad news . . . you seemed so friendly and I really need someone to talk to right now . . . I was hoping . . . wondering if maybe you could . . . if you'd like . . . could we get together for lunch?"

I checked my calendar. By nature I'm an impulsive person so I've had to learn to be very disciplined about checking. My partner, Suzanne, had written herself in in red. That meant it was important, priority and unalterable. "I can't do lunch," I said, hating to disappoint her. "What about dinner? That good Chinese restaurant at the Chestnut Hill Mall? Six-thirty?"

"Seven," she said. "If I can get a sitter . . . plan on it, okay. I'll call if there's a problem." In the background a child's cry rose to an urgent and insistent wail. "Oh Lord! That's Emma. I've got to go. See you there."

I tried not to think about what awaited me at seven. I was sorry for Julie Bass and willing to help her, but the last thing I wanted to go near was another murder, even in a role that only involved being a shoulder to cry on. In my gloomier moments I wonder if I have some sort of fatal attraction that draws death to me like filings to a magnet or perhaps my own personal cloud. Then there was the fact that letting Julie unload her grief and pain would bring back some of my own. In a wry corner of my mind, a Monty Pythonesque character was urging "Line up and be flogged, it's good for you."

There's a strong Puritan streak in my family that says you don't shun other people's troubles to avoid pain to yourself, but sometimes I get tired of the world's troubles and want to just say no. I want some cheerful person to clap me on the shoulder periodically and urge me to not worry and be happy. It's only a dream. In reality, if someone did that I'd probably yell "don't touch me" and punch him in the nose. It was too late, anyway. I hadn't said no. By 8:30 the phone was ringing, people were arriving, and I was too busy to think about anything but work.

At five I forced myself away from the desk and went to my health club, where I submitted myself to the heartless ministrations of a beautiful youth named Aaron, a pearl in the murky world of aerobics instructors. Aaron has the startled eyes and diminutive grace of a faun. He is lithe and muscular and tireless. The ladies love him. He does more to ensure regular attendance than fear of spreading thighs or drooping butts ever did. At 5´11˝, I tower over him, and I know my chest is bigger than his. He makes me feel like a Clydesdale next to an Arabian stallion, but at the end of the hour my muscles are humming, I'm drenched with sweat, and I know I've had a good workout. That's what I go there for. Lately he'd been into boxing aerobics and boy, what a way to get your aggressions out!

I pulled into a parking space at the mall, muscles still trembling, my stomach growling for food. Suzanne is still trying to lose her postbaby pounds, and her idea of lunch is a pouch full of sprouts—for both of us. Doughnuts and sprouts aren't enough to sustain this full-grown woman. Julie Bass was leaning against the wall outside the restaurant, looking even more forlorn than she'd looked the day before. Her hair needed washing and her skin was so pale it looked waxed. Without the wall to hold her up, she looked like she would have collapsed. I grabbed her firmly by the arm and steered her into the restaurant.

"I really appreciate this," she said. "Your mom's always telling me how busy you are. I know I'm imposing. It's just . . . I don't know . . . I'm feeling so shaky these days and you seem so together. I guess I just felt like being around someone who isn't falling apart. Your mother has been great but she's kind of intimidating . . . you know what I mean?"

I nodded. Of course I did. "This business about the car. Do you want to talk about it?" I said.

She shook her head, a dazed motion, more like she was clearing her head than replying. "To tell you the truth, I don't know. I don't understand . . . what's happening. It was bad enough knowing he was dead. But that someone killed him? That it might have been deliberate? I guess I don't want to think about it. I'm . . . I'm having trouble . . . focusing on anything right now." She picked up her napkin, shook it out, and put it in her lap. Then she picked it up and put it back on the table. "I don't know how we're going to live now that Cal . . . I know it was stupid of me . . . but I let him handle everything . . . about the money, I mean."

I had a badly tuned engine once that ran the way Julie Bass talked. It would rev up and then fade out until it almost died completely and then rev up again. It—her speech, not the engine—was the product of controlled hysteria. Julie Bass was right out on the edge of control. It was there in the trembling of her hands and the taut muscles in her neck. In the stiff set of her head. She'd had two major blows in a week—first losing her husband in a fiery crash, and then learning it was no accident. She should have been at home in bed, under the care of doting relatives or loving friends, being plied with tranquilizers or whiskey tea and soup. Instead, in the way of twentieth-century women without extended families, she was soldiering along alone, trying to make the best of things in a world that expected people to grieve on their own time and then gave them no time.

"Are you worried about money?" I said. It seemed to be weighing heavily on her mind.

"I don't know. I guess. Maybe. I mean, I really don't know what to say about that, either. I have a lawyer, of course, and he's looking into it, but it seems that things are in kind of a muddle. Cal made all the investments and I guess he made some bad ones or something. The lawyer wasn't too clear. You'd think, being a banker, that he'd know better, wouldn't you? Your dad's been trying to explain things to me. . . ." She smiled her sweet smile. "He reminds me so much of my own father . . . he'll make a wonderful grandfather, won't he?"

"If we ever give him the chance." A waiter came and took our order. I had to order for Julie. She couldn't seem to make up her mind.

"Oh, but isn't your brother planning to—" she began.

"I don't know. We've never discussed it." I couldn't stomach a discussion of Michael and Sonia and children. It was too revolting. "What about life insurance?" I asked, steering the conversation back to finance.

She blinked and put the napkin back in her lap. "I know he was well insured. Because of the girls, he was always careful about that . . . only it will be awhile before we see any of it, especially if . . ." She trailed off, thinking better of what she'd been going to say. "I guess I'm going to have to get a job . . . only finding someone to care for the girls . . . and Emma's so clingy . . . and I haven't worked since I was married . . . Cal didn't like . . . I just don't know . . . I don't know how to begin. Resumes, want ads, work clothes . . ."

"It's too soon for you to think about things like that," I said. "Give yourself some time. . . ." The waiter brought our food and two glasses of seltzer with lime.

"I know . . . but . . ." She picked up her fork, rearranged the food, and set it back down again, leaving the food uneaten.

"The bills . . . the girls . . . the house. And I find the financial stuff so confusing." She stared at me, wide-eyed and helpless. "I don't even know how much money he made."

"That will all be in your tax returns . . . and there must be some kind of pay statements. What about his boss at the bank? I'm sure he can help you out."

Her voice dropped to a whisper and her eyes dropped to her plate. "I don't think he would . . . he didn't . . . I don't think he liked Cal very much."

"His boss?" She nodded.

That was the way things went all through dinner. Julie expressed her fears, I offered advice, she offered confusion. I'd chosen a place where the food was great and I was scarfing it down with gusto. Julie's portion was rearranged, that was all. "You've got to eat," I said, knowing I hadn't eaten for weeks after David's death. "It takes strength to deal with all this stuff."

She dropped her fork into the untouched food. "I can't. Can we get out of here? I'm too restless to sit still."

"Why don't you take it home? You might get hungry later."

"I couldn't . . . can't . . . it makes me sick. . . ." She shook her head, pushed back her chair, and half ran from the room.

I paid the check and joined her in a haphazard stroll around the mall. I'm not much of a shopper. Too impatient and besides, when you're a tall woman, nothing fits. When you have a big chest, nothing fits. When you have long arms, nothing fits. I have a nice, womanly body, and clothes shopping makes me feel like a freak. My partner, Suzanne, buys most of my clothes. If she sees something while she's shopping, it appears on my desk. Not so much, since marriage and the baby, but enough to keep me covered.

I drifted in Julie's wake through the natural cosmetics store and the expensive lingerie store and through the door of Barneys, where the simplest little shirt is an investment, not a purchase. Julie's fluttering white hands drifted over the luxurious fabrics like a pair of doves, plucking an ice-blue silk jacket and skirt off the rack, and selecting a matching blouse, with the assurance of a born shopper. The clothes she held were so tiny they wouldn't have covered my elbow. Carrie's clothes had been like that. Laughably small. "I'm going to try these on," she said.

I cooled my heels, studying expensive hair ornaments, until she appeared again wearing the clothes. The price tags added up to about the same as my monthly mortgage payment. She looked like a million dollars and I told her so. "I think I'll get the outfit," she said. "If I'm going to work, I'll need some clothes."

"But you were just saying you didn't know how you'd pay your bills," I said.

She shrugged. "So this will be another bill I don't know how to pay, won't it?" She headed for the dressing room, hesitated, and turned back. "Don't be mad at me, Thea. I need something . . . right now . . . to cheer me up. I . . . it's so hard . . . you understand, don't you?"

I nodded. What else could I do? I did understand. I didn't approve. I thought it was folly. But each of us has our own forms of comfort. I turn to work, and occasionally to my friend Jack Daniel's, and now I have Andre. But Julie didn't have anything. So if an armload of blue silk made her happy, who was I to criticize?

We walked out to our cars together, two girls on a night out, strolling through the chilly April darkness. To look at us, you would have thought we didn't have a care in the world. I had an African beaded wrap to tie up my hair and Julie had a full bag and an empty heart.

Julie's car was an expensive green Lexus. Another thing she would have to maintain on a diminished income. She put her packages in the trunk, slammed it shut, and turned to say good night. In the harsh yellow glow of the streetlight, I saw tears on her cheeks. Instinctively I put an arm around her. "I'm just so scared, Thea."

"Scared about what?"

"The police. Questioning me. About Calvin's death. They're acting like they think I did it."

"Did it?"

"Killed him," she said, her voice trembling. "Because the car was tampered with. They wanted to know if I was in Connecticut with him. But, Thea, I wasn't with him!"

I slipped automatically into interview mode—I do it so much—and asked the next obvious question. "Do you know of anyone who might have wanted to kill your husband?"

"Everyone," she said. "Calvin was not a very nice person."

CHAPTER 4

I GRABBED HER elbow, steered her back inside, and found the nearest bar. Once we were settled in the darkest corner and supplied with bourbon and Scotch, I asked the question that had been perched on the tip of my mind for ten minutes. "What do you mean by everyone?"

Her answer was slow and hesitant. "I hate to say this—I know you're not supposed to say bad things about the dead—but my husband Cal, while he had many good qualities—he was charming and handsome and a good provider—well, to be honest . . . he was . . . could be . . . an absolute stinker, Thea."

She was already halfway through her drink, whether for courage or from habit I couldn't tell, and she was drinking on an empty stomach. I signaled the waiter and asked if they had anything to munch on. His weary acquiescence told me two things—that they had snacks for their customers and that they served them only grudgingly. It's one of the many things in life I don't understand. Why have snacks available and then act like it's a chore to serve them? I also don't understand people slowing down to stare at an accident and why I always chose the longest line in the grocery store. But a life without things to learn is an empty life.

She picked up her glass and took another drink. "He was so charming and romantic when we were dating. I was swept right off my feet. I'd never met a man who made me feel so safe, so cared about. All the little details of my life were important to him. I thought it was sweet that he paid so much attention to what I wore, to what I said, to other people's reactions to me. It's true what they say, you know, about love being blind." The Scotch was leveling her out. Where before her conversation had revved and dipped, now it was running at fairly high, but steady, rpms.

The waiter put a bowl of mixed nuts on the table and Julie seized a handful. "What I thought was so romantic," she said, chewing hungrily, "was obsessive control. He had opinions— inflexible opinions—about what I should wear, who I should so-cialize with . . . I mean, with whom I should socialize, what I should say, how the house should look. He wanted to remake me in his image of the perfect wife. At first, I tried to humor him . . . to make him happy. I loved him so much! He wanted me to be the mother of his children . . . to quit my job and stay home and have his babies. . . ."

She stopped. "You don't have children, do you?" I shook my head. "Well, have you ever met a man who wanted to have children with you?" She didn't wait for a response. "It's the most amazing feeling . . . having someone who wants to have children with you." She clasped her hands over her midriff. "It gets you right here. I don't know how to describe it. I felt like I was bathed in a kind of holy light . . . oh, I know that sounds hokey. . . ." Her voice dropped so low I had to lean forward to hear her. ". . . but it was magical to think that someone loved me, valued me, that much.

"By the time I realized that it wasn't really love, that it was ownership, Camilla had been born, and there wasn't anything I could do. She needed a father."

"You didn't consider leaving him?"

She tried a gay little laugh but it fell flat. "It would have destroyed my parents. There's never been a divorce in my family. And they thought so highly of Cal. They always worried—you know how parents will—about me marrying a suitable man. One who would keep me in the style I was used to. I kept telling them that I could take care of myself, that I had my education. That's what women of our generation do, isn't it? And then I went and let myself become dependent on Cal, just like I swore I never would."

The tears were there again and she blinked them away as she grabbed more nuts. Now that the drink was releasing her, she was hungry. Too bad we hadn't saved her dinner.

"You want to order a sandwich or something? I think you should."

She shook her head. "These are fine," she said firmly. Her tone deterred argument. "Calvin Bass was a handsome, brilliant, charming, ambitious, obsessive, intolerant, arrogant, scathingly critical man who imposed his standards on everyone around him." Her voice was so flat she might have been reading from a script, but I didn't think these were things she'd said many times before, though she might have thought them. The lack of emotion was necessary if she was to get the words out. "Cal was an avid tennis player, golfer, and car nut. He was a banker, a vice president at the Grantham Cooperative Bank. And he was in Connecticut taking that racing course because I arranged it for him as a present."

"But you didn't kill him?"

"You are joking, aren't you?"

"You said everyone wanted to kill him. . . ."

"Not me." She dabbed at her eyes with a tissue, leaving a

black blot of mascara on her cheek. "I wanted him to change. . . ." Her voice dropped again. "I wanted him to love me . . . to be happy with me. With me and Camilla and Emma. My brother Duncan once threatened to kill Cal if he didn't start treating me better, but Dunk wouldn't hurt a flea. He's just very protective of me."

"Was your husband abusive?"

Her delicate arched eyebrows rose over her big eyes and she stared at me nervously. "Physically?" She hesitated, weighing her answer, then answered in a rush. "Not very often. Nothing that was front-page news. I mean, he wasn't abusive, he was just impatient when things didn't go right . . . his way . . . the occasional shove, twisted arm, wrist gripped too tightly, hair pulling . . . rough sex. Calvin was as demanding about sex as he was in every other way. It was his right, on his schedule, to meet his needs."

I'd known another banker who was just like that. A wham-bam-thank-you,-ma'am guy who'd never even entertained the notion of foreplay. The first man I'd slept with after David died, he almost put me off men for life. I wondered idly if it was part of the job description. If it's not in *Playboy* or the *Federal Regs*, forget it.

Julie drained her glass and signaled the waiter for another drink. "No," she said, "mostly he was emotionally abusive. I was inadequate, incompetent, an unfit mother. That I'd deceived him. Married him under false pretenses." She took another tissue out of her purse and dabbed at her eyes. "When Emma was born, he didn't speak to me for a month because she wasn't a boy."

Her round red eyes and pink chapped nose made her look a little like a rabbit. She pulled out a mirror, stared at her face, and put it away again. "God, I'm a fright," she said. She scrubbed at the mascara spot below her eye. "Not that it matters now that Cal . . ."

"Did you tell the police about this, about how Cal alienated people?" I interrupted, hoping to stave off tears. "That there might be a lot of people who disliked him?"

The waiter set down her drink, removed the empty glass, and looked at me. I shook my head. I'm very careful how much I drink when I'm driving.

"Not really. I didn't get a chance to tell them anything. It wasn't much of a conversation . . . mostly they just came to bring me the news . . . about the car, I mean . . . and I guess to see my reaction, since they kept watching me and I was sitting there wondering how they expected me to act. And all the while I was feeling this odd numbness . . . like I was the one who was dead, and wishing they'd go away."

"I know what you mean," I said. "I've been there . . . that waiting politely for them to leave you alone so you can scream and cry and fall apart. . . ."

She nodded. "I knew you'd understand. . . ." Her voice died away and then she smiled, a humorless, cynical smile. "And they wouldn't go. I guess I did the right thing, though. I offered them some coffee and when I got up to make it, I fainted. Woke up with some guy bending over me who had the worst garlic breath I've ever smelled." This time her smile, though slight, was genuine. "I almost fainted again."

"They didn't ask you questions about Cal?"

"A few. I think they were scared to. They were . . ." She tilted her head, searching for words. ". . . cautious. Afraid I might faint again. I did tell them that people didn't like him. That he was hard on people. Maybe I mentioned some specific names, I don't remember. I didn't tell them about Dunk, though." As she said it, she watched my face, looking to see if I was on her side. A little bit of iron crept into her voice when she talked about her brother. "Because he's my brother. The one person who's always on my side. There's just the two of us now, you see. Now that our parents are dead. We're very close.

Dunk's always been kind of like a second father to me. Dunk Donahue, the terror of the north." Her pale, expressionless face grew more animated when she mentioned her brother.

"You said he's up in New Hampshire?"

She nodded. "Near North Conway."

"Couldn't you go up there and stay with him for a while?"

"He's got a small house and kids of his own, Thea. It wouldn't work out. And his wife works. And Dunk works all the time. He's incredibly busy. Fleet manager for a trucking company, Verrill Brothers." Her eyes fell to her watch. "Oh my gosh! I had no idea it was so late. The sitter's got a curfew and I've got to run or I'm going to miss it." She reached across the table and grabbed my hand. "Thanks for listening. I really needed that tonight."

"Wait," I said, "do you have someone who could stay with you? You shouldn't be all alone with this stuff." She shook her head, grabbed her purse, and was gone before I could say anything, a little unsteady on her feet.

Cynic that I am, even in the midst of reflecting on poor Julie's plight, I noticed that she had neither paid nor offered to pay for dinner or the drinks. Well, she'd had a lot on her mind. And despite the silk suit, a lot of fear about her finances.

I drove home with the sun roof open, letting the cool air revive me, called André, and dropped into bed. I told him I'd had dinner with Julie but I didn't tell him about her troubles. Though we've reached a pretty good accommodation about not interfering in each other's lives, I knew what he would say: "Don't get involved." He claims he can spot trouble a mile away and that I'm a magnet for it. I wasn't in the mood to be told that I shouldn't offer a comforting shoulder to a woman who'd just lost her husband. It made me feel a little bit deceptive but not more than I could live with.

I closed my eyes, the sound of his voice still in my ear, expecting to dream about him. Instead, I dreamed that Aaron the aerobics instructor was chasing me around a race track, leaning out the window of a neon car with a number on the side, yelling encouragement to me as I jogged around vigorously punching the air. I woke up with sore arms.

CHAPTER 5

SUZANNE AND I had our heads together, struggling with the wording of a proposal we were about to send out, when my secretary, Sarah, stuck her head around the door. "Sorry to interrupt you busy ladies, but Thea's mother is on the phone and says to tell you that someone named Julie Bass has been arrested for killing her husband and they're holding her until they can extradite her to Connecticut." Suzanne cocked her head sideways and looked at me quizzically and with the beginnings of irritation that always seemed to be with her these days.

"Tell her I'll call her as soon as I'm through," I said. Sarah nodded and withdrew.

After that, though I tried my best, my concentration was shot. Suzanne didn't bother to control her annoyance. Normally a patient woman, the sleepless nights of a new mother were taking their toll. Sleepless nights and something else bothering her that she wasn't ready to tell me. After seven years, I know her well. "Thea, I don't care if it's your own mother who's been killed. We're up to our ear tips in work around here, with not a whole lot of worker bees to help us out. There is no time right now . . . I repeat . . . absolutely no time to be gallivanting around the countryside trying to solve mysteries, so I hope that's not what that phone call is all about. Am I making myself clear?"

"As if I wanted to."

"With you it's not desire," she reminded me, "it's your be-lief—your wrongheaded but admirable belief—that it's your job to fix the things that go wrong in other people's lives. So you won't say no. Especially to your mother. You're just a girl who can't say no."

"Woman."

"Girl," she said. "Women learn how to say no. Now repeat after me, I will not get involved."

I raised my right hand, solemnly swore that I wouldn't get involved in anything that would interfere with my work, and wrenched my attention back to the proposal. In a brisk fifteen minutes we'd whipped it into shape and dropped it on Magda's desk. Magda was Suzanne's gloomy Hungarian secretary. She eyed the proposal skeptically. "This is for the last time, right?"

"Right," we both chorused.

"Yes," she said darkly, pulling the draft up on her screen, "and I was born yesterday."

As if on cue, an infant's wail came from Suzanne's office. "Not even Junior was born yesterday."

Magda, who, however much she may complain, dotes on Suzanne and regards Paul Eric, Jr., as her surrogate grandson, smiled. "He's a very good baby."

"Yes," Suzanne said. "Now if I could only find some very good day care for him."

Suzanne went to tend her very good baby and I went to call my mother.

"You took your time," she said.

"I had to get something in the mail."

"It couldn't have been that important." I didn't pursue it. I'd have better luck arguing with the Registry of Motor Vehicles than with my mother.

"What's going on? Julie's been arrested?"

"Look in the paper. It's a screaming headline. I wonder that you missed it."

"I haven't read the paper." She persists in acting like I sit around all day, drinking coffee, reading the paper, and schmoozing with my girlfriends, even though she's always telling me she thinks I work too hard. "She was devastated by his death," I said. "How could they possibly think she did it? Tamper with a racing car? She's the type of woman who looks like she has trouble figuring out which end of the screwdriver to use." I felt a twinge of guilt at indulging in such a gross form of sexual stereotyping.

"We both know the police don't always use their common sense," she said.

"What about the children? What's happened to them?"

"Her brother came to get them."

I thought about poor, helpless Julie in the clutches of the police. Of last night's snatches of befuddled conversation. Even though she had nothing to hide, I hoped she had a lawyer who was protecting her. Even I'm intimidated by the cops sometimes, and I'm as tough as nails. "It's terrible. Does she have a good lawyer."

"You don't, for even a second, imagine that she did it?" my mother snapped. "And don't fool yourself that the police will figure it out. They always take the easiest course." She knew it would irritate me but she can't help herself. It bothers her to know that her daughter is in love with a policeman. "I've sent your father over to see what he can do for now, but of course what she'll need is a criminal lawyer, which he'll take care of. And someone to do some—"

Oh no, I thought, here it comes. I had to get off the phone

before she made the inevitable suggestion. "I'm sorry. I've got a frantic client on the other line. I've got to take the call," I said quickly, "I'll talk to you tonight," and disconnected before she could respond. I looked around for Bobby, one of our professional employees, but he'd taken an early lunch. I borrowed the paper from his desk and there it was, in stark black and white: "Grantham Wife charged in Connecticut Race-Car Death." It was creepy to think that while Julie was pouring her heart out to me last night, a stealthy net of cops was closing in on her.

I tried to put the whole thing out of my mind and go back to work, but images of Julie's frightened and bewildered face intruded between my eyes and the pages. I had finally thrust her out of my mind once and for all and was working efficiently when Sarah interrupted me. "There's a Julie Bass on the phone and she says she can't call back. You want to take it?"

I grabbed the phone. "Julie. Good God! What happened? Are you all right?"

"I don't know. It was so sudden. I got home . . . they came . . . early this morning . . . we were all asleep . . . woke the girls . . . I tried not to go with them, tried to explain that I couldn't leave the girls . . . they dragged me out, screaming . . . my babies were crying, clinging to me . . . we were all so scared." She gasped for breath. "This big cop pulled them away and held them. They were screaming and struggling. Oh . . . God! Thea, you should have seen their faces. I won't forget if I live to be a hundred. How could they possibly think . . . This has been the worst day of my life!" Another gasp. Her face floated before me, those huge brown eyes wide with terror, an image of Camilla and tiny Emma, confused and half asleep, being forcibly restrained by a stranger.

She rushed on, perhaps afraid that at any moment they'd be cutting her off. "Your father was here. So kind. He made them put me in a c-c-cell by myself but he couldn't get me out. I'll go crazy if I have to stay in here long. Cold. Ugly. It smells. Can you come and see me, Thea? Please? I'm so scared! I need a friend so much right now." This time her speech was like a machine gun. Short rapid bursts interrupted by abrupt silences. "I don't know . . . I think . . . I'm afraid that I'm losing my mind. This is so awful. I can't understand any of this . . . will you come?"

"Yes. Of course. I'll be there as soon as I can." I grabbed my purse and left.

Despite Sarah's amazed stare as I rushed by her desk, it was an unusually early departure only by my own standards. Most of the rest of the world goes home at a civilized hour. I fed myself into the enormous clot of traffic that oozes reluctantly around Route 128 between four and seven every day, popped in some road music, and tried not to feel guilty about what I was doing. My oath to Suzanne didn't mean ignoring urgent human need.

By the time I got there, I was worn out from struggling against the aggressive incompetence of Massachusetts drivers, people who believe yield is for the other guy, red means go, and are willing to risk their own lives and the lives of others to cut a second or two off their commute. Although there were no-smoking signs posted, the place smelled like cigarettes, disinfectant, and fear. An expressionless, balding cop told me that Julie already had a visitor and I would have to wait.

Naturally, I had brought work. After I'd cooled my heels for a long time—long enough to recognize that I was starving, having been so distracted by work and Julie's dilemma that I'd forgotten to eat lunch—I got up to ask how much longer I might have to wait. I was halfway across the room when an attractive, dark-haired man who looked like he'd just lost his best friend rushed into the room, crashed into me, stared blankly through me, and left without apology, absently brushing at his shoulder.

I muttered a few ladylike expletives at his departing back. "You can see her now," the balding cop said, and ushered me into Julie's presence. Since our phone call, she seemed to have pulled herself together, if the fragile, trembling control she exhibited could be called together. She started to tell me what had happened, stopped, and suddenly put her hand up to her mouth like she'd just realized she'd forgotten something urgent.

"I need you to do something for me," she said, looking around nervously. "Something very important."

"Of course," I said. Short of engineering a jailbreak, I was willing to do anything I could to set her mind at rest.

"Go to my house. The key is under the pot of pansies on the porch. Upstairs in the bedroom closet is a briefcase of old letters. I don't want the police to find them. . . ." She looked up from her clenched hands. "Not because they're incriminating. I know you believe I'm innocent. But they're terribly embarrassing."

"What—" I began. This sounded like a very bad idea.

Her voice dropped to a lower register. "Cal and I were doing some marriage counseling. One of the things the therapist had us doing was writing letters to each other. Very frank, intimate letters. We were very open about our anger and dissatisfactions with each other as well as our intimate needs and desires . . . you can see why I don't want anyone reading them. Terribly embarrassing and they could so easily be misconstrued, misused. . . ." Her voice dropped even lower. "I'd hate to have Cal's memory tainted with those disclosures . . . to have everyone in town know the private details . . . the intimate . . ." She choked off her words and grabbed my arm. "Say you'll get them."

"No touching," the guard called.

Cowering, she let go but whispered a frantic "Please?"

I'd sworn I wouldn't get involved and here I was being asked to do something that *had* to be illegal. And if I got caught, it not only wouldn't help Julie, it would probably ruin my career. Maybe not that much of a career, by type A standards, but it suited me. Suzanne's words echoed in my ears as I tried to avoid

Julie's pleading brown eyes. Couldn't I be sorry for her and sympathetic without getting involved?

"I can't," I said, staring at the light switch over her shoulder. "It's too risky."

"Oh God, Thea, please!" Tears welled up and poured down her face. She reached for my hand, shot a nervous look at the guard, and pulled it back. "You don't understand, do you? If they get their hands on those letters, every intimate detail of my . . . our . . . private lives will be the source of sniggering jests all over town." She wiped her eyes and met mine with a challenging stare.

"You have a boyfriend, don't you? A cop, right? Your mother's mentioned him. . . ." She hesitated. "I'm not sure she . . ." Julie stopped. "What I'm trying to say is, how would you feel if all the Maine state troopers knew the intimate details of your relationship? How would it feel to know they were staring at you . . . at parts of your body, and thinking, 'yeah, she's a hot piece. I know just the way she likes it and I'm just the guy to give it to her.' " She swallowed.

"Well? You know that's how it would be. Could you stand it? Because I know I couldn't. If it weren't for Emma and Camilla, I'd—" She ran a nervous hand through her hair, swallowed, and raised her eyes to meet mine, her voice dropping to a whisper. "There's no one else I can ask. If you don't help me . . ."

In the face of her desperation, I couldn't say no. She was right. I wouldn't want cops rooting around in my personal life, either. "All right. All right. I'll get them if I can. Do you need anything? Should I pick up anything while I'm there?" She shook her head. Said nothing, but her gratitude shone in her eyes.

"Was that your lawyer who was just here?"

She didn't seem to have heard me. She sat in her chair, her

arms wrapped tightly around herself, as if that way she could hold herself together. I couldn't begin to imagine how frightening this must be—being dragged out of your house and away from your children by the police, accused of killing your own husband.

"The girls . . . they've never been away from me. Never, not even for a day." Her exhaled breath a sigh. "My babies. I wonder how they're doing. Emma's so sensitive, so fearful and shy. With someone who doesn't understand her . . . Dunk's a good uncle but he doesn't have much patience and Emma takes patience. I tried to call him but I didn't get any answer. And it's so hard to make phone calls. There's no privacy here. I feel like a prisoner. . . ."

Her eyes swept the room with disdain. She lifted her chin proudly and tried being brave. "I know. I know. I *am* a prisoner. I'm in jail, for God's sake. How could I not know? But I'm innocent . . . and aren't we supposed to be innocent until proven guilty?" Her voice had risen from a low, confiding whisper until she was practically shouting. "They all treat me like I'm scum. The way people look at me! You can't imagine . . . how will I stand . . . it might be days before I can get out of here. Days! I keep throwing up and they just stand around and watch me . . . as though being scared and sick was a sign of guilt!"

Her fragile control deserted her. She rocked in her chair, growing more and more agitated, her fingers flying around like pale birds, tugging at her hair and clothes. Suddenly she pushed herself back, ran around the table, and threw herself into my lap, gripping me around the waist, clinging like I was her last hope. "You've got to help me. Get me out of here! Oh, God! Please! Thea, get me out of here!" Her grip was tighter than Scarlett O'Hara's corset.

"No physical contact with the prisoners is allowed," the guard boomed from the door. Julie cast a glance over her shoulder and clung tighter. "Help me, Thea! Don't let them touch me." The cries were pathetic and heart-rending, like the keening of a wounded animal.

The officer grabbed Julie's shoulder and tried to pull her away. "You'll have to let go or your visitor must leave."

I considered a dramatic rescue. Something from an old Western—too much TV as a child, I suppose—but as I had neither gun nor horse, I settled for size and decisiveness. "Please don't do that. Don't pull on her like that," I said firmly. "She's distraught. I think she needs a doctor." I regretted the word distraught as soon as it left my lips.

The officer rolled her eyes. I could imagine what she was thinking. That it was good for a spoiled country club set wife who'd toasted her husband to have a taste of reality. But I don't go in for shock therapy myself and I didn't believe Julie had committed any crime. She backed off a few feet and said, "Okay, if you can get her to sit down . . ."

"She should see a doctor," I repeated.

"The doctor was just here."

"What did he say?"

The guard shrugged. "That she's dehydrated and exhausted. That he'd be back with something to calm her nerves and settle her stomach. He was very solicitous." Her smile was malicious.

I felt Julie's hands fall away from my waist. "I'll be okay, Thea," she whispered. "Get the letters. Please!"

I said good-bye, unhappy about the state I was leaving her in yet knowing there was nothing I could do about it, and drove to her house. As I was parking, I saw someone hurrying away down the sidewalk. It was the same man I'd seen at the jail. Curious about him, I jotted down his license number as he drove away. I already knew two things about him—that he was a doctor and that he had good taste in cars.

I found the key where Julie had said it would be and let my-

self into the silent house. The scattered bits of toys and cloth-
ing against otherwise impeccable neatness spoke of a hasty departure, as though the family had suddenly been swept away by
a genie. I picked my way carefully through the semidarkness,
not wanting to advertise my presence by using lights. The mas-
ter bedroom was pure *House Beautiful*, with deep white carpet,
a mahogany king-size bed with tall pineapple posts, a huge double dresser, a second dresser with doors and drawers, a writing
desk in a white curtained alcove, and an armoire entertainment
center hiding an oversized television set. Someone had left dirty
footprints on the white rug. Thinking about cops and footprints, I slipped off my own shoes at the door.

The his-and-hers closets were in a separate dressing area. I
slid open the first door to reveal a row of pinstriped suits, shut
it, and opened the door on the other side. The faint scent of lily
of the valley drifted from the carefully hung clothes. I went back,
closed the dressing room door, and switched on the light. On
the floor of the closet, back in a corner, was a letter addressed
to Julie. Another was beside it, stuck into a black loafer, but no
briefcase. I picked up the letters and tried the other closet. Not
there, either. I went back to the first closet and found a battered
brown briefcase underneath some balled-up sweaters. I shoved
the letters into it, shut the door, put on my shoes, and went
downstairs.

I put the briefcase in my trunk with all the other junk, jam-
ming it underneath the beach chair and the picnic blanket and
my dry cleaning, which I keep forgetting to take in. I was about
to leap in and roar off into the sunset in search of a sandwich
when I remembered the house key in my pocket and went back
to put it under the plant pot. On my way up the steps, I saw
something white fluttering in the grass. I picked it up and saw
that it was another one of Julie's letters, though I was sure I
hadn't dropped any. Before I had time to reflect on why it might
have been there, I heard a car pull up at the curb and someone

started running toward me. I shoved the letter down into my bra and bent to replace the key under the pansies.

"All right, lady," a voice called. "Put your hands on your head and turn around slowly."

Andre says if you want to get along with the cops, you do what they say without arguing, so I put my hands on my head and turned around slowly. "Are you police officers?" I said. "Have I done something wrong?" One way cops keep the upper hand is by making you feel ridiculous. It's hard to assert yourself when you're standing there looking like an idiot with your hands parked on top of your head and the buttons on your blouse gaping like a fool's mouth. I slowly lowered my arms.

"Yes, ma'am, we're police officers." He flapped a badge in my face. "You have some kind of identification?" The speaker was a wide man with a dark mustache and a receding hairline. He wasn't in uniform, but the two men behind him were. Not Grantham uniforms, either. Connecticut. They all looked like they wanted to cuff me and throw me in the car. All except their leader. He was staring at my chest like he wanted to pat me down for weapons. I hoped the letter wasn't showing.

"In my car. My name is Thea Kozak."

"Your address, Ms. Kojak?"

"Kozak." I told him my address.

He shook his head. "You're kind of a long way from home, aren't you?"

"Not really. Grantham is home. That is, I grew up here. My parents live here."

"Their address?" he growled again. I told him. He shook his head. "Nobody named Kozak on that street."

"McKusick," I told him. "My maiden name was McKusick."

His eyes dropped to my ringless left hand. "You mind telling us what you're doing here?"

It was a good question. One I intended to ask myself once I

was out of this mess. What was I doing here when I knew I should have stuck with "no"? Being Thea the Fix-it Lady, just as Suzanne had predicted. Wasn't I breaking my promise to her? And why was she so grouchy lately? All questions for another time. He was waiting impatiently for an answer. Stick close to the truth, that's my motto. Especially since I don't lie well. "I'm a friend of Julie's," I said. "She asked me to come by and see that the house was secure."

"What were you doing just now, as we drove up?"

"Putting the key back under the plant pot."

"She keeps a key under a plant pot and she's worried about the house being secure?" he said to his companions. They grinned obligingly.

I wanted to say "Yeah, the broad is much too dumb to have killed her husband," but I refrained. Experience has shown that most cops don't appreciate my sense of humor.

"You've been in the house?" I nodded. "Did you take anything?"

"She said she didn't need me to pick up anything."

"That's not what I asked. Did you take anything?"

I lied. "No."

He jerked his chin toward the Saab. "That your car?"

So far, he'd asked perfectly reasonable questions, but I could feel my temper rise. Partly because of the way they'd treated Julie, so they already had one strike against them. Partly because except for Andre and my friend Dom Florio, I don't like cops, so that was two. And partly because I don't like men who only stare at my chest and never at my face. And that's what he'd been doing. So he'd had his three strikes and he was out.

"The Saab?" I said demurely, though it was the only car besides his in sight.

"That's right. The Saab."

"It's mine," I said cheerfully. "I love it!"

"Save the testimonials for someone who cares," he growled. He must have taken lessons, to have cultivated such an indifferent tone.

I wanted to stick out my tongue and wave my hands beside my ears and say, "Nya, nya, you're a real big man when you have your stooges behind you," but I didn't. My mother taught me to curb such impulses. This was one case where she was right.

"Why don't we step over there, find that identification of yours, and take a look inside the car?" he said. It wasn't an invitation.

My heart sank. I knew my rights. Growing up a lawyer's daughter has given me that. One of them was that they had no right to search my car without probable cause; and probable cause didn't arise from finding me putting a key under a flower pot more than a hundred feet from the car. But knowing your rights and knowing what to do aren't the same thing. I was in a tight situation without a lawyer in my pocket. My dad was across town. If I opened the car to get my license, would that be inviting them in? Then there was the downside, which was that if I didn't cooperate, they might arrest me on some pretext and then get a warrant to search the car. If I let them search now, I might get lucky and they'd miss the letters.

Keeping my pose of good girl scout, I said, "Certainly, Officer. I'm afraid it's an awful mess," in my best demure and innocent way, and led the parade over to my car. They all shifted nervously when I stuck my hand in my pocket and hauled out my keys. I'm sure I don't look like the gun-toting type but we live in uncertain times. I unlocked the car, got out my briefcase, fished out my license, and handed it to my inquisitor. All the while, the stooges kept their hands near their guns, waiting for me to pull my own gun out of the case and blow Mr. Hot Eyes away. They seemed a little disappointed when I didn't.

It must be hard to live on the edge all the time. Like being half aroused. Irrationally, the idea of pale blue balls floated through my mind. I almost couldn't keep the smile off my face. Lately my irreverent side had been working overtime.

I apologized for the Dunkin' Donuts bags and the Burger King bags and the empty Styrofoam coffee cups, the empty plastic salad containers with bits of dead lettuce swimming in murky dressing, the three empty boxes of Bridge Mix and the apple core and the old newspapers. Usually I clean my car on weekends, otherwise the mound of trash would overwhelm me, but I'd been busy. I vowed that as soon as I got home, no matter how late, I'd hoe it out. My mother would die of embarrassment if she ever had to ride in my car. Besides, I have the vague feeling that clean cars are like clean underwear. I wouldn't want to get in an accident and have emergency personnel haul me out of the wreckage through a mountain of greasy wrappers and the dregs of a dozen cups of coffee. I could picture the headlines: Slightly damaged car condemned by Health Department.

"Mrs. Kozak?" Someone dropped a heavy hand on my shoulder and interrupted my reverie about trash. I glanced sideways at it. He was a nail biter. "May we look in the trunk?"

My stomach clenched as I nodded and said brightly, "Go right ahead. But I warn you, it's as bad as the rest of the car." And I never once uttered the words "take your hand off me, you pig." Under my jacket, I was sweating. It was only a matter of time before it soaked through. I felt like there was a giant red light on my forehead flashing "guilty" into the deepening darkness. I watched as they pulled out the beach chair, my rain boots, the picnic blanket, a spare raincoat, an umbrella, a canvas tote bag full of books, the shopping bag with my dry cleaning, the briefcase I'd just stowed in there. Hot Eyes held it up, initial side away from him. I beamed mental messages at him, telling him not to turn it around. If he did, my goose was cooked.

"What's in here?"

"Stuff I keep thinking I'll get around to reading. Boring financial stuff."

"You don't mind if I look?" he said, reaching for the zipper.

I considered grabbing the case and running but the image of the stooges with their eager hands by their guns deterred me. Well, Thea, I thought. This is it. Your golden opportunity to go to jail. Look at it as a chance to see how the other half lives. Or an opportunity to keep Julie company. A chance to see Andre mad. My stomach tightened. Bright smile in place, I said, "Of course not."

Slowly—or so it seemed to me, for whom time had become deranged—he unzipped the case, stuck in his hand, and pulled out a sheet of paper. I held my breath, waiting for the explosion as he discovered intimate details of the relationship between Julie and Calvin Bass lurking in my trunk.

"Very interesting," he muttered. I leaned over and looked at the paper. The heading was the Metro-Boston Real Estate Board and the page was covered with charts and graphs about demographics and sales prices.

"I'm glad you think so," I said. "I find it all rather dull." Relief was followed by a sense of futility. I'd taken the wrong papers. Hot Eyes and his companions were bound to find the right ones soon, and there was nothing I could do.

He put the papers back in the briefcase and the briefcase back in the trunk. "Okay, let's put this stuff away and get on with what we came to do." They piled my stuff back into the trunk and slammed the lid. "You can go, Mrs. Kozak, but let me give you some advice. The next time a murder suspect asks you to go to her house and do anything, talk to the police first. You could have gotten yourself in a heap of trouble."

"I'm sorry," I said. "It never occurred to me that there would be a problem."

He just walked away, shaking his head, the Connecticut

cops behind him. I could almost hear him thinking "dumb broad." I wanted to scoop up a handful of the gravel, dirt and leaves from the gutter and fling it after him, but it would have been stupid. I was lucky that they hadn't dug farther into the case and found the letters I'd stuck in there. Otherwise, I'd just risked an ulcer for a bunch of old statistics.

I got in the car and started the engine. In the aftermath of fear, though, I was shaking too much to drive. I closed my eyes and put my head down on the wheel, waiting for the trembling to stop. All that for nothing. I hadn't gotten what Julie sent me to get. I took a deep breath and reviewed my search. No. I hadn't been careless. Hot Eyes wouldn't get them because the letters hadn't been there. And if they weren't there, someone had gotten to them before me. Maybe that was what the guy I'd seen leaving had been doing. It explained the letter I'd found in the grass. A strange chore for a doctor. Though if Julie had asked him to get her letters, why had she also asked me to do it? Because she didn't trust him to follow through?

It would have bothered me more at any other time. Now I was too shaken by my constabulary encounter to dwell on it. To dwell on anything other than pulling myself together and getting out of there. I'm always amazed at how much fear takes out of me. I put the car in gear and drove home.

CHAPTER 6

THE NEXT MORNING I took a green plastic trash bag, pulled on rubber gloves, and made my car a safe and decent place. By the time I was showered and dressed and driving to work, I no longer feared being in an accident. The EMTs would find me prepared. I was so conscientious I even carried my Styrofoam cup inside and threw it away and got the crumbs from my chocolate doughnut on my desk instead of the car seat. I was a woman reformed.

I hit the stack of messages waiting for me with all the zeal of the converted. I was hot, I was ready, the world had better watch out. At 9:30 my secretary, Sarah, looked in and shook her head. "Whatever you had for breakfast, I want some," she said. "At the rate you're going, there will be nothing left to do tomorrow."

"There's always something to do. Anyway, tomorrow I'm going to New Hampshire, I've got that meeting at Northbrook, so I have to be sure I leave you enough for two days."

"That's never a problem."

I was working frantically because I was avoiding thinking

about Julie, languishing in her cell and worrying about her children. I assumed it was only a matter of time before her lawyer had her out on bail, but the hours must seem very long. My hours were flying. By eleven, I'd had a headmaster looking for advice on handling a pregnant student, another school where a Buildings and Grounds employee had exposed himself, and a third where a minority student had claimed discrimination after being disciplined for cheating. Just another happy day at EDGE Consulting.

Sarah stuck her head in, rolled her eyes, and announced, "Your mother is on the phone. Another crisis." Mom is a bit peremptory and Sarah often runs interference for me, so when she can't, I know I've got to take the call.

I pressed the button, said hello, and got an earful. "They're sending poor little Julie off to Framingham today and you've got to do something."

"Framingham? Why Framingham?"

"It's the only women's prison we've got."

"What about bail?"

"There's some problem ... seems she told a guard the minute she got out she was grabbing her kids and disappearing. . . ." There was a pause. "You've got to do something," she repeated.

"What do you want me to do?"

"Find some way to get her out of there—some alibi or evidence or something."

"Mom, for years now you've been telling me to keep my nose out of other people's business and not get involved. To stay away from violence and murder. . . ."

"Well, if you've got the experience, you might as well be useful," she interrupted. "It's not like I'm asking you to do something dangerous. And she needs the help. The poor girl has no one. . . ."

"The poor girl has her family and her friends. She has her

brother. She has you and Dad . . . I hardly know her."

"I suppose you're too busy gadding about having tea with headmasters to help an innocent girl in trouble. . . ."

My teeth were clenched so hard to keep from screaming at her that I was afraid they'd crack. I thought of all the time I'd spent in the last few years helping people because of the "Thea will fix it" flaw in my nature. And all of the grief I'd gotten from her for living so dangerously. But I was a recovering nice girl. I was learning to say yes and no when I wanted to, not when other people wanted me to. "Mom, this is crazy. You don't know what you're asking. I am not going to get involved in this business. It's a job for the police."

"Yes, and we both know what kind of job they'll do, don't we?"

She has a talent for making me lose my temper. "I have to go," I said, choking back all the things I wanted to say, and slammed down the phone, fuming.

I was not going to let my mother push me around and I was not going to get involved and I couldn't explain, even to myself, why it was that I called up the Grantham Cooperative Bank and made an appointment with Eliot Ramsay, Calvin Bass's boss, for that afternoon.

It meant skipping lunch but what the hell, I'd had my chocolate doughnut, that ought to be enough for any girl. Suzanne had informed me that I couldn't call myself a woman unless I could think for myself, which wasn't what I was doing here. Suzanne. That was another problem I'd have to deal with someday soon. She was not herself and I didn't think it was just postpartum depression. She had something on her mind she wasn't sharing. That always made her edgy. As soon as I had a chance, I was going to corner her and make her talk. Praying for light traffic, I told Sarah I was going to get lunch and do some errands, and hit the road, arriving at the bank with five minutes to spare.

There are people in the world who keep you waiting because they're busy and there are people who keep you waiting to establish their importance. Eliot Ramsay was one of the latter. Even though I could see through the partly opened door that he was busy rearranging his magnetic desk sculpture, he kept me waiting ten minutes. No skin off my nose, though. I enjoyed talking with his secretary, Sherry DuBose, one of those omnicompetent people who can answer the phone, type like Superman, send papers off in six directions, and still be pleasant company.

Because secretaries often know a great deal about what's going on, I was open with her about the purpose of my visit. She admitted she was shocked about the accusation and concerned about Julie's well-being. "I don't think she's had a very happy life," she said.

I was about to ask what she meant when the door opened and Eliot Ramsay emerged. Ramsay was a small, wiry man with graying dark hair and a dapper, controlled mustache. The hand he offered was manicured. His suit was well cut, conservative and expensive. Not a Ken doll but a Ken's boss doll. My impression was confirmed when he glanced at his reflection in the glass and gave the immaculate suit a tug. Appearances mattered to Eliot Ramsay. He ushered me into his office, asked the purpose of my visit, and expressed his deep sorrow both at the loss of a valued employee and at Julie's ordeal.

I asked him for a frank assessment of Calvin Bass, as an employee and as a person.

He leaned back in his maroon leather chair, tented his fingers, and stared at them as he spoke. "Cal was a very ambitious man. Very demanding of himself and others. Rather intolerant of mistakes and of people less driven than he was. Impatient. We didn't socialize much outside the office, so I can't really comment on his personal life, but he struck me as the classic work-hard, play-hard man. I expect he was as driven and demanding in his private life as he was in his professional life."

I resisted the urge to lean back in my chair and tent my own hands. I was struck by the fact that he wouldn't look at me when he spoke. "You say that you didn't socialize. No business lunches? No golf or tennis? Company parties?"

His laugh was perfunctory. "Well, of course we did those things. Men ... coworkers ... professional coworkers do. I meant we weren't friends. I didn't know him outside a business context."

"You did play tennis and golf?"

"Squash and golf. But ..." He hesitated, torn between a banker's discretion and his urge to say something bad about a man he hadn't liked. Meanness won. "It wasn't pleasant. Cal had a pleasant social veneer but he couldn't always conceal his cutthroat attitude. Winning was very important to him." He untented the hands and held them palms out in a defensive gesture. "Don't get me wrong. Calvin Bass was a hell of an employee. An incredibly hard worker, and he was tireless in his efforts to build us a portfolio of secure mortgage investments. Of course, we are a local bank and try to make our investments serve the community, but Cal took the lessons of the eighties to heart. He didn't like to take chances. He was very conservative. Very conservative. And very sure of himself." He said it matter-of-factly but there was a nervous flicker in his eye that suggested there was something more he wasn't saying.

"You approved of his practices?"

There was that flicker again. "Of course. They were the bank's policies."

"Do you know Julie Bass?"

"A lovely girl. I'm shocked they could even consider that she would do such a thing."

"Why is that?"

I caught him off guard. He'd assumed I'd be satisfied with his platitudinous declaration. "Well, uh, she's such a good wife and mother. A homemaker, in the old-fashioned sense of the word. And so delicate. It's impossible to imagine a woman like Julie doing such a thing. Even contemplating such a thing."

I let it go. Admittedly, I'd thought the same thing myself, but it seemed offensive coming from him. "How did Calvin Bass get along with his coworkers?"

He touched his mustache nervously. "Just fine. I'd say they admired or respected, rather than liked him."

"He wasn't very likable, was he?"

He touched the mustache again. Again the internal debate. Again malice prevailed. "No. He was too ruthless and demanding. And competitive. And critical. Very sure of himself." I heard it as arrogant and pigheaded. He looked quickly at his watch, uncomfortable, as though he'd said too much. "I'm afraid that's all the time I have. Good luck, Mrs. uh . . . Kozak. I hope you're able to help Julie."

I got up, too. "Thank you for your time, Mr. Ramsay. I just had one more question. Was Mr. Bass in any financial difficulty?"

He straightened his coat sleeves and didn't meet my eyes. "Not that I know of." I was firmly and inexorably led to the door and dismissed.

As I passed Sherry's desk, she handed me a piece of paper. "You dropped this, Ms. Kozak." On it she'd written "Call me at home tonight" and her number.

"Thank you," I said.

I was backing carefully out of my parking space when a blue Taurus SHO came from nowhere and missed me by inches. Eliot Ramsay, without even registering my face, gave me the finger and a blast of the horn and shot out of the lot in a cloud of dust. "And a hearty heigh-ho Silver to you, too, pardner," I muttered.

I went back to the office and put out a few more fires, then rushed to my club, struggled into some Lycra, and let Aaron put me through my paces. On the plus side, Aaron gives the best workout I've ever had; on the minus side, everyone thinks so, and his classes are getting overcrowded. I'm too big to move about safely in a crowded room. I have a wide wing span and when I kick out my leg, I really cover some ground. I've found that the right front corner is a good spot for me. Unfortunately, so has this uncoordinated little twit with raccoon makeup and bright red fingernails. I sometimes end up standing behind her when she squeezes in front of me at the last minute. She's always off beat and doing her own thing with her arms. If we weren't such a civilized society, I'd kill her and eat her.

On the way home I felt so righteous that I skipped my usual greasy burger in favor of a salad and flavored seltzer. I knew I'd feel virtuous until about nine, when I'd become ravenously hungry, but I'd be at home then, where there is nothing, tempting or otherwise, to eat. Lately Suzanne has been lecturing me about reforming my eating habits; any day now I expect a healthy heart cookbook and bags of quinoa and low-fat granola to show up on my desk.

I cruised in, pleased to see that the red eye of my answering machine was staring at me, unblinking. I shed my work clothes, putting them carefully on hangers just as my mother taught me to do, and put on shapeless old sweats. To celebrate the fact that it was Tuesday and my favorite TV program was on, I poured myself some Jack Daniel's, got the portable phone, and curled up on my soft leather couch.

Sherry DuBose wanted to get one thing straight from the start. "Normally, I would put office confidentiality first," she said. "I'm a discreet, well-trained professional secretary. I'm talking to you because I'm so damned mad at that jerk that I want to hurt him, so you may want to take what I say with a grain of salt."

I'll take it any way I can get it, I thought. "What did he do to make you so mad?"

There was a pause. A sigh. "I don't like to talk about my troubles," she said. "This is just so you'll understand. My daughter April was born with a congenitally short leg. It's not a tragedy. She handles it well. Wears a special shoe and it doesn't keep her from playing soccer like a fiend or riding her bike or anything. She's a real trouper. But it does need treatment. Anyway, she had to have surgery in the fall. One of several they'll have to do. I planned for it. Saved up my vacation and my sick leave and my personal days, made sure I missed the fewest number of days possible, so some days I was with her and some days my husband was. On the days I worked, I came in early and left late, so I wouldn't get behind. . . ."

The anger in her voice was loud and clear. "Then she got an infection and had to go back to the hospital. She was terribly sick. I missed three days in a row and that bastard, who has always said he understood family came first and who knows I do the work of any other two people in that place . . . when he wrote up my yearly evaluation, he gave me a bad performance review because family demands had made me miss too much work, so I didn't get a raise."

"I'm sorry," I said.

"Not as sorry as I am. I'd look for another job, but I provide the insurance. . . ." She left the rest unsaid. We both knew about insurers and existing conditions.

"Did Ramsay and Calvin Bass get along?"

"Not lately. Well, let me back up a bit. Calvin Bass didn't have friends at the bank, he had underlings and coworkers, and he treated his coworkers like servants or morons and he treated his underlings like serfs. He was very up front about it. It was clear that no one was as good or as bright or as hardworking as Saint Calvin. That wasn't Ramsay's style; he's more the underhanded, backstabbing type, smooth to your face, steal your ideas when your back is turned. You can't trust anything Ramsay says. At least with Cal, you knew where you stood. It might be low in his estimation, but he was honest about it. Ramsay never meets your eye."

"I've noticed."

"You're a quick study," she said. "What I wanted to tell you was that Ramsay and Cal had a big fight the week before he died. Something about mortgage applications. The FDIC inspectors are coming next week. I couldn't hear most of it, only when they raised their voices, but from what I overheard, it sounded like Ramsay was afraid the records might show lending discrimination. I couldn't hear Ramsay's proposed solution but whatever it was, Cal disagreed. Vehemently. And I heard Ramsay telling Cal not to . . . these are his words, not mine, 'fuck things up for everybody.' "

"Could Ramsay have disliked Calvin Bass enough to want to kill him?"

Sherry was silent for a minute. "You have to understand," she said, "that I can't imagine any situation in which one person decides they're justified in killing another, except to protect my child, though I realize from the news and TV that plenty of people do. Eliot Ramsay is devious, underhanded, and absolutely devoted to his own interests, but I don't think he's a killer. I don't think he has the guts. So my answer to your question is no. However, I will say that Cal Bass was a dedicated philanderer and a son of a bitch. He had a way of being critical that was very hurtful. Very personal. His disapproval could be devastating. If you don't believe me, ask Rachel."

"Who's Rachel?"

"His assistant. She wanted his job; he wanted her body. It was a standoff, as far as I know, but I did once hear her tell her friend Lois that, 'if that pig lays a hand on me one more time, I'm going to kill him.' He stole all her best ideas and then treated her like a stupid bimbo. Cal had her in tears more than once, and Rachel is tough."

"Full name?"

"Kaplan. Rachel Kaplan."

"Married?"

"No."

"Think she'll talk to me?"

"Well, she thinks she's the perfect professional woman and the soul of discretion, but if she's drunk enough, she'll talk. Try her Thursday night at Popovers. If she doesn't pick up some guy, she'll be working on getting drunk."

"He ever make a pass at you?"

"He made a pass at every female between ten and fifty. I think someone once told him he looked like a Kennedy and it went to his head."

"Doesn't sound like it went to his head. It sounds like it went south." Sherry DuBose laughed out loud and then I heard her say something to someone in the room.

"My husband said that was a good one."

"Maybe this is a silly question, but did anyone like Calvin Bass?"

"His secretary, Rita. But she's new. He went through secretaries like some people go through jelly beans. No. Doughnuts. Because doughnuts, like secretaries, have holes, and Cal Bass thought he had a calling when it came to filling holes." She laughed, choked, and mumbled "Excuse me" into the phone. I heard voices in the room, then she came back. "My husband says not to descend to Cal's level."

"You were telling me about Rita?"

"Poor little thing! Rita still thinks he walked on water. She cried all last week because he was dead."

"Was she sleeping with him?"

"I don't know but I wouldn't be surprised. Most of the others did."

"Was he attractive?" I said, realizing that I had no idea what Cal Bass had looked like.

"Devastating. Gorgeous. A hunk. And so driven and calculating. You have to admire a man who knows what he wants and is ruthless in going after it, until he steps on your face. He had a certain predatory charm but underneath he was a gilded dog turd. I always felt sorry for his wife."

"Why?"

"For all the reasons I've already told you. Because he treated her the same way he treated his employees. Demanding, scornful, and condescending. He treated her like a slightly simple child. Once she called him with a medical emergency involving one of the children and he yelled at her not to bother him when he was working. I wouldn't have put up with it, but I think she loved him. I've got to go put my daughter to bed. You want Rita's number?"

I took Rita's number and leaned back, ready to spend some quality time with my friend Jack and ponder on what I'd heard, but Mr. Graham Bell's invention buzzed in my ear. A seductive man's voice, asking for me. I admitted that's who I was and he identified himself as Bennett Landry, Julie's attorney.

"She asked me to touch base and see if you were able to do what she asked." He sounded as if he had no idea what that was.

"You can tell her that I checked the house and everything was secure but that was before the police got there." I wasn't about to admit to some stranger, even a stranger working for Julie, that I'd removed anything from the house.

"I'm worried about her," he said. "She seems disoriented and depressed and extremely anxious about the children. Do you . . . uh . . . I know this is awkward . . . but I'd just like to have some reactions from friends of hers . . . like you. Do you know of any reason why Julie might have been in Connecticut that weekend?"

"Was she in Connecticut that weekend?"

"That's what the police say."

"I really don't know Julie very—"

"What about his friends, his coworkers. Do you know if any

of them might have had a grudge against him? Or of anyone who might have wanted to hurt him?"

"I'm sorry, Mr. Landry. I hate to disappoint you when I know you're trying to help Julie, but I'm pretty useless as a source of information. I've only known her for a few days and I never met him at all."

There was a long silence on his end of the line, punctuated by a thumping sound. I imagined a pinstriped man drumming restlessly on the desk with his pencil.

Then he said, "Julie said you were a good friend." His voice was accusing.

"Only a few days," I repeated. "I'm concerned about her, of course, but I don't know her well. Maybe some of her closer friends could help."

"Give me their names," he said eagerly. "I'll call them."

"You'd have to get them from Julie. . . ."

"The only names she gave me were yours and your mother's."

Probably Julie was so upset she wasn't thinking clearly. Maybe my mother would know. "Ask my mother," I told him. "She knew Julie pretty well. Maybe she can suggest some people."

"I'll do that," he said. "Thanks for your time." I had the impression of him rushing off.

"Wait," I said. "I have two questions for you."

"Yes?" A reluctant, hesitant response.

"Was Calvin Bass well insured?"

"I don't think that's your business," he said.

"Two-way street," I countered. "You want me to help you, you'll answer my questions."

"Help me how? You just said you didn't know anything."

"I know Cal Bass was almost universally disliked by the people he worked with."

"And . . ."

"And I'm waiting for an answer to my question," I reminded him.

Another long silence after which he grudgingly allowed that Cal Bass was worth more dead than alive.

"Second question," I said. "How did he die?"

"Fire," Landry said. "He burned to death when the car caught fire."

"Thank you. Give me your number and I'll call you if I learn anything."

"Why should you be learning anything?"

I shrugged, even though he wasn't there to see it. "I'm very good at asking questions."

He gave his number so reluctantly that I decided his hesitation wasn't due to caution or legal considerations, it was just his personal style.

I wanted to get back to Jack and it was almost time for my program, but I had to call my mother first. The idea of Julie having no friends troubled me. Once again, I found myself in a hesitant conversation. I asked my question. Mom was silent, a calculated, disapproving silence. "I'm glad you've found time in your busy schedule to try and help her. . . ." she said.

"Mom, I'm only asking because her lawyer called. . . ."

"Your dad says he's a good lawyer. You'll like working with him."

My turn to be silent. Finally, I said, "I'm not working with him." I spat it through gritted teeth. "I just wondered about her friends."

Another silence. Then, she said, "I don't know. I'll call you back."

Unanswered questions swirled around my mind like dustballs stirred up by a draft. Why had Julie sent two of us for the letters? Why had her doctor, of all people, picked them up? Why did the police think Julie had been in Connecticut? And what, exactly, had happened to Calvin Bass? Over all the questions, Julie's scared face and my mother's disapproving one hovered, watching me.

Ms. Thea "fix-it" Kozak decided she had to go to Connecticut and learn the TRUTH, especially since I could combine my field trip with a long-overdue social visit. I called my friend Ellen Bradley and asked if she and her husband George, who lived near the track, would mind some company on Saturday. Ellen and George were delighted, especially when I said I might bring Andre. All my friends are hoping I'll find Mr. Right and have another chance at happily ever after. And Ellen had called several times, trying to invite us down.

After that I paused to sip my drink but the ice had melted and the bourbon was too watery. I dumped it down the sink and fixed another one to sip while I called Mr. Right. He answered on the first ring: "Lemieux."

"Hi, handsome," I said. "I was going to be in the neighborhood tomorrow and I wondered if it would be convenient to stop by."

"I have a girlfriend," he said. "She lives down in Massachusetts but she's very jealous. I don't think it would be a good idea."

Just the sound of his voice made me want to crawl into the phone and snuggle up next to his ear. "Seriously, folk," I said. "Will you be home if I arrive on your doorstep around five?"

"Make it six and you've got a deal."

"You're a hard man, Lemieux."

"Especially when I think of you."

Yeah, right, I thought, though my pulse rate seemed to be increasing. "What should I bring?"

"I'll cook, you bring wine and clean underwear."

"Clean underwear?"

"Didn't your mother ever tell you . . . ?"

"More times than I can count. So I'm invited to spend the night?"

"It would give me great pleasure."

"I'll bet. Say, have you got any connections with the Connecticut State Police?"

"Why? You got a ticket?"

"Nope. Dead body."

"Theadora . . . you aren't. . . ."

"No. No way. It's for one of Mom's friends. I just need to know how this guy died. The details of the accident, I mean. He was taking a racing course. . . ."

"You're not going to do anything stupid?"

"That's why I'm calling you, honey, instead of putting on my cloak and dagger."

He sighed. "Give me the basics and I'll see what I can do. And, Thea—"

"Yes, sweetie?"

"Don't do anything stupid."

"You already said that."

"Come live with me."

"I'll think about it." I was just irritated enough to suggest that that was stupid, but every day in every way I'm getting better at keeping my mouth shut. Besides, when he isn't being overprotective, he's a great companion. And in this case, he'd argue his concern wasn't overprotection, it was common sense. We shared some intimate details about what we planned to do with each other on the morrow and disconnected. I had a fatuous grin on my face, but what the heck. I was alone.

I tried calling the number Sherry DuBose had given me for Rita, but the woman I reached was hysterical. She mumbled something about an angry call from Eliot Ramsay and papers missing from the files and being fired and hung up on me.

I was deeply immersed in the trials of a bunch of homicide detectives when my mother called. She rambled on for a while about trying to locate Julie's friends and how difficult it seemed to be before she delivered her bombshell.

"l heard a terrible thing from Mrs. Pulsifer today, that nasty old gossip." Mrs. Pulsifer was the source of all my mother's rumors. "She says that the talk at the hospital is that Dr. Durren was having an affair with Julie Bass, and that he's the father of her younger child."

"Who is Dr. Durren?"

"Oh, I forget you don't live here anymore. Dr. Thomas Durren. He's the ER physician over at the hospital. Isn't it dreadful what people will say about you when you're down? They were just as horrid about your sister, Carrie. At least you haven't done anything to be gossiped about. At least not here in Grantham." There was an implied "yet" at the end of the sentence.

CHAPTER 7

WEDNESDAY DAWNED CLEAR and cool. I carried my coffee out onto the deck and listened to the waves and the shriek of gulls and inhaled the salty tang of the air. It was one of those days when it felt good to be alive. I didn't even mind that I had a long drive ahead of me, midway up New Hampshire on the Maine–New Hampshire border, to the Northbrook School. It was good driving weather.

I was meeting with the headmaster and his trustees at eleven to discuss a marketing study. Like many of our client schools, Northbrook was doing all right but getting nervous about their market niche. I wasn't nervous. I'd been through these meetings so many times now that there were few surprises. But it was all new to them, and in their honor I was wearing my most conservative consultant gear—navy suit with an executive blouse, plain jewelry, and shoes with only a suggestion of a heel. My independent hair was trying to pull loose from its confining barrette, but the barrette, like me, was tough and experienced.

Spring wasn't as far advanced in the mountains, and the trees on Northbrook's campus had only buds instead of leaves.

In the gardens, perennials were just beginning to peek out to see if it was safe to emerge. Crocuses were starting to bloom and daffodils were budding. Even still shaking off the grip of winter, it was a lovely campus—a mix of white clapboard houses with green shutters and red-brick Georgian buildings. Vast expanses of green lawns, crisscrossed with paths, surrounded the buildings, and from its location on a hillside, it looked out over the valley like the lord of the manor. The students who passed seemed animated and happy. I was a little sorry to have to go inside.

The meeting went well. Both the headmaster of school and the trustees seemed eager to have EDGE doing some work for them. They were an unusual group in several ways—first, because they lacked the arrogance and self-importance of many such boards, second, because both the head and the board seemed to genuinely love the school, and finally, because there was no tension between the head and his board. I was tempted to tell them that they didn't need us—all they needed to do was let prospective students and their parents see the campus and see their own enthusiasm—but it was a fact that their applications had been down slightly and they were concerned about their continuing ability to attract the kind of students who made Northbrook so lively and desirable.

They invited me to stay for lunch, which was not a sit-down affair in the trustees' room but a trip to the dining hall. By the end of lunch, I knew that if I did the study, one thing I would recommend was a better cook. From the amount of food that I saw being thrown away, I thought the students would agree. Their liveliness and good cheer were even more impressive given that they were fed on grade-B slop.

After lunch, the headmaster took me on a tour of the campus. He led me proudly through the new theater, through the gyms, through the music facilities and the arts center, and through the science labs. Usually, such a tour reveals some weaknesses in a school. Typically, private schools do not have science facilities as good as those in public schools, and sometimes other facilities or classrooms seem shabby, cramped, or outdated. Northbrook seemed to have no such problems. Everything was up-to-date, well maintained, and inviting. I couldn't imagine a student not being impressed. The only deterrent I could see was tramping through the snow in the winter. New England had just come through a serious winter and most of us still cringed at the sight of our winter coats and boots. I mentioned this to him as we strolled across the campus.

He looked abashed. "It's such a nice day I forgot to show you the tunnels."

"Tunnels?"

"Underground. Or partly underground. They connect the buildings."

"Are you kidding?" I said. "This place is amazing."

"We think so, too. We're able to do all this because we've got an unusually large endowment. An absolute fluke, really, how we got it. You'll like the story." We had just come to a bench in the sunshine, looking out over the valley. "Let's sit here," he suggested, "and I'll tell you the story of Northbrook's fortune."

The headmaster, a man called Benjamin Franklin Rhodes III, was a short, slightly rounded man in his fifties, who moved with the vigor and enthusiasm of a much younger man. He had a bounce in his step and a gleam in his eye that made me jealous. "Once upon a time," he began in a storytelling voice, "on a snowy evening, an elderly gentleman was driving past Northbrook when his car skidded on a patch of ice, went into the ditch, bounced out, and ran into one of our gateposts. Some students who were out having a snowball fight heard the crash, ran to the scene, and pulled the man out of the car just seconds before it exploded."

I loved stories that began with once upon a time, and sat,

staring out over the peaceful valley, imagining the snowy night. "They were just boys," he continued, "and they never thought about the possibility that they could aggravate injuries. They just pitched in as a group, hauled him out, and carried him to the infirmary, and while the nurse checked him out and determined that, apart from cuts and bruises, he seemed remarkably uninjured, the boys fixed him cocoa and cookies. Over cocoa and cookies, he regaled the boys with stories about his adventures as a miner in the West."

The headmaster smiled. "As luck would have it, the snowstorm turned into a major blizzard and the accidental visitor was unable to leave Northbrook for several days. He spent the first night in the infirmary and after that moved to the headmaster's house. He took his meals in the dining hall with the boys. . . ." He caught my look. "It's not usually as bad as today," he said. "Our cook is down with a bad back and I'm afraid her assistant isn't quite up to the task. The old man's name was Foster. Edwin Foster. He'd had an interesting and adventurous life in the West around the turn of the century as a mining engineer— made a fortune at it—and now he was all alone in the world. A widower without children. So the students adopted him.

"Claiming that he was an orphan boy—they'd just finished a production of the *Pirates of Penzance*—they went to the headmaster and asked if there was some way Mr. Foster could remain on campus. There was an empty faculty suite at the time, the trustees were agreeable, and so Mr. Foster became a geology teacher emeritus, spent five wonderful and productive years here at Northbrook—he actually did teach and he was gifted— and when he died, he left his enormous fortune to the school."

"What a wonderful story."

"Isn't it? I never knew him. He was before my time. But there are a few faculty members left who did. They all say that knowing Edwin Foster was a privilege and an experience that enhanced their lives."

There was a note of finality in his voice and an impatience in his wiggling foot that said it was time for me to leave him to his other chores. I stood and held out my hand. "Thank you, Mr. Rhodes. It's been a delightful visit. Northbrook is certainly an impressive place. Where would you like to go from here? Do you want to look at the materials I brought and get back to me? Would you like more information about anything?"

He checked his watch. "I'm meeting the trustees at two. We'll see what they have to say and then I'll call you. I can't speak for them, of course, but it seems to me that we can definitely use your help."

He walked me back to my car, we shook hands again, and I rolled a bit regretfully down the drive and out through the gate. Northbrook was the first school in a long time that had made me wish I was a kid again. I wished I had no more cares in the world than the complexities of French grammar and which flannel shirt to wear.

It was only two. The drive to Andre's would take maybe an hour and a half. And, being a workaholic like me, he never came home early so I had time on my hands. If I drove another half hour north, I might be able to find Verrill Brothers Trucking and Julie's brother, Duncan.

I stopped at Malone's Kwik-Stop for coffee and directions. The woman behind the counter, probably only my age though she was shapeless and had a hard-used look, was happy to give directions. "Go on up this road 'bout two miles and you can't miss it on the right. Big sign with orange letters." She paused and studied me carefully. "You aren't lookin' for a job there, are you, honey? Because if you are, then forget it. They pay some of the best wages around here but far as I can see, they're still in the last century, it comes to hiring women. Nobody's sued 'em, I guess, 'cuz no one's about to tangle with ole Dunk. He'd make life hell on earth for any woman worked there."

"Duncan Donahue?"

Her expression was frankly curious. "You know Dunk?"

I shook my head. "His sister. I wanted to ask him some questions about her."

"I hope you aren't from the state or anything. Dunk's real protective 'bout Deanna. Always was. So if that's it, I was you, I wouldn't mess with him. Dunk's got some temper on him."

"I don't know Deanna. I came to ask him about his sister Julie. She's in trouble."

She gave me a puzzled look. "Maybe you've got the wrong guy. Dunk's only got the one sister. Deanna. Little bitty blond thing with huge eyes and a face like a baby doll? Looks so lost and pitiful you feel like you oughta take her home and feed her?" I nodded. "That's Deanna, then. Don't look a bit like her brother, what with him big as a house and got that red hair. So she's changed her name to Julie, has she? Probably thinks it's more classy. Always was a climber, that Deanna."

"What do you mean?"

"Mind if I get myself some coffee? If you're trying to help Deanna, there's things you ought to know. That'll be eleven seventy-five," she told the man behind me. She took his twenty, gave him his change, sold him a lottery ticket, and poured herself coffee.

By the time the cashier, Cindy, had finished her story, I knew more about Julie Bass's early life, at least according to local gossip, than I could ever have imagined wanting to know. According to Cindy, Deanna and Duncan were abandoned by their father when Deanna was very small, left in the uncertain care of an alcoholic mother. The mother died when Deanna—Julie, that is—was only sixteen. After that, her brother raised her, and he raised her to make something of her life, or, as Cindy put it, to think she was better than she was. Deanna had not had dates because Duncan drove even the boldest boys away.

Between Dunk's protectiveness and her own shy nature,

she'd been so aloof she'd gotten a reputation as a snob and person who thought too well of herself. It didn't help that she was academically talented and ambitious, quietly winning things like the school math prize that, in the community's opinion, ought to have gone to a boy. When she got a college scholarship, there was a lot of talk about it being unfair either because of Duncan's bullying or Deanna's machinations, but whatever the reason, Deanna had left town and never returned. From what I'd heard, I didn't blame her.

"Thanks, Cindy," I said, heading for the door and the fearsome Duncan Donahue.

"You're welcome," she said. "I hope I haven't offended you, being a friend of Deanna . . . uh . . . Julie's and all, but she was always so good at putting on an act, I thought you oughta know. What I mean is, don't let that fragile exterior fool you. She's no dope and she can be tough as nails. Back when Verrill Brothers used to sponsor a race car and Dunk was in charge of it, Deanna was a member of the pit crew, and that dainty little babe could hold her own with the best of them."

CHAPTER 8

SMIRKING MEN AT Verrill Brothers Trucking were happy to send me down a dimly lit, battered corridor to the loading dock where they said I would find Duncan Donahue. Forewarned is forearmed, so I was expecting their behavior, thanks to the helpful Kwik-Stop clerk. She was wrong, though. They weren't so much still in the last century as still in adolescence. The hall was lined with pinups of air-brushed improbable bodies and I thought, as I marched past them, that if there were any women employed at Verrill Brothers, even as secretaries, they'd have themselves a pretty nice sexual harassment case. If this wasn't an atmosphere hostile to women, I'd never seen one.

As I neared the end of the corridor, a commotion of male voices, yelling and cursing, penetrated right through the heavy metal door. I stuck my head out just as someone went flying by and crashed into the wall beside me. A man with blood streaming from his nose clawed his way up the wall, scrambled to his feet, and pushed past me. I turned from watching his retreat to find a gigantic man with blazing red beard and hair bearing down on me with a crowbar in his hand.

"Where the fuck's Jimmy gone? And what the hell are you doing out here?" he bellowed, waving the crowbar.

Pleased to meet you, too, I thought, battling my urge to turn and run. I didn't know anything about Jimmy, though I assumed he was the fleeing man, so I just stated my business. "I'm looking for Duncan Donahue."

"What the hell for?" The rasp in his voice would have scraped the shell off a turtle.

I was ready to take my toys and go home. This wasn't any fun. The circumstances didn't look auspicious and I hate people who try to intimidate me. I'd come a long way to help Julie, though; it didn't make sense to leave without trying to talk with her brother, even if he did have the manners of a junkyard dog. I didn't waste any time on pleasantries; I got right to the point.

"I want to talk about your sister Julie."

The ruddy giant laid a grimy hand on my shoulder and gestured with his chin toward the battered door. "In my office," he said, and steered me none too gently through some doors and into a chair. He dumped the crowbar in a corner, dropped himself into a chair across the desk, and subjected me to a crude third degree. "What are you, a fuckin' cop?" I shook my head. "One of those snooping social workers then? Her kids are fine, thank you, and no, you can't see 'em without showing me some kind of a court order. You got that?"

I shook my head again. He wasn't making this easy. "Look, Mr. Donahue, I'm not a social worker or a cop or anyone who's trying to hurt your sister. I'm a friend of hers. That is, I'm trying to be. I haven't really known her very long. And my mother told me I had to help."

To my surprise, he smiled at that. His smile was pleasant and with it some of his fierceness dropped away. For the first time, I saw the shadow of a resemblance to Julie. "You're a pretty big girl to be doing what your mamma tells you."

"You haven't met my mother."

"How is she? Julie, I mean," he asked with almost boyish eagerness. "Is she doing okay?"

He must be talking to her, I thought, he had her kids, but not wanting to alienate him further, I tried to answer the question. "She had a hard time that first night . . . when I saw her . . . there was a doctor in to see her. Look, I think we both know that jail is not a nice place, Mr. Donahue. I haven't seen Framingham, but it can't be nice, either. I expect it's an especially awful place for someone as sensitive as your sister. And you know how she worries about the children. The important thing is to get her out. I came to see you because Julie seems to have trusted you and confided in you. I don't believe she's guilty . . ."

"You're damned right she's not guilty!" he roared.

". . . but it's difficult to talk with her while she's in jail. Her lawyer asked me for help. I'm trying to find out who might have wanted to harm Calvin Bass. To give the police an alternative . . . another suspect. . . ."

"You make it sound like she's a suspect," he said, the genial look vanishing. He leaned across the desk and glared at me, the heat of his anger scorching me from five feet away, the bulging veins in his forearms seeming to pulse with it.

Someone knocked on the door, opened it, and stood there, not quite meeting Donahue's eyes. "Rooney sent me for the wrench," he muttered.

"Well, goddammit, go get it then. Can't you see I'm busy?" The man sidled into the corner and grabbed a large wrench. "You're gonna bring that right back, aren't ya, Joe," Donahue said. "I don't want to have to come looking for it." Cringing before Donahue's dark look, the man nodded and slouched out, leaving black fingerprints on the door.

"We're dealing with a real-life situation here, Mr. Donahue," I reminded him. "They did arrest her. So they think they have reason, don't they?" He didn't like that, but he held his tongue. With difficulty. I could tell he wanted to yell at me again. Feeling more and more out of my league, I persisted, "Do you know of anyone who wanted to hurt your brother-in-law?"

"I would have," he said. "My brother-in-law Calvin was a horny scumbag who had to dip his wick into everything that moved. He cheated on my sister and bullied her and put her down until he broke her spirit. I didn't shed any tears when I heard that fucker was dead. No sirree! Except for leaving Julie alone with those two little ones, but Cal wasn't interested in being a father anyway. Practically went nuts when the second one wasn't a boy! He only used 'em for show, know what I mean? He used to rag her somethin' awful about how she had to dress and behave and how the girls had to dress and behave and how she had to talk and what clubs to join." He stopped abruptly. "You get my drift?"

"He was very controlling?"

"I guess that's what you'd call it. I think a man's got to keep a woman under control, don't get me wrong, but there's a kind of a deal that goes along with that, and he didn't keep the deal. Plus he was a complete shit to live with. You can quote me on that. Never missed anything. The house had to be just so and his food just so or the man would have a fit. She was the sweet-est little thing . . . Dee . . . Julie was."

Now that I had him going, Dunk, as he urged me to call him, was on a roll. "She changed her name?"

"Bet your ass." I never bet my ass on anything, but I didn't tell him that. The phone rang.

He snatched it up, barked his name into it, listened for a minute, and pawed through the papers on his desk. "Thursday! Listen, dickhead, I've got a business to run here. A trucking business. Which means I need my trucks. You said Monday." He listened again. "Did you try Bilodeau? Well, try him. If I'd known you'd take this long, I'd have done it myself. No, ass-wipe, sitting in an office hasn't made me forget a thing. I can still put an engine together faster than you can take a piss." He listened again. Barked a laugh. "I just might take you up on that. Okay. Okay. Try Bilodeau and get back to me. I'll bet he's got something lying around." He threw the phone down. "Where were we?"

"You were telling me about Julie changing her name."

"That was Cal's idea, too. Fell for her when she was named Deanna, but it wasn't classy enough for him, so he suggested Julie. Told her never to let on that she'd come up the hard way. The two of 'em invented a whole story for her about her rich family and her proper upbringing. Guess a smart mill town girl pulled herself up by her bootstraps wasn't good enough for Mr. Calvin 'self-important' Bass. No way. He's got to take a real smart, capable, college-educated girl like that and make her act like some kind of country club twit. Way he had her behavin', you wouldn't think the girl had a brain in her head. He even had her believin' she didn't."

"Where did Julie go to college?"

"You don't have to sound so surprised," he said, frowning. "Dee was determined to get out of here and make something of herself. Until she met that jerk. Best damned mechanic on my crew, but she wanted to leave this town behind and do something respectable. Not that I blame her. We come up hard, me and Dee. I guess it was harder on a girl, growing up poor like we did, treated like trash 'cuz we didn't have a father and our mother was a drunk. Dee went to Wheaton. Studied economics and sociology. Honors and everything. She was going to be a smart social worker and help people like us."

He shook his head. "Then she meets that asshole and love turns her into mush. 'S funny, you know. How all that ambition could vanish and leave her just like a piece of clay. All his fault, you know." He glared at me as though I might dare to disagree, unconsciously clenching his freckled fist, the muscles in his arm dancing, but it was unnecessary show. It was already very clear to me that sensible people didn't disagree with Dunk Donahue. At least not openly. Even when he was calm, anger seemed to hang around him like a red cloud.

Dunk's story of their childhood was a far cry from the life of privilege Julie had described—described so well it sounded like she'd come to believe it. His was a different story than I'd gotten from Cindy at the Kwik-Stop, though I recognized the characters. It wasn't helping me any, though. I tried to change the subject. "What about their financial situation? Did Julie talk about that?"

He shook his head. "That's another dumb thing my sister did. She's perfectly competent to handle money but she let him do it. I don't know what came over her. It was like she ran out of confidence or something. I don't know. All through high school she worked like a dog to get out of here. She was going to set the world on fire . . . and then she up and marries that guy and . . . I dunno. It's like he brainwashed her or something. My wife and I, we were both always saying to her, Dee, you've got to keep a job, some means of support. Suppose the guy walks out on you? But she wouldn't hear it. Said it would never happen."

He shook his head. "Real dumb for such a smart person. My wife Brenda, she says she thinks Dee married her dream of how life was supposed to be but then Brenda likes to read those women's magazines that're always preaching that psychology shit. Whatever the reason she married him, she discovered that it was no better than what she'd come from. Worse, if you ask me. But she wouldn't have killed him. She's not the killing type. And she wanted those girls to have a father. That was more important than what he was doing to her, even if he did have her so skinny and nervous she couldn't even eat anymore." He shrugged. "But I don't know much about their finances. They lived well. He wasn't generous, though. He made her account for every penny. Lately she said he'd been real nervous about spending. That's all I can tell you."

"Did you ever hit him?"

"Once. He had her up against a wall, choking her, because she'd forgotten to pick up his favorite shirt at the laundry and he wanted to wear it. I couldn't help myself."

I tried to steer the conversation back to my original question. "Do you know of anyone else who might have wanted to harm Cal?"

"Not specifically, but I expect it's everyone who knew the guy, except maybe his golfing buddies. The husbands of some of the women he slept with, maybe? He wasn't particular about their marital status. Or some of the women he'd rejected. You know how they are. I don't know this for a fact, of course, but I expect he didn't get on very well with the people who worked for him, either. He probably treated them the same way he treated Julie. Badly."

"You don't know any particulars?"

"Julie didn't talk much about his work. I don't think she knew much."

Other than Dunk himself, I was coming up empty-handed. "What about girlfriends? Anyone you can think of that I should talk to?"

"You're asking me about Cal's girlfriends?"

"Julie's girlfriends. Friends. The women she socialized with."

"Dee . . . Julie isn't much for girlfriends. She's always been sort of a loner." There was a pause as he reflected on the conversation. "Hey, wait a minute, lady. You aren't suggesting that I might have done it?" He leaned over the desk and peered at me. "You sure you aren't a cop?"

"I'm sure. Did she ever talk to you about Thomas Durren?" It was a long shot, a casual question. I wasn't prepared for his reaction at all.

A thundercloud rolled across his face. A quick reach behind him and he had the crowbar in his hand without even looking.

My nose tingled as I remembered the man on the loading dock. Jimmy. "You said you were her friend, and now you're trying to slander my sister." His voice dropped to a growl. "Let me tell you something, missy. If you have any notions of sharing that with the police, you'd better forget about them, you know what's good for you. We Donahues have to look out for each other." He set the crowbar on his desk, like a peculiar paperweight, but kept a hand on it. "Why did I tell you all that stuff for, you go and ask a question like that?"

I shrugged. I had no answer for him. And questions of my own, like why I'd wasted my time coming up here. The man was a tiresome bully. "I'm leaving," I said, getting up.

"Sit down," he said, patting the crowbar. "Sit down and tell me about how you won't say anything about Durren to the cops."

I stayed standing, comparing the distance around the desk for him to the distance to the door for me. "I don't have to tell the police anything, even if I were so inclined, which I'm not. I don't know anything about Dr. Durren except his name. But frankly, Mr. Donahue, it seems to be no secret—the rumor about Durren and your sister is all over Grantham. It's a pretty small town, you know. I expect some helpful soul has been willing to share it with the authorities."

"You sure you're not with the police?" he asked again.

"If I were with the police and you asked to see some identification, I'd have to show it to you." I waited to see if he'd ask. He didn't. "Julie volunteered for my mother at the hospital. Mom introduced us because she thought Julie needed a friend. . . . I lost my husband a few years ago in a car accident. She thought I might be able to help."

"Cops won't look beyond the ends of their noses, now that they've got her," he said bitterly. On this subject, at least, he and my mother were simpatico. "Especially once they find out she knows—" He bit the words off abruptly, reddening, trying to cover the breach with the awkwardness of one unused to watching his words. "Forget it. Damned cops." Donahue stared at me suspiciously, something in his look making me very uneasy—like he still didn't believe that I wasn't a cop. "You came all this way just to talk to me?"

"No. I had to see some people at the Northbrook School today. You know Northbrook? I was already close and I had some time, so I came." It sounded lame to me and from his look, I could see he thought it was lame as well. "I'm a consultant," I added. He didn't say anything but I sure didn't like the way he kept looking at me. I took a step toward the door. "Thanks for seeing me. If you remember anything Julie might have said that you think could be helpful, please call me." I offered him a business card.

He took it without looking at it and set it on the desk. "I don't think you're—" He was interrupted by the phone. "Don't leave," he said. A longer call this time, which required another rummage through the papers and then he read several things to whoever was on the other end. As soon as he hung up, there was another call. He turned his chair around so his back was to me. All I could hear was the murmur of his voice, except for one phrase. I heard him say ". . . send someone to talk to me?" and then ". . . cover for me if I have to go out."

While his back was to me, I edged toward the door, had my hand on the knob when he swung around. I stopped. A strange mood had overtaken him. He seemed to have forgotten that I was there. He grew pensive, rubbing his beard and staring at the wall behind me. He muttered to himself something about Durren. Suddenly he picked up the phone, started dialing a number, and then glared at me. "You have to go," he said rudely. "I've got work to do."

He gathered together enough manners to see me out, getting up, taking his coat, opening the door. He was even gracious enough to leave the crowbar behind. As we walked down the bawdy hallway, he cast the occasional sidewise glance to see if I was observing the decor. I stared carefully straight ahead. He said good-bye at the entrance and then stood watching as I walked to my car. His farewell was civil enough, but I couldn't shake a lingering sense of menace as I drove away.

CHAPTER 9

I STOPPED TO buy daffodils but got seduced by scented Stargazer lilies, which reminded me of hot summer nights. Bought some red wine. A sinful chocolate cake. A huge can of salted nuts with no peanuts. All the trappings of a big evening, first class all the way. Carrying my offerings, I presented myself at Andre's door, all the ups and downs of the day ousted by anticipation. I felt a little tingle of excitement when I heard his footsteps. Then the door opened and the tingle became a rush. Around Andre, my normal self-control sometimes vanishes like morning mist. This was one of those times.

He took the flowers and the wine, the nuts and the chocolate cake. Admired the cake, opened the nuts, put the flowers in water, and opened the wine to let it breathe. As he moved around the kitchen, I leaned against the counter, admiring his shape under his clothes, the firm line of his jaw, his sturdy forearms, the sexy arch of his brows, and tried not to drool. My mother would have been shocked at the ideas running through my head; Anaïs Nin would have been envious. I wanted him to sweep everything out of his way and pounce on me. He knew it, too. I'm no good at hiding my feelings from him.

Without being asked, he fixed me bourbon on ice, fixed one for himself, set them both on the coffee table, and seized me. "You need kissing," he said.

I didn't argue. "That's not all I need," I said, when I came up for air.

"First," he said, plunking himself down on the couch, "tell me about your week. Any further developments in the suburban wife racing car murder?"

"I'm trying to drag you off to bed and you want to chat about murder? Where are your priorities?"

"I can prioritize just fine," he said, patting the cushion beside him. "Come on over here and set a spell and tell me about this Julie Bass business."

He looked good enough to eat and there was a teasing glint in his eye that I'd seen often enough to know he wasn't going to budge from the spot until he made me talk. "I think this is cruel and unusual punishment," I said, sliding in close to him and putting my head on his shoulder. "But all right. First I will tell you about the angry red giant."

He shook his head. "Nope. No sex talk until we get this other stuff off the table."

"Idiot," I said, "the angry red giant is a person."

"I thought only men felt that way."

"Are you going to let me talk?" He nodded.

Until I began to talk about it, I hadn't realized that my encounter with Duncan Donahue had upset me so much. Seen from a safe distance, his irrationality and anger were even more frightening. Andre is a good listener and a thoughtful questioner, and when I was done telling him about Julie and Cal Bass, Donahue, and the people at the bank, I felt much better. It's one of the things I love about him. He can be as hard and pigheaded and macho as anyone and sometimes he drives me to distraction when he closes down and refuses to talk, but most of the time, I find my respect renewed and realize how lucky I am to know him. If I tell him I'm scared, he won't think I'm a wimp; I can admit I'm confused and he knows I'm not scatter-brained.

When I finished spitting out Duncan Donahue, he shook his head. "Jesus, Kozak, you sure know how to pick 'em. Promise me you won't go near him again."

I promised. I was glad to. Duncan Donahue scared me. I wondered if he had scared Cal Bass. It didn't sound like it.

"Close your eyes," Andre said. I closed them and felt his hands gently massaging the muscles at the back of my neck, moving up my neck to the back of my head and slowly down to my shoulders, pressing out the tension. "You're very tense," he murmured. If I'd been a cat, I would have purred. I was begin-ning to dissolve into a big, relaxed heap when he resumed the questions, but it wasn't so hard this time.

He took me through a description of my meetings with Julie, of my visit to her house and encounter with the police, Cindy at the Kwik-Stop and the details of my interview with Julie's brother. "You have considered the possibility that she might be guilty, haven't you?"

"Try suggesting that to my mother."

"I'm suggesting it to you," he said with an edge in his voice. "Think about it. You've told me the guy was an insufferable bas-tard and his wife was probably having an affair . . . and that while she seemed helpless to you, others have suggested she wasn't helpless at all, especially around cars. You ought to be prepared for the possibility that she killed him."

I considered what he'd said. "Yes and no."

"Meaning?"

"Meaning he was an abusive SOB who made her life miser-able, so I can imagine her thinking about getting rid of him. But she struck me as genuinely sorry that he was dead."

"Which she might have been even if she did kill him."

"And extremely helpless."

"That's not what everyone says."

"I'm not naive, Andre. But people can change. They can be intimidated into believing they're helpless, even when they aren't."

"I know that."

"And she wanted a father for her kids."

"A role the lover might have fit into nicely. He married?"

"I don't know," I said impatiently. "I don't . . . didn't want to know any of this stuff. I think I'm letting myself be drawn in . . ."

". . . because your mother told you to."

I gave him a dirty look. "Will you let me finish?"

He put his hand on my thigh. I could feel the heat right through my skirt. "Did you start without me?" he asked.

I sighed. Now I was the one who wanted to talk. "I've been trying to start. You're the one who's been holding back," I said. "Anyway, as I was saying . . . hey! Stop that! It tickles. I got started on this thing because Julie reminded me of Carrie . . . that lost quality she had . . . a sort of stubborn helplessness that kept her from taking sensible care of herself. Carrie was like that and Julie is like that. But what keeps me involved is curiosity. It's more complicated than just a husband-and-wife thing."

"*Just* a husband-and-wife thing?" Andre said.

"Yes, dear," I said patiently. "The whole business is a true mystery, with a lot of questions that need to be answered. There's a story there. Something was going on with Cal Bass. . . ."

His hand drifted farther up my leg. "Why do you care?"

"Because motive or not, lover or not, miserable life notwithstanding, I don't think she did it."

"What if she did? Say she did have motive, opportunity, and the ability to commit the crime. Are you prepared to accept that?"

"You already asked me that." We were back where we'd started.

"You never answered so I'm asking again. Look, I know that loyalty and friendship can keep you from seeing . . ." He raised his hand to make a gesture but I captured it and put it back on my leg.

"I'll be disappointed," I interrupted. "And I don't think I'm being foolish or naive here. Though if Julie is found guilty my mother will never speak to me again."

"Which wouldn't be all bad." He stroked the inside of my thigh in a way that was terribly distracting.

"Right. Did you get that information for me?"

"Information?"

"Information. You remember. I asked you to find out about the accident."

"Find out about the accident?" His hand stopped moving and pulled away. He looked like I'd just asked him to shovel out a barn.

"Relax, trooper. I don't mean wave your badge in people's faces and ask penetrating questions. I mean a little favor. Use your contacts. Find out the details of the crime from the Connecticut police?"

"I can't do that."

"You already said you would. The other night. On the phone." Instead of pressing the point, I leaned over and nibbled on his ear. "Of course you can," I whispered. "You guys do it all the time. Use the old-boy network. I'll make it worth your while."

"Ma'am," he said, "are you aware that I am a sworn officer of the law?"

"You're not in uniform."

"On an undercover assignment."

"Just where I want you, trooper. Under the covers."

"Detective, not trooper." He slipped a hand back between

my thighs. I closed them tightly, trapping it there.

"Mmm," he said. "Thighs like a steel trap."

"Blame it on Aaron."

"Aaron?"

"My aerobics instructor. Will you help?"

"I don't think Aaron needs any help. These thighs feel fine to me."

"Andre . . ."

"I'll see what I can do."

"I already know what you can do, but I'll sit through another demonstration."

"Sit?"

"If you want. Or stand. Or lie. Lean against the wall. Tie myself in knots like a pretzel. Shall I suggest other possibilities?"

"And you'll be very careful?"

"During the demonstration?"

"Thea . . ."

"Very, very careful."

"No heroics," he said. "No dramatic interventions. No more entering the premises of crime suspects. . . ."

"No," I agreed.

"That was really stupid," he murmured.

"Thanks," I said. "I know."

"I mean it," he said. "You have to be more careful. This is not your problem."

I was so weak with desire I would have promised anything. "I promise," I agreed. "If things look the least bit dangerous, I'll call my favorite cop."

"And who might that be?"

I unbuttoned his shirt and rubbed my face on his chest. In my honor, he'd omitted the undershirt. "Of course, his line might be busy, or he might be out of the office. Then I'll call my second-favorite cop."

"Florio?"

"Who else?"

"I mean it. About being careful."

"Shut up," I said, stopping his talk with a kiss. "I've been missing you." He buried his scratchy face between my breasts. Andre has such an aggressive beard he has five o'clock shadow by three. Too much testosterone or something.

"You want me to shave?"

"I want you to leave whisker burn over my entire body."

"Masochist."

"You say the most romantic things."

"This blouse must have at least a hundred buttons," he muttered.

"Rip it. Tear it. Pretend we're posing for the cover of a bodice-buster novel."

"Having Fabio fantasies, are we?"

"Andre Lemieux fantasies are good enough for me."

"Only eighteen," he said. "There!"

"Thirty. I'm thirty, not eighteen."

"Buttons, dammit. Oh, God, look at those luscious pillows of flesh. . . ."

"I love it when you talk dirty."

"That's not dirt, that's trash."

"Shut up and kiss me, you big oaf." I wrapped my arms and legs around him and clung like a burr.

Some time later, one of us suffering from whisker burn and both of us suffering from rug burn, we dragged ourselves into the kitchen and made dinner. The wine had had enough time to breathe and steaks and salad tasted like ambrosia. There's nothing like a little exercise to work up an appetite. We took our decadent chocolate cake to bed with two forks and managed to make quite a dent in it. Neither of us is petite and we don't have dainty appetites.

Eventually I snuggled into his arms and went to sleep. I only woke once, from a dream where Dunk Donahue was chasing me through a cemetery with an ax. Just as the ax was descending toward my head, Andre muttered some soothing sounds and pulled me close and Dunk Donahue vanished from my thoughts.

CHAPTER 10

WE ALWAYS HAVE a hard time getting out of bed in the morning despite being slaves of duty. The temptation to stay is just too great. Why would I want to leave the embrace of a warm, sexy man to walk across a cold room, pull on cold clothes, get in a cold car, and drive off into a cold gray dawn with three and a half hours of driving ahead of me? When our watches beeped, we only snuggled closer. Finally we managed to drag ourselves into the shower and make ourselves fit for the workplace. It took awhile. There's something awfully seductive about hot water and soap.

When we got to the kitchen we discovered that the cupboard was bare, except for leftover chocolate cake and salted nuts. We were in the mood for your basic lumber Jack and Jill breakfasts, so we headed for Benny's Diner. Good food, plenty of it, and someone else does the cooking and the dishes. We'd just pounced on our poached eggs and hash and home fries and three buttermilk pancakes, juice and coffee when a trooper Andre knew came in and asked if he could join us.

"Thea Kozak, this is Roland Proffit." Proffit had a grip like an unpegged lobster. When he finally gave my hand back, I felt like I should stick it in a bucket of ice.

"Pleased to meet you, ma'am," he said, sliding in beside Andre. "I heard Lemieux'd got himself a good-looking girl-friend, but they didn't half do you justice."

I could feel the heat of a blush coming up my neck. "Thank you," I muttered.

"She's very shy," Andre explained. "Smart, too."

I tried to kick him under the table and got Proffit instead. Proffit gave me a smile so broad it narrowed his gray eyes almost to slits. It was a pleasant, friendly smile, but something about Proffit suggested a cat about to pounce on its prey. Genial on the surface but with a restless undercurrent in the way he watched everything, his pale eyes jumping continuously to us, the other patrons, and the street, and in the tense set of his wide shoulders. Unlike Andre, who, as a detective, gets to wear civvies, Proffit was in uniform, every inch a state trooper, everything starched and pressed and shined.

"I hear you've got another moose story," Andre said.

"It's a peach," Proffit said. "Human nature's a funny thing, you know? Every time I think I've seen it all, someone does something even stupider. Goes like this. Police get a call from this woman on her car phone. Says she's hit a moose and needs help. They send out the cops, send out the ambulance, all that stuff. We know what a moose can do. They're not petite creatures," he said, watching me closely to see if I needed things explained. One of those down easterners who distrust people from away.

"When they get there, they find this drunken babe—no offense, ma'am, but she was a babe—in a little red sports car. Convertible with the top down even though it was colder than a bastard and she's wearing about enough clothes to cover her little finger. She's practically blue and too drunk to notice it. And she's got a moose in the backseat."

"In the backseat?" I said, knowing that was my line.

He nodded. "Yup. Then she tells the officers that the reason it's in the backseat is that it was in the road and wouldn't get out of her way no matter how much she honked, so she decided to back up and run into it, to scare it off. It went over the hood, over the windshield, and got stuck in the backseat, one hoof wedged between the seat and car. She thought it was kind of cute." He shook his head. "It's a wonder it didn't end up on top of her and bye-bye chickie."

I winced at the "chickie," but I have no patience with people, male or female, who won't use their brains.

"Roland collects moose stories," Andre said. "He once had to comfort a woman who thought she'd killed one of Santa's reindeer. And there was the assistant attorney general going north to do a title search. Swerved to avoid a moose and rolled the car, and then refused to go in the ambulance unless all the papers came, too."

Moose stories were fun but the clock was running. Time for me to hit the road, preferably sans moose. I did take the time to clean my plate while the guys talked shop and then I said my polite good-byes. In deference to Proffit's bachelor ears, I didn't bother to tell Andre what I'd be missing until we were together again. It was only going to be forty-eight hours. With cold showers, I could wait that long.

I was zipping along on 95, blessing the sixty-five-mile-an-hour speed limit even as I exceeded it, when a black van loomed up in my rearview mirror, coming closer and closer until we were almost sharing a seat. I was in the slow lane and the passing lane was clear but knowing that some drivers are numb as stumps, I moved over to let him pass. He moved over with me and stayed on my tail. Annoyed, I pulled back into the right lane. This time, the van pulled alongside and bumped the side of my car. I swerved out of the way and hit the horn to wake him up, but he bumped me again and stayed there, pressing steadily against my car.

Recognition brought a stab of fear and an adrenaline surge. This was no careless or inattentive driver. This was someone trying to force me off the road, and there were no other cars in either direction.

My sweaty fingers slipped on the buttons on my car phone, as I pressed *SP while I clung to the wheel and tried to keep the van from pushing me down the steep bank. Behind the dark tinted glass, the driver was invisible. We were both slowing down, most of the way into the breakdown lane, when the van accelerated, shot past me, and pulled in at an angle in front of me, forcing me to a stop and pinning me there. I was trying to give a coherent account of what was happening to the police dispatcher when Dunk Donahue appeared at my window, a gun aimed at my head.

"Shut up and get the fuck out of the car." The lurch of my stomach made me regret my big breakfast.

"You said you weren't a cop!" he roared as he grabbed my shoulder, his fingers digging deep as he hauled me out of the seat and slammed me against the car. My silk blouse shredded and the sleeve nearly came away in his hand, leaving my shoulder bare. If there was such a thing as wardrobe insurance, I'd be a good candidate.

"I'm not a cop!" I said as forcefully as I dared with a gun only inches from my face.

"A stoolie then. You looked pretty buddy buddy with that cop at breakfast."

Realization that he'd been following me and spying on me zipped through me like an electric shock. "I don't know what you're talking about."

"Why were you having breakfast with the state police?" he demanded in a furious voice. The gun bobbed and jumped in his hand like a living thing, shiny and lethal and so frightening it filled my view until it was all I could see—just the gun and below it the red-streaked skin of my shoulder. I struggled to stay calm; to treat him like the reasonable man he wasn't.

"I don't know what your problem is, Dunk. Or why you're holding that gun to my head." Keeping my voice calm and level. Informative. Conversational. Trying not to scream. "I was just having breakfast with my boyfriend and the other guy, the trooper, just happened to come along. I'd never met him before."

"That's not how it looked to me."

"I can't help how it looked. I'm telling you how it was. I was having breakfast with my boyfriend, Andre Lemieux, and Trooper Proffit came along and joined us." I raised my voice, hoping, with the car door open, that the dispatcher might still be listening. That's the beauty of those little microphones. You can talk without taking your hands off the wheel. Or your eyes off the gun. "What's the matter with you? Here I am, just driving along Route 95 in Gardiner and suddenly you're trying to drive me off the road."

"Pipe down, missy," he ordered, waving the gun just inches from my nose. "I can hear you just fine." He reached past me and pushed the door shut.

We've all seen a thousand guns on TV, a steady, lifelong diet of them. The real thing, I was discovering, was very different. A gun holds your attention, grows until it fills the whole space before your eyes. This one was so close I could smell the oil used to clean it. I wondered if I could snatch it and throw it away—a fine time to be imagining heroics—and realized that if my hand moved, his hand would move . . . and that would be it. I thought about how I'd promised Andre I'd be careful.

Sweat was soaking my blouse—what was left of my blouse—profuse, cold, drenching sweat, running down my arms and down my sides. Unbidden, my mother's annoying line—that horses sweat, men perspire, and women glow—popped into my head. Under stress, my mind reacts oddly, producing strange thoughts. Well, Mom, right now I was glowing like a beacon.

I hated this great red beast of a man who was making me sweat. Hated him so much I was almost as mad as I was scared. I wanted to scream and swear until I blew him off the face of the earth. But, discretion being the better part of valor, I piped down. I didn't want to die beside an interstate because a misguided attempt to help someone had mixed me up with Duncan Donahue. Death in the breakdown lane might be a great headline but it wasn't how I hoped to end my days. Nor was this the time.

"Okay, let's go through this again," he said, his face so close I could see the rusty stubble, the moles, scars, wrinkles. The whites of his small eyes were as red as his face. "The guy you spent the night with. Who's he?"

"My boyfriend."

"What does he do?"

"He's a detective with the state police."

Dunk Donahue's red face radiated anger. I could see how badly he wanted to hit me, just for something to do. Up close and personal, as they say, he smelled of stale sweat and old beer and cigarettes. I figured he'd probably slept in the van. Even though there was a cool breeze, he was sweating, too. Much as I hated him at that point for making me afraid, I could see that he was almost as scared as I was. Scared and confused. He wasn't used to doing his menacing in such public places.

"You're from Massachusetts. Why would you have a boyfriend in Maine?"

"I met him when he investigated my sister's murder," I began, but this wasn't the time for long stories. "Look, the Maine police don't have any interest in this. Julie lives in Massachusetts, the crime was in Connecticut. . . . This doesn't have anything to do with you. Why don't you believe me? I'm telling you the truth."

He hesitated, the gun wavering. "I don't get it," he said. "You're in New Hampshire on business and then coming to Maine to see your boyfriend. Why'd you come see me?"

"I told you. I was trying to help Julie . . . I thought you might know something useful. . . ." Fear does strange things to the vocal cords. My voice came out little and squeaky. "I thought you might know of someone who wanted to hurt Cal Bass . . . or something about his business. Something . . . anything we could give to the police so they'd see Julie isn't the only possible—"

He shoved the gun into his waistband, grabbed my arm, and twisted it up behind me, pressing my face into the car. I yelped involuntarily from the pain. "You'd better be telling me the truth, missy. I'm not going to let anyone hurt my sister."

I struggled with my temper. "Use your head, Dunk," I said. "The only one here hurting your sister is you! Forcing me off the road and threatening me at gunpoint isn't going to help Julie. If you don't believe I'm who I say I am, look in my briefcase. Look at the letters, the papers. Just a big bunch of Northbrook stuff."

He just grunted and jerked my arm. I bit back a groan and tried again. "We both know the most important thing for Julie's peace of mind right now is to know that her daughters are safe, right? That's the one thing you can do for her. If you go around acting like a mad dog, you won't be allowed to keep them."

I was trying to make him be reasonable but my words had the opposite effect. He gave my arm another vicious twist and spun me around again, leaning into my face. "Watch who you're calling names, you big bitch. Now, I'm going to let you go this time. If you know what's good for you, you won't say anything about this. Not to the Maine police or the Massachusetts police or the Connecticut police. Or your boyfriend. Get it? No one. You'll forget this ever happened. I won't let anyone hurt my sister. You try to get those kids taken away and I swear, I'll come after you. . . ." He spat the words out, his breath hot and foul. From what I'd seen of him at work, he was so accustomed to controlling people through intimidation that it wouldn't occur to him that I might not do what he said.

In the distance, like the chimes of freedom, I could hear a siren wail. "Bitch!" he yelled. "You called the cops." His face went purple with rage, folding in on itself like a withered apple. The hand with gun came up.

I felt an eerie distancing, a sense of being outside myself watching the scene, a sense of time slowed down. My whole body was cold, tense, anticipating. This was it. Just as I was beginning to allow myself to consider the possibility of a life beyond work—a life with Andre—I was going to die on a dusty roadside.

He swung the gun toward my head. I ducked, closing my eyes, heard the clang of metal and the thud of flesh as he hit the car instead. He stared at his bloodied fist and at me, and if looks could kill I would have died on the spot. The wailing grew louder. "You'd better not say anything," he said. He gave me a tremendous shove that sent me sprawling into the travel lane. I heard the screech of brakes, the blare of a horn, as I rolled sideways, clawing for purchase on the asphalt. A woman in a red Cherokee gave me the finger as she sped away. Donahue sprinted for the van and roared off in a shower of gravel.

The force of my fall left me breathless. I scrambled away from the traffic on my hands and knees and sat on the sandy asphalt, too shaken to get up, my mind still full of the blaring horn, the screeching tires, and the sensation of rushing metal inches from my head. Slowly, tentatively, I rubbed my hands together, dusting the gravel off. Most of it was imbedded and would have to be picked out. I felt like I used to when I fell off my bike. Badly scraped hands and knees and seriously wounded pride.

A police car alive with lights pulled up behind me. A trooper got out, ran over, knelt down. I looked up into Roland Proffit's worried gray eyes. "Thea? I heard on the radio . . . Good God, what happened?"

"I'm okay," I said. "I'm okay. He didn't shoot me," and promptly burst into tears.

"*Who* didn't shoot you?"

"Duncan Donahue. He came in his van and forced me off the road. He had a gun. I've never seen anyone so angry. But he didn't shoot me. . . ." The words were almost inaudible through my sobs. Mortified, I struggled for control.

"Let's get you up," he said. Bending down, he put his hands under my elbows and gently raised me. "We'll go over to my car and you can tell me all about it."

I held my swollen, sandy, oozing palms stiffly in front of me. Little rivulets of blood were running down my ruined stockings. I've had my clashes with cops. They can be real stinkers. They're the ultimate authority figures and heaven knows, I have my problems with authority figures. But when you're dazed and shocked and hurt, no one can be kinder or understand better. I was happy to let him help me up; happy to lean on him as I hobbled to his car. My legs felt unreliable; the aftermath, I knew, of having had a gun pointed at my head.

He asked enough questions to put a description of Dunk and his van on the radio, then gave me time to pull myself together, as he produced a first aid kit and tended to my battered hands and bloody knee. "Good thing you don't play the piano for a living," he remarked as he picked gravel out. I felt like the hapless heroine of a silent movie, ready to clap my hand to my breast and declare Trooper Roland Proffit my hero. "I could take you to a hospital." I shook my head. "You ready to talk about it?"

"He had a gun," I said in a small voice.

Proffit nodded. "Scary, aren't they? Do you know him?"

"I met him yesterday. In New Hampshire. At Verrill Brothers Trucking. I was stupid. I went there to ask about his sister. . . ." As I told my story, anger creased his brow and darkened his eyes and I could see that he was ready to go out and slay dragons or at least Duncan Donahue on my behalf. Even a modern woman like me gets a thrill from that kind of protective anger.

"What do you want to do now?" he asked. "Sure you don't want to see a doctor?"

I shook my head. "I'm okay." I wanted to say that I'd felt more battered than this after a wild night with Andre, but I knew I'd better not. Andre is a very private person. "I'm fine. A little shaken up and sore, that's all."

He stared at the ripped off sleeve and the muscles in his face tightened. "I could call Andre. . . ."

I shook my head. I didn't want to make a big deal out of this. "I just want to go to work now."

"What about Donahue?"

I thought about Julie, in prison, worried about her kids. "I don't know if you can do this," I said slowly, "but I really don't want to press charges. It's a huge hassle for all of us. As well as the last thing his poor sister needs right now. I just want to be sure he stays away from me."

He nodded, a hard look in his gray eyes. I knew he wished I'd asked him to throw the book at good ole Dunk. "Pressing charges is the best way. . . ."

I shook my head. "I know you're right. If it were just Donahue . . . but he's got Julie's kids. She trusts him. The kids know him. If they take them away and send them to some anonymous foster family, it will be that much worse for her."

"Are you sure? What about you? What about what's good

for you? For other people? Not letting that guy run around loose, waving guns in people's faces. . . ."

My brain felt mushy and slow. He was right but so was I. I didn't know what to say. "Couldn't you just . . . uh . . . threaten him? Hold this over his head somehow?" I felt stupid, like I was asking him to do something improper. I didn't really know what I wanted. I longed for clarity and precision but felt wobbly and indecisive. "I know I'm not being very clear."

"I understand," he said, in a way that assured me that he did, that he knew how I felt, and while he might not approve, he would do as I asked. "I'll take care of it. I will speak with Mr. Donahue and let him know that he has made a very big mistake."

I had no doubt that he would. I was inside a special circle of protection and Duncan Donahue was going to rue the day he'd tangled with me. "Thanks, Trooper . . . uh . . . Roland . . . for rescuing me. I feel better now."

He gave me a quick, warm smile. "That's what I'm here for." He handed me carefully out of the car and steered me to my car, a strong, supporting arm around my shoulders, glaring at the scrapes and scratches on the shiny red paint. He opened the door, waited until I was in, and carefully closed it behind me. I felt like I was going to my junior prom. I felt safe and grateful and served and protected, as well as battered and sore and worn out. He motioned for me to roll down the window. "You take it easy now," he said. "You seem okay now but something like this can really shake you up. Sometimes you don't feel the effects right away. You start to feel shaky, you pull off the road and get yourself a cup of tea or something."

I nodded. I started the engine, gripped the wheel cautiously with my swollen hands, and accelerated into the traffic. Where had all these people been when I was cowering before Dunk Donahue's wrath? The sun poured in through the sunroof, warming me up so that my shivering gradually stopped. I was driving on auto pilot, my mind filled with images of the last few days. I had no reason to conclude that Donahue had killed Calvin Bass, but one thing was certainly clear—he was capable of that kind of calculated violence. Had I just foolishly asked them to let a murderer go free? Even with the sun beating down and the heat on full, a shiver went through me that left me cold for a long time.

CHAPTER *11*

IN THE PARKING lot outside my building I pulled on a sweater to cover my ruined blouse, thankful the skirt I'd worn was a murky print that was none the worse for wear after skidding along the ground, and got a spare pair of stockings from my emergency kit. The kit is another of the organized overlays I've imposed on my undisciplined personality. I never go anywhere without spare pins, buttons, stockings, double-sided tape for gaping blouses and sagging hems, barrettes, tissues, aspirin, and Band-Aids. I should have been a girl scout.

Upstairs, things were jumping. The phones seemed to have St. Vitus Dance and when I passed her desk, Sarah gave me a cynical smile, bit back a comment about my bandaged hands, and held out a stack of pink slips thick enough to paper a wall. "Northbrook wants a proposal from us ASAP," she said. "That note is on top."

I read it and sighed. They wanted something for a meeting next week. With all the proposals we'd sent out lately, we were like fishermen who bait a bunch of lines and cast them all out, then wait. If all our fish bit at once, we were going to be in serious trouble. I dumped my briefcase and the pink slips on my desk and headed for the ladies' room to do a little more restoration on my hands. On the way I met Suzanne and her baby.

"For someone who just got her ashes hauled, you don't look very cheerful," she said.

"That's the strangest expression, isn't it?"

Her eagle eyes lit on my hands. "What happened?"

"I fell off my bike."

"And I was born yesterday."

"I don't want to talk about it."

"Thea. . . ."

There's no sense in trying to evade Suzanne's questions. Her perceptive skills are what make her good at this business, and we've worked together so long she knows when I'm being evasive. "I had an unpleasant run-in with Julie Bass's brother."

She's a good enough friend so she's honest when she thinks I'm being foolish. "Oh, Thea. Not again! You promised." And she was genuinely annoyed. "Remember what I told you. . . ."

"That we have too much work for me to get myself landed in some hospital and if I do, you won't come visit me, right?" She nodded. "Don't worry. I'm being very careful. Between you and Andre, I don't dare be anything else."

"This is careful?"

I skipped the long version. "He didn't shoot me, Suzanne."

She rolled her eyes but let it drop. "Well, I guess we have to be grateful for small favors, don't we? Isn't it a madhouse out there? How did we ever get ourselves into this mess?"

"By being good at what we do."

"And how can I say that was a mistake?" She was about to say something else when Paul, Jr. yawned an enormous yawn and began to wail. "Okay, little guy," she said, "I get the hint. Mealtime." She laid him on her shoulder and he snuggled into her neck, making hopeful sucking sounds. "Catch you later." She bustled off and I bustled right after her, wondering when I was ever going to get a chance to talk about what was going on in *her* life.

The calendar said I had a late-morning meeting. There was the Northbrook proposal to prepare. I sorted my pink slips into piles and more than half of them were urgent. As with everything at EDGE, the clients may take six months or a year to make up their minds to work with us and then they want results right away. Some of them. Others, like Northbrook, act fast and expect us to act faster. I sighed and picked up the phone.

I was halfway through the stack and feeling very efficient when Suzanne walked in and dropped the *Globe* business section on my desk. A small article was circled in red. The headline was: MURDERED BANKER TIED TO MORTGAGE IRREGULARITIES. A typical article. After the headline, it didn't say much—just that in the course of a routine review of the Grantham Cooperative Bank, the FDIC had uncovered a number of missing mortgage applications that their investigation indicated might have been in the possession of the late Calvin Bass.

I shrugged and pushed the paper aside, picking up the phone for another call, but the article kept nagging at me. Not by what it did say, which wasn't much, but by what it suggested. As I waited, on hold, for someone whose time was more valuable than mine, I thought of the argument Sherry DuBose had told me about between Bass and Eliot Ramsay, and Bass's secretary's hysteria on the phone about Ramsay and some missing papers. I wondered if there was someone I should share my speculations with, but before I could think about it further, my secretary, Sarah, stuck a note in front of me. "Your mother is on Nine and she says it's urgent!"

Why should she be different from anyone else? And anyway, lately, with her, everything was urgent. I nodded, gave up on the person who was keeping me on hold, and pressed the button. My mother's distressed voice exploded from the phone.

"Someone broke into Julie's house and tried to burn it down!" I almost asked what she wanted me to do about it, but I'd hear that in due course anyway.

The story was shocking. Someone, unnoticed by the neighbors, had broken into Julie's house, torn the entire place apart, and then set it on fire to cover up the destruction. An alert neighbor had seen the smoke and called the fire department, but not before the downstairs had been seriously damaged and many of Julie's and the children's things destroyed.

"As if that poor girl hàsn't been through enough, losing her husband and then being charged with the crime . . . without having vandals breaking in and destroying her home! People these days! Honestly, a bunch of predators just waiting for a chance to take advantage. . . ."

Mom went on talking but I was following my own thoughts, wondering if it really was vandals or if someone was looking for something, like maybe the missing mortgages. Wondering if Calvin Bass was really responsible for the missing papers or if Ramsay was taking advantage of his death and inability to defend himself to get rid of a big problem. Probably something I ought to take to the police, but what would I say? I have this hunch about the papers? And had they—the police—considered whether Ramsay might have had an interest in eliminating Cal Bass? I could imagine how that would go over . . . by the time I'd finished my first sentence they'd be looking at me like I had two heads. No. Before I said anything to anyone, there were questions I wanted to ask Rita and Sherry, like why missing mortgage applications might have someone's Jockeys in a twist.

"Isn't that just the saddest thing?" my mother said.

"I'm sorry. I wasn't paying attention. What's so sad?"

"I didn't call just to pass the time of day," she said huffily. "I want you to do something about this."

"Do something about what?" I asked wearily, trying to keep my irritation out of my voice. Getting annoyed with her would only prolong things. Maybe it was a good thing Andre and I didn't live together, though lately I'd begun to wonder about it. Together, we never got enough sleep, and when I'm tired, I'm grouchy. "I'm doing all I can. I have a job to do, you know. Right now, I'm absolutely swamped. I've got deadlines. . . ."

"Too swamped to help a desperate person in trouble, I suppose."

"Mom, I'm doing all I can. Yesterday I went to see her brother—"

"Duncan. Yes. Julie just adores her brother. She talks about him all the time."

"I don't know why. He's a madman. He nearly killed me."

"Don't exaggerate, dear. It's unattractive. Anyway, as I was saying when you weren't listening . . ."

I wasn't the only one who wasn't listening, but when Mom has an agenda, she's all output and no input. I gave up the effort of getting her attention and tried to sound involved. "Did you get me the names of Julie's friends?"

"That's what I've been trying to tell you, if you'd been listening. Julie doesn't seem to have had any close friends. I talked to two women she plays tennis with at the club yesterday. One of them told me Julie was a cold fish who was friendly only when she wanted to be; the other said she'd tried but Julie was so distant she got the impression that Julie wasn't interested in being friends. And then when I was talking to one of Dr. Durren's nurses about those scandalous rumors, you know what she said? She said Dr. Durren kept a picture of Julie and the children in his desk drawer. That's how good a friend he was. Isn't it just the saddest thing? If you ask me, it's his wife who's the real cold fish. Won't do anything to further his career, never comes to hospital functions with him. . . ."

Sarah was standing in the doorway, pointing at her watch. "Mom, I've got to go. I have a meeting. I'll call you tonight."

"Don't call. Come for dinner," she insisted. I agreed just to get her off the phone. It only meant another two hours of driving, one down, one back, on top of the three and a half I'd already driven today.

Luckily, the meeting was in our conference room, so I didn't have to drive anywhere for that. A smooth, efficient meeting, which reminded me that I've been in this business long enough to know what I'm doing, a confidence I've worked a long time to achieve. I came out of the meeting feeling comfortable that Bobby and Lisa, our two professional employees, were ready to run the focus groups and our telephone team was prepped to handle a survey questionnaire, and at least the work portion of my life was under control. I went back to my unfinished stack of urgent slips, reflecting on the fact that the downside of success is more work to be done and still the same number of bodies to do it. Still, it was better than last year at this time, when I was worrying about where the money for the payroll was going to come from.

I'd stopped by Sarah's desk to mooch one of the granola bars she keeps in her drawer when Suzanne buzzed by. "All set for next week?" I nodded. "What about Northbrook?"

"They want a proposal," I said glumly.

"Come on. Where's the old Kozak enthusiasm?"

"I'm hungry. I can't be enthusiastic when I'm hungry."

"Other people eat these things called meals, you know. Sarah, haven't you got something to toss to this ravening beast?"

Sarah opened her drawer and looked in. "Sorry," she said, "I seem to have run out. Lisa might have something."

"I thought feeding Thea was part of your job," Suzanne said a little shortly.

Sarah only shrugged. Sometimes she could get rather huffy about what was and was not her job. "Maybe you need to hire someone else. . . ."

My heart sank. If Sarah quit I would be in serious trouble.

She was a wonderful secretary. "Don't even joke about leaving," I said. "You'll give me heart failure. I'll just go hungry."

"You got any food, Bobby?" Sarah said, tapping impatiently on her keyboard.

"A banana and an orange. You want 'em?"

Sarah gestured at me. "Thea does."

Bobby glanced nervously at the three of us and hurried off to get the fruit. He stuffed it unceremoniously into my hands. "Don't let her quit," he said, "I just couldn't take that right now."

Usually I'm the wade-in-and-sort-it-out type, but I wasn't feeling up to it today. The delayed effects of my encounter with Duncan Donahue and too little sleep and a long drive had worn me out. "Thanks, Bobby," I said. "I'm going back to work." I retreated to my office, leaving Suzanne to figure out what was going on with Sarah.

An hour later, I was up to my elbows in papers, putting together ideas for Northbrook, when Sarah leaned in the door. "Don't take it personally," she said. "It's my husband again. Sometimes I get so mad at that jerk I'd like to rip his head off and I take it out on the people around me."

"I thought you were going to use that stairclimber he got you until you had thighs like Wonder Woman and then you were going to crack his head like a nut?"

"I said that?" She shook her head. "Well, it worked out like everything else around our place does. I finally get the kids to bed and the dishes done and get everything cleaned up and then I'll be changing into some workout clothes. The minute he sees me doing it, he makes a beeline for the machine and starts working out. Then he complains that I don't use it enough. If that man had a personality half as nice as his thighs, I'd be a happy woman. I'll buy some granola bars tonight. I'm going grocery shopping anyway."

"You don't have to."

When she smiled, Sarah was awfully pretty. "That's why I'm going to do it. Because you and Suzanne worry about offending me . . . you worry about asking me to do too much and you're willing to let me know that I'm valued here. And Bobby . . . he's sweet! He was so worried that I might quit, he sneaked out and got me flowers. Now I'll go away and let you work."

"Thanks, Sarah. And hold my calls, will you? I've got to get some work done."

She did, but half an hour later she buzzed me on the intercom. "Sorry to disturb you. There's a guy named Eliot Ramsay on the line. He says it's urgent. You want to take it?"

"I'll take it." Half curious and half annoyed that everyone in the world seemed to think their business was urgent today, I pressed the button and said, "Hello?"

"I believe you have something that belongs to me," he said brusquely.

"Excuse me?"

"The papers. The ones you took from Bass's house. They're mine and I want them. If you don't turn them over to me immediately, I'm notifying the police."

I didn't like his tone one bit and I had no idea what he was talking about. All I had were three of Julie's letters and some outdated junk. But even if I had had something valuable, Eliot Ramsay was about the last person on earth I would have admitted it to, the way he was behaving. "Mr. Ramsay, I don't know what you're talking about. Julie Bass didn't give me anything."

"You're lying," he said. "If I don't have those papers back in my office by tomorrow morning, I'm calling the police."

"You can call anyone you want, Mr. Ramsay," I said. "The police. The F.B.I. The Pope. It won't help."

"I know you were there," he said. "A cop told me."

"I don't know what you're talking about."

"Sure you do. Don't bullshit me, lady. You were in the ouse. You took 'em," he said.

"Of course I was in the house. Julie asked me to check on it. Did your cop also tell you they searched my car?" I said. I waited or an answer.

"Bullshit," he said. A tiresome man with a tiresome vocab-lary.

"And that they didn't find anything? Ask your cop buddy. 'm not a magician, you know. I can't make things vanish into hin air. I haven't got your papers, Mr. Ramsay." I did have some ntimate letters. But they were none of his business. Maybe the ld financial crap was his, but it wasn't worth a threatening hone call and the ruder he got, the less cooperative I felt.

"We'll see about that," he said.

"Fine," I said. We both hung up in a huff.

I tried to go back to work but my concentration had been lestroyed. I scraped the papers into a pile. They'd have to wait ntil tomorrow. At dawn. It was the only time I had. I like to :laim I'm only a type B+ personality, but no one believes me ex-:ept my mother, and she thinks I'm an easygoing B-.

On impulse, I called Rita, Calvin Bass's former secretary, nd asked if we could meet for a drink after work. She agreed with surprising alacrity; I'd expected her to be suspicious.

I left work a few minutes early and, despite my bandages and oruises, submitted myself to an hour of Aaron's torturous rou-ine. I had a lot of poison to work out of my system. The little :wit who stands in front of me stared with avid curiosity at my oruised shoulder and knees and bandaged hands. They all hurt nd made me extremely disagreeable. I thought about using the bicycle excuse again, but then she might ask me if I'd like to go for a ride some time, she seemed like that kind of person. "My husband," I said. "Sometimes he just loses control. But he's a good man, really." She turned quickly away and after that avoided meeting my eyes.

An hour later, pumped with endorphins and soothed with Advil, having sweated Duncan Donahue out of my system and worked up an appetite for my mother's cooking, I hit the road.

CHAPTER 12

WHATEVER HER OTHER qualifications were, Rita hadn't gotten her job because of her experience. She was young, no more than early twenties, and seemed even younger because of her naive, confiding style. She was sitting where she'd said she would be, at a table near the door, in the bar of the Grantham Inn, wearing a skimpy two-piece pink knit outfit that on someone fuller figured or older would have been cheap. On her it was rather sweet. She had long, dark hair, elaborately styled with elastics and a bow, demure, glossy lips, pink cheeks, and a round face and upturned nose that, despite my dislike of the word, had to be called cute. The only thing that detracted from youthful perfection was the sawing of her jaw as she worked her gum.

I'd chosen the inn because it was a place a woman could go alone and not be bothered. A respectable bar, if that's not an oxymoron. When I introduced myself, she waved me into a seat across from her and waited expectantly. Obviously, no one had ever taught her that you don't discuss your employer's business with strangers.

When the waiter arrived, I asked if she'd like a drink and she ordered a ghastly combination of liqueur and ice cream, beaming like a kid with an ice cream soda. "It's very good of you to be willing to talk to me," I said. "I'm not trying to be nosy. I just want to help my friend Julie."

She nodded, a vigorous bob of bow and curls. "I feel real bad about that," she said. "I don't think she could have done it, do you?"

"No, I don't. But convincing the police of that is another story. I'm trying to find other suspects, starting with people who didn't like Mr. Bass—"

She interrupted before I could finish. "But that's everyone. Nobody liked him at the bank. I mean, respected, maybe, but not liked. Except me. People were afraid of him."

This was like taking candy from a baby. "When we talked the other day, you'd just had an upsetting call from Mr. Ramsay. Have things calmed down about the missing papers?" She nodded. "Did they find them?"

She shook her head. "Mr. Ramsay apologized for yelling at me. He says Cal . . . Mr. Bass . . . must have taken them."

"Why would he have done that?"

She shrugged. Shrugs and nods seemed to be her primary methods of communicating. "Because Ramsay . . . Mr. Ramsay had made some changes that Mr. Bass didn't like."

"What makes you think Mr. Ramsay changed them?"

"I heard them arguing about it."

"You heard the argument?"

Another shrug. "Not the words. The door was closed. But I could see their faces." She snapped her gum for emphasis.

"Angry faces?"

She nodded, tasted her drink, and cast a disparaging look at my Stoli and tonic. "You ought to try one of these."

"It looks good," I agreed, "but too filling, and I have to go to my mother's for dinner."

The curls bobbed. "Yeah, I know how that is. They can be real crabby if you don't eat, huh?"

Now I was the one who was nodding. "If you couldn't hear them talking, how do you know Ramsay wanted them changed?"

She snapped her gum thoughtfully. "Oh, I heard that before they shut the door. Like, Ramsay . . . Mr. Ramsay . . . goes 'it's no big deal, you just add a couple lines of explanation here and there,' and then Cal . . . Mr. Bass . . . goes, 'Eliot, that's illegal and you know it,' and Mr. Ramsay goes, 'who'd ever know? You'd rather have us accused of discrimination?' and Cal starts to say something about decisions being perfectly defensible and notices the door's open. He comes over, asks me to get him a Coke, and then closes it. So that's like all I heard."

"Do you know what the papers were?"

"Some kind of mortgage forms."

"Did you ever actually see them?"

She shrugged. "I see so many papers every day. I don't know if I saw those papers."

"Do you think Calvin Bass took them?"

She shrugged.

"Can you think of any reason why he would have taken them?"

"Keep 'em away from Ramsay . . . Mr. Ramsay?" she suggested. "Keep him from changing 'em?" But she was only guessing. "I know Mr. Ramsay went ape . . . uh . . . crazy when he couldn't find 'em."

"Did you see the story in the paper today? The one suggesting Mr. Bass might have been involved in some mortgage irregularities?"

"Irregularities?"

She was genuinely puzzled. Probably she'd only heard the word used in connection with laxatives. "Done something wrong," I explained.

"When it came to his work, Cal ... Mr. Bass ... was like arrow straight. I mean, that's why people didn't like him. He never cut no one ... anyone ... any slack. It was like done right or it was done over."

Was he a hard person to work for?"

"Everyone thought so. He was nice to me, though. Tried hard not to get impatient."

It was hard to imagine being cruel to Rita, except maybe about her gum. It would have been like kicking a baby. "Besides Ramsay, can you think of anyone else who might have taken the papers?"

"Rachel Kaplan, maybe?"

"Who's she?"

"Cal's assistant," she said, surprised I didn't know.

"Why would she take them?"

She grinned and snapped her gum. "To get him in trouble. She wanted his job." She hesitated. "I would have, like, had to quit. Still might, if they promote her. I couldn't work for her. She's a bitch."

"How so?" I didn't like it when women called each other bitches, even when it was true.

She drank some more while she considered my question, then set her glass down and stared sadly at the pink froth in the bottom. "Would you like another?" She nodded and I signaled for the waiter.

"The guys ... the men ... just come right out and tell you if they don't like something. You know, like, they'll say, 'Rita, this isn't right, you'll have to do it over.' And I can handle that, 'cuz, like, I'm still learning and I know that. But with Rachel ... Ms. Kaplan, she doesn't like to be called by her first name. It's unprofessional, she says. She's like your best friend one minute, wants to hear all about your weekend or your boyfriend, telling you your work is fine and all, and then it's like she's stabbing you in the back, saying to Mr. Bass, 'that Rita is really hopeless, she can't get anything right.' I mean, I don't mind being told I did it wrong, 'cuz I know I'm just learning and I want to get it right, but she'd never say it was wrong to my face. So I wouldn't want to work for her, see. Besides, she's sneaky." She announced this last with a decisive nod. Her bow, peeking up from behind her head, reminded me of a Scottie's ears.

"Sneaky?"

"I've seen her going through the files—not her files but like other people's—when she thinks no one's looking. And sometimes taking things out—"

"What's her relationship with Mr. Ramsay? Did he question her about the missing papers?"

She shook her head. "They didn't used to get along that well. Ramsay . . . Mr. Ramsay's really one of those men who think a woman's place is horizontal, if you know what I mean. And Ms. Kaplan's real ambitious and she's not too good at hiding it. But lately they've been pretty tight."

"Do you think they're sleeping together?"

A man passing stopped at our table, staring down at me. "I haven't seen you around here before, have I?" he said.

"No," I said, impatient at the interruption.

"I'm Jerry," he said, "and you're—"

"Busy," I said.

"Not too busy for a drink, I hope?" He included Rita in his predatory smile.

"Afraid so," I said, turning back to Rita. "We were talking about Rachel Kaplan," I reminded her. "About whether she was sleeping with Mr. Ramsay. . . ." Jerry spun angrily on his heel and strode out of the bar. I guess things in Grantham were changing. I used to be able to come to the inn with my friends and carry on uninterrupted conversations. Some people just don't realize that the whole world isn't a dating bar. You can hardly buy cereal these days without an approach.

Rita stared at me, wide-eyed. "Whew!" she said. "What did you say to him?"

"I said I had a contagious social disease. About Rachel . . ."

"And Ramsay?" She shrugged, unwilling to comment, but the unspoken opinion on her transparent face was that she couldn't imagine anyone wanting to have sex with Eliot Ramsay. "I don't know." She paused, then burst out, "It would be like humping a weasel." I almost fell off my chair. "I'm sorry," she said, "that was awful. Forget I ever said it. But Rachel likes men." She gave me a conspiratorial grin as something occurred to her. "In a way, she's just like Ramsay. I mean, she thinks men are only useful when they're horizontal. I never thought of that before. They're a lot alike, aren't they?" This insight seemed to delight her, and she celebrated it with a generous measure of her new drink. Her cheeks were considerably pinker than when we'd started talking.

"That poor guy," she said. "You don't really have a . . . you know . . . a disease, do you?"

I shook my head. The only disease I had was an allergy to jerks. "I told him we were busy, that's all. I guess he's not used to getting turned down. What about Cal Bass? Do you think Ms. Kaplan slept with him?"

A much more vigorous shake of the head this time. "Oh, no! He wouldn't have slept with her. He's . . . uh . . . uh. . . ." She searched for a word, sucking thoughtfully on her straw. "Particular. And she's got a mustache."

Time to slip in the zinger. I did it, even though it made me feel mean. "What about you? Did you ever sleep with Cal Bass?"

Her sweet face crumpled and her dark eyes filled with tears. She pulled a teensy purse out of her lap and searched for a tissue. The bag looked too little to hold anything useful. I pulled one out and handed it to her.

"Thanks," she mumbled. "Do I have to talk about this?"

"It's up to you."

"Oh, I guess I don't mind. It's a relief to tell someone, really. I did. He was so kind to me and such a hunk and I like had this huge crush on him and so when he hit on me, I said yes. It was so romantic! He like took me to this great place on the river—this condo—and there were candles and champagne. . . ." She stopped. "I know. It was foolish. When I got this job, my dad took me aside and told me—excuse the language, this is just how he talks—he says to me, 'Rita, you can do well there but there's one thing you gotta remember—girlie, you don't shit where you eat.' I know he was right because afterward I got to thinking about how Cal had a wife and those two sweet little girls, and I told him I couldn't do it no . . . any more."

I had to leave or I'd be late for dinner. I signaled for the check and told Rita I had to go. "Can't keep my family waiting," I said.

"Thanks for the drinks," she said. "I think it's nice of you to try and help Mrs. Bass." I was heading for the door when she called me back. "Wait. There's something else, something I didn't tell you." She had the look of a kid confessing to stolen cookies. "It wasn't just me . . . my decision . . . about not sleeping with Mr. Bass again, I mean. That is, I was trying to do the right thing and all, but he wasn't. And much as I liked him, I didn't approve of what he was doing."

She was frowning like she was about to reveal something sordid, something I really didn't want to hear, maybe about Cal Bass's sexual practices. Before I could tell her that she didn't have to share very personal things, she'd come out with it. "The real reason he didn't try to sleep with me again—not that I would have—is that he had a new girlfriend . . . woman friend . . . and I think it was pretty serious, too. She called him all the time."

I waited, but that's all she had to say. "Do you know who the woman was?"

A vigorous nod. "Someone he met when she came in for a

loan to buy some commercial property. A very rich-looking woman. Like from those TV soaps, you know, her clothes, I mean. I think her name is Nan Devereaux, but I could check. . . ."

"That would be great, Rita," I said, taking a card out of my purse and giving it to her. "Check on her name and then call me. Either number is fine." I really had to rush. I had visions of falling soufflés and overdone beef and my mother's irritated expression.

"I can't believe he's dead," she said. "He was such a vibrant man. So alive. I think he had more energy than anyone I've ever seen. He worked so hard." She shook her head and looked sadly at her second empty glass, but I could tell she'd had enough. A novice drinker, she was already beginning to slur her words. I turned again to leave, but Rita, having begun her confession, had more things to get off her chest.

"I don't know whether this means anything to you but I think he might have been in over his head financially. He was always getting calls from credit card companies and people like that, and after those calls he was always red-faced and flustered, like he was angry. I think his wife must have run up a lot of bills."

"I'll look into it," I said, beating a hasty retreat before she could come up with another stunner. Maybe I should have stayed and listened; it was obvious she wanted someone to talk to, but my head was already spinning, and not from the Stoli. I knew it was naive of me to hope that someone would just give me the vital fact that would make everything suddenly clear. A friend of mine who does divorce law says that listening to the stories from people who have been married for years, you'd swear they'd been in two different marriages. I think it's always that way when you're trying to learn about someone by talking to other people. You get the subject through their lens. Still, it would have been nice if any two things I learned about Julie Bass matched up.

What did I know? That she was a fragile blossom who could dismantle a race car in nothing flat; she was an economics major who knew nothing about money whose husband kept her on a miserably tight financial rein while she ran up astronomical bills; she was gracious and socially adept and didn't have any friends. At least Cal Bass was easier—he was a handsome, competent, driven perfectionist whose tomcat activities and abuse of his wife made him lower than pond scum.

I shook my head to clear it, which didn't help a bit, and drove to my parents' house to get some food. Once again, I got more than I'd bargained for.

CHAPTER *13*

IN TYPICAL LINDA McKUSICK fashion, my mother had a dinnertime surprise for me. Not a peach cobbler or a fresh raspberry pie or something deadly and chocolate. Nor what I would have appreciated most, a reprieve from her pressure to get involved in Julie's affairs. Quite the opposite. Tonight it was Dr. Thomas Durren, and thanks to my mother's advance PR work, Dr. Durren was under the impression that I was there to help them get Julie out of jail. My mother led me across the room and announced, "This is my daughter, Thea, the one I've been telling you about."

He leapt to his feet, seized my hand before I could stop him, saw the bandages, and dropped it like a hot potato. He was the same guy who'd bumped into me at the police station, the one I'd seen hurrying away from Julie's house. There was no glimmer of recognition on his face. Durren was sad-eyed, sallow, and had a cold, moist handshake that left me feeling like I'd been handed a dead fish. "Thank goodness," he said, regarding me with his spaniel eyes. "At least someone is trying to help her. She needs your help so badly! It's absurd, of course, but everyone acts like her guilt is a foregone conclusion. Your mother tells me you've done this sort of thing before. I'll do anything I can to help. Just tell me how." Despite his cooperative words, he spoke so softly I had to bend forward to hear him. Softly and in a rush, as though communicative speech was learned late in life and rarely used. Well, what did I expect? He was a doctor. An ER doc. Accustomed to dealing with people desperate for his help, where brusque, monosyllabic communication was adequate for the job. Doctors are not high on my list of favorite people.

I manufactured a pleasant smile, wishing I could twitch my nose or sprinkle pixie dust or rub a magic lantern and vanish, but there was nothing I could do. For the second time today I was trapped. At least this time no one was holding a gun to my head or threatening to throw me into oncoming traffic. Perhaps I should learn to be grateful for small favors. I sat back and studied the man who was allegedly Julie Bass's partner in adultery.

My first impression was of a delicate elegance, almost too effete to be attractive. Partly it was his clothes—the exquisitely soft Italian leather shoes, the silky cotton sheen of his shirt, the careful drape of a fine wool jacket. His face was nicely chiseled, with pale skin over fine bones. Dark, aggressive eyebrows cut a straight line over moist brown eyes. I could picture him as a boy, hand to breast, reciting "Excelsior." He was undeniably attractive, yet something in his manner was uninviting. There was a cool reticence there, rather than warmth. A more-than-professional detachment. I wondered what it was that had drawn Julie and how he was with his patients. Perhaps, after Cal's demanding aggression, his reticence was appealing.

Oh well. Once a worker bee, always a worker bee. I took a deep breath, repressing annoyance at my mother's trap, and went to work, trying to find out whether Dr. Durren knew anything that might be helpful.

"How long have you known Julie, Doctor?" I asked.

"I hate to rush things, but I'm afraid we've got to eat right away," Mom said. Traces of annoyance on her face reminded me that I'd kept her from the orderly progression from drinks to dinner that she considers civilized. Dr. Durren held my chair, the very soul of courtesy.

"I'm sorry you didn't have time for a drink," my father said, pouring wine into my glass. "What happened to your hands?"

"Yes," Mom echoed, "what have you done now?"

What had I done? There it was. The implicit assumption that everything was my fault. I gritted my teeth so hard it was a wonder they didn't break, then held out my gauze-wrapped palms and gave a nonchalant shrug. "My bike skidded. All that loose sand they haven't swept up." I tried to switch the conversation back to Julie Bass. "About Julie, Dr. Durren . . ."

"Call me Tom. Please. You were asking how long I'd known her?"

"When did you find the time to go bike riding?" my mother interrupted. "I thought you were very busy at work?"

"I am. Work hard, play hard, that's my motto. I just don't sleep. Dr. Durren . . ."

"You do look tired," she said. "Suzanne's working you too hard again."

I choked on my angry responses. It was a waste of time to argue with her or explain. I'd told her Suzanne and I were partners till I was blue in the face. "Dr. Durren," I said again. "About Julie . . ."

"Well, Doctor," Dad said, "now that we've got you here, I might as well take advantage of the situation. What does someone who is directly affected think of health care reform?"

Dr. Durren's eyes shifted nervously from one of us to the other, wondering whom he should answer. He chose age over beauty. "I don't see how the bureaucracy could get much worse," he said, "and that's our biggest problem. Having to get approvals for treatment from people who have no idea what we're talking about, practically on a day-to-day basis. Any doctor will tell you that. If doctors could use their time to treat patients, instead of wasting so much on the phone, they could deliver medical care a lot more efficiently. It even affects my practice in the emergency room."

"I hear you!" Dad said.

"Dr. Durren . . . Tom . . . about Julie Bass . . ."

"More mashed potatoes?" Mom said, offering him the bowl.

"Sure. Thanks," he muttered with his mouth full. "This is delicious. I'm sorry my wife couldn't join us."

It seemed like that would have been rather awkward, but what did I know? "Tom," I said, "how long—"

"Thea, let the man eat," Mom said.

I hadn't driven an hour to admire Dr. Durren's table manners, which were quite good. Besides, this had been her idea, not mine. "Mom, I'm sorry. It's been a long day. I'd just like to get to the point here."

"A long day bike riding, while poor Julie is languishing in Framingham."

This was what I got for lying. Still, her reaction if I'd told her about Duncan Donahue and the gun would have been harder to take, though it might have bought me some peace from her persistence. Maybe not. I'd tried to tell her earlier today and she'd ignored me. "I didn't do this today," I said mildly. "I was in New Hampshire yesterday on business and I stopped in to see Duncan Donahue—"

"Julie is so fond of him," Durren said.

I wanted to say "I don't see why," but that would have required half an hour of explanation and they were hardly letting me get a word in. Maybe it was all the driving, or the drink I'd had with Rita, or delayed effects from the morning's attack, or sheer frustration, but I was losing my concentration. My back hurt and all the cuts and scrapes throbbed. My eyes wanted to close; my mind said bedtime. I was too tired and too grouchy and in too much pain to keep up a pleasant facade much longer.

"Yes," I said, "I guess Julie and her brother are very close."

Durren nodded. "Was he helpful?"

"Somewhat. He didn't know much about Cal's work life, of course. So far, all I know is that he was difficult to work with. And a philanderer. Cal, I mean. Did you and Julie ever talk about that, Tom? Did she confide in you?"

"Thea, really!" Mom said. "Why ever would Julie tell Dr. Durren about her personal life?"

I wanted to throw mashed potatoes at her disapproving face and ask what Dr. Durren was doing there, if he wasn't supposed to know anything, but I didn't. "She had to talk to someone," I said. "And people sometimes talk freely to doctors."

"Properly brought up girls like Julie keep their troubles to themselves."

"I hope not," I said, wondering what she'd think if she knew about Deanna at the race track; the drunken mother and missing father, and being raised by Dunk Donahue. Some proper upbringing.

"Why?"

"Because if no one knows anything about her life, we can't help her."

My mother's chin went up. "I don't think we need to resort to common gossip . . . interfere with poor Julie's privacy. . . ."

I found myself saying something Andre had said to me when Carrie was killed. "In murder cases, Mom, there isn't any privacy. Think about Carrie. Protecting Julie's privacy will only serve to hide the real killer."

"We're not talking about your sister." There was silence until she said, "Does anyone want any more roast pork? No? Tom, will you help me clear?" Both men started to get up and Mom actually giggled. "I'm sorry, Doctor. I meant my husband."

Dad shot me an apologetic look and reached for my plate.

"Maybe the two of you would like to wait for coffee and dessert in the living room?" he suggested.

That was all I needed. Dim lights and soft couches. I'd be asleep in an instant. On the other hand, I'd have Durren to myself. "Thanks, Dad. We'll do that."

Once again, Dr. Durren was there to pull back my chair. Feeling a bit like Queen Victoria, I led him back to the living room, let him get comfortable on the couch, and then fired off my first question. I didn't have much time. "What was your relationship with Julie?"

"We were friends," he told his clenched hands. With a visible effort, he unclenched them and laid them on his knees. They were beautiful. Long and slender yet conveying a sense of strength and competence. Hands you'd feel comfortable placing yourself in. Physically, that is. Emotionally, I'd have preferred a dog. Maybe Julie had liked him for his hands.

"Did she confide in you?"

He shrugged. "A little." I had to lean forward to hear him.

"Do you know any reason why she would have killed her husband?"

He raised his eyes from his hands and gave me a disapproving look. "She didn't kill him. Julie isn't the violent type. She's a true lady. . . ."

"What was her relationship with her husband like?"

He just sat and stared at his hands. "I had no idea we'd have to go into that sort of thing," he said.

I wanted to shake him. "What can you tell me about Julie's marriage?"

He raised the dark eyes again, sighed, and lowered them again. "She wasn't happy with Cal. He was . . . he wasn't a very kind man. She was afraid of him. But she never would have dreamed of killing him. She was a gentle soul. And I believe that despite his brutish behavior, she loved him."

"Did she ever express anger toward him? Ever say she'd like to hurt him?"

"Never."

"And she didn't talk to you about his work . . . his friends . . . there's no one she ever—"

"I didn't say that. . . ."

". . . no one she ever mentioned who might have had a grudge against him?"

Dr. Durren squirmed uncomfortably. "What you said at dinner. It was true. He wasn't a faithful husband. That hurt her badly." He sighed and sank deeper into the upholstery.

"Did she ever mention any names?"

He shook his head.

"What about their finances? Did she ever talk about their finances?" Another shake. "What about his work at the bank, his relationships with people there?" No response. My frustration was reflected in my posture. I was leaning forward, stretching toward him as though I could physically break through his reticence. "Look," I said desperately, "is there anyone you can suggest that I should talk to? Friends? Neighbors? Anyone who knew her well?"

"She was a very private person. She tried to keep her troubles to herself."

He was behaving like Julie's plight was tea table conversation. Didn't he understand how serious this was? "Dr. Durren," I said. I couldn't bring myself to call him Tom. Tom was my dad's name. It was a friendly name and this man wasn't friendly. Maybe he just didn't understand. "I know you want to help Julie or you wouldn't be here. To help her, we need information. Details about her life. Details about Cal's life. I'm not trying to be nosy. I believe in privacy just like the rest of you, but to help her we need to have something to offer the police as an alternative. We can't just go to them and say that we believe in her innocence."

It didn't work. "I can't see how anyone could think for one minute that she . . ." he began.

"You went to her house and took those letters, didn't you?" I asked. His response was a blank, unwavering stare. "Did you know that you dropped some? I found two in the closet and one by the front steps." Two dull red spots appeared in his cheeks, but otherwise his expression didn't change.

It was hopeless. On the one hand I had the police, whose take on the matter was clear. Abused wife with knowledge of cars arranges for a well-insured unfaithful husband to take driving course, tampers with car, and presto, all her problems are solved. On the other hand I had my mother and Dr. Durren, who thought it would suffice to declare that Julie was a lady and refused to discuss anything important, and Dunk Donahue, ready to bash anyone who disagreed with him over the head with a wrench. To use the sports metaphors guys are so fond of, I was on the losing team and all my efforts to rally my players were falling on deaf ears. An unacceptably non-PC expression.

"What is your relationship to Julie?"

He stared at me coldly. "That's none . . ."

". . . of my business?" I finished. "The police will certainly think it's some of theirs. You're her motive. Woman kills husband so she can be free for her lover. Especially if the husband is an abusive philanderer. Surely you can see that?"

His stare remained cold. "You wouldn't understand," he said. "Julie was . . . is . . . a remarkable woman. So proud and sensitive. Private. She had needs . . . feelings . . . that Cal Bass could never appreciate. She needed an understanding friend. . . ."

"Were you sleeping with her?"

"No." I didn't believe him.

"Did you know she was going to Connecticut?"

"She didn't—" He stopped. In the silence, I heard the swing of the kitchen door and approaching footsteps.

Suddenly he raised his head and his eyes were fierce. "She didn't go to Connecticut to hurt him. It was because of the other woman. . . ." He clamped his mouth shut and looked nervously around to see if anyone else had heard.

He got up and began to pace. "Forget I ever said . . . look, you've got to help her. She's innocent!" As a knight in shining armor, he wasn't much, but there was a truckload of feeling in his final declaration. At least now I understood why he'd been willing to risk getting the letters. Not as her doctor but as her lover. At least it was something he could do for her.

Dad appeared at that moment with a tray but it didn't matter. Dr. Durren had shut down. We were a pitiful crew of know-nothings, and we had a long way to go if we were going to help Julie Bass. A long way. Yet the people who claimed they cared most were unwilling to try. Over coffee and dessert, I pondered what to do next. I had a few more questions but by the time the linzer torte had been handed around and adequately admired, Dr. Durren's beeper went off and he escaped.

I was fed up with wasting my time on people who wanted to help only if it didn't involve any pain, effort, introspection, or honesty. It's the TV effect. Everyone thinks murderers are caught in an hour minus commercials. The coffee had resuscitated me just enough to recognize how tired I was. I thanked them for dinner and tottered out to the car, ready to put the whole messy business out of my mind.

My resolve lasted about a mile. That was when I remembered that it was Thursday night. The night that Sherry Du-Bose had told me I could probably find Cal Bass's assistant, Rachel Kaplan, at a bar. So what if I felt like I'd been worked over with a two-by-four? It was better to get it over with than to drive back another time. I groaned, pulled into the parking lot at Popovers, and called Sherry on the car phone.

At her friendly hello, I said, "Hi, it's Thea Kozak. Sorry to bother you again. How do I recognize Rachel Kaplan?"

She laughed. "Look for someone who's a cross between a banker and a hooker." I heard a male voice in the background. "Dan says that she has hair like a poodle, eyes like a frog, and a look of perpetual dissatisfaction, but she's not that bad! She was wearing a fitted magenta power suit when she left work. And I'll bet you dollars to doughnuts that she's changed her proper white blouse for a low-cut camisole. I wouldn't be single again for a million dollars."

Rachel wasn't hard to spot. She was sitting at the bar with her purse on the stool beside her. A transparent trick to keep the seat open for an available man. I marched up, stared innocently at the purse, and asked if anyone was sitting there. She twitched with annoyance but removed the purse. Her body language said more eloquently than words that she didn't welcome the competition.

Rachel Kaplan was small and wiry with bright dark eyes, short curly hair, and the kind of turned-up nose lots of girls in upper-middle-class suburbs get for their eighteenth birthdays. Sherry was right. She had shed her blouse and the deep plunge of her suit jacket revealed tantalizing glimpses of flesh and black lace. An attractive package marred by the suggestion of a perpetual pout on her face.

"Save my seat?" she asked. "I'm going to the ladies." I nodded as she slid off her stool and teetered away on heels almost too high to walk in.

Ten on a Thursday night. Popovers was popping, the band heating up for another set, and Rachel Kaplan was already unsteady on her feet. The place favored inky darkness punctuated by vivid pink and blue neon lights, the darkness ringing with the artificial laughter of desperation. A meat market. A place that, despite the noise and music and laughter, depressed me. A balding man with a belly drooping over his belt tried to take Rachel's seat. "Someone's sitting there," I said.

"Yeah, me," he said, sliding onto the stool. "So, what's your name? I haven't seen you here before."

"Someone is sitting there," I repeated.

"Come on. Don't be like that. I'm Bob. Bob the broker. What about you?"

"Someone is sitting there."

"Can't blame a guy for trying," he said, and went in search of greener pastures.

When Rachel came back and slid onto her stool, I said, "It's a jungle out here, isn't it?"

"You can say that again. This crowd seems to go directly from innocence to impotence with nothing in between."

"You come here often?"

"It's the only place around that has any life at all."

She might have been a cop, the way her eyes never stopped searching the crowd. I ordered a Stoli and tonic and asked what she'd like. Her eyes narrowed suspiciously. "I just don't like to drink alone."

She relaxed. "A gibson."

"My name is Thea. I'm a consultant."

"I'm Rachel. A banker."

"Banker, wow, that's still pretty much a man's world, isn't it? They make you wear a tie to work?"

"Just about. We're making some headway, though."

"What bank?"

"Grantham Co-op."

"Isn't that the bank where that guy got murdered?"

She needed some fortification before she could talk about it. "I worked for him," she said. "He was a shit. Married but he put the make on anything that moved. I don't blame her for killing him."

This was too easy. As easy as Rita. If I wasn't careful I'd get overconfident and blow it. I knew Rachel Kaplan wasn't stupid.

I tried not to seem interested. Sipped at my drink and looked around. "The band any good?"

Rachel shrugged. "Too loud but they seem to be able to hit most of the notes."

"So, this guy who was killed. You think the wife did it?"

She considered it while she surveyed the room again, disappointment clear from her face. The pickings did seem slim. "You wouldn't think so, a little bitty thing like her. She seemed so helpless. Underneath, I think she was pretty tough. And living with him must have been hell! She did it or she hired someone."

"You worked with him?" She nodded, her eyes darting to the door, noting who came in, and then back to her glass, dismissing the newcomers. "Was he hard to work with?"

"Cal Bass was one of those old-fashioned assholes who believe that women are good for only one thing." Rachel's language grew less refined as the drink took hold and she warmed to her subject. "He saw us as just holes to be filled and believed he was the one with the God-given duty to fill them. I mean, there I am with my MBA and three years of banking experience and he's like the big bad wolf saying 'want to see my etchings, little girl?' I'm killing myself to do a good job there and he pats me on the head like he does his children and then takes all the credit for my good work." She tilted her glass and drained it angrily. "There were times I could have killed him myself."

I laughed. "But you didn't, did you?"

"Are you kidding? What I know about cars wouldn't fill a thimble." Rachel was thoughtful. "No, if I'd wanted to kill him, what I would have done was let Nan Devereaux know, anonymously, of course, what kind of a guy her new loverboy really was. She's a woman who doesn't like to be crossed."

The bartender cruised by and asked if we wanted more drinks. I was dying to know more about Nan Devereaux but I didn't want to seem eager, so I ordered another drink and so did Rachel. "What about you," she said. "Got a man in your life?"

"Yeah," I said, "a cop. You can imagine what that's like—phone ringing at all hours of the day and night—someone always knowing when he spends the night with me . . . and dates getting broken and being scared to death when he doesn't call and he said he would . . . but I sure feel safe when he's around."

Her grin was sloppy and her eyes were getting glassy. She laid a manicured hand on my arm. "I've always wanted to sleep with a cop. Is it any different?"

It must have been the atmosphere. Or I was just too tired to be sensible. I was halfway through a second drink and I had miles to go before I slept. If I didn't slow down, I'd be into a third and then into the ditch. "I've only slept with the one," I said, "but I've got no complaints."

If I didn't derail this topic I'd be swept into a long conversation about cops and sex. There are a lot of people out there who assume all cops are real studs. Comes from reading too many novels. Cops are like everyone else—some are studs and some are duds and most fall somewhere in the middle. "I slept with a banker once. A real bummer." She nodded vigorously. I tried to get back to an earlier subject. "This Nan Devereaux? That's the wife?"

Rachel's laugh was a short, derisive bark. "Wife? That's Julie. Pallid little thing wouldn't say boo to a goose. I'm talking about Nan Devereaux, his latest conquest. Unless he was hers. I bet she's got as many scalps on her belt as he does . . . uh, did. Maybe more. Lives in Dover. Money of her own. Pots of it. And she cleaned out her husband when they divorced. Cal used to salivate just thinking about all that money. I gather he's at the anemic end of old Yankee money that's still yielding a meager five percent. At least, he always seemed abnormally interested in money, even for a banker. All he had to do was hear someone talking about a hot investment and he was all ears."

She picked up her drink and lowered the level significantly, setting it down a little unsteadily on the bar. "God, it's dull tonight." I was afraid she was going to switch back to dating and cops, but she was interested in her subject. "A little convenient eavesdropping yielded the information that Nan was pretty mad at Cal on Friday. When she called, she just about scorched Rita's ear off with her language. Rita is . . . was . . . Cal's secretary. So maybe she killed him for revenge. Killed him or had him killed. Swatted the old boy like a fly. Nan, I mean." She shrugged her shoulders and fortified herself with alcohol again. "In any case, it means there's a job open at the bank. And they'd better give it to me. God, this place is like a tomb." She craned her neck around hopefully. "Usually there's something. . . ."

"It's usually livelier? I haven't been here before. I was visiting my folks and decided to stop in. After dinner with them, I needed a drink."

"The pickings are usually a little better. Bob the broker try to hit on you?"

"You might say that. Did you see the article in the *Globe* about the missing papers?"

"Don't bother with Bob. He's impotent."

"And it's common knowledge? How sad."

She shrugged indifferently. "You seem awfully interested in the bank."

I forced a laugh. "I grew up here in Grantham. Had my first savings account there. I guess I think of it as my bank."

"That's kind of sweet," she said. "I find it hard to have fond feelings about any bank."

"Do you think he stole the papers?"

She answered my question, but I could see she wasn't interested in talking about the bank any more. "It's not like him . . . if he did, he had a good reason. However much of a sleaze Bass was in his private life, he was a straight arrow about banking. Rigid. Inflexible. He couldn't see a creative or practical solution if it bit him on the ass. It was another reason I hated working for him. And it drove Ramsay crazy. Eliot would sell his mother to make a buck."

The door opened and a noisy group came in. Her eager, bleary eyes checked it out. "Oh, there's Jon Piper, waving. Wish me luck." She slipped off the stool and teetered away.

I hate to waste good alcohol, but I'd had enough. Enough of everything. Banks. Bars. Family. Julie Bass. Men like her brother, who push me around. Murders without clues. I paid the check and left.

I always think I ought to be able to stand at the door and whistle and have my car come galloping up, like the horses in those old westerns, but it never works. I had to walk all the way across the parking lot. Halfway to the car, Bob the broker appeared and grabbed my arm.

"You weren't very nice to me in there," he said.

"Let go of my arm."

"Come on," he said, thrusting his meaty face at me. "Be nice. You're alone. I'm alone. Let's do something about that."

"I want to be alone," I said icily. "Take your hands off me and get out of my way." I stuck my hand into my purse and found the alarm that Andre had given me. Hit the button and a tremendous sound burst out.

He reeled back. "What the hell is that?"

I didn't bother to answer. I jerked my arm out of his grasp and ran to my car. I always have my keys ready when I cross parking lots at night. That's just good sense. It shouldn't be that way. I shouldn't have to worry about my safety because other people lack self-control. But I'm not about to risk myself as a political statement. I'm careful. Most of the time. I jumped in and slammed the door, ignoring Bob's fists beating against the glass and his angry words. I could have called the police on the car phone, but it would have been a major hassle and taken up more time. I only wanted to get home and crawl into bed. I jammed the car into reverse and backed up. If I ran over the guy, the world would not be a poorer place.

CHAPTER 14

My answering machine was blinking like a startled albino rabbit when I dragged my leaden body through the door. I dumped my stuff on the counter, shaped my hand into a gun, pointed, and shot. It wouldn't die. I gave up and pressed the button, ready with a pencil and paper to make a list of people who needed to be called back.

It was the usual grabbag of messages, including one from Andre, the essence of which was that he thought I shouldn't let Duncan Donahue off the hook. I'd turned my attention to whom I would call first before the machine came to an end. No one, I wasn't in the mood for any more conversation. I was brooding about Andre's message. "Oh, honey," I told the stolid piece of plastic on my counter, "I know you're doing this because you care, but can't you see I have to make these decisions for myself?"

In seconds, my mind took off like a runaway horse, dragging me into both sides of an imaginary conversation with Andre. And then, abruptly, I reined in my thoughts. He'd be here tomorrow and we could have this discussion then. I was tired and sore. I needed R & R.

I went into the bathroom and prepared to give myself some hydrotherapy, carrying the phone with me in case I changed my mind about returning calls. Aaron's current infatuation with weights had left me aching every place that Duncan Donahue had not. I turned on the water, threw in a handful of bath salts, and the doorbell rang. I pulled on my robe and went to answer it.

I know better than to just open my door. My life's been too adventurous for that. I peered through the spy hole. There were two men on the doorstep. Sports jacketed and tough-looking. They hadn't come to borrow a cup of sugar. "What do you want?" I called.

"Police, ma'am," one of them replied, holding up a folder with a badge. "From Connecticut. Investigating the death of Calvin Bass." It was an odd time of night for a visit. I knew that when the police were working a fresh murder, time was of the essence. But the murder wasn't that fresh, and why did they want to talk to me?

I settled them in the living room and offered them coffee, which they refused. Curious. I might not be Starbucks, but I make good coffee. Most cops never refuse coffee. I tried to excuse myself, saying I would go get dressed, but the larger, older one stopped me. "No need to bother," he said, "we only need a few minutes of your time." He immediately launched into a series of questions, most of which I didn't know the answers to.

"You have to understand . . . Officer—"

"Detective," he said.

"Detective. I've only known Julie for a week and I never even met her husband."

He persisted despite my disclaimers, acting like he didn't believe me. I've spent a lot of time around cops because of Andre and my own misadventures, and there was something about the situation that didn't ring true. My sixth sense said these guys weren't cops, especially when one of them asked me about the bank papers.

"The only thing I know about them is what I read in the paper," I said. "What do they have to do with Bass's murder? You think someone killed him over mortgage applications?" At least that would be a break for Julie.

They ignored my question. "Young lady, do you know what it means to be an accessory to a crime?" the older one asked. I shook my head, wondering where he was headed. "Well, miss, it means that if someone commits a crime and you help them—either beforehand or afterward—to commit it or cover it up, you can be guilty of a crime yourself. You wouldn't want us to have to arrest you and take you to jail, would you?"

Oh, spare me, I groaned inwardly. What did this guy think? That I was born yesterday? Under other circumstances I might have argued with him about how stupid his threat was and how he didn't have the authority to arrest me in Massachusetts anyway, but I was alone with these guys in my apartment late at night and it wouldn't have been prudent. We've got plenty of laws to protect us, but there are still cops who do what they want.

Anyway, by now I was almost certain that they weren't cops of any sort, so they might be particularly inclined to do what they wanted. "May I see that badge again, Officer?" I said.

Instead of answering, the smaller, uglier one weighed in and clinched it. "Come on, sweetheart, stop holding out on us. We know you've got 'em. Just give us the papers and we'll be on our way."

But the papers were a federal matter, not one for the State of Connecticut. "Oh my God!" I said, jumping up. "The bathtub . . . I left the water running." I sprinted into the bathroom and locked the door behind me, shutting off the water just as it was about to go over the side. And as I stood there, trembling and wondering what to do, I spotted the phone on the edge of the sink. Trusting my instincts, I dialed 911 and asked for help, explaining, as I struggled back into my clothes, that I had let two men into my condo because they said they were cops, that I didn't think they really were, they wouldn't let me examine the badge they'd flashed more closely, and I was scared.

For better or for worse, I am not unknown to my local police department, and they promised to send someone over right away. I hoped they really meant right away and not in half an hour. My visitors seemed to be getting less friendly by the minute.

One of them was banging on the door. "Hey, lady. You all right in there?"

"I'll be right out." I hid the phone in a stack of towels and reluctantly opened the door. The ugly one was right outside the door, close enough to have peered through a keyhole, had there been a keyhole to peer through. I hoped he hadn't heard me on the phone.

"You did say you wanted coffee, didn't you?" I said cheerfully, bustling past him and into the kitchen. "It always amazes me the way you policemen drink coffee. My boyfriend Andre— he's a Maine state trooper—and all his friends are the same way. It's one thing I make a point to never run out of."

I tried to stay cheerful despite the menace of their presence—kind of like cooking with a cobra on the counter. I made coffee the elaborate way—grinding whole beans from the freezer, opening a fresh gallon of spring water, using an unbleached filter, refilling the sugar bowl—anything to take up time, increasingly nervous and hoping the police hadn't put me on the bottom of their priority list or been diverted to something more important. My hands were shaking; I hoped they hadn't noticed. Bad guys are like bad dogs—they sense fear and it goads them to attack.

One of them—the one who looked like everyone's genial uncle—joined me in my pretense, asking about my boyfriend and answering my questions about his work, but the other—the blunt, ugly one—lounged against the counter grinding his fist rhythmically into his palm. He was watching me like a hungry cat watches a bird, eyes narrowed and glittering. I could almost see his tail twitching as he got ready to pounce, almost hear the rattling growl in his throat. He'd shed his jacket, displaying weightlifter's arms. A tattoo danced on his bicep. Where the heck were my rescuers? I was beginning to understand the expression "sweating bullets."

Finally, he ran out of patience and pounced, grabbing my arm roughly. "Let's stop playing nice-nice and cooperate with Uncle Mikey, all right? We know you took those papers out of Bass's house. Now where the hell are they?"

"I don't know what you're talking about." I didn't. The papers I'd taken turned out to be dull old industry reports, the kind of stuff you save to read someday and then never do. I couldn't imagine anyone wanting them, but I would have gladly given them away to get these guys out of my house, if it weren't for Julie's letters. For all I knew, these might be cops pretending to be bad guys pretending to be cops.

"Hey, Mikey, take it easy," the other "cop" said. "You don't want to hurt the lady." He didn't interfere, though. Just leaned back and folded his arms. "Good coffee, ma'am."

Mikey did want to hurt the lady, twisting my arm until I screamed. "That's just a taste of what it's going to be like if you don't play ball with us." His breath hissed hot in my ear.

That was twice today big bullies had twisted my arm and threatened me. Tears welled up in my eyes. I blinked them away. No way I was going to let him see that he'd made me cry. I had enough sense to be scared out of my wits. I could scream but the neighbors wouldn't hear. These condos were too well built. So instead of telling him that I wouldn't play ball if his was the last team on earth—why did these guys always have to talk in sports clichés anyway?—I kept a lid on my temper and tried to make him understand that I didn't have the papers and I didn't know what he was talking about. "Honestly, Mike, if I had them, I'd give them to you. Please. Stop. You're hurting me!"

He dropped my arm but before I could breathe a sigh of relief and rub the pain away, he backhanded me across the face, swatting me as casually as I might swat a fly. "Get real, lady!" he said. "We know you've got 'em."

"But I don't." I felt like a kid accused of a crime one of my siblings had committed—frustrated and helpless to defend myself in the face of parental certainty. Feeling helpless brings out the worst in me. I pulled myself up, steadying myself on my hall table, grabbed the first thing I touched—a heavy ceramic cat—and hurled it at his head. He ducked and it smashed on the tile floor behind him, which made me even madder. I liked that cat.

He came at me, smiling, and hit me again in a manner so casual I thought he must do it all the time. "Go ahead, honey," he said, "I just love it when people fight back." His pale gray eyes were dancing. The only nice feature in his ferret face. He had a nose too thin to breathe, cup-handle ears, a receding chin. Maybe people's rejection had turned him mean and all he needed was understanding. Like O.J. and the Menendez brothers. His hair needed washing. He smelled. He was enjoying himself.

I went for his nose, determined to break it. Caught him off guard, managed to draw some blood. He muttered a stream of curses, nothing I hadn't heard before, grabbed my wrist, and we struggled. I was no match for him—my own fault, I keep putting off weight training—and Mike took every indecent liberty he could. "Too bad we don't have more time," he said. "I like 'em wild and crazy." It was time for a gang of feminist guerrillas to burst through the door and take indecent liberties with *his* body. They didn't. His buddy just stood and watched.

Just because I was outclassed didn't mean I had to make it easy. I broke away, staggered down the hall to the front door, grabbed an umbrella, and pointed it at him menacingly. He laughed and pulled out a gun. "Drop it, sweetheart," he said. I dropped it. I might be pig-headed sometimes, but I wasn't so stubborn or blind with rage I couldn't see that an umbrella was no match for a gun.

Having a gun pointed at me focused things nicely. I might as well give them the papers I did have. They were useless, but maybe they wouldn't realize that. Maybe they'd take them and go away and I could lie down on the floor and cry and throw up and wet my pants without witnesses, and spend the rest of the night showering away the filthy sensation of Mike's roaming hands.

I was only trying to keep the briefcase away from them because some of Julie's letters were in it. And because I hate to cooperate with bad guys. There was no sense in getting myself injured or killed or even covered with sweaty fingerprints to protect someone I hardly knew from some embarrassment. From a wrongful murder conviction and prison, maybe, but not from embarrassment. I have a finely developed ability to prioritize. Besides, if my guess was right, these were Ramsay's people, and Ramsay didn't give a damn about Julie Bass's personal correspondence.

"All right," I said. "I'll give you the briefcase."

The older guy heaved himself away from the counter. "You're a very sensible young lady," he said.

I grabbed my car keys and headed for the door. "Hold on," the ugly one called. "Where do you think you're going?"

"The papers are in a briefcase. In my trunk."

Mike held out his hand. "Give me the keys. I'll get it. Which car?"

I gripped the keys tightly, the rough serrations cutting into my fingers. Even though it was perfectly sensible to hand them over instead of getting shot, I couldn't seem to relinquish control. He gestured angrily with the gun. "Come on, girlie, we haven't got all night."

The doorbell rang.

"Don't answer it," he ordered.

"Watch out, Officer," I yelled, "he's got a gun!" I jerked the door open and hurled myself through it.

There was a shot. I dove for cover, the cop outside dove for cover, and the two faux cops almost trampled me as they ran out. I lay in the cold, prickly shrubbery and shook. Another quiet Thursday evening chez Kozak. My neighbors must be praying that I'll move. The flashing strobe lights on the patrol car burst on my overwrought senses like Fourth of July fireworks.

My old friend Officer Harris picked himself out of a yew bush and ran to the car. "Are you all right?" he called over his shoulder.

"Don't worry about me," I said. "Go get those bastards!"

"Stay where you are. I'll be back," he called, his spinning tires churning up a shower of gravel that fell around me like hail stones.

Not knowing how long he'd be, I decided I wouldn't wait for him lying facedown on the ground. I got up. Slowly, carefully, treating my body as if it was made of glass instead of bruised and swollen tissues. The front of my sweats was a tangle of leaves, twigs, and bits of bark mulch. One of these days I was going to have to reform. If the body is a temple, mine had been desecrated.

I pulled myself onto a kitchen stool, folded my arms, and put my head down on the counter. My heart was still galloping, my body racked with the tremors of an adrenaline rush. I closed my eyes. Mike's ugly, amused face floated on the insides of my lids, the cynical smile, laughing eyes, stained teeth. He reached for me with dirty fingers. "Get out of my head, you creep!" I yelled.

It was too uncomfortable on the stool. I was cold. I limped into the living room, spread a wool throw over myself, curled up in a ball. I couldn't stop shivering. The incident wouldn't leave me alone. I was second guessing myself, trying to think how I could have handled it better. I hate losing. I hate it. I hate being pushed around and intimidated. Maybe it was time to get a gun and learn to use it. Maybe it was time, as Andre kept urging, to stop getting myself involved in things like this. Time to settle down and lead a regular, careful life. Time to stop helping. By the time Officer Harris came back, I'd worked myself into a deep funk.

Officer Harris and I first met when someone tried to break into my condo one night, and left me a calling card in the form of a large hunting knife, just days after a good friend's mother had been murdered with a similar knife. Our second run-in, when someone tried to burn both me and my condo, had been more acrimonious. Harris, cutting me no slack for being burned, concussed, and frightened, had bullied me and treated me like an idiot. I'd responded with a determined lack of cooperation. Over time, though, we'd reached a working accommodation. Sometimes.

He came in bursting with his own adrenaline high, posted himself at my head, and started firing off questions. "Who were those men and why were they here?"

I pulled my head out from under a pillow and stared at him, overwhelmed by his energy. "They wanted some papers that I don't have."

"What papers?"

"Papers allegedly missing from the Grantham Cooperative Bank." I was proud of myself for saying allegedly.

"Who were they?"

"They said they were cops. From Connecticut. One of them had a badge. . . ."

"Easy as pie to get," he muttered.

"I was careful," I said defensively. "Your wife would have let them in, too."

He shrugged, started to say something, wisely thought better of it. "Why did they think you had the papers?"

I could confess to removing things from Julie's house, or I could fudge. I opted for less than the truth. No wonder stalwart upholders of the law find me irritating. "You'll have to ask them."

"When we catch 'em," he said. Only then did he seem to notice my fetal position and bruised face. "Are you okay?"

"I've felt better."

"Come on, get up," he said, "I'll take you to the ER."

"I'd rather have a root canal without anesthesia. You could make me a cup of tea, though."

He turned on his heel and headed for the kitchen. "Coffee smells good," he said.

I closed my eyes, listening to the comforting sounds of him bustling around the kitchen. The rush of water against the metal of the tea kettle. The hiss and click of a burner. A cupboard opening and shutting. The sound of a mug on the countertop. His foot kicking the stool. A muttered curse. "Hey! What's this?" And then he was back by my side, looking anxious.

"There's a trail of blood from the kitchen to here. What's going on?"

"Maybe you're bleeding."

"I'm not bleeding," he said. "Are you?"

"I don't know."

"What do you mean, you don't know?"

"Harris," I said, irritation warring with exhaustion, "it's been a bad day. An awfully bad day, so don't push me. Please.

I mean I don't know. Do you think I'm bleeding?"

He rolled his eyes heavenward. "Well, somebody is. Where does it hurt?"

"Everywhere," I said unhelpfully. "Really. I got hit by an armed man this morning and then there was this guy. . . ."

His breath hissed out through his teeth. The look on his face was a man mentally rolling up his sleeves for an unpleasant task. Mike the Thug might have thought a chance to cop a cheap feel was fun, but Harris didn't look like he relished the idea of touching me one bit.

"Relax. You don't have to touch me," I said. "I'll just go in the bathroom and check things out." I stood up and took about two shaky steps before my body betrayed me. My mind might still be working but the rest of me, sensibly recognizing that I was in shock, knew that it was time to rest and be still. I grabbed his arm to keep from falling and collapsed back on the couch. I huddled there, shivering and sweating.

"I'm calling you an ambulance," he said.

I grabbed the arm of the couch and pulled myself up. "Don't you dare!"

Before he could act, his radio crackled. He listened and asked if he could use the phone. He came back shaking his head. "Looks like we're not going to be asking those two anything. They just drove themselves into a tree going about ninety. They're history."

"That's too bad," I said. "I wanted to kill them myself."

"We were talking about blood," he said.

"I try not to," I said. It was getting harder and harder to hang tough. I wanted to cry. I wanted him to put his arms around me and tell me I was okay. I wanted my pain to go away, especially the pain in my leg.

"My leg," I said. "Hurts."

"Which leg?"

"Left." He ran a hand down my leg.

"Ouch!"

He pulled it back ruefully, staring at the blood.

"Relax," I said. "I don't have any dreadful diseases."

He grabbed the waistband of my sweats and jerked them down. I gasped. "Relax," he said, "I'm a cop. I've seen it all. . . ."

I was wearing sturdy black cotton underpants. Bigger than my bikini bottom. Utilitarian. Unerotic. Only a few bits of lace. "That's what Andre always says, too."

"Why don't you marry the guy and go live someplace else?" Harris muttered.

"That would make your life too easy. Ouch! Careful. . . ." I closed my eyes, unwilling to look at the ugly, oozing red gash on my thigh. In the kitchen, the kettle raised its voice in song.

"Be right back," he said. I lay on the couch, feeling exposed and vulnerable, the shriek of the kettle grating on my taut nerves, the pain in my thigh expanding on exposure to the air.

I limped to the bathroom and, leaning heavily on the sink, began sifting through the medicine cabinet for first aid materials. I'm not always a good scout, despite good intentions. I'm often unprepared, but this time the search was rewarding. I found antibiotic cream and adhesive tape and gauze bandages. Lined them up on the sink. Sat down on the toilet and tried, with shaking hands, to fix myself up.

"You ought to have a doctor," Harris said.

"Don't start that again," I said. "You know how I feel about hospitals. We've been through this before. It's superficial and I'm current on all my shots."

"Then stop fiddling. I'll do it," Harris said, pushing my hands away.

"I don't understand how I cut myself right through my clothes," I said.

"Not a cut," he grunted as he swabbed at the wound with antiseptic. "Bullet."

The sting was sharp, hot, piercing. I gasped. Tears welled

up in my eyes. "I've been shot?" I said in disbelief. "They shot me?" Once the tears began, they were unstoppable.

"I hope it was them and not me," he said grimly, tearing open the gauze. "I'm going to have to put this in my report."

I nodded. I knew that. "Distract me," I said. "Tell me about something besides crime."

He laid the gauze gently over the wound and tore off some tape. A decent, capable guy. A good cop. "I have a new baby," he said.

"Boy or girl?"

"Girl. She's twelve days old. Miranda. She's beautiful."

"Your first?" He nodded. "So you guys aren't getting much sleep these days?"

He shrugged. "It's worth it. Puts things in perspective, though. And makes me careful."

"Oh yeah, real careful. If I were you, I wouldn't go home and tell my wife I'd been shot at tonight."

"I won't. I'll tell her I had to rescue this dippy broad who let two strangers into her place because they told her they were cops. There," he said, getting to his feet. "Now come drink your tea while you tell me everything that happened."

It wasn't exactly tea and sympathy but by the time I'd told my story and had my tea, I felt a little less shaky. My leg was stiff and sore and I was badly bruised. Before he left, Harris fixed an ice pack for my face. I walked him to the door so I could lock it behind him and stumbled off to bed. As I was struggling out of my clothes, I knocked the letter I'd found by Julie's front steps to the floor. The one I'd fished out of my bra and dropped on the dresser.

Curious, and by now feeling that I had a right to know everything that was going on, I picked it up and read it. It was not, as Julie had claimed, a letter from her husband. It was a letter to Julie from Thomas Durren. A sickly romantic, intimate, and sentimental letter. There was no longer any doubt in my mind that Julie and Dr. Durren had been lovers. Yet I could have sworn, from what she'd said and how she'd acted, that Julie cared for her husband despite his faults and was genuinely sorry about his death. It was a puzzle, but one I was too weary to consider.

On the other hand, after all that had happened, I was no longer so concerned about protecting Julie's privacy. Tomorrow, somehow, I was getting rid of that briefcase and everything in it. Maybe I'd send it to Julie's lawyer. I really didn't care, as long as it was out of my hands. It seemed like everyone involved was either a thug or a liar, including Julie herself. I was fed up with the whole business. I turned off the light and sank into an exhausted sleep.

CHAPTER 15

IF YOU'D ASKED me when I groaned and turned off my light, I would have said that I was never getting out of bed again. That was how tired I felt. But I surprised myself, bouncing out of bed at an early hour, surging with energy and ready to slay dragons or wrestle weasels. I was bouncy only until I landed on my feet. Then the nerve cells in every part of my body sent swift and desperate messages to my brain saying, "gently, gently."

I limped gently to the bathroom, showered gently, changed the bandage on my leg, swallowed some Advil, and finished drafting a proposal for the Northbridge School. Applying the every-cloud-has-a-silver-lining theory to my own life, I noted that at least I wouldn't have to do aerobics for a few days. The morning dawned gray and gloomy as I drank strong coffee and labored at my desk. When it was finally a civilized hour to call, I phoned Andre to confirm that he was still coming—people have the rude habit of getting murdered at inconvenient times—and went to work. Neither of us mentioned Dunk Donahue, and I didn't mention my nocturnal visitors. Andre worries about me.

The DJ was hosting a call-in of the ten most erotic songs of all times and playing the nominations to get our reactions. Some of the suggestions were pretty good and soon I was speeding down Route 128 with the windows down and music blasting, rocking orgasmically in my seat. Another car whirled past me and I saw that the man at the wheel, his face a mask of bliss, was rocking in just the same rhythm. Safe sex for the nineties.

Sarah was going to have a fit, I thought, as I left the North-bridge proposal on her desk, and there was still time to get more work done before the phones started ringing, crises were reported, or I had to head out to the King School. At least I liked the people at King. I was staying busy because it was my way of not dealing with the things at work that were worrying me, like Sarah's moodiness and Suzanne's secretive irritability. Sooner or later I was going to have to start asking them questions. It was my job. I was the fix-it lady.

Like me, a lot of people arrived at work early. I could tell by the time the phones started to ring. I spent an invigorating hour handing out advice and making appointments before Suzanne and the baby arrived. I held out my arms and Suzanne handed him over. Normally, though I found him cute and cuddly, I had no desire to imitate Suzanne. This morning, as I kissed his soft, sweet head, I felt a strange melting inside, imagining holding a child of my own. And Andre's.

Suzanne, always a fine reader of minds, grinned wickedly. "Baby lust," she said. Her teasing look changed to exasperation as she stared at my face. "What happened this time?"

Not wanting to worry her, I said, "Would you believe I hit myself in the face with a hand weight?"

"And why are you limping? You also dropped a weight on your foot?"

I was only half listening, thinking that I'd been up for hours and still hadn't done anything about the briefcase. "You wouldn't believe what Aaron put us through yesterday. I think I'm getting too old for this."

"Older, maybe, but apparently not wiser. Is there something going on that I should know about?" She didn't have to say she didn't believe me. Of course, I could have asked her the same question. "Okay, play the strong-and-silent type," she said, and changed the subject. "I'm considering a long weekend in Bermuda. Just me and Junior and Paul. Any problems with that?"

"Just jealousy."

"Aren't you and Andre off to San Diego soon?"

"Barring emergencies," I said. "He's talking about living together again."

"Well, Paul is talking about a new job." Her innocent statement dropped like a bomb between us.

Suddenly there were butterflies in my stomach. I liked this life, this partner. I didn't want Suzanne quitting and moving away. Butterflies and a peculiar sense of relief. Now I knew why she'd been so touchy lately. "New job where?"

Her smile was huge. "Southern Maine. It's a great opportunity for him. We could just move the whole business. . . . Oh, but you've just gotten your condo all fixed up, haven't you? And what would we do without Lisa and Bobby? Darn it. Everything's so complicated. Love. Life. Work. And motherhood. Motherhood makes all the rest of it look like a piece of cake." I handed the baby back, picked up my jacket, and shoved some papers in my briefcase. "Hey, wait a minute!" she said. "I've finally worked up the courage to talk about this and you're leaving?"

"Believe me, I'm not trying to avoid you. Not after all the anxiety I've experienced, trying to guess what's going on with you. Got a ten-thirty meeting at the King School. We'll talk when I get back?" She nodded, relieved, and I rushed out into the gray day, quickly checking my shoulder for drool.

It was a heavy, gray day. Much warmer, the air thick and sticky, with a damp clinginess that sent me straight to the air conditioning. It was the season of unpredictable weather—warm one day, freezing the next. As the Advil wore off, a slight headache nagged at my temples. I knew it would get worse as the day went on until my head was filled with little dwarves pounding on anvils. The low pressure would give a lot of other people headaches, too. By rush hour, the whole world would be cranky. But not as cranky as I'd be. The rest of the world hadn't been manhandled—not personhandled—twice in the last day. And probably most of their partners hadn't just announced they might be leaving.

I was feeling exceedingly depressed and put-upon when I pulled through the gates at King. Even though I was moving heavily and felt like those same dwarves had been clog dancing on my body, my spirits rose when I walked into the room. It was good to see my old friends again, good to feel wanted and appreciated. The head, Denzel Ellis-Jackson, a strikingly handsome man, was one of the few people I'd ever met who made me feel petite. Arleigh Davis, head of the trustees, was a blunt, practical, energetic person, absolutely devoted to the school. Her rock-solid calm in the face of calamity—and King had had its share—was a model for us all. And there was Yanita Emery, the assistant head. Yanita had come to me, tired of being assistant dean at a junior college where they'd treated her like a token. I'd sent her on to King even though I'd wanted to hire her myself—I do have my unselfish moments—and she was thriving under her heavy load of responsibility.

One thing I could always count on at King—sensible refreshments. We sat in the great hall of what had once been a turn-of-the century mansion. The high ceiling and thick walls kept things cool, silent fans stirred overhead, and there was good iced tea and crabmeat sandwiches. In such a pleasant atmosphere, it was easy for us to agree on a strategy for writing some grant proposals King wanted our help with, and in record time I was lightly fed, cooled, complimented, and back in my car with pleas to get a speedy start on their work ringing in my ears.

South of the city with time on my hands. A dangerous combination. My conversations with Rita and with Rachel Kaplan buzzed in my head and impulsively I decided to drive to Dover and see if I could locate the mysterious Nan Devereaux, the new woman whose presence in Calvin Bass's life had been so threatening to Julie. Who had, according to Dr. Durren's reluctant admission, made Julie so nervous she'd followed her husband to Connecticut. Being a partner in a firm where getting work depends on selling myself, I've learned to be bolder than my upbringing allowed. Now I know that "nothing ventured, nothing gained" is often true.

The worst thing that could happen would be that she'd refuse to talk with me. That's probably what she would do— refuse to see me—but I've been surprised before. Sometimes, especially when there's been a sudden shock, people need to talk, and often their circumstances haven't let them.

I found the address in the phone book and got directions from a friendly gas station attendant. I was a little surprised they allowed gas stations in Dover, but even the very rich drive cars, or have them driven. The gas station was so well disguised as a little chalet I half expected Heidi to prance out when I stopped to ask directions, golden braids bouncing, and offer me goat's milk for my health. She didn't, though. Only a handsome, thick-necked jock-type in a ragged college sweatshirt and shades with two-day stubble and awesome pecs. Something for the matrons to salivate over. On such a gloomy day, it was a miracle he could see to pump the gas, but he was very nice about directions.

Nan Devereaux's house, looming at the end of a long drive, was big enough for about twenty-five people. The double cherry doors were solid and elegant and sported knobs and knockers that cost as much as my condo. A tiny, frowning maid answered the door, ascertained my business, and left me standing in the hall while she went to see if Ms. Devereaux would receive me.

The Hall, and it was a Hall with a capital H, was high and paneled with dark wood. The gleaming floors were dotted with gorgeous Oriental rugs. I stood on one of them, not wanting to mar the gleam with my damp shoes. On the walls and going up the stairs, a collection of dour ancestors glared down at me. Not a pleasant face in the lot. The maid was gone a long time. My leg hurt and I wished I could sit down, but I hadn't been invited.

From somewhere in the house, I could hear a woman talking. A one-sided conversation, so probably she was on the phone. A long, steady murmur with pauses. Then, so suddenly I jumped, the voice rose, loud and angry. "No, that is not what I told you at all. I think my instructions were perfectly clear. I told you to sell them all and that's precisely what I meant. So don't bother me with any more questions, just do as I asked and send the money to my bank." A crash as a receiver was thrown down, missed the cradle, and clanged to the floor. Then silence.

Finally, I heard footsteps coming my way and a tall, willow-thin woman in black slacks and a flowing white tunic came striding toward me. She had luminous blue-green eyes, pale blond hair pulled into a gleaming chignon, and cheekbones to die for. She stopped a few feet away, swept me with a supercilious glance, and reluctantly held out a bony hand. "Nan Devereaux," she said. Despite the icy appearance, she had a voice made for telephone sex.

"If you'll follow me?" She turned without waiting for a response and glided out of the room. She walked like a ballerina, head high, chest forward, toes turned slightly out. I followed her to a cozy sitting room, all pale yellow walls and creamy furniture, with deeper yellow drapes drawn to shut out the gloom. She waited while I chose a chair and then sat on the sofa across from me. As she settled back among the cushions, her tunic draped itself around her body in a way that left no doubt she wasn't wearing a bra. Her elegant hands were carefully arranged in her lap, her long pink nails sporting a French manicure that looked like she'd been scraping off human flesh.

"Inez says you've come to talk about Calvin Bass," she said. "You've got a hell of a nerve!" I didn't respond but waited to see what she would do. If she was going to throw me out, why bring me in here? The shadow of a smile rustled her thin lips. "I've never met a female private detective before. I find it rather amusing."

I didn't want her to get the wrong idea. "I'm not a licensed detective, Ms. Devereaux. I'm just trying to help Julie out."

"The little mill-town princess? How noble of you."

Too bad he was dead. From what I'd heard about Calvin Bass, it looked like he and this icy snob were made for each other. Not wanting to spend any more time with her than necessary, I got right to the point. "What was your relationship with Calvin Bass?"

"Lust," she said bluntly, watching for my reaction. "I was very attracted to him and I believe the feeling was mutual. We had an affair. He lied to me, of course, as men in his situation will. He told me he and his wife were separated. That I couldn't call him at home because he'd just moved to a new place and was having trouble getting a phone installed. Don't look at me like that, Ms. Kozak. I'm not some sweet young thing, claiming I was led astray. I went to his place with him. A condo, nicely if sparsely furnished. There was no sign of a wife. By the time I'd figured out that he was still living with her, I didn't care. I was enjoying myself."

"He told you about his wife?"

"More like I told him and he admitted I was right. It was rather sad—marrying a girl he believed was his social equal only to find it was all a veneer and he was married to a mill-town girl with pretensions who turned out to be a clinging vine. He said he was drowning in her helplessness and dependence yet afraid to leave her, for her sake and the sake of the children. He didn't think she could handle it."

She shrugged her wide shoulders. "Pathetic. It's such a cliché, isn't it? Ah, here's Inez. Would you like some tea or lemonade?"

"Lemonade."

"I'll have tea," she said. "And don't forget the lemon, Inez." The silent, frowning Inez went to get it.

"If you want my opinion, I think she did it," she went on, with a decisive bob of her elegant head. "That kind of obsessive jealousy and dependence can cause quite desperate behavior. I expect she found out about me and simply couldn't handle it."

She settled into a more comfortable position with a soft rustling of silk, caught her reflection in a mirror, and smiled fondly at herself. "Perhaps I'm being too trusting, telling you all this. But I haven't anything to hide."

It was precisely the kind of statement that made me assume she did have something to hide. But then, I was already wondering why she'd been willing to talk to me. She was neither grieving nor naturally generous—the two circumstances under which I might have expected cooperation. No. Nan Devereaux thought she had a placid fish on her line and I agreeably took the bait.

"But why kill her husband, if she wanted to keep him so desperately? Why not kill you, instead?"

Before she could answer, Inez reappeared with a tray, which she set on the table between us. Nan swooped gracefully forward and poured herself tea as Inez offered me lemonade. It was made from real lemons, rich with pulp, and just enough sweetener. Oh, to be rich enough to have someone who would squeeze lemons.

She waited until Inez was gone before she spoke. "The insurance, I suppose."

"Was he well insured?"

She smiled. "He never mentioned it. It wasn't the sort of thing we talked about. Actually . . ." she paused for effect, "we didn't talk all that much." She left the rest to my imagination. If she could have read my mind, she would have been disappointed.

"When was the last time you saw Calvin Bass?"

Her hand clenched her knee and then relaxed. She glanced at her reflection again, raising her head to tighten her chin, and smiled again. I realized she was older than I'd first thought. Closer to forty than thirty. When she didn't hold her head high, I could see the beginning of crepey skin on her neck. Something she'd no doubt attend to in time.

"I was supposed to go to Connecticut with Cal that weekend. Does that surprise you?" Her smile was mocking. "You're not shocked, are you, Detective? You look shocked. He was going to take his racing course and I was going antiquing and then we'd have the nights together." Her voice curled around the words, caressing them. It was an amazing voice, low and husky, with little catches and breathless pauses. Its contrast with her appearance made it doubly arresting. A petulant note crept in. "But at the last minute, he called and said his cousin was going to be there, too, had suddenly taken him up on a long-forgotten invitation, and it would be awkward if I went, so I stayed home. And then . . ." She stared at her reflection.

She seemed to be gathering herself to say something. There was tension in her posture that hadn't been there before, tension and a suggestion of playing to an audience. Her hand rose like a conductor about to start an orchestra. "Then I had an appointment with my doctor . . . my gynecologist . . . and she told me that I had genital warts! And I could only have gotten them from Cal. Shall I tell you how they treat them?"

She didn't give me a chance to reply before launching into

a vivid description of having the warts burned off chemically, one by one. It was enough to make a woman celibate. "If he hadn't died in that crash, I would have killed him myself, the little shit!" She set her cup down hard on the table, sending tea cascading over the glossy surface. "A thoroughly nasty business."

Her bravura performance over, she folded her hands together again and gave me a perfunctory smile. "That's why I agreed to see you, so you'd know exactly what kind of a man he was. So you'd understand why that pathetic little creature killed him. Because he deserved killing. He was a thoroughly detestable man." She rose to her feet. "I'd like you to leave. I don't want to talk about him any more. About Cal . . ."

Her voice lingered on his name, then rushed on. "He was handsome, he was charming, he projected the rakish charm of a sexual pirate, yet he was an educated and cultured man. But what I didn't see at first was that underneath he lacked substance. I thought he was a mover and a shaker but he was a user and a taker. If you came here to see if I killed him, the answer is no—why should I?—but if you want to know if I'm sorry, I'm not. Not one bit. I thought I was building a relationship with that two-timing slimeball. I'll think of him fondly while I spend the next month with my feet up in stirrups."

"If I could just ask you a few more questions?"

She shook her head. "I think I've said enough." She touched her forehead lightly, as though the business pained her. "I'm sorry."

She must have rung a bell I couldn't see, because Inez appeared again. "Ms. Kozak is leaving, Inez. Will you see her out?"

I left my almost untouched lemonade reluctantly and followed Inez. Nan Devereaux sank back down on the sofa, kneading her forehead gently with those predatory fingers and watching her reflection in the glass. It had been a good performance. It would have fooled a lot of people. But I spend my life interviewing and I could see that for all of her protestations of hatred, Nan Devereaux was, or had been, in love with Calvin Bass.

CHAPTER 16

BACK AT THE office, I jumped out of the car, eager to make up for lost time. My battered body responded with an all-encompassing ouch. A scintillating, reverberating, unignorable ouch, reminding me that I had to slow down. Reminding me also of my nocturnal visitors and the briefcase that was still in my trunk. I couldn't imagine, from the little I'd seen, that I had anything worth dying for, but someone had cared enough to hire those two faux cops. And they had died. Maybe Dr. Durren had taken them along with Julie's letters, but if everyone was so sure I had the papers, I'd better look again. I popped the trunk and grabbed the case. It was battered brown leather with CAB in faint gold letters. Upstairs, I dumped the papers out on my desk, set aside Julie's letters, and started going through them.

The first twenty sheets were like the ones the police had pulled out when they searched my trunk—real estate sales data and census data for various suburban towns. Very boring. Very innocuous. The twenty-first was the original copy of a mortgage application. So was the twenty-second, the twenty-third, and the twenty-fourth. I yelped an overused expletive and dropped the papers like they were hot. This was, as my mother would say, a fine kettle of fish. Especially since I was in the kettle with the fish. I stared at the forms, rubbed my temples, and tried to sort out where I stood. The incipient headache was becoming full blown.

I was extremely lucky that the cops who'd searched my trunk had been so lazy. Extremely confused about whether I was lucky or unlucky that I hadn't given them to the faux cops. And extremely unlucky that I now had in my possession documents that the federal government, the Grantham Cooperative Bank, and some bad guys wanted—which I most certainly didn't want and didn't know what to do with. Worst of all, I didn't understand what it was about these dull-looking papers that got people so excited.

Feeling paranoid, I took the case and locked it up in the safe. Suzanne and I bought one after an unscrupulous employee tried to steal our client lists and other vital documents. Another example of how the life of an educational consultant is never dull. Then I called for help.

Help was in the form of Delayne Hatsis, the loan officer at my bank who'd helped me with the mortgage on my condo. Since then, we'd become casual friends. Delayne played a wicked game of tennis and was sometimes willing to go to late movies or spontaneous dinners on week nights. In other words, unmarried. And smart. She invited me to come to her office at the end of the day so she could take a look at the papers and seemed excited at the prospect. "This is as close as I'll ever come to real cloak-and-dagger stuff, I'll bet."

"Real cloak-and-dagger stuff is a lot like a math test," I told her. "Scary and boring all at the same time. Tennis is more fun. So are movies."

"So you say. You ought to try my job."

"Well, I'll be over at four and you can take a walk on the wild side, but don't get your hopes up."

"I'm polishing my dagger," she said. With her slight southern accent, she made it sound like a genteel activity.

There was one more thing to do before I got back to work, something to prepare for tomorrow's trip to Connecticut. I called a former coworker from my brief stint as a journalist, who now worked for the *Globe*, and asked if he could locate photos of Calvin Bass, Nan Devereaux, Dr. Thomas Durren, and Elliot Ramsay and fax them to me. On the off chance that he might have done something newsworthy, I also included Dunk Donahue, but I wasn't optimistic. The fleet manager for a New Hampshire trucking company wasn't likely to have done anything very newsworthy, unless mug shots counted.

Reporter to the bone, he said, "Is there a story in this?"

"Maybe. I don't know yet."

"You got some inside info?" He'd once had the desk next to mine and I could picture the too-eager, slightly avaricious look on his face.

"Not yet, Larry. I'm still digging."

"What's your angle?"

"Friend of the accused."

"What's she like?"

"I've only known her a week."

"Newfound friend, eh? I thought you were out of the newspaper business? I heard you'd become a consultant." He made consultant sound like garbage collector, when in my opinion, it was reporters who were the garbage collectors.

"I am. I just happen to think she's innocent."

"*Cherchez la femme,*" he said. "Remember, a high proportion of murders are committed—"

"Spare me," I said.

"You'd better share what you learn, Thea. The information highway is a two-way street, you know."

"Right now I'm looking at some real estate with prime frontage," I said, goaded into tantalizing him. I liked Larry, but he had an attitude problem. He always had to get more than he gave. Now I'd owe him and he wouldn't let me forget it. He gave me his home phone number and rang off, promising to fax the pictures if he found them.

I was up to my elbows in revisions of the Northbridge stuff when Sarah buzzed. "Detective Andre Lemieux, Maine State Police, on Three," she said.

I grabbed the phone. "Don't you dare tell me you're not coming."

"I'm not even breathing hard yet."

"Andre . . ."

"I'm a little slow today, that's all."

"That's what happens when men get older."

He let that one go without a comment. I could tease him with impunity because I knew he didn't suffer from performance anxiety. "Just called to let you know I'd be a little late," he said, "and to remind you to buy food."

"Oh, man of little faith."

"A little salmon on the grill with chives and lemon butter? Potatoes baked with herb cheese? A little Caesar salad? Lemon cheesecake?"

"You think I run a restaurant? And what about cholesterol?"

"I think when you put your mind to it, you're a great cook. Just thinking about you makes me hungry. . . ."

"Are you alone?"

"What kind of a question is that?"

"The kind of question a woman asks who would rather not have your comments overheard by a roomful of cops."

"Oh," he said.

"Oh? What kind of an answer is that?"

"The kind of answer a man gives when he doesn't want his conversation overheard by a room full of cops. See you later." He left me with a buzzing line and a foolish smile on my face.

I'd barely begun to work again when Suzanne came in,

dropped Junior in my lap, and plunked herself down in a chair. "What's this for?" I said.

"Feeding your baby lust. That's how we mothers are. We can't stand the idea that someone else might still have a waist or be free of stretch marks or be sleeping through the night."

I wanted to be cool, but today Paul, Jr., with his wide, curious eyes, his huge grins, and his happy baby noises seemed quite wonderful. "Michael and Sonia are getting married," I said.

"Ugh," she said. "Are you a member of the wedding?"

"Oh yes."

"When?"

"Labor Day weekend."

"If they have a baby, it will have three heads and eat maidens for breakfast," she said.

"I've always assumed she's such a hostile environment she'll just curdle his sperm. I don't think I'm in grave danger of becoming Auntie Thea."

"Yeah," Suzanne agreed, "it would have been different if Carrie. . . ." She stopped, looking stricken. "I'm sorry . . . forget I said that. It's all those nights without sleep. My manners are ragged."

"It's okay. I've been thinking about that, too. About Carrie. That's why my mom is so wrapped up in this Julie Bass business. . . . That's why I'm so wrapped up in it myself, even though she has me so mad half the time I could scream. This isn't about Julie Bass. I don't know her. It's because Julie reminds us so much of Carrie. It's about people life has dealt a bad hand to, who need some help with their cards. . . ."

"You're not doing this because of Carrie," she said.

"I am."

"You think you are. You tell yourself you are, to justify it. You're really doing this to please your mother."

"Thank you, Dr. Freud."

"You don't need this, Thea," she cut in. "This is your mother's crusade, not yours. Let her handle it."

"I tried."

"Obviously not hard enough," she snapped. "You're thirty years old. It's time you stopped letting your mother run your life."

"I don't let her run my life."

"What do you call this mess you're in right now? Someone else's life? You've got your career. You've got Andre. If you have spare time, you could try reading or relaxing. Movies. Biking. Hikes. If you can't control your need to do good, join Big Sisters or volunteer at a soup kitchen or something. Getting beaten up by thugs is not normal behavior."

"How did you . . . ?"

Suzanne sighed, a long, exasperated exhalation. "So I was right. Good God, Thea! When are you going to learn to be careful?"

I bent down and nuzzled the baby's head so she couldn't see my face. I was close enough to tears that I was afraid I was going to have to hand him back and rush to the bathroom before I made a fool of myself.

"I'm sorry, Thea," Suzanne said, and I realized she was the one who was crying. "I just want you to be careful. I couldn't stand having to bail you out of any more hospitals. You're my best friend. I couldn't do this without you." She started to cry harder. "Ignore this. Please. It's just all these hormones. I feel like an alien in my own body sometimes."

"Don't worry. I've become a medicophobe anyway." I pulled a box of tissues out of my drawer and pushed it across the desk. "While we're having truth time, what's this about Paul changing jobs?"

"He's being considered for the headmaster's job at the Coatsworth School." She hesitated, torn between her ambitions for her husband and her loyalty to me. "It's time for a move. He's been an assistant long enough."

My stomach knotted, the way it does with a sudden shock. I nodded. "I knew there was something going on." I wanted to yell at her, to tell her she couldn't do anything to upset my life because I liked it just the way it was. But she was already upset and I knew the only sure thing in life was change. Besides, we were close enough so that she already knew what I was thinking, just as I knew what was going through her head. We could have talked about the weather and still known what the subtext was. "He's certainly qualified. How serious has it gotten? When will you know?"

"A few weeks. You know how these searches go, back and forth while everybody looks you over, but he's in the final three, and he says he gets good vibes." Suzanne really wanted this for Paul.

"At least, with their endowment, he won't be under pressure to raise money," I said.

"No. They're looking for someone to spend money."

"They could hire us."

"Except for nepotism."

"I'm not a nepot and neither are you. Besides, these places hire their sisters and their cousins and their aunts all the time."

"And the headmaster's house . . ."

"Ooh la la! It's a mansion!"

"Yeah." Suzanne dabbed at her eyes and grinned. "Lots of lead paint for Junior to chew on."

"Pessimist!"

"I'm just trying not to want it too much."

"You've got to stop calling him Junior. It's an awful name."

"You prefer pumpkin? Oh, Thea," she said, "I don't know what I'm going to do. None of this is working."

"None of what?"

"I wasn't kidding when I said I feel like an alien. He's such a good baby. It's not his fault. I can't go on like this, working at our pace on only four hours sleep a night. I go home and sit down and cry. Paul is at his wits' end. He wants me to quit. I don't think he understands. You can't take something that was your whole life for years and suddenly chuck it and become a full-time mom."

"Women do."

"You don't think I should. . . ."

"No. Of course not," I said quickly. "It's my life, too, you know. But you could take it easier."

"How?"

"Do less work. Do you remember, when I married David, how I discovered having fun? And how frustrated you were that I suddenly wasn't working day and night? The business didn't fail."

She shrugged. "I guess I can try. I'm just overwhelmed by everything and then the possibility of moving on top of it all. Paul is being so good to me. Last night he made dinner. Music. Candles. Everything. He put Leonard Cohen on. You know. 'Suzanne.' And I was so grateful that I couldn't stop crying. . . ."

"Excuse me," Sarah interrupted. "A Dr. Durren on the phone. You sick?"

"It's business, not pleasure."

"Since when was going to the doctor a pleasure?" she muttered, and retreated. Something was bothering Sarah, something more serious than her ongoing dissatisfaction with her marriage. When I felt more energetic, I was going to have to find out what it was. Actually, from the look of things, we were going to need group counseling.

"I'll leave you alone," Suzanne said, getting up and taking the baby out of my lap. Where he had been was slightly damp.

"We're not done with this discussion," I said. "How can we

move? We need Bobby and Sarah and Lisa and Magda . . . and I'm worried about you."

"We'll talk about it," she said quickly. The pained look on her face said she wanted to put it off as long as possible. So did I.

I punched the button. "Dr. Durren? This is Thea Kozak."

"I need to talk with you," he said. "It's urgent."

I looked at my calendar. "Sometime on Monday?"

"Now," he insisted. "I'm downstairs."

I stared gloomily at the papers on my desk. I wasn't making progress anyway, I was just treading water. "I can give you a few minutes but that's all. I've got another appointment. . . ."

"I'm in the parking lot. In my car," he said, and disconnected before I could ask what car. Not that it mattered. I already knew it was a Porsche with an MD plate. Hard to miss.

As I passed Sarah's desk I told her I was meeting someone downstairs and would be back in half an hour. "If you're not back," she said, "what shall I do? Call the cops? Send out a St. Bernard?"

"Pour gasoline on my desk and set it on fire," I said, and hurried out.

It's hard to be subtle when you drive an electric-blue Porsche. It didn't seem to go with his retiring nature. Maybe he was having an early midlife crisis. Maybe Mrs. Durren bought it to spiff him up a bit. Maybe he bought it to impress Julie? My, I was having nasty thoughts today. I opened the door and climbed into the comfortable leather passenger seat.

Durren sat gripping the wheel, looking like he'd just lost his last friend. "Anything new?" he asked eagerly. "Anything that will help Julie? She can't stand it much longer . . . away from her children . . . Framingham is an awful place and that lawyer doesn't seem to be doing a damned thing for her. Can't seem to get her bail. They're holding her to let Connecticut make a case for extradition. And no one is trying to help."

"Rendition, I think. Not extradition," I corrected. All my life people have been casting me in the role of fixer. I know. Ann Landers says people can't do anything to you that you don't let them. But she expects a lot from us. I was trying to break the habit and people like Durren helped. I found his assumption that it was my job to fix things for Julie infuriating. Especially when he'd been so unhelpful himself.

I shook my head. "The best I've been able to do is identify some other people who were angry at Bass. About stuff at the bank, mostly. Except for his brother-in-law. You don't really think someone is going to call me up and confess, do you?"

He grabbed my wrist. "You've got to do better," he said. "She needs your help."

"Cut that out," I snapped, snatching my hand back. I was sick of being manhandled. The word had taken on new meaning this past week. The way things were going I might as well have been wearing a big sign that said "Hit me! Maul me. Jerk me around."

He stared at me, astonished. "I'm sorry. I'm just so upset . . . I wasn't thinking," he muttered. I would have taken his head off but he looked so pathetic it would have been like kicking a puppy.

"How long have you and Julie been lovers?"

"Who told you that?"

"Oh, come on, Doctor. Don't be naive. Everyone in town is talking about it. There's even a rumor that you fathered her second child. Besides, I've read one of your letters . . . the one you dropped on the front lawn."

"I what? I dropped . . . What letters?" he sputtered. He fell silent. This wasn't news. I'd already mentioned the letters. Maybe he thought his bluff had worked.

"I had hoped . . ." he began. "The letters, I mean. That they'd stay private." He must have decided he could drop his pretense of the interested "friend," because his face took on the fatuous look of a lover. "I wish she were mine. Emma is a doll. But she's not. Our . . . our love . . . our relationship . . . is a more recent thing." He said it proudly. Defiantly.

"You didn't do her any favors being so careless," I said, trying to shake him out of his smiling reverie.

He was startled. "What do you mean?"

"Julie sent me to the house to get the letters . . . the ones you took. I saw you leaving but I didn't know why you were there. As I told you last night, I found two on the floor of the closet. I found the one outside just as the police arrived." In response to the question on his face, I said, "And yes. I read one. Can you imagine what the police could have done with them? Or if they'd found you there with the letters?"

He just stared at me, the picture of offended virtue. "You had no right to read that." Irritating, selfish booby. Did he really have no concept of the harm he'd almost caused with his carelessness? This was life and death, not privacy and etiquette.

I tried to puncture his facade. "Did Bass know about you and his wife?"

He shrugged, still irritated. "I don't think so. He was too busy catting around. But even if he had, he wouldn't have cared. He didn't care about Julie and the girls, except as possessions. The proper accessories to a banker's life."

"Most men," I observed coolly, "don't like other men screwing their possessions."

"Excuse me?" Durren fussed with some lint on his blue blazer. "You needn't be so crude," he said. "Julie wasn't happy as an accessory. She was . . . is . . . a real flesh-and-blood woman. She had needs, dreams, desires that weren't being acknowledged. . . ."

"You ought to know."

He drew back like I'd hit him. "What's that supposed to mean? I thought you were her friend?"

"Doctor, please. We're both adults here. Let's not play

make-believe. I hardly know Julie. You must know that. You must have known who her friends were. . . ."

"Then why are you doing this?" The confusion in his voice was genuine.

"Because my mother asked me to. Because Julie needs help and there doesn't seem to be anyone else to do it. Because there's something so vulnerable and needy about her. Someone has to take care of her. Except for you and my mother and that awful brother of hers, she doesn't seem to have any friends. Because everyone thinks she did it and I don't. Because she reminds me of my sister, Carrie. I . . . couldn't . . . didn't . . . help Carrie . . . I guess I'm still trying. . . ." There it was. I might resent people who expected me to help, but in the end, the compulsion to fix things, to put things right, was in me, not them.

"Carrie is dead," he said. It wasn't a question. Even though I'd been unkind and snappish to him, he understood about Carrie and he was sorry. Maybe he wasn't such a bad guy after all. Self-centered and ineffectual, but with a good heart? His elegant hand closed gently over mine. I looked away from him, blinking back tears. I couldn't help it. It had been a hard twenty-four hours. Mixed up images of Carrie and Julie Bass hovered before my eyes, small and blonde and projecting an irresistible air of helplessness. Two women who cried out to be saved—even when they resented our meddling—and we couldn't seem to save them.

I pulled my hand back and straightened up. I wasn't one for wallowing in self-pity. Now that we'd declared a temporary truce, I probed a little, trying to see if Dr. Durren knew anything that might be helpful. "Did Julie know anything about these mortgage applications that her husband is supposed to have taken?"

He shook his head. "Cal kept her in the dark about his work. All she knew was that he'd put some papers in her closet. Papers he said were very important. Papers the FDIC was going to want on Monday . . . the day after the . . . after his . . . after he . . ."

I found the idea of a doctor who was unable to speak the word death a bit ironic.

Durren went on. "I disliked the man intensely. For what he did to her. I admit that. Still, it was a horrible way to die. To have something go wrong with the suspension and crash and burn like that. I wouldn't wish it on my worst enemy." He shuddered. "I've seen too many burn patients. It's horrible. Horrible."

"Do you know how Julie found out about the racing course? Was it from Cal?"

"It was from me. I learned of it through the Porsche Club."

"Porsche Club?"

"When I bought the car, my wife thought I should join . . . uh . . . meet people. . . ."

Durren was getting uncomfortable again. He'd come to pick my mind and now I was picking his. He began toying with the keys and fiddling with dials on the dashboard. "I really have to get going," he said. "I've got to get back to the hospital." He confirmed my worst prejudice about doctors—that my time was worth nothing, I could be interrupted or kept waiting endlessly, but his time was precious. "I just stopped by because I was hoping for some good news. I talked to her this morning. She's a wreck . . . as you can imagine. I'm so desperate to help her and there's nothing I can do."

It was as close as he'd ever come to saying please. Now that he was here—now that I had him in my power, as they used to say in old movies—I wasn't letting him leave. "The other night at my mother's you were saying something about Julie going down to Connecticut and then your beeper went off and you never finished. Julie went down there? While her husband was taking the course?" He nodded. "Did Cal know she was coming?"

"Cal? Of course not."

"Why did she go?"

"There was another woman. With Cal there always was another woman, of course, but she'd heard him on the phone, booking a room, and something seemed different—maybe just the fact that he wasn't trying very hard to hide it from her. Oh sure. He told her he was going to be taking the course with a cousin of his. But we all know about these cousins, don't we? Julie was afraid this one was serious. That he was going to leave her. She said he'd changed. Grown harsher, more critical and, at the same time, more oblivious, more uncaring. Disinterested. Withdrawn from their lives in areas where he'd been obsessive. There had been some nights when he didn't come home. He hadn't done that before. Having a father for the girls was very important to her. Important enough to tolerate all he put her through. . . ."

"So she went down there?"

"Yes."

"And was he with a woman?"

Durren shook his head. "He was sharing a room with his cousin."

"Did you go with her?"

"I'm a physician," he said huffily. "I work on weekends. I was at the hospital on Sunday when that accident happened."

"And Julie? Where was she?"

"As far as I know, she was home on Sunday."

His attitude that even though he said he loved her, he didn't have any obligation to support Julie annoyed me and made me want to provoke him. "But the car wasn't tampered with on Sunday, was it?"

"I'm a physician," he repeated, "I know about the human body, not cars. And I work Saturdays, too. It's in my contract, covering the weekends. . . ." He sounded resentful, but I didn't know whether it was of me or of having to work weekends. Or maybe just that I was taking up his time when he wanted to be off. For all his concern and sincerity, there was something of the petulant child about Dr. Durren.

"What's this?" I asked, patting the dashboard. "Your midlife crisis?" Durren didn't respond.

"So you don't know whether Bass was with a woman or not?"

"She said he was with his cousin," he growled.

"A male cousin?"

"Yes." He spat out the word between clenched teeth. "Julie doesn't lie. . . ."

I thought of some of the things Julie had said to me. About her rich father and her privileged upbringing, and changed the subject. "Does your wife know about your relationship with Julie Bass?"

"My wife has no interest in me or in anything I do," Durren said bitterly, "although, for reasons which I cannot ascertain, she wishes to remain Mrs. Doctor Durren."

There was no response to that. "Do you know anything about this cousin who was there with Bass? Name? Age? Place of residence?"

"No. Nothing. Julie probably does." It had obviously never occurred to him that the cousin might be an important witness. He checked his watch impatiently. "I really must go. People will be waiting. About the car," he said abruptly. "Something I can control. No surprises. No disappointments. No demands. Just a satisfying, predictable response. An antidote to the rest of my life." I got out and he was gone almost before my feet touched the pavement.

Another choppy little piece of my day gone. I went upstairs and worked for about two nanoseconds and then it was time to remove the clandestine documents from the safe and go see my banker. I like the sound of that—my banker—it makes me feel like someone important. I wasn't feeling important in general, though. I was feeling frustrated and confused. And sore.

Delayne looked like an African princess. Her skin was rich, dark chocolate. Short-cropped hair revealed a perfectly shaped head atop a long, graceful neck. Her arms and legs were endlessly long and slim and gorgeous and her eyes black, shiny, slightly slanted and exotic. She carried herself like the model she could have been, moving with a stately grace as she came to meet me.

Early on, she'd made the decision to take pride in her heritage, and her walls were decorated with bright tribal fabrics and African sculpture. As she'd said to me once, "Some people try to play the assimilation game. And they blend in. Not entirely, but they blend. I don't blend. I'm never going to meet anyone who doesn't notice that I'm black . . ." She'd paused. ". . . and beautiful. So I'm making a political statement, a social statement, and"—she lowered her voice—"scaring the heck out of 'em."

"Have a seat," she said, waving at the row of chairs facing her desk. "Some days I look over at these chairs and I feel like a high school principal. I've been known to rap on the desk, too. Some people have no sense of order." She slid into her chair and waited, her hands clasped loosely on the blotter in front of her. Waiting like that, she looked like a high school principal.

Her suit was heavy silk, the color of the caramel in a Milky Way bar, with a honey-colored silk blouse underneath. She had a string of amber, turquoise, and honey beads, and two chunks of amber in her ears, complete with bugs. She tapped her earlobes. "Disgusting, aren't they? All day long people have been staring at my ears and making faces they think I don't see. But Delayne sees all."

"What does Delayne see here?" I took out the mortgage forms and handed them to her.

She smiled warmly and gathered them in. "Cloak, or dagger?" she said.

"You tell me."

She started out smiling but the smile dissolved into a frown of concentration as she worked her way through the pile. I might as well have not been there. All her attention was focused on the papers. Finally she looked up. "Equal Opportunity Lending," she said, in words of all caps. She pulled out a few applications and spread them on the desk in front of me. "See how these are paired? You've got minority applications and white applications with approximately identical financial pictures, only in each case, the minority application was denied and the white application approved."

"Bad?"

She nodded. "Bad. Very bad indeed. If I were the guy in charge of the lending department, heads would be rolling, probably mine included. Or, if I were a CYA type, I'd be hoping this just disappeared."

"CYA?"

"Cover your ass."

"Oh."

"And you said these were removed from the bank's files by an employee?"

I nodded. My stomach was doing a little knotting number again. I had the feeling Delayne was about to give me some more bad news. "Just before the FDIC was supposed to do an audit."

Delayne shook her head sadly. "A real mess. You don't want to get involved in this, Thea. This is federal stuff. The FBI investigates messes like this. If I were you, I'd put that briefcase in a box and ship it UPS to the fibbies with a note that you found it by the side of the road. Or leave it by the bank door."

I was thinking about the faux cops and Cal Bass's accident. "But surely these aren't the kind of thing people kill each other over? A bunch of loan applications?"

She shook her head. "I've given up being surprised at what

people kill each other for, Thea. There are people out there killing over a jacket or shoes or even a look. As for these . . ." She shrugged. "Discriminatory lending is serious business. It's a criminal offense. A federal criminal offense. Or it could be. And an employee whose carelessness brings the FDIC investigators into a bank is not going to be a popular person. People could lose their jobs. And then there's tampering. . . ."

"Tampering?"

She held out an application. "You see these faint little chicken scratches in the margin? These pencil marks? Someone was worried about what to do with these. Very worried. Someone was trying to figure out how to alter them. And that is a criminal offense." Delayne frowned. "As far as I'm concerned, I never saw these papers and I never talked to you." She made shooing motions with her hands. "If you know what's good for you, neither did you. Get rid of 'em." She no longer looked pleased about her cloak-and-dagger experience.

I left her office, toting the tainted files, feeling like it had been a very sorry day. Several times on my way to the car, I looked back over my shoulder, expecting that at any minute a carload of fibbies would come roaring up and cart me off to jail.

CHAPTER 17

SKIPPED AEROBICS, passing up the opportunity to watch Aaron cavort and sweat with a touch of regret. He makes me feel like a dirty old lady, but having lustful thoughts can contribute to a healthy sex life. Andre was coming tonight and I didn't need any more stimulus for lustful thoughts. I already ached from head to toe; I didn't need Aaron for that, either. What I needed aerobics for was to sweat the anxiety and anger out of my system. In my present battered state, though, the pain outweighed the benefits. I went to the grocery store instead.

Andre always needles me about my refrigerator with observations like if I got snowed in, I'd starve, or was I trying to invent a new form of penicillin? So what if I don't keep food in the house? I have other good qualities. I'm kind, quick-witted, and loyal. And I hate grocery shopping. The too-bright lights make my brain malfunction and the grade-B music sets my teeth on edge. But there's some truth to the contention that the way to a man's heart is through his stomach—at least in Andre's case. He'd even ordered his dinner at Mama Thea's restaurant.

I parked in the crowded lot and got a cart, wincing at the

length of the checkout lines. The aisles, jammed with tired shoppers in a hurry, looked like a bumper car course at a county fair, as people shoved each other's carts around to get at the food. I dutifully bought potatoes and herbed cheese and salmon fillets and lemons and chives and butter and my favorite quick-and-dirty Caesar salad mix: romaine, endive, and radicchio. Bacon and eggs and strawberries for breakfast. I had to buy the berries. They smelled real. Then it was on to the bakery.

I have a soft spot for baked goods. Mom used to bake bread when we were little, and a thick slice of bread hot from the oven, slathered with butter, is as close to heaven as life gets. If I ate as many baked goods as I liked, I'd be a 5′11″ collage of soft spots. But the smell of baking bread is soothing and seductive, and I came away with a cart groaning under the weight of foc-cacia and cheese bread and herb and sun-dried tomato bread, whole wheat, raisin and pecan rolls, and croissants, regular, chocolate and strawberry and sweet cheese. The lemon cheese-cake Andre had requested. Chocolate chip cookies to eat in the car. Thick slices of pizza rustica for snacks, layered with cheese and hot ham and red peppers and spinach. I was light-headed just thinking about how much fun it was going to be.

I've learned a few things over the years about caring for a damaged body. I chose the store with grocery boys—average age seventy-five—who wheel the cart out and load the car. Sweet, chatty, avuncular men who call me young lady and make me yearn for simpler times and smaller towns. Too bad you couldn't take them home to unload at the other end, but maybe I expect too much from life. One thing I expected that I was going to have, though—a quiet evening with Andre without anyone ring-ing the doorbell or barging in and pushing me around.

Back home, I let myself in, turned off the alarm, dumped the groceries on the counter, and left it all sitting there while I went to change. There was no surreptitious breathing, no sound out of the ordinary. Just the appliances doing their thing and the hiss of the ocean outside on the rocks. There was no one in my living room. No one in the bathroom. No one in my closet. No leering, evil eyes watched me as I changed into leggings and an oversized silk shirt, switched on ZZ Top, and sashayed through the rooms, putting things away and starting dinner. Tomorrow I would be back on the case, sorting out poor Julie's life, but tonight belonged to me.

When the doorbell rang, I was lounging on the couch, drinking white wine and listening to Marcus Roberts playing smooth jazz. The potatoes smelled delicious, the salmon was marinating, and the salad was waiting to be dressed. The peep-hole gave me a rather fish-eyed view of Andre, holding a florist's bundle.

"Dahling!" I said, opening the door. "Are those for me?"

"Nothing's too good for my girl," he said, handing over the flowers with a flourish. "And as soon as you've put them in water, I want to hear all about those two guys who were here last night. You said you were being careful. . . ."

"How did you know—" I began, but of course I knew. "Harris, right? The police brotherhood?"

"Fellowship," he corrected. "Brotherhood is non-PC, isn't it?" He hesitated, knowing how prickly I could be. "Were you planning to keep it a secret? Did you think I wouldn't notice . . . ?" He broke off abruptly and seized the flowers. "I'll put these in water. Sit down. You look tired."

"Tired? Not ravishing? Not gorgeous? Just tired?" He looked tired himself. Tired and like a man with something on his mind. Something besides good food, good company, and good sex. I'd been looking forward to an evening relaxing and having fun; Andre wanted to talk. I felt a tightening in my stomach, and a mix of relief and irritation. So we'd do both. We'd play. We'd talk. That was what relationships were all about.

We've had our conflicts about my taking risks. Andre's instinctive protectiveness wars with my determined independence.

We've worked that out pretty well—I've agreed to be more careful and he's agreed to be less controlling—but things still come up that we disagree about. I didn't know if that was it, but there was something on his mind.

"Ravishing, gorgeous, and tired," he said, setting a vase of roses on the coffee table and sitting down beside me. "We need to talk."

"Now? Don't you want to eat first?" Up close, I could see his five o'clock shadow, dark along the firm edge of his jaw. I reached out and touched it.

He caught my hand and held it. "Better to clear the air. I've got things on my mind," he said.

"You want some wine?" He nodded. I poured a glass and handed it to him. He was watching me carefully with his policeman's observant eyes.

"They hurt you," he said.

"It's nothing. . . ."

"Any time you're hurt, it's something to me."

Maybe Sarah was right. Maybe I was neurotic. Maybe there was something wrong with all the rushing about and pushing myself so hard and never taking the time to just be, to have my feelings, to think about where I was in the world and what I wanted instead of what I had to do. When Andre said that, something inside crumbled and all my fear and pain and repressed desire to be comforted and cared for tumbled out. Like a frightened child, I threw myself into his arms and buried my head in his shoulder.

"I was scared," I said. "Scared and angry."

"Tell me about it." His arms locked around me and pulled me closer. For the first time in days, I felt safe. Safe and comforted. I took a deep breath and cleaned my emotional closets. I told him everything. About the false police and the papers I'd taken from Julie's house and how just having them might get me in trouble with the Feds. How stupid I felt for having taken them and now I didn't know what to do. About Julie's brother—though he already knew about that. About the other people at the bank and how everyone had disliked Cal Bass and about Bass's girlfriend and about Dr. Durren and why we were going to go to Connecticut and do some investigating of our own. When I was done, I felt so much better I was practically giddy with relief.

"So that's the story," I said. "Are you hungry?"

"I still don't understand why you're mixed up in this at all," he said.

"I told you. Because she reminds me of Carrie. . . ."

"I don't think that's it, Thea. I think you're letting your family push you into this. It's not your problem. . . . You've got to stop thinking you can save the whole world, Thea. You can't. No one can."

He was right. And he was wrong. I'd made it my problem. "You don't understand," I said. "My mother just asked me to do a little—"

"I can't believe how you let her manipulate you," he interrupted. "When you know what she's like. If this is so important to her, why doesn't she do it herself?"

"She wouldn't know how. . . ."

"And neither should you. And how many times has she asked you to stop getting involved in other people's problems? Until one comes along that matters to her. Someone should do the world a favor and shoot that woman!"

"You should be the last person on earth to advocate shooting someone, Detective!"

He held his hands out defensively in front of him. "Look, forget it. I'm sorry. It's just that I can't stand the way she manipulates you into doing her dirty work for her. I thought you'd gotten over that."

I shrugged. "So did I . . . after Carrie . . . but then, she's my mother. I guess it's kind of like malaria. I think I'm over it and then it comes back and there I am sweating and shivering and right back in the grips of it again. I don't think anyone is ever entirely cured of family."

"Did you consider just saying no?"

"Of course. But you haven't met Julie. She seemed so helpless . . . . and then it turned out she really didn't have any friends, just that belligerent lout of a brother. . . ."

"You're not Mother Teresa, you know. You can't go around taking in all the world's strays."

"You're saying I shouldn't help people?"

He rubbed his forehead like it hurt. "No. No. Of course not. It's one of the best things about you, your loyalty, your generosity. How can I say this? I just wish you'd take better care of yourself. Be generous to you." I felt his chest heave under my head, felt him gathering himself. "You should have seen the two of us, when Roland told me about Donahue . . . about what he did to you! That man is lucky he's still walking. . . ."

"You saw Donahue?"

"I exercised the greatest self-control." I knew that was all he was going to tell me. "You know I can't stand it when you're hurt," he said. "I want to be there. To help you. To put the bandages on your little fingers and toes."

I'd been holding my breath and now I let it out. We weren't going to have a fight. He was just telling me he'd been worried. "And thighs."

"Oh, yes. And thighs." He sighed.

"I'm trying to be careful."

"The things you do when I'm not around," he said, shaking his head. "You're going to give me an ulcer if you keep this up. I don't know what I'm going to do with you. Throwing a vase at a man with a gun. . . ."

"I didn't know he had a gun. And it wasn't a vase. It was a cat. That dumb, grinning ceramic cat that used to sit by the door."

"Nitpicker." He gave me a diabolical grin and pulled out his handcuffs, dangling them in front of my face. "I think I've got it," he said.

"Got what?"

"The solution." He clicked a cuff around my wrist and the other around his own, fastening our wrists together. "From now on we aren't going to be separated."

"Cute," I said. "Like Siamese twins. These are going to make things very difficult. . . ."

"Where some people see a problem, others see a challenge," he said.

"Mister, you are always a challenge. And sometimes a problem. I guess you're going to help me fix dinner?"

He shrugged. "Whither thou goest . . ."

"Everywhere?"

"We'll see." His hand was warm through the thin silk. I tried to work up some irritation at the handcuffs, at the questions, but I couldn't. I was too happy just to have him here.

"I feel so safe," I murmured.

"You ought to. You've got your own cop only an arm's length away."

"Come closer," I said. I wanted to be connected, wanted to be even more connected. I didn't know what had come over me but I was practically intoxicated with lust, overcome with the rushes of sensation his hands were producing. He was on the same wavelength now—getting mad at each other seems to naturally segue into other passionate activities—and we managed nicely, despite the cuffs. Getting undressed, at least, though a couple times our gyrations had me laughing so hard I almost slid right off the buttery-soft leather of the couch.

Afterwards, I looked at our linked arms and burst out laughing. "We look like a clothesline."

"Clothesline?"

My shirt, his shirt, my bra, and his T-shirt all dangled from our arms. "Nobody better come to the door."

"And the phone better not ring."

"We're never going to get this stuff back on."

"Who cares?"

"Well, I'm not going out on the deck to cook the fish dressed like this."

"Undressed, you mean."

"Keep correcting me and you aren't getting any dinner."

"Who cares?" he repeated, but his stomach betrayed him by rumbling.

"You are hungry!"

"For you. Come live with me. I can't go on like this much longer."

"I'll consider it if you'll take these things off." I jerked my arm impatiently, half amused, half angry. They were beginning to make me feel vaguely claustrophobic.

He lay there on the couch beside me with an insolent grin. "Can't. I don't have the key."

"Where is it?" I had mortifying visions of having to drive back to Maine this way or going into the local police station to ask for help.

"Out in the car."

"Out in the car! How could you . . . ?"

"I forgot."

"Forgot?" Suddenly I wanted them off right now. I struggled to sit up. "Get dressed. We've got to go get it."

He covered me with his body and pressed me back down onto the couch. "What's the rush?" he whispered, nuzzling my neck. "I said I wasn't going to let you go." I tried to push him off but he captured my free hand and pinned it down. I could feel him hard again against my leg, searching, connecting. His breath roared in my ear, his rocking head scraping against my

heek. Then it changed to a faint moan, a gasp, and a drawn-
ut groan of satisfaction.

This time we weren't on the same wavelength at all. A panic
d never experienced filled me, tightening my chest until I
ouldn't breathe. It didn't matter that this was Andre, a man I
oved and enjoyed having sex with. I was trapped by locks. Held
own and overpowered by another big man bent on controlling
ae and I couldn't escape. I pulled my arm free and beat on him
ith my fist. "Let me go. Let me go!" My voice was shrill with
esperation.

He raised himself with his free arm and stared down at me,
is satisfied look changing to astonishment. "Thea? Hey, calm
own. Calm down. What's the matter?"

I couldn't calm down. I couldn't breathe. I couldn't think
ationally. Like a bottle of soda that's been shaken, my panic
lowed up and out and I couldn't stop it. "Please. Let me up,"
gasped.

He rolled sideways into a sitting position, his face still etched
ith confusion. I jumped up and tried to run away, but I only
ot to the end of my arm, which I practically jerked out of its
ocket before the cuffs caught me and pulled me backwards. I
ollapsed onto one knee on the rug, naked and trapped, and
uried my face in the clothes strung along my arm. "Help me."

Andre knelt beside me. "Thea? I don't understand. What's
oing on? Did I scare you? Did I hurt you?"

I was confused, disoriented, having trouble breathing. "I
.. don't . . . know. Suddenly. I felt so strange . . . something
appened . . . I was trapped . . . panicked. You were holding me
own and I couldn't get away. Too many people . . . doing that
o me . . . lately."

"I didn't mean to," he said, struggling to understand.
I thought we were having fun. You're not saying I'm like
hem. . . ."

"You were having fun. I was having a panic attack."

"You don't have panic attacks, Thea." He said it firmly, as though that was the end of the discussion. "You've just had a hard week. You've been hurt. Traumatized." Implicit in his words was the phrase "you'll get over it." At the same time, good cop that he was, and used to dealing with people at the limits of control, he was soothing me with warm and gentle hands.

"Maybe I do now. Have panic attacks. There's been so much happening lately. All these men pointing guns at me and trying to push me around. . . ."

"I'm not one of them, Thea," he said, hurt by being lumped together with my attackers.

I had to straighten this out or we'd have a fight. I didn't want that. This wasn't something rational, this shattered feeling. I collected my scattered wits and tried to explain. "That's not what I meant. . . ."

"You're not saying that having sex with me gives you panic attacks?"

"No. This isn't about sex. It's about handcuffs . . . and power . . . being overpowered . . . trapped . . . feeling helpless. I feel like my life is falling apart."

He reached over and gently pushed back some hair that was sticking to the tears on my face. "I think we should go get those keys, don't you?"

"Please."

Getting undressed had been easy and amusing. Getting dressed was harder. A recent survey showed that sixty percent of men prefer bras which fasten in the front. Well, mine did and it still gave us a hard time. But we managed. Finally, panting and almost restored to good humor, we were dressed. Not neatly but at least we were decently covered and I could breathe again. We went out to his car and I waited patiently while he searched for the key. There was a scary moment when he thought it was lost but then he found it and set me free.

He steered me back inside and poured me another glass of wine. I curled up in one corner of the couch and sat, clutching a pillow defensively.

"You look about twelve years old," he said. "What did you mean when you said your life was falling apart? This thing with Julie Bass?"

I shook my head. "Everything. Sarah is grouchy all the time. Suzanne is talking about moving. . . ."

"What about the business?"

"I don't know. She doesn't know. She's not talking about it yet. Paul's considering a new job."

He nodded. He knew how important my job, Suzanne, and all the people I worked with were to me. "You don't know what's going to happen and you're scared."

I nodded. "I used to have my family. And David. Then I didn't have David any more. And since Carrie . . . since she died, I don't feel like I have my family any more. Not in the same way. And so what I have is my work. And you. And I'm scared of having you and scared of losing my work. And please, could we not talk about this any more?"

"Tough luck, lady."

"What do you mean?"

"You've got me whether you want me or not."

"But you're not here when I need—" I stopped. The decision not to live together was mutual and insurmountable.

"And you're not there when I need . . . and we both need to do something about that," he said. "But not right now. Let's eat. I'm starving."

"Right. The way to a man's heart and all that."

He struck himself lightly on the chest with his fist. "You're already in my heart, stuck right here in the middle of this squishy, bloody muscle."

"Ugh. How romantic."

He gave me a look the Hallmark people would have died for.

"Do you have any idea how I feel about you?"

"Do you have any idea how strongly your feelings are reciprocated?" The intensity of the moment crackled around us like a storm of personal lightning. Then he refilled our glasses and touched mine lightly with his. He didn't say anything. There was nothing more that needed to be said.

Andre cooked the fish while I finished the salad and set the table. It was fun to watch him eat. No picking and aimless cutting for him. He takes a twofold view of food—he eats to sustain his big, solid body, and he eats because he loves to eat. Like my mother, I enjoy feeding people. Feeding him brings out all my maternal instincts. I practically beam as he packs it away.

"You're grinning like a fool," he said.

"Don't call names."

"Is there any more bread?"

"Not for you. You're getting love handles."

"Puhleez?"

"Oh, all right. But only if you tell me what the Connecticut police said about the accident."

"Nothing. They aren't revealing any details. Not even to me."

"Well, thanks for trying."

We worked our way through the potatoes and the bread and the fish and the salad and a substantial portion of the lemon cheesecake and opted for an early bedtime. We were just drifting off to sleep when the doorbell rang.

"I'm not answering it," I mumbled, burrowing deeper into the covers.

"No one rings the bell at this time of night unless it's important."

"No way. Probably bad guys. I've had enough of bad guys this week. I'm sleeping."

"You want me to answer it?"

"Sure. Scare away the baddies and come back to bed. It's cold without you."

The bell rang again. Whoever it was wasn't going away. "I'll be right back." He reached for his pants.

All the commotion had broken the thread of sleep. I gave up, pulled on a robe, and followed him. The door was open, letting in a blast of chilly air. Standing on the step was a young girl in a brown leather jacket. Pale faced, with lank brown hair. Her nose was purple and she was shivering.

"I need your help," she said through chattering teeth. "May I come in?"

CHAPTER 18

KAREN OSGOOD LOOKED like a born victim—her shoulders had a perpetual defensive slouch and she flinched at quick movements like a cornered animal—so I was amazed that she'd had the courage to seek me out. But she had, and now she sat on my couch, adding a whole new layer of complication to my life.

Her first words, after declaring that she needed my help, were delivered with a belligerent thrust of her head. "I'm sorry to burst in on you like this but I didn't know what else to do. You've got to help me find Jon. I think something's happened to him."

I was still struggling to get my eyes open but Andre, a policeman to the bone, was awake, aware and alive. "Why did you come here?"

The girl flinched and looked at me. So far she'd avoided looking at Andre. "You are Thea Kozak, aren't you?" I nodded. "Because," she told Andre's shoes, "she's investigating his cousin Cal's death. And Jon was with Cal that weekend . . . they were taking that driving course together . . . that is, Cal was treating him to a driving course . . . and then Jon just disappeared. In all he confusion after Cal's car crashed, Jon checked out of the motel and disappeared."

I didn't want to hear any of this. I could feel the first black fingers of a headache reaching into my brain. I had too many headaches lately. Probably a brain tumor. "I don't understand. Why me? How did you find me? Why didn't you go to the police?"

"I went to see Julie." Her voice dropped like someone had pulled the plug. She leaned wearily against the door jamb, her face as white as the paint. "She gave me your name. Could I come in? Please? It's cold out here . . . and I've been driving all day."

I didn't want this problem-bearing stranger in my house in the middle of the night, but thanks to my mother, my manners are pretty hard-wired. I stepped aside and motioned her in. Andre stood silent but I knew his mind and his eyes were already on the case.

I turned on the living room lights and settled her on the couch. "Would you like something to drink? Coffee? Tea?"

"Tea, please." The slight catch in her voice suggested tears weren't far away. "And . . . could I have something to eat?" She said it in a rush, embarrassed at the audacity of her request.

We were all silent as I fixed her a sandwich, and one for Andre as well, since he was always hungry. Tunafish. At least I always have that. She seized the plate greedily. "Thanks," she mumbled around a mouthful. "I haven't eaten all day."

We waited a little longer while she finished chewing. As soon as she was done, Andre pounced. "You got Thea's name from Julie Bass?"

Karen flinched like he'd accused her of a crime. "Yes." Her voice was almost a whisper. "When Jon didn't come home I called her but even though I left a couple messages, she never called me back. I waited a week . . . I didn't want to be any trouble or anything. Julie was always nice to me but Cal . . . well, I could tell he didn't think I was good enough for Jon. He made me feel stupid and ugly. So I didn't want to talk to him . . . but finally I couldn't stand it any longer. I was so scared. That's when I tried to call Cal at the bank and they told me he was dead and that Julie had been arrested."

"Don't you read the papers?" Andre asked.

"Sometimes. Not always. Not those first few days when Jon didn't come back. When I wasn't working I was . . ." She hesitated. "Drinking. Anyway, it's only a local paper. It doesn't pay much attention if it's not local news."

She pulled a tissue out of her pocket and scrubbed at her nose. "I couldn't believe it. That they could think Julie was the killing type, with her so darn refined she don't even like to raise her voice. I mean, it's silly, isn't it?" She looked around for a response, but we didn't have one. It was late. We were weary. We just wanted her to get to the point.

"Well, she wouldn't kill somebody and not especially somebody she loved, like she did Cal," she said defiantly. "So then I called the police and they said she was at Framingham. So I found out when visiting hours were there and I borrowed my father's car and drove down to see her. To ask if she knew anything. She was a wreck . . . you should see . . . never mind. But she didn't know what happened to him. She said she was surprised that Jon had been there but I'm not sure I believed her. She said maybe you'd know something. That you were trying to find the real story. So do you? Know anything about Jon, I mean?"

She stared at me with sorry eyes that begged me not to disappoint her. I shook my head. "I've never heard of Jon until just now."

The tears in her voice were in her eyes now, brimming over and trickling down her face. She made no move to wipe them away. "It's not like Jon not to come home. . . ." She hesitated. "Or at least call. Not after all this time."

"He's disappeared before?" Andre said.

She stared at the tips of her scuffed Doc Martens. "Well, yeah. Sometimes. But he'd always call . . . after a few days. I mean, he'd never go away for weeks like this and not get in touch. . . ."

"Does Jon have a job?"

"He's a musician," she said defensively. "He has gigs."

"But not that weekend?" She shook her head. Slowly, confused, as if she wasn't sure. "What about the following week?"

"That's when I started getting worried. At first I figured he was just holed up with the rest of the band, working on songs or something. They'd do that sometimes. . . ." Her glance challenged us to accept that as normal. "But he'd call . . . when he remembered that I get worried. Only then I get this call from one of the guys, wanting to know where he was . . . saying that he'd like . . . not shown up or anything. That's when I began to get the feeling . . ." She broke off and ducked her head nervously, watching us through her hair as though she expected an attack.

"What feeling?" I said.

She just sat there, twisting a strand of hair around her finger. Finally she said, "My mood ring turned black. And then I got this weird hollow feeling like I was all black inside, too. I get intuitions," she said defiantly. "People don't believe me, but I do."

At this rate, we'd have a coherent story by dawn. "Did Jon call you while he was at the course?"

She shook her head. Her hair had fallen forward, hiding her face. From behind the curtain came a small, sad voice. "No. He wouldn't have. He was mad at me, see, because we'd had a big fight about him going. About the money, see. About him paying for the course."

"Was it a last-minute decision to go?" I asked.

"Well, yes and no. Cal had asked him a couple months ahead

and Jon said no, but then the weekend before he called Cal and said he'd changed his mind. He wanted to have an adventure, see. He was blocked. Thought it might help with writing songs to do something different like that. Only I got real pissed at him because he was supposed to help my sister move and they were going to pay him and everything. And we needed that money. I can pay the rent and all and I don't mind, but Jon's always needing something like strings or picks or a new bridge or some CD he's gotta have to study their technique. So I told him he shouldn't go, he should stay home and earn that money."

She shook her hair back from her miserable face. "He said Cal was paying and it was something he had to do. Then he told me to fuck off and left. I haven't seen or heard from him since. And he always comes back." She put her hands over her face and sobbed.

"What makes you think he didn't just take off on a whim to go have another adventure?" Andre said. "Or because he was mad at you?"

" 'Cuz that's just how he is. He wasn't all that mad," she said. "He says sometimes I act too much like his mother. I'm used to that. He always comes back. He needs me. I take care of him." She blew her nose again, her words punctuated by the little hiccuping breaths that come from crying. "Anyway, it's not that. The one thing in this world that Jon really cared about was his band, Live Bait. Even if he was going to . . . going to . . ." She sucked in a breath and continued in a shaky voice. ". . . leave me, he'd never leave them. And none of them has heard from him either. Not a word."

"I wish I could help you," I said, "but I don't know anything about Jon. What's his last name?"

"Bass. Like Cal."

"Did you file a missing persons report?" Andre asked.

"Oh yeah. With our local police. They were real concerned. Said if I was patient my wandering minstrel would come home."

"What about the Connecticut police?"

"Pretty much the same thing," she said bitterly. "They said they'd ask around but I had to understand they were real busy with a murder on their hands."

"We're going down to Connecticut tomorrow. I'll be glad to see if I can get you any more information." I had her write down her name and address and a phone number where I could reach her.

"Do you have a picture of him?" Andre asked.

She pulled out her wallet, took out a photo, and paused, staring at it. Slowly, reluctantly, she offered it to Andre. "You'll give it back, won't you?"

"Of course." He handed the picture to me. Jon Bass was a younger, stockier version of Cal, with slightly longer hair and a mustache.

"Is this a recent picture?"

She nodded. "Christmas."

"How are Jon and Cal related?"

"Cousins. Their fathers were brothers."

"He still has the mustache?"

She shrugged. "Far as I know." She yawned, not bothering to cover her mouth, and bent down to untie her boots. "I hope you don't mind if I crash here. I'm bushed. No way I could drive back home tonight." Off came the shoes and socks. Her feet were dirty.

Over her bent head I looked at Andre and made a helpless gesture. What was I supposed to do, throw her out in the street? He grinned and mouthed "Mother Thea." I made a face at him. It looked like we had an overnight guest. Sometimes the audacity—or obliviousness—of the young astounds me. Here was a girl so timid she cowered if you looked at her, yet she saw nothing odd about inviting herself to spend the night with total strangers, and it hadn't occurred to her that it might be an imposition or inconvenience. Such utter self-absorption makes me feel like an old fogey. So I said an old fogey thing. "It would have been nice if you had called first."

She cowered, but her answer was unsatisfying. "I didn't have your number," she said. "I forgot to get it."

"Then how did you find me?"

"Your mother."

I gave up. Reforming the lost generation was beyond me. Miss Manners could do it. "You can sleep in the guest room. The bed's made up. I'll get you a towel and there are spare toothbrushes on the second shelf."

"That's okay," she said, fishing one out of her purse. "I brought my own."

"You want to borrow a nightgown?" She was maybe 5´2˝ and couldn't have weighed much over a hundred, so she would have disappeared in anything of mine. I was just being polite.

"S'okay," she said. "I don't wear one."

Andre and I said quick good nights and retreated to the bedroom. He had a malicious grin plastered on his face that infuriated me. "Look," I said, sounding about as defensive as Karen had, "I didn't ask for this. What was I supposed to do?"

"I didn't say anything."

"You didn't have to. It's all over your face."

"Your problem is that you're just too tenderhearted."

"Who answered the door?"

"It might have been important. . . ."

I narrowed my eyes and gave him my best hard-boiled P.I. glare. "You think this isn't important?"

He slipped a chilly hand into the front of my robe. "I know what's important. . . ."

"Hey!" I grabbed his wrist. "Are you trying to change the subject?"

"We have a quota to meet," he said, kissing me. "Store it up for the long, cold week."

"I really don't give a damn about anybody else's problems," I said, kissing him back.

He untied the robe and slid it off. "That's my girl," he said.

But later, during pillow talk, I asked him, "What about this Jon Bass business? Is it important?"

"Can we save all that stuff for tomorrow?"

I wiggled in under his arm and buried my face in his shoulder. "Where is this relationship going?" There's nothing I love more than a bare, hairy chest.

"To sleep."

"No fair. That was a serious question."

"You want a serious answer?"

"I don't know. I'm kind of sleepy."

"I want to live with you," he said abruptly. "Or I want you to live with me. I don't know if it will work—we're a pretty independent pair—but I'd like to try. I want to come to bed every night knowing I can have you beside me like this. Not just sometimes. All the time. I want to be able to throw a leg over you and feel your skin. I want to curl up like spoons when it's cold. It feels safe. It feels real. It feels good."

"So you want me in your bed. That's good. What about the rest of the time? What about in the morning when I'm the world's biggest grouch? And there's this habit I have of getting involved in other people's problems. You going to try and cure me of that?"

"I want to chase you around the breakfast table," he said. Then he got serious. "You know it bothers me. Worries me, this compulsion you have to fix things for people. But it's who you are. It's who we both are, in our own ways. I'm learning that . . . or trying to. I didn't say it would be easy. You know there's a part of me wants to lock you in a tower and keep you safe, but there's also a part that knows a locked-up, restrained, subdued Thea wouldn't be the woman I love. But when the kids come . . . then you've got to be more careful." His voice rumbled deliciously under my ear.

"Kids? We're already talking about kids?"

"Someday. Right now we're still practicing." There was a long silence. I snuggled against him and listened to him breathe. It was easy to put everything else out of my mind. "I confess," he said, "sometimes I have this powerful urge to make you pregnant. . . ."

"Against my will?"

"Not like that. It's not a rape fantasy, it's a procreation fantasy. You know how physically attracted to you I am . . . and sometimes that just spills over into this desire to make a child . . . our child. You'd be so gorgeous pregnant. A little girl, I think. A wild, wayward, stubborn, generous beautiful little girl. . . ." His voice trailed off.

No other man had ever talked to me like this. It hit me at gut level. There was something profoundly erotic about being wanted not just for sex but for a merging of genes and the creation of a whole new generation. It stunned me, left me breathless with desire.

In the back of my mind, I heard a small voice, Julie's voice, echoing what Andre had just said. I heard her voice asking if I'd ever had a man want to have children with me. It was a most amazing feeling. Get out of my head, Julie, I thought, slamming a mental door on her voice. This was my life. This was Andre. It was different.

"Let's practice," I said.

CHAPTER 19

ELLEN AND GEORGE Bradley looked like they'd just stepped from the pages of a glossy fashion magazine, an image the Range Rover in the driveway did nothing to diminish. Even their sons, dressed in turtlenecks, cardigans, and khaki pants, were picture perfect. Assembled on the steps to greet us, they could have been waiting to be photographed by Bachrach, ready to adorn the paneled walls of their perfect house.

Even though I'd warned him not to judge them too soon, I could tell Andre was uncomfortable. Like a lot of Maine people, even intelligent and sophisticated ones, he gets uneasy as soon as he crosses the river in Kittery. Suzanne says they're all secret vampires and can't cross water or they'll die. So why does she want to go and live there? Maybe she doesn't. Maybe it's just a case of "whither thou goest." She did wait a long time for her happily ever after.

It didn't take long to break the ice. The Bradleys' gloss was just habit. It wasn't their fault they'd been raised in a Talbots world. Underneath, Ellen and George were really nice. I should know. Ellen was my roommate my freshman year, and we were not goody-two-shoes types. And I introduced her to George, who was an old friend from high school. In a way, the surprise is not that George is a Talbots type but that I am not.

"I hope you're ready for an adventure," George said, a twinkle in his eyes. "I've arranged for you to drive today."

"Drive?"

"On the track," George said.

"You'll love it," Ellen said. "It's more fun!"

I stared at her incredulously. "You've done it?" Ellen has chin-length precision-cut brown hair, pretty dark eyes, and an air of delicate reserve. Her hems never drag, her blouses never get stained, she never has a hair out of place, and her stockings wouldn't dare run. Looking at her, I find it hard to remember her shinnying down a sheet from our dorm window to sneak out with George. But she did.

"Of course. No sense in living this close and not taking advantage of it. George thought I was crazy until he tried it himself."

"Hey!" he interrupted, "I was the one who had to convince you."

Ellen just smiled and looked down at the two restless boys. "After you shake hands with Ms. Kozak and Mr. Lemieux, you can go play until Claire comes." She looked at Andre, a little uncertain. State troopers aren't common in the circles she travels. "I'm sorry, I forgot to ask. What should you be called? Officer?"

"Detective," he said, "but you can call me Andre." He looked awfully handsome today and I could tell that Ellen thought so, too.

She presented her boys, the oldest first. "This is Owen." Owen was delicate and dark, like his mother. He stepped up to the task, made eye contact, and acquitted himself well. "And this is Seward." Seward looked like half the boys on the prep school campuses I visit—medium size, not quite beefy but giving an impression of bulk, ruddy-cheeked, and blond. He gave my hand a cursory shake and turned to Andre.

"My dad says you're a policeman."

"That's right."

"Do you carry a gun?"

"Sometimes."

"Do you have it today?" Andre shook his head. "Darn," the boy said. "I was hoping you'd show it to me."

Andre went down on one knee so he was at the boy's level. "I didn't know I was going to meet a gun fancier," he said. "Do you have a gun?"

Seward shook his head. "Not a real one. My dad does, though. Did you ever shoot anyone?" Andre nodded. "Did you kill them?"

"Don't believe what you see on television," Andre said. "Policemen try very hard never to use their guns. Guns are very dangerous things."

"Seward, dear," Ellen said, "you're making our guest uncomfortable. Run along and play now. Claire will be here soon and she's taking you to the new Disney movie. Did you remember that Dad and I are going out today?"

Seward's pose suggested an internal war between curiosity and manners. It was a credit to Ellen that manners won. He mumbled "nice to meet you" and raced away, pausing about ten feet away to call back, "I'll bet you did kill 'em," before disappearing around the corner of the house.

"You're lucky," George said. "Once he starts to give someone the third degree, he usually doesn't let up. I think we're going to have another lawyer in the family someday."

"Would you like some coffee or juice while we're waiting?" Ellen asked. "Thea?" I shook my head. "Andre?"

He shook his head. "Do I get to drive, too?"

"Of course. Of course," George said expansively. "I didn't know if you'd want to. I figured, being with the police, you'd already had your share of this kind of thing."

"I've taken driving courses. It's fun," Andre said. "I'm not sure Thea thinks so, though."

So he'd been reading my mind again, the dastardly intruder. I suffer from a constant tension between wanting to be known and understood and wanting absolute privacy. But I couldn't argue. He was right. A flock of butterflies were beating their delicate wings against my chest and stomach.

"You don't have to go fast," he said.

"Where's the fun in that—" George began, but Ellen quelled him with a look. She was good at that. Her air of impeccable certainty discouraged people from arguing with her. She'd had it at eighteen and the first time I saw her use it on our dorm mother I was green with envy.

We were still standing on the steps when an ancient VW bug chugged into the driveway and rolled to a stop. It was Pepto-Bismol colored where it wasn't pocked with rust and sported a jumping frog on the hood. A smiling young woman with pinkish-red hair climbed out the passenger side and bounced over to us with the energy of someone who has eaten her Wheaties. "Sorry I'm late. Something funny in the engine. Jerry looked but he couldn't figure it out." She shrugged, an elaborate, full-body gesture. "Cars. Can't live with 'em, can't live without 'em." She stuck out a small hand with purplish-black nails. "I'm Claire." Gave us a taste of an electrifying grip and stepped back, craning her neck around the yard. "Where are the Munchkins?"

"They hate it when you call them that," Ellen said. "Out back, probably hovering by the new trampoline. I won't let them use it unsupervised." She rolled her eyes. "They think I'm such a dinosaur."

George dangled a set of keys. "Here. No offense to the rust-mobile, but I'd feel safer if you took the Lexus."

Claire seized them and pocketed them in a flash. Andre raised an eyebrow and grinned at me. I wasn't sure whether he was thinking about her abilities as a shoplifter or whether he was envisioning someone like this caring for our offspring someday. Any way you looked at it, Claire was a piece of work. I couldn't imagine Ellen leaving her children with this woman.

This time it was Ellen who read my mind. While George drew out his wallet and piled money into Claire's hand for lunch, a movie, and snacks, Ellen said, "Claire's taking a semester off from Vassar while her mother recovers from surgery." In other words, intelligent, educated, caring, and responsible. Well done, Ellen, I thought, wondering how to put a lock on my mind. Or was my face transparent today? I'd have to ask Andre.

"Okay, troops," George said, "let's take these detectives to the track. I sort of told the owner why you were coming . . . I hope you don't mind. He's going to be waiting for us." We all climbed into the Range Rover and rolled away.

The track owner, Tony Piretti, seemed to be on great terms with George, if friendship can be measured in back slaps and shoulder pats. He told his secretary that he'd be back, grabbed his coat, and gave us the grand tour. Half the time, it seemed like he was speaking a foreign language, but the place was interesting. I was still waiting for a pause in the eloquent narrative to ask my questions when he led us through a door to a man waiting beside a BMW parked on the track and announced it was time for us to drive.

"Relax," he said as I opened my mouth to object, "we can talk over lunch. Nick's only available this morning, and I couldn't send a friend of Ellen's out with anyone but Nick." I was becoming as predictable as a Quarter Pounder with Cheese. He introduced us to Nick and bustled away before I could speak.

Before I knew it, I was firesuited, helmeted, and belted into the driver's seat. I took a deep breath, let it out slowly, and looked over at my instructor for direction. "I've never done this before," I said.

"Most people haven't." He didn't exactly inspire confidence. Maybe he did in men. He had receding rusty hair, a florid face, a loose-lipped grin so confident it was almost demented, and bold blue eyes that looked at me like I was wearing nothing but the seat belt. Years of squinting into the sun had given him crows feet on top of crows feet. "It helps if you start the engine."

I shot him an angry look and turned the key. The engine roared to life. "I assume you know how to drive standard." I nodded. "Then ease her out onto the track and let's see what happens. The biggest thing people have to learn—the thing that surprises 'em most—is braking. That's what it's all about. Normally, you were here for the course, we'd give you some classroom time on braking theory. But you're not, so we'll just make do."

We made do. The first time around, I felt like a little old lady out for a Sunday drive. At least I did until Nick laughed and said, "Scared? I'll bet you go faster than this on the back roads at home." Under his abrasive needling, nudging, and coaching, I got around again at a more respectable pace, learning to work the accelerator and the brake together. The third time, he made me go faster than I felt I could control. Guess it wasn't like skiing, where you're trying to stay under control, because Nick had me right out at the limits of anything that felt safe. "Use your eyes. Use your eyes," he kept saying. "Think where you want to be, going into that turn. And now where?" I was just beginning to feel comfortable when he said, "Time to learn about skidding."

I said, "No way, José," but before I knew it, I was skidding toward the outside wall and visions of a crisply fried Cal Bass being joined by a crisply fried Thea Kozak danced in my mind even as I followed Nick's calm instructions and brought the car back under control. But somehow, in the process of steering through the skid, I discovered I was having fun. "Can we do that again?" I asked.

"Sure thing, darlin'," he said, giving me another wide, loopy grin. "As many times as you want."

I did it a couple more times. "This is fun."

"I don't know what it is about skidding, but women just seem to love it. We had us a little more time, I'd show you how to spin 'er completely around."

"With you driving, you mean?" He nodded. I brought the car to a stop. "Then show me."

We traded places and Nick gave me a driving demo that rivaled any Tilt-a-Whirl I've ever been on. Through it all, he kept up a calm, steady explanation of what he was doing. When he braked, when he accelerated, how to steer through the curves. Not oversteering, not understeering. Terms like upshifting and downshifting and apexes tripped like Shakespeare off his tongue.

By the time I was back on planet earth again, I understood what Ellen had meant. It was exhilarating and more than a little terrifying. I came back flushed with adrenaline, a little shaky about the limbs, and grinning like a fool, still caught up in the rush. George stood waiting like a proud poppa. "Like it?"

"Of course she liked it," Ellen said. "Look at her! Flushed with power. She looks gorgeous. Who needs Elizabeth Arden when you can race cars?"

"Don't get carried away, Ellen," her husband said, but I could tell from Andre's face that I did look different.

I leaned against the car and gave Andre my helmet, shaking out my hair. "Careful out there, mister. This stuff could get addictive."

"Yes," he said. "It could." He wasn't talking about racing, either. Then he grabbed the helmet and got in the car. I watched with my heart in my throat as he roared around the curves a lot faster than I'd dare go, and knew exactly how he felt when he and Nick, both laughing, climbed out of the car. He had exhilaration all over his face. When we were done, George and Ellen drove and then we joined Tony Piretti and an instructor who had worked with Calvin Bass for lunch.

I felt like a wet blanket, asking about a death at the track after the wonderful experience we'd just had, but that's what we'd come for. Not just for fun. Although I could see where having fun might be addictive. Sometimes I wonder if I have my priorities straight.

"I'm sorry," I began, going against all the advice which says to begin interviews on a positive note, "I know this is hard for you, but could we talk about the accident?"

"It was no accident," Piretti growled. "Someone deliberately tampered with that car. And with my business! You can bet we keep those cars under lock and key these days." He stabbed his salad for emphasis, sending a mass of spinach over the side.

"Not that we were ever careless." He cast a quick glance at George. "Were we, counselor?"

"Nope," George said with a decisive waggle of his head. "Always kept 'em inside a fence, and with security guards."

"Even at night?" I asked.

"Especially at night," Piretti said. "That's when we're most like to get some asshole—pardon my French—with a snoot full who decides he's Mario Andretti, climbing over the fence and trying to get a car. . . ."

"Hey," Billy interjected, "what about that guy Bass was arguing with on Saturday?"

Piretti scratched his head. "Guess I didn't hear about that."

"Security practically had to pry them apart."

"What did he look like?" I asked.

Billy shrugged. "I didn't see it. I only heard about it from one of the security guys. I asked him where he got his shiner and he said trying to pull Paul Bunyan off one of the paying guests. Didn't say anything about a blue ox, though."

"What, exactly, was done to the car?" Andre interrupted.

"You want to know exactly?" Piretti said. "I'll give you exactly. . . ." He launched into an explanation that was way over my head and, from her glazed look, over Ellen's, but Andre and George and the instructor leaned forward raptly as he discoursed on suspensions and undercarriages and tension and torque and adhesion, on understeering and oversteering and overconfidence and assholes and walls and firewalls and explosions. He ground to a halt with a shake of his head, paused for breath. So much for the Connecticut cops wanting to keep things under wraps.

Still wound up, Piretti sputtered on. "How he ever got out on that track without a firesuit . . . would have protected him from some of the burns . . . any of you ever handled someone with bad burns?" His eyes lit on Andre. "Trooper?" Andre nodded. He's seen a lot of nasty things. He doesn't like to discuss them. "The smell," Piretti went on. "You never get it out of your head completely. We don't barbecue any more."

Ellen looked like she was going to throw up. George leapt to her defense. "Did you have some questions you wanted to ask, Thea?"

"What about his cousin?" I said. "How did he react?"

"Like you'd expect," the instructor, whose name was Billy, said. "He was in shock. Horrified. He was white as a sheet and he kept saying 'Oh my God! Oh my God! It could have been me. It could have been me, Calvin.' " His head bobbed, embarrassed. "It's not as bad as it sounds. See, they'd flipped a coin to see who would go first . . . so it could as easily have been him. They seemed to be pretty good friends. You could hardly tell one from the other, especially once they were suited up and had their helmets on. The way I told 'em apart was that Calvin—

the one who got killed—he had a real bossy way of talking, while Jon was quieter and sort of spacy."

"What about the mustache?"

Billy shook his head. "Neither of 'em had a mustache."

"What happened to the cousin . . . Jon, was it? . . . after the accident?"

Billy shrugged. He was younger than Nick but had that same cocky arrogance, though he was doing his best to rein it in. The guys who teach you sailing, skiing, rock climbing, river rafting, they're a lot alike. Overgrown camp counselors, perpetual Peter Pans, omnicompetent, great with people, showing just the tip of that edgy superiority. He had a fabulous shock of wheat-colored hair that hung over half his face. I wondered how he could see to drive.

"When he left here, he went in the ambulance to the hospital. I guess the cops talked to him there . . . no offense, sir," he said, with a glance at Andre. "And then I guess he just drove away. He didn't come back here. I suppose he could have finished the day, but I don't guess he felt like driving after that. We never saw him again."

"That's not quite right," Piretti interrupted. "He went in the ambulance with his cousin and then the police gave him a ride back here to get his car."

"Oh yeah," Billy said. "I forgot about that. I saw him out in the parking lot. I asked how his cousin was doing and he gave me this odd look and said he didn't make it. He seemed to be in a big hurry to get away."

Acting on a sudden, chilling hunch, I got the pictures of Cal and Jon Bass from my purse and laid them on the table. "Are these the two guys we're discussing?" Piretti and Billy said yes. "Which one of them got killed?"

They bent over the photos, passing them back and forth a few times, discussing details. Jon's mustache confused them. Finally Billy stabbed Jon Bass's picture with a decisive finger.

"This one," he said. "The one with the scar by his eye. Calvin."

Andre's eyes met mine across the table. "Time to go talk to the cops," he said.

"Hey. Wait a minute. What's going on?" Piretti said.

"You pointed to wrong Bass," Andre said. "That's Jon."

They stared at us with troubled faces. "This one is Calvin Bass," I said, "and you think he's the guy who walked away?"

Billy picked up the photos again and studied them with a troubled face. After a minute he set them down again. "I don't know," he said. "This is too weird. I'm sure the guy who wasn't in the car called the guy we pulled out Calvin. I'd swear to it. But . . ." He brushed back the wayward shock of hair and stared at us with two very troubled eyes. "The guy in the parking lot didn't have a scar."

"And Jon Bass's live-in girlfriend says he never came home," I said.

In the silence, Ellen drew a sharp, shocked breath. "What do you mean?"

We told them about Karen Osgood and the missing boyfriend. Piretti struck himself in the forehead, a half-mocking gesture, and groaned. "This is all I need." He picked up the other pictures I'd left on the table. "Got any more surprises in here?"

"I hope not," I said, as he looked at them.

"Who's this?" he asked, holding out a picture of Dr. Durren getting an award.

"Thomas Durren," I said. "Emergency room doctor at our local hospital. Why?"

"Looks like a guy I used to race with years ago. Skinny, long-haired kid with nerves of steel. A real wildman. If you told him something couldn't be done, he'd do it just to prove you wrong. I think his name was Durren." He scratched his head and thought about it. "Yeah, it was. Chuck Durren. Is your guy a wildman?"

I choked back, "When pigs fly," deeming it unsuitable. Even behind the wheel of a Porsche, Durren was prissy. "Farthest thing from it. A control freak. Shy, quiet, and so cold he makes ice cubes nervous."

Piretti shook his head. "Can't be the same guy, then. People don't outgrow Chuck's kind of crazy. Not in my experience." He handed back the pictures. Although he continued to be polite, it was clear Andre and I had worn out our welcome.

I was coming back from the ladies' room when I heard Ellen's voice around the corner, sharp and argumentative. "But I don't understand. She keeps putting herself in danger. Why on earth does she do it?"

I paused, curious, to see who would respond. It was Andre. "You know she's lost two people in the last few years . . . two people that she loved. . . ."

"Of course I know that," Ellen said, "but I should think that would make her more careful. . . ."

"So when it happens to someone else, Thea knows how it feels. She understands their pain . . . their confusion . . . their sense of loss. She tries to help them make sense of it. . . ."

"But to get involved like this. . . ."

"That's who she is," Andre said. "The oldest child. The responsible one. The fixer. Thea believes it's her job to make things right—to put order back in the world, especially for people who seem helpless or friendless or needy."

"You make her sound like a saint," Ellen said. "The Thea I know is no saint. A good person, but no saint. And doesn't it worry you? I mean, all those risks she takes. Why don't you make her stop?"

I could hear the smile in Andre's voice. "Can anyone stop the women in that family when they set their minds on something?"

"But surely, if she loves you, she'll do what you want . . . do it for you," Ellen insisted.

"I'm afraid she sometimes has to answer to a higher authority . . . her conscience," Andre said.

"I guess," Ellen said doubtfully. "I know George would just put his foot down and—"

"Oh, I've put my foot down," Andre said. "She stomped all over it."

"Hi, guys," I said, coming around the corner. "Ready to go?"

We rode in a somewhat subdued silence back to the Bradleys' house. After agreeing we'd meet again for dinner, we picked up my car and drove off in search of the police station.

CHAPTER 20

THE CONNECTICUT POLICE weren't very happy with the news that Andre and I had to share, especially since Calvin Bass's body had been cremated. Identification, they said, hadn't seemed to be an issue, since the cousin was there and identified the body and everyone at the track agreed. We got to tell our story to the local cops and again to a couple of state cops, all of whom were initially irritable and supercilious until they learned that Andre was one of them.

I was on my best behavior. I didn't once complain that they treated me like Andre's decorative appendage, even though I was the one who'd figured things out. I just sat politely with my legs crossed at the ankles, not the knees, and spoke when spoken to. I could tell Andre was proud of me. He didn't once give me the kick under the table, our secret code for "put a cork in it, Thea."

Partly I behaved because I was tired of the whole nasty business and eager to drop it into their laps; relieved that someone else would have to contact Karen Osgood with the bad news. Partly I behaved because of the conversation I'd overheard between Andre and Ellen. I felt so lucky to have someone like Andre, who understood and supported me even when he didn't like what I was doing. And partly because the conversation had shifted to a discussion of whether Calvin Bass had tampered with the car himself. I was sick and discouraged at the idea that Bass might have killed his cousin and then just walked away, leaving his wife accused of the crime, his children fatherless, and Karen Osgood desperately waiting for the man who never came back.

The big Connecticut detective who'd been asking questions leaned back in his chair and folded his hands over his expansive gut. "Why would Bass want to disappear?" he said. He looked at Andre for an answer.

"Because he was in trouble at the bank?" I suggested. "Because his personal finances were in disarray and this was a perfect opportunity to start over with a clean slate? Because he thought he had nothing to lose? Maybe to run away with his mistress?" I threw this last in as an afterthought, though I couldn't imagine Nan Devereaux running away with anyone.

"What trouble at the bank?" he asked Andre.

Andre's foot came to rest against my leg. He knew what was going on in my head. "There was a problem with some missing mortgage applications," I said. "When the FDIC did a routine audit. His boss thinks Calvin Bass took them."

The detective finally looked at me. "Just what is your interest in all of this?"

"Julie Bass is a friend of mine." It sounded a little too defiant.

"Oh," he said, tapping his fingers. His belly shivered a little.

"What kind of a car was the cousin driving?" I asked.

"Blue Chevette rust bucket," he said.

I remembered something I'd forgotten to ask during lunch. "How would whoever tampered with the car have known that Calvin Bass would be the one to drive it?"

Andre gave me a little approving nod. The detective looked at me curiously. "The names of the drivers and their scheduled driving times for Sunday were posted on a trackside board on Saturday afternoon. All our killer had to do was be able to read."

"And to get inside to read the board," I added.

"Went up before they closed for the day. Anyone could have seen it."

"Did anyone see Julie Bass there? Reading the board?"

He shrugged. "She was seen at the motel. And we know that she's an experienced mechanic."

"Did you find her fingerprints on the car?" He shook his head. "Anywhere at the track? Did anyone see her near the track?"

He took his feet off the desk, dropped them with an abrupt thump onto the floor, and stood up. "We'll take it from here. Thanks for coming by and sharing this stuff with us. Complicates our lives, of course, but still. . . ."

We were being dismissed. "What about the fight in the track parking lot? The one where the security guards had to pry some guy off who was attacking Bass?"

The detective looked blank. "Didn't hear about that one. I'll have someone check with the guys. . . ."

"Excuse me," I said. Andre kicked me in the ankle but I ignored him. "How can you assume that Julie Bass killed her husband? Assume it with enough certainty to keep her locked in jail and away from her kids . . . when her husband isn't even dead? When her husband was having a very public fight with another man the night before he was killed . . . or supposedly killed . . . and you don't know anything about it? This is the most slipshod, half-assed, careless investigation—" Andre kicked me again and I shut up. I even managed to shake hands and say good-bye with a manufactured smile.

Back in the car, he gave me one of his "boy, can you be a

ain in the ass" looks but he didn't say anything. Nothing. Not
a word. I didn't care. I was mad at the whole world.

We were halfway to George and Ellen's before he spoke.
"Thea, how do you expect to get along with people when you
all but call them incompetent assholes to their faces?"

"I didn't all but call them anything. I straight out called
them incompetent assholes." He sighed. "And," I went on, before he could interrupt, "they were calling me a mindless honey,
the way they addressed all their questions to you."

"Well, naturally they assumed, since I was there, that I
knew—"

"And that I knew nothing, when I'm the one who—"

"You don't have to tell me that, Thea. I'm just saying that
you could take it a little easier. You don't have to prove that
you're always right . . . all the time."

"You mean you weren't shocked that they didn't even know
about the fight in the parking lot? That they'd accused Julie of
killing someone who isn't even dead?"

"We're not sure. . . ."

"I'm sure."

"That's one of your problems, Thea. You're always so sure
that you're right."

I put a hand on his arm. "I'm sorry. I didn't mean it that way.
Please, let's not have a fight. I know I make mistakes . . . I know
I'm not always right. It's just that sometimes I get tired of doing
everything for everyone when it's someone else's job. And when
I get tired, I get cranky." I pulled my hand back and dropped it
in my lap. A minute later, he reached out and put his over it.
We weren't going to fight.

I tried to pull myself together for dinner with Ellen and
George, but I could sense, from the looks that passed between
them and Ellen's conversation, that they'd been talking about
us, and, more particularly, about me. Things were awkward
until we started talking about driving.

"I was right, wasn't I, Thea?" Ellen said triumphantly. "Admit it. You loved it, didn't you?"

"I'd do it again." Recalling the feeling made me smile.

"You should see your face," Ellen said.

"Ellen looked just the same way the first time she drove," George said. "Took me weeks to convince her to try it, and then she was hooked."

"Like skiing. When you're right out there on the edge of control and it's working. Do you still ski, Thea?"

I shook my head. "She works all the time," Andre said.

"Do you ski, Detective?" George asked.

"I like it. I'm not very good."

"You know. We've got a place up at Stratton with a spare bedroom. You guys should come up for a weekend sometime. Seward is dying to ask Andre more questions about his . . . about being a policeman," Ellen said, "and we'd like to see more of you. Thea and I used to have so much fun. . . ."

"Ellen knows all the secrets of my misspent youth," I said.

"Hey, what about me?" George said.

"And George knows all the secrets of my misspent high school days." That seemed to please him, though I knew far more secrets about George than he knew about me. "And we'd love to come up and ski sometime. We need to take more time off." It was an easy offer. Winter was a long time away.

We decided to drive back after dinner, even though they urged us to stay the night. It wasn't that they were bad company. They were cheerful and kind and decidedly pleasant. But Andre and I wanted to be alone—not to hop into bed and make whoopee, though we probably would—but to talk things over and puzzle things out. Even though neither of us had mentioned it to the other, the disappearance of Calvin Bass weighed heavily on our minds.

Andre drove. He's better at staying awake than I am. I put the seat back and dozed. I felt beat up, discouraged, and confused. We were on the Mass Pike around Stockbridge when an idea hit me like a ton of falling bricks. I sat up suddenly and almost startled Andre off the road when I said, "I think I know where he is."

"Where who is?"

"Calvin Bass."

CHAPTER 21

IT WAS AFTER midnight when we arrived at Edgewater, the unfinished condo complex along the Grant River in my hometown of Grantham, a condo complex that had been taken over by the Grantham Cooperative Bank when the developer went belly-up. Everything was dark as we cruised along the narrow street behind the condos that fronted on the river. It wasn't really a street, just a glorified driveway, lined with garages and islands of landscaping, modern ministreet lamps and minidriveways for guests or the second car.

Andre was remarkably patient with me, never once reminding me that we were looking for a needle in a haystack. True, it was a big needle and a small haystack, but we were both weary and longing for bed.

I knew I'd hit a homer as soon as I saw it—a red Mercedes sports car parked beside one of the garages—even before I saw the NAN on the license plate. "There he is," I said. "That's Nan Devereaux's car. I'll bet Jon Bass's little Chevette is in the garage."

Andre yawned. "So what do you want to do now?"

"Talk to him."

"Why bother? Why not just call the police and let them take it from here?"

"Because I found him. Because he's indirectly made my life miserable and I want some answers. Once the police get here, there will be no chance of that."

"All right," he said, "but we're calling the police now, agreed?"

"Oh absolutely," I agreed. "I don't want to take any chances on letting him get away again. Just as soon as I'm sure he's here. . . ."

I marched up and rang the bell. A sleepy voice said, "What the hell . . . ?"

"Calvin Bass?" I said. Before he had a chance to think, he'd said yes. I nodded to Andre, who picked up the car phone and called the Connecticut police.

"Who the hell is it?" the voice demanded.

"I'm a friend of Julie's. I want to talk to you. Can I come up?"

"Go to hell," the voice said.

"It's me or the cops. You choose," I said, lying without compunction.

"All right. Come up." The buzzer buzzed and Andre and I went in.

Cal Bass and Nan Devereaux made a handsome couple in their matching bathrobes. Thick, white terry with hotel monograms on the front. "Hello, Nan," I said. "Andre, meet Mr. and Mrs. Sheraton."

"You!" Nan hissed. She didn't seem pleased to see me again. Not that I cared. I wasn't interested in Nan Devereaux, except perhaps to be astonished at how a woman suddenly roused from sleep could look so good, nor in the array of expensive luggage that was standing by the door, ready for an imminent departure. I was there to confront Calvin Bass.

Like Nan, he looked awfully good for a guy just roused from

sleep. Maybe they hadn't been sleeping. They did both have what might be taken for a healthy postcoital flush. I stared at him—this hunk, this paragon of business, this prince among men, this slimeball. "What were you planning to do?" I demanded. "Just walk away, leaving your kids with your despicable brother-in-law and Julie in prison for murdering you?"

He shrugged. "It was a chance for a brand-new start, so I took it. Things were falling apart. . . ."

"What things?"

"My marriage. My job. My life."

"A responsible person stays and works things out. He doesn't just run away. Were you planning to hide for the rest of your life?"

He shrugged again. "I was planning . . . I *am* planning . . . to be Jon Bass. That's all."

"What about Julie and your kids?"

"What about them? Julie's a pathetic clinging vine and it turns out I'm not cut out for fatherhood. I don't like kids very much." He said it with such scorn I wanted to hit him. But if my feelings were written all over my face, it didn't matter. He was looking past me at Andre, who was standing by the door, arms folded. Maybe he was assessing his chances of escape. They were about the same height—Andre's an inch or so taller than I am—but while Bass was slim to normal, Andre was a big guy, and none of it was flab. Andre was making no effort to keep his opinion of Cal Bass off his face. He thought Bass was lower than a dog turd. Bass didn't like what he saw; he switched his gaze back to me.

"What's your angle in all this? Someone paying you to find me? You're no friend of Julie's. Julie doesn't have any friends. She's too weird."

"You're wrong," I said. "She has friends. Friends who aren't going to let you walk away and leave her in the mess you've created."

"Bullshit," he said. "Don't 'poor Julie' me. She ought to go down for something. Julie and that freak brother of hers. Even if they didn't kill me, they did kill Jon."

"What makes you think so?" Andre said.

"Well, that freak Duncan was there, wasn't he? Practically took my head off in the parking lot. Goddamned security guard had to pull him off. Julie must have set it up . . . how the hell else would he have known I was there?"

"Maybe he was acting on his own," I suggested. "Maybe he'd had enough of the way you were treating his sister."

"Me? Treating her? All I was trying to do was help her make something of herself. All I ever tried to do. Not my fault she was hopeless."

"So you thought it was okay to just fade away and abandon her to whatever fate the courts hand out?"

Another shrug. Indifferent. Unconcerned. "They'll never convict her. And she'll have the insurance money. She can marry her doctor and live happily ever after." He seemed to have no notion that perhaps the jig was up, that his plan was blown.

"And your kids?"

"Oh, she's a good enough mother. . . ."

"And Jon's girlfriend, Karen?"

"That pitiful little drudge? Spare me."

"What about the bank? Those papers?"

"I did my best," he said. "I took those papers so Ramsay couldn't tamper with them, but the slippery bastard managed to turn it around and lay it all off on me. I tried to go back to the house and get 'em, but someone had taken them. The cops, I suppose. . . ." He turned to Nan. "In light of this unexpected turn of events, perhaps we should advance the time of our departure?"

He stopped dead, staring out the window. "Oh Jesus! You did this, didn't you?" Turning my head, I saw the reflection of red and blue lights. "Why? I haven't done anything."

"Maybe it was Ramsay who tried to kill you," I suggested.

Bass shook his head. "Eliot's a shark, all right. But only a sand shark. He hasn't got the guts for murder."

I thought about my nocturnal thugs. I wasn't sure I agreed. "Haven't done anything? Just killed your cousin. Let your wife be separated from the kids and dragged off to jail. Let your cousin die unacknowledged and just walked away. Let his girlfriend and his family suffer and worry, not knowing what happened to him? Let your wife and family mourn, believing you'd died a horrible death? Not to mention all your affairs and the stuff at the bank. . . ."

"Hey, wait a minute!" he yelled. "You don't think . . . they don't think . . . but I didn't kill Jon. I told you. That was someone trying to kill me. I was supposed to drive first. Only I let Jon go instead . . . and then, when I saw that he'd taken my helmet . . . and he was already dying . . . I just saw my chance and I took it." He stared at us, dumbfounded. "You've got to believe me. Someone tampered with that car. . . . It must have been Julie's cretin brother. There was no way either one of them was going to let me have a divorce."

"Divorce?" I said.

"So I could marry Nan," he said. I looked around. Nan was nowhere to be seen.

"Listen, you miserable excuse for a human being," I said, "that business about people not letting you get a divorce. It's bullshit. We have no-fault divorce in Massachusetts. All you have to do is to be willing to fight about property, instead of just having your own way, or, as it appears you've planned to do here, just walking away and leaving all your responsibilities behind. And what about your cousin Jon? Did the feelings of the people who loved him really not matter at all?"

I might as well have spoken to my foot. Bass wasn't listening. He was fretting about my accusation that he might be responsible for anything that happened. "It wasn't me," he repeated. "None of it was me. I didn't do anything. Look, give me a break here. So I made a mistake about Jon. So I lied to the cops. That's not some big-deal crime or anything. I'd be willing to talk about that. . . . It was just the shock and confusion of the moment. I was in a bind there. I saw an opportunity and took it. There's nothing so bad about that."

"Cal," I said. He stopped babbling and looked at me hopefully. "Save it for the judge, okay? I wouldn't care if they put you in a roomful of rats and lost the key." Andre opened the door to a gaggle of Grantham cops and we went home to bed.

CHAPTER 22

"ARE YOU THINKING what I'm thinking?" I asked Andre over breakfast.

"That it's almost time for bed?" he said, grabbing the last slice of toast and slathering it with jam.

"That and something else."

"I ate the last piece of toast and didn't offer you any?"

"I'm used to that. Try again."

"That Bass didn't do it?"

"Yeah." I reached over and swept a bit of jam off his cheek. "But who then?"

"Who had the most to gain from Bass's death?"

"The most? Hard to say. Julie, of course, would have been comfortable financially and free to marry her lover. But he isn't free to marry her. And she loved her husband. Or had once loved him. And she cared about having a father for her kids. Her brother? He would have removed a threat to his beloved sister. Eliot Ramsay would have removed a threat to his reputation and had a convenient fall guy for those troublesome loan applications. . . ."

"Your mother?" Andre suggested.

"My mother?" I considered for a minute. "Oh, I see. But I don't think so, Andre. She knows nothing about cars . . . the guys at the garage have to show her how to open the hood. She's never even put air in a tire." Andre has a thing about my mother. I admit it. But she started it. She was going to have a conniption if we decided to live together. Worse, she would have to stop referring to him as "Andy" or "that cop."

He reached over and put a hand over mine. "You're cold," he said. "What about the boyfriend, then?"

"Durren? I doubt it. He's such a wimp. Handshake like a dead fish. Cringes when I use unladylike language and he's always picking imaginary lint off his clothes. I can hardly see him sneaking down to Connecticut in the dead of night, much less crawling under a car and disabling it."

"He got the letters."

"Yes, and dropped one in the front yard."

"Stranger things have happened."

"Like this?" I said, standing up and slowly unbuttoning my shirt. I turned away from him and walked toward the bedroom, dropping clothes as I went. Andre came behind me, collecting them, muttering about always having to pick up after people.

Later, lying in the bed, he said, "Come live with me and be my love."

I sighed. "I may have to do that," I said. "I'm finding it increasingly hard to live without you. . . ."

"That's all I ask. That you'll think about it." He rubbed his stubbly face across my stomach.

"But what if we find out that it's all physical?"

He stopped rubbing and grinned up at me, his sexy eyebrows arching. "You mean, sex and food? You mean, what will we talk about on long winter evenings?"

"Mm-hm."

"I will read you Dickens and you will tell me all the gossip

on the private school circuit. I will share all the nefarious do-
ings of Maine's felonious residents and you will strum your lute
and sing madrigals. I will braid you hair into a Medusan masterpiece and you can tenderly clip my toenails."

"Yuck!"

"Okay, I will tell you about my 'misspent youth' and you tell
me about yours."

"But I didn't misspend my youth."

He twisted an imaginary mustache. "You're still young and
there's no time like the present."

"We can speculate on the sex life of my brother Michael and
his chronic Sonia."

"Or wonder why my sister can't seem to stop having children."

"Speaking of having children," I said, "something strange is
happening to your body."

"Happens whenever I think about sex and I'm near you and
there's only one cure. . . ."

I didn't bother to tell him there was more than one cure. I
was happy to see things from his point of view for a change. Despite a healing wound on my thigh and residual scrapes and
bruises from my encounter with Duncan Donahue, I felt great.
We cured his problem in the good old-fashioned way and went
back to sleep. And we slept and slept and slept.

Around two in the afternoon the phone woke us. I didn't
want to answer it. It was such a perfect day anything would have
been an intrusion, but Andre insisted. It was my mother and she
was in an awful state. "Oh, Theadora, I don't know how this
could have happened. I'm so upset. I hope you'll forgive me.
Please say you'll forgive me!"

For a fraction of a second, I expected her to confess to killing
Calvin Bass, that is, Jon Bass, just as Andre had suggested, but
not for long. "I've gone and invited everyone else and suddenly
I realized that in all the confusion of this past week . . . all these

awful things happening with Julie . . . that I forgot to invite you."

"Invite me where? Invite me when? Ouch!" Andre had chosen that moment to peel off the bandage. "No. Mom. I'm okay. Just an old bullet wound. What invitation?" Her squawk could have been heard across the parking lot. Andre grinned diabolically and went to get surgical supplies.

"Relax. I was joking. What invitation?" I listened to a garble of explanation and apology and my spirits began to sink.

"And Sonia's whole family. I've only met her parents, but this time her brother and his wife and her sister and her husband and their children, and her aunt, and of course your Aunt Rita and Uncle Henry, and so I don't know how . . . you know I'm not disorganized . . . but somehow, when I was straightening up my desk, there was your invitation, buried under some things. I'd totally forgotten to mail it."

There was a caterwauling sound from the other room as my smoke alarm went off. "Damn," I said. "I'm sorry, Mom, I've got to go. The smoke detector's gone mad. I'll call—"

"Wait, Thea," she wailed. "Don't go yet. The dinner. It's tonight! Six-thirty, because of the children. Don't be late. Bring some of that great bluefish pâté you make. I promised Sonia. And darling, this is an engagement party, so do dress accordingly."

I hung up the phone, using all my self-control to keep from slamming it, and stormed into the living room. Andre, looking even better than Jim Palmer in his briefs, was standing on a chair, holding a candle under the smoke detector. "You are a fiend!" I said, trying to knock over the chair. "Stop that. I cause any more trouble and I'm going to get run out of this place on a rail."

He waved his hands to disperse the smoke, hopped down, and set the candle on the counter. "Got you off the phone, didn't it?"

"What am I going to do with you?"

Ignoring my question, he waggled a box of Band-Aids in my face. "Dr. Lemieux will see you now."

"I hate doctors. You know that. And besides, I'm annoyed with you."

He disappeared into the bedroom, reappearing in the doorway a minute later with his white handkerchief on his head, folded into a little white cap. "Nurse Lemieux will see you now." The white cap, white briefs, and foolishly happy smile were too much for me. I went into Nurse Lemieux's office and shut the door and when we came out, we were both wearing foolishly happy smiles and it was time for a very late lunch.

Andre made grilled cheese and tuna sandwiches while I dug through the freezer for a piece of smoked bluefish. You can buy bluefish pâté in fancy stores for lots of money, or you can do it the Kozak way: dump a chunk of smoked bluefish into the food processor. Dump in a package of cream cheese. Add a tablespoon or two of lemon juice. Bottled horseradish to taste. A bit of salt and pepper. If it seems too thick, thin it with cream. And voilà! A two-minute culinary masterpiece. Delicious served with slices of English cucumber.

After lunch we showered and did dishes and then it was time for Andre to leave. I'm not the clingy type, but I had a hard time letting him go. It wasn't any easier for him. "I'm sick of saying good-bye to you," he said.

"I told you I would consider your suggestion." He gave me the kind of kiss that usually means we delay his departure another hour. "Now don't start that," I said, pushing him away.

"Just something to remember me by."

"I couldn't get the memory of Nurse Lemieux out of my head in a thousand years." I watched him get in the car and back out, thinking about the white briefs and the white cap and his broad chest and furred stomach and warm and gentle fingers and I was lonely before the car was out of sight.

I went inside and opened my closet and thought about what

to wear. What was an appropriate outfit for a dinner that made me want to throw up? I had a little time before I had to start thinking about that. I pulled on jeans and a jacket and went to walk on the beach.

I skipped rocks and found a few shells, and then I lay down on a sheltered patch of warm sand and watched sea gulls wheeling in the sky overhead, shrieking their raucous cries. There wasn't a cloud to mar the clear, wide blue. I dozed in the sun's soothing warmth, but not for long. Being still, in mind or body, is not in my nature. With Andre and all his absurd distractions gone, the complex questions of the day before came flowing back. It wasn't my problem any more. I'd done my bit. I'd found other suspects, questions, possibilities, scenarios, and shared them with myriad police. If Bass's story was true, Julie might not be off the hook, but at least the cops had enough information to consider other suspects. Maybe her lawyer could make enough out of that to get her out on bail.

Tonight I could fill my mother in. Now, since the police couldn't be counted on to do it, I'd better get in touch with Julie's lawyer and, while I was at it, with Durren, because he seemed so worried.

Julie's lawyer was shocked, surprised, and more than a bit confused. I would be, too, if I suddenly found myself defending somebody who was accused of murdering a man who wasn't dead. He wanted to ask me a lot of questions. I told him to contact the police instead. I felt like I'd been wearing a heavy pack and now it was getting lighter and lighter, until I felt like I was floating. When I left my message on Durren's answering machine, I was so light I almost grazed the ceiling.

CHAPTER 23

IF I WERE a pessimist, I'd say life has it in for me. Instead, I'll just say that when I came out of the shower, the phone rang and fate whacked me with a big wet codfish, full in the face. Maybe it was a whole bucket of fish. The fish came from Andre, calling me from the road. I thought it was just romance, that he was calling because he missed me and he couldn't wait until he got home to say so. But no.

"Thea? It's Andre. . . ."

"Couldn't wait till you got home, sweetie?"

"Listen, what are you doing right now?"

"I just got out of the shower." I waited for him to comment on that. His response surprised me.

"Is your door locked? Your front door? The deadbolt and the chain? And the patio door?"

"I think so. Let me check. What's up?" I carried the cordless phone with me while I checked. Everything was secure. I reported this to Andre.

"Good."

"Good why? Why good? Why am I suddenly supposed to be worrying about locked doors?"

"I've been thinking," he said, "about how many loose ends there still are. Like how someone's still going to want those papers. Maybe more than ever, now that Cal Bass isn't dead. Do you still have them there? With you?"

I tried to remember. Had I left them at the office? No, because I hadn't gone back after my meeting with Delayne. No, they were back in my car. "They're in the car," I said.

"I know this is awkward," he said, "but I'd feel a whole lot better if you didn't have them at all. If you turned them over to the police. I could call Harris, have him come by and get them."

I pictured myself being led into the cell beside Julie. I have a slightly warped view of women's prisons, formed from too many of those C- movies, the ones where they have long scenes of the women showering naked together under the malevolent eyes of sadistic matrons. "And the next thing they'll do is arrest me, Andre. It's not so simple. I'll be in a terrible mess if anyone finds out I've got those papers . . . that I took them out of Julie's house. . . ." I shook the phone in frustration. "Dammit, Andre, I was having such a wonderful day, thinking this mess was over and I was free."

"I wish that were the case," he said. "But just because you've decided you're out of it doesn't mean everyone else knows you're out of it."

"Look, I'm not some Disney character, you know that. I don't believe wishing will make it so," I said. "But I've done my bit. What more does all this have to do with me?"

"There's still a killer out there." There was something in his voice. A hesitation.

"There's something more, isn't there? Something you're not telling me." I was getting scared now, my spirits plummeting in direct proportion to the amount they'd risen earlier.

"Yes," he said reluctantly.

"Are you going to tell me or do we play twenty questions?"

"I'm sorry," he said, "I wasn't trying to play games. I was just thinking about the best way to put this."

"In simple words. One after the other. Come on, Andre, you're making me a nervous wreck."

"I'm sorry," he repeated. "It's about Duncan Donahue. I got a call from Roland Profitt a few minutes ago. The police went to question Donahue today about his confrontation with Bass down in Connecticut and . . ."

". . . and he's gone missing," I guessed. "But what does that have to do with me? If he's after anyone, he's after Bass."

"That's the logical thing to think. But we don't know if the guy thinks logically. I mean, look what happened to you before. If he still believes you're one of us. . . . You'd assume he'll go straight for Bass, especially if he's the one who tampered with the car, but what if he decides you're the one who can lead him to Bass?"

"Isn't Bass locked up somewhere?" I asked.

Andre made a funny noise, kind of a verbal shrug. "They didn't really have anything to hold him on. . . ."

"What about perjury? Obstruction of justice? Misappropriation of bank papers? What about causing excessive pain and suffering? What about being an asshole generally?"

"Naturally, if I had my way," Andre said. He didn't have to say more. We were both familiar with the irritating vagaries of the legal system. "The thing is—please don't hate me for this, Thea—I would just feel a lot safer if you didn't stay there tonight. If Julie knows where you live, her brother probably does, too." He had a hard time spitting it out. He didn't want to break the spell of the day any more than I did, and he knows how I react to being told what to do. I overreact. Negatively. But this time I was in no mood for trouble. I didn't feel brave and I wasn't interested in being pushed around or shot at any more. I just didn't know where to go.

"I can't stay at my mother's, Andre, I just can't. I'd rather go to a homeless shelter. And Suzanne has the baby. It wouldn't be fair to bring any danger near her. And I couldn't face a motel. Not after last night. Not alone. . . ."

"But you would stay someplace if it was the right place?"

"Like where? Damn. Oh S-word!" I was trying to dress as we talked and I'd just put my thumb through my panty hose.

"Are you all right?"

"Just a run in my hose, dahlin'. You were saying?"

"You could go stay with your second favorite policeman."

My second favorite policeman, Dom Florio, was a detective on the Sterling police force. We'd met when my friend Eve Paris's mother, Helene Streeter, was brutally knifed on the street near her house. I'd gone to comfort Eve and ended up getting sucked into the investigation. Helene Streeter, feminist psychologist and champion of battered women, had been one of my heroes. Dom was one of the investigating detectives, and he'd bullied and cajoled me into maintaining my role as family confidante to assist with the investigation. In the end, it nearly got me killed, and it cemented our relationship forever.

Dom and his wife, Rosie, disabled after being hit by a drunk driver, had become like a second family to me. Sometimes I thought they were more like parents than my real parents. Dom is the guy I know I can always call if I need him, and he'll just come, no questions asked. As Andre knew, with them I would be both safe and welcome. My motto has always been, if you can't have your favorite cop by your side when you're in trouble, then you'd better have your second favorite.

It was an inspired suggestion. I considered it as I sorted through my closet, the phone clamped between my chin and my shoulder. There was a spot on my green silk blouse. The purple suit was missing a button. I couldn't wear black, it would reveal my true feelings about the union and my mother would have a fit.

"Well," Andre said, after an extended pause, "what do you think?"

"The flowered silk. I'll look like an overgrown ingenue, but it's the only thing that's whole."

"Theadora, are you trying to be annoying?"

"I'm sorry," I said. "I'm trying to get dressed and there's something wrong with everything. And I don't want to go to this stupid party. It's going to be miserable. I want to go to bed and sleep for twelve more hours, not make small talk with a bunch of strangers I know I'm not going to like. You're right. Going to Dom's is a good idea. I'll call them as soon as I—"

"I've already called," Andre said. "They were delighted. They're expecting you after dinner." He said it nervously. He was expecting me to blow up.

But I was the new, reformed, happy, compromising Thea Kozak, a woman who tries to get along with people. "Thanks," I said. "That was very sweet of you." I wish I could have seen the look on his face. "I've got to go now. Got to get dressed and pack a bag. If I can find anything. . . ."

"Your navy-blue silk skirt. The long, swirly one. White satin blouse and that vest with all the embroidery," he said. "And leave your hair down. That's how I'll be thinking of you. The most beautiful woman at the party."

"I'll call you when I get to Dom's."

"You'd better."

"Andre. Wait. What am I looking for? I mean, what should I be watching out for?"

"Nothing, I hope. Just keep an eye out for someone following you . . . Donahue's van . . . you know what it looks like."

"And what am I supposed to do if I see it? Pull over and call for help?"

"Drive to the nearest place with lots of people . . . convenience store, gas station, police station, and then use your phone to call for help. Don't just pull over to the side. If someone threatens you while you're in the car, put on your flashers, lean on the horn, flash your lights, do everything you can to call attention to yourself. And don't stop until you're surrounded by people."

"You're making me paranoid. Should I be on the lookout for Bass, as well? There's no one around with a better reason to hate me."

"I hope not. I would think he'd be trying to minimize his trouble. Just be careful, okay?"

"I'll be careful." I'm always careful, I told the unresponsive silence around me. The bed, the carpet, the curtains, none of them cared. People were always telling me to be careful, and I was, but trouble just seemed to have a way of finding me. Short of retreating to a cave and never coming out again, I didn't see what I could do differently. My hideous stuffed cat, its Velcro feet stuck together so it clung to the back of a chair, grinned at me. I picked it up and hurled it across the room. That's what I keep it around for. It was gift from a guy I dated briefly. A guy even more awful than the cat.

I pulled out the flowered dress, held it up, and looked in the mirror. Ugly. So I followed Andre's suggestion, adding big, clanking earrings and a silver necklace. Put on heels, had second thoughts, took them off, put them on again. So what if I towered over everyone else? I was tall. I asked the mirror, mirror on the wall again, and got a better reaction. Then I threw some stuff in a suitcase, rechecked all the locks, set the alarm, and left. In the car, I checked the location of the flashers and the horn, things I rarely use, and checked my purse for my alarm and Mace.

Mace and bluefish pâté. Who said my life wasn't normal? As I drove, I tried to recapture some of my earlier good humor.

After all, I was on my way to celebrate my brother's engagement. An occasion for rejoicing. I'd been married once, and it had been joyous. But I didn't feel that way about Michael and Sonia. They brought out the worst in each other. I couldn't help wondering whether there might be someone out there who was better for each of them. And though it gets fainter with time, the prospect of marriage for others brings back memories of my own. And that still hurts. I expected to enjoy the party about as much as I enjoy being sutured, maybe less.

I wasn't paranoid. I just checked the mirrors frequently for an ominous black van.

As I passed the hospital, I stopped, on impulse, to see if Dr. Durren was there, just in case he hadn't gotten his message. Passive and hangdog though he might be, he was about all Julie had, and with the shock she'd had, learning her husband was still alive, and her brother perhaps involved, she would be more in need of support than ever. I worried about her ability to withstand this latest blow. It wouldn't hurt her to have a visit from her doctor.

They paged him for me and reported that he'd be out shortly. I knew what shortly could mean in an emergency room—I've spent way too much of my life in such places—and I idly thumbed through the magazine collection: an ancient *Ladies Home Journal, Reader's Digest, Road and Track*, and *Highlights for Children*. Better than some hospitals had to offer. But nothing that interested me. I tried an article on sport/utility vehicles, but my mind was too full of stuff to concentrate. Still clutching the magazine, I drifted back and made desultory conversation with the bored nurse.

"Is it usually this quiet on Saturdays?" I asked.

She shook her head. "Not at all. It's never like this. Last Saturday was busy, but the week before was wild. We were shorthanded that day and then there were two auto accidents in a row with personal injury. EMTs rushing about, blood everywhere. People screaming. Dr. Wood just about went out of his mind. He's not as calm as Dr. Durren. But we handled it."

"Oh, Thea. There you are." Thomas Durren came toward me, his hand outstretched, moving as silently and gracefully as a cat. Neither the nurse nor I had heard him coming. I dropped the magazine and took his hand. "Something's happened?" he asked eagerly. I nodded. "Let's go somewhere a bit more private." He steered me into a treatment room, offering me a chair while he leaned against the table. "What is it?"

"Did you get my message?" I asked.

"Message?"

"I left it on your machine. But of course, you've been working. There have been some astonishing developments in Julie's case. . . ." I considered how to tell him, what to tell him, and settled for the simplest version. "Calvin Bass isn't dead. He wasn't driving when the car crashed. His cousin was. They looked a lot alike. When he saw what had happened, he simply pretended to be his own cousin and walked away."

"Walked away?" His voice was faint, like a man in shock. He looked like he was in shock, too. His face was deadly pale. "He's not dead?" He ran a hand slowly through his hair, wincing as if it pained him. "What does this mean for Julie?"

"I don't know. You'll have to ask her lawyer. I'm not sure anyone knows what to think, right now. The existing Connecticut charges are no good, of course. But I think they're holding her here on a fugitive warrant or something. Of course, if the car was tampered with, as they assume, then it doesn't matter whether the murderer killed the right person or not. There was an intent to kill and someone was killed." I shook my head. "So I don't know where it goes from here, except it also appears that Julie's brother was there—in Connecticut—he had a fight with Bass in the parking lot."

Durren looked like he wanted to cry. "That would be almost as bad, for Julie. She adores her brother. He's the only family she has."

I should have stayed and comforted him, but I didn't know how and I didn't have time. He seemed so shattered by my news. "I'm sorry," I said. "I didn't mean to upset you . . . only you seemed so anxious for any news." I gave up. There was no way to comfort him. The situation was too bizarre. "I wish I could have done more for her but short of getting someone to confess, which no one seems eager to do, I'm afraid I've done everything I could think of." He didn't seem to be listening. "I have to go. Dinner at my mother's. It's an engagement celebration for my brother. I just thought you'd want to know. About Bass, I mean."

He shook off his confusion, walked me back to the nurse's station, and said a rather formal good-bye. I headed for the entrance. When I looked back, he was staring blankly after me, holding the magazine I'd been reading. He sketched a feeble wave, crossed the waiting room, replaced the magazine with the others, and made the small stack neat.

CHAPTER 24

THERE WERE NO black vans in the hospital parking lot and none as I drove across town. Although my parents' street was crowded with cars, none of them were black vans, either. I could tell I looked good because Sonia gave me three dirty looks before I even got the bluefish to the kitchen. I'd never thought of her as the jealous type. Jealousy is an emotion that takes energy and passion; Sonia never seems to have any energy and her passion is all for herself. Well, it was no skin off my nose. I wasn't there to be admired or disapproved of; I was just doing my familial duty.

I passed bluefish, fetched drinks, chatted with Sonia's relatives, admired children, and made aimless small talk until my jaw ached. Meeting her family made it easier to understand Sonia. A more self-involved crew I've never seen. They all wanted to talk and it was all about themselves, their interests, worries, illnesses, disabilities, opinions. Nothing reciprocal. No other-directedness. No curiosity about the people they were meeting. Just me and I and we, and I have, we want, we are, we need. I almost lost my composure in the middle of Sonia's sister's plantar wart story. I was about to excuse myself when she segued into another story.

"This looks like such a nice neighborhood," she said. "Did you grow up here?" I said I had. "Well, you know, it's funny, but I saw something coming in that I've never seen in my neighborhood." I could see the criticism coming right off. Braced myself for it. "There was a man right out there on this nice street working on his car. All we could see were his feet sticking out. Wearing fancy shoes and suit pants!" She went off into peals of laughter.

I didn't understand why she was laughing. I depend on my car and don't think car trouble is funny. Not many of us keep mechanic's coveralls in our trunks. If something goes wrong we wade in, business suits or not. "Excuse me," I said, "I think my aunt needs me," and scooted away.

It was a thoroughly rotten ending to a day that had begun so well. I was working my way across the room, trying to get to Uncle Henry and Aunt Rita—my favorite relatives—when Mom seized me by the arm, hauled me into the kitchen, and asked if I'd done anything to help Julie. Although she'd hired people to serve and clean up, she looked frazzled and anxious. Her normally full face had a pinched look. I realized that for all her social adeptness, this party was an awful strain. She was trying hard to please Sonia even though it couldn't be done.

The air was rich with lamb, asparagus, and warm bread. A bowl of minty green jelly trembled on the counter. Pots steamed gently on the stove. Dinner was going to be wonderful.

"I don't know if I've helped or not," I said.

"What is that supposed to mean?" she snapped as she tied an apron over her shiny silk dress.

"I found Calvin Bass. He's not dead," I said.

A cut-glass dish full of olives crashed to the floor, glass shards and olives skittering everywhere, the inky black juice running along the cracks between the tiles. Ignoring the mess, she stood staring at me. "That's a disgusting thing to say, Theodora. How could you?"

Did she think I was making this up? "It's true. He was taking the racing course with his cousin Jon. A cousin who looked a lot like him. It was the cousin who was killed. Bass identified his cousin as himself and walked away."

"How do you know? I mean, how did you find out?" she said, stooping down and trying to gather up olives and glass indiscriminately, the hem of her dress trailing perilously close to the pool of juice.

"Here. Use this. You'll cut yourself," I said, thrusting a brush and dustpan at her. "I went down to Connecticut yesterday. Andre and I went to the track with George and Ellen Bradley. You remember George, from high school? And after we'd all done some driving on the track, we had lunch with—"

"I just don't understand you," she interrupted. "You say you're so busy at work that you never have time for fun, yet every time I talk to you, you've just come back from some outing where you've been playing. Biking, until you fell off, and now you're playing at being a race car driver when you say you're too busy to help Julie . . . and now this nonsense about Calvin Bass not being dead. . . . You don't realize how lucky you are, when other people have such trouble. . . ." She stood up and held out the dustpan. "Here, you clean this up. I've got to get dinner on the table."

She wasn't going to let me talk, nor would she listen if I did. She'd called me in here only to complain. I knelt down, carefully tucking my skirt out of the way, and swept up the mass of olives and glass, mopping up the juice and tiny glass shards with wet paper towels. Time suspended, inside a shimmering haze of fury, I worked meticulously at getting every bit of glass, waiting for the return of enough control to speak.

"I'm sorry, Mom," I said, "I lied to you. I didn't fall off my bike. I hurt my hands and skinned my knee when Julie Bass's brother forced me out of my car at gunpoint and then threw me into the travel lane of a highway. But I was lucky. He didn't shoot me and the car that was coming missed me by a few inches. And Julie Bass's brother did that because I went to talk with him, to see if I could help Julie, and he didn't believe I was her friend, so he followed me and saw me eating with Andre and another trooper and he thought I was a cop who was trying to trick him. But I'm lucky, Mom, because he didn't kill me." I spoke slowly and carefully through an anger that left me breathless.

I crossed the kitchen and dumped the dustpan into the trash. "I'm really very lucky, Mom, and I do have a lot of fun. For instance, that same night, two thugs came to my door, claiming to be Connecticut cops. Only they weren't cops, Mom. They were two guys looking for some papers I'd taken out of Julie's house because she asked me to. Two guys with fists and guns they were ready to use . . ." She was standing across the room, staring at me like I'd gone mad, her spoon frozen in the air above a pot, her mouth slightly agape.

"But I got lucky, because I have such a fun life, don't you know, never doing anything for anyone else. He hit me a few times and twisted my arm and scared me to death but because I'm so lucky, when he shot me, it only grazed my leg." I pulled up my skirt and showed the Band-Aid. "So it bled a lot and hurt like hell, but, Mom, I have such a happy, easy life that I didn't get killed." Her mouth opened and shut a few times, like a landed trout, but no sound came out.

Dad burst through the door at that moment, carrying a tray of empty glasses. "The natives are getting restless out there. . . ." He stopped at the sight of our tense faces. I continued as though he wasn't there.

"Then yesterday, when I could have slept late and stayed home and read a book, or gone out and had all that fun you think I'm having, I drove to Connecticut and back so I could go to the race track and find out what really happened there the week-end Bass was killed. It was a good day. No one hit me and no one shot me. I did find out, by questioning the people at the track, that the man who was killed was not Calvin Bass, but his cousin, Jon Bass, who was there with him taking the course. And that Cal Bass identified his cousin as himself and then walked away and disappeared. Wait!" I interrupted as she made a sound that was the beginnings of speech.

"Then I found Calvin Bass, when the police wouldn't have known where to look. I found him because, when I wasn't roller-blading and eating bonbons and watching TV, I had inter-viewed a bunch of the people he worked with, and I'd located his girlfriend, who inadvertently let it slip that he had a cozy lit-tle place by the river where he took his lady loves. No, wait. . . ."

Absurd as it was, I wanted to be factually accurate. "It was his secretary who told me the place was by the river. You don't appreciate me, really. You know that? While you have been call-ing me up and whining about how I don't do anything to help poor Julie, I have conducted endless interviews, spent countless hours, and driven hundreds of miles, all while holding down a more than full-time job."

"Thea, we—" Dad began.

"Wait!" I held up my hand. "Before you say anything, let me finish. On her behalf I have been stalked, rammed, run off the road, terrorized, slapped, beaten and shot, because you think I ought to be helping her. And every time I talk with you, you complain because I am not doing enough. Now would you please tell me what more it is that you would like me to do?" I was as close to hysteria as I have ever been, yet cold to the core with a shaking fury that tightened my vocal cords until I could barely speak. When I finished, I was trembling and as winded as if I had just run a hard race.

"Thea!" Dad's low, furious voice cut across the kitchen like a whip. "How dare you! We have a houseful of guests and a family celebration under way. This is not the time to indulge in a hysterical outburst."

I stared at the two of them. Two of the people I thought I loved best in the world. At their tight, furious faces. "She asked what I was doing for Julie. I told her."

"That's no excuse for this . . . for this . . ." He sputtered as he looked for proper, lawyerly words. "This dreadful, undisciplined attack on your mother. You should be ashamed. You've upset her terribly. Really, I thought you'd learned some self-control, being in a business like yours." He set the glasses down on the edge of the sink with a crash.

"I was trying to make her understand—"

"You were attacking her. Viciously. I heard you. . . ."

I put the dustpan and brush, still held out stiffly in front of me in one tense, white fist, back in the cupboard. A piece of glass stuck in my finger like a tiny dagger. I pulled it out and dropped it in the trash. One small, perfect drop of blood rose from the spot. I watched it, mesmerized, as it swelled and stopped.

Metal clashed on metal as my mother attacked her pots. Dad was still watching me in the uneasy way you watch a potentially dangerous stray.

"I'd just like to understand why you two care more about Julie than you do about me." I choked on the words. "Why whatever I do, it's never enough."

He groaned. "Don't start up with that what-about-me crap now. We don't have time for it."

"I know."

In the other room, I kissed Henry and Rita and murmured something about a broken pipe emergency and having to leave. I did the same to Michael and Sonia and a few other people I bumped into on my way to the door. I retrieved my coat and purse from the closet and drifted outside and into my car, oblivious to the rain that was starting. We were working our way toward the longest day of the year, still eight weeks away and yet so much nearer than on those dark, close days in December, and even with the rain, there was a lingering sense of light in the air. I felt strangely detached, light-headed, dazed. Recovering from the effects of a powerful drug. Mechanically I put the car in gear, switched on the wipers, and headed home. I wanted to speed—wanted my car to respond to the explosive rage I felt inside—but the rain and heavy traffic kept me doing a nice, legal 55.

Route 128 isn't so much a loop around Boston as a cup handle, one side of the loop being precluded by the presence of the sea. As it swoops around, an aging, high-speed road plagued by too much traffic, other roads connecting more far-flung places rush to meet it, disgorging intrusive streams of traffic into the already far too clotted lanes. Sometimes Massachusetts drivers send me into a rage with their antics but tonight I hardly noticed, responding like an automaton as people around me played their absurd, death-defying, high-tech game of chicken. A game where if someone wants your spot, he just puts himself there and to hell with you.

When it came, it came at me so suddenly I didn't even have time to think. It was at the merge where traffic comes in from the left instead of the right, pouring into the high-speed lane beside me. A vehicle, materializing suddenly on my left, brushed the side of my car with a metallic *clunk*, horn blaring. I glanced in the rearview mirror, saw a window of open space beside me, and jerked the wheel sharply to the right.

My car responded, moved over, and when I turned the wheel to correct the veer, it didn't respond. I just kept turning right, heading for the breakdown lane and the guard rail, across a lane of heavy traffic. I hit the flashers, I hit the horn, glancing frantically in the mirror for an opening that didn't exist, breaking, sawing at the unresponsive wheel, slewing through a blare of lights and horns, distorted by the rain. There was a bone-jarring *thunk* as I was hit, the car spinning, turning, careening toward the rail, driver's side first now.

Time seemed endless, meaningless, gone into slow motion as I rocketed through the cacophony of sounds and lights. The tearing rasp of metal on metal, the window beside my head dissolving in a spiderweb of cracks. The car tipping, tipping, making me seasick as the ground came up and slammed into me, hurting my head. Then I was over, upside down, down on the other side and over again. I was at a carnival, the ride spinning and tilting and going upside down and the belt cut into my shoulder and my lap and my lap was full of something, someone, an enormous pillow that filled my lap and wanted to smother me and pressed me back in my seat.

I clung for dear life . . . for dear, dear life, my lively, fun-filled life . . . something sharp cutting my arm, the hot flow of blood, and I'd been cut on the arm before and I pulled it back and screamed and screamed and screamed and suddenly everything was still and the ride had stopped and I was a little bit sideways and all around me the metal was groaning with the agony it had just endured.

A small voice in my head was giving orders, orders beyond the comprehension of my conscious mind. "Get out of the car. It might blow up. Get out of the car. It might blow up."

Years ago, on a stormy winter night, the kitchen in our house caught fire while we were making popcorn in a frying pan. My mother, conditioned by years of worrying about such an emergency, stood by the door and repeated, like mantra, "Everyone must get out of the house. Everyone must get out of the house." While she stood and chanted, the rest of us put out the fire and cleaned up the mess. She didn't get us to leave the house to burn down, but she did manage to instill a lifelong fear of fire. I struggled with my door but it wouldn't open.

Fighting my way free of the air bag and seat belt, I crawled across the seat, pushed against the other door. It wouldn't open either. I pushed out the remaining glass with my feet and dragged myself out onto the ground. Cold, damp, sloping ground with thorns and bristly grass, soaked by the now-heavy rain. I scrambled a little way up it on all fours, slipping and sliding, and looked back. The car had rolled down a long slope, coming to rest with its last jarring bang in a ditch. Up above, I could see people milling and hear the commotion of voices above the hiss of traffic. Below me, the car gave a metallic groan and shifted.

If it was going to blow, I was still too close. I clambered on up the bank away from the road, which wasn't as steep as the one I'd rolled down, grappling weakly for handholds and footholds on the slippery grass, collapsing at last in a mass of trees, where the emerging leaves gave some shelter from the heavy downpour.

Through the murky darkness, I saw a figure approach the car. I was about to yell "I'm up here" when it bent not to look inside the car, but to do something to the exposed underside. Rising on the damp air came the gurgle of liquid. I saw the flash of a lighter shielded by a hand and the figure hurried rapidly away.

Voices on the opposite slope, the crash of running feet. People coming to my rescue. What I could see, that they could not, was that beneath the car, flames were licking at the grass, leaping up the car, spreading like a wide orange blanket. I grabbed a tree trunk and pulled myself up, tottered toward them, my voice a deafening roar in my ears. "Get back! Stay back! The car's on fire."

My voice was drowned out by the *whoosh* of the fire as it swept over the car. My car. My beloved car. With my beach chair, picnic blanket, the dry cleaning that never made it, and a briefcase of mortgages belonging to the Grantham Cooperative Bank in the trunk. Flames licking out the windows like greedy tongues, curling over the sides, out of the engine. I was rooted to the spot, staring at the car that was supposed to have been my funeral pyre. A small explosion, like the pop of a cap pistol. Then a rushing roar, a sound that seemed to hold and tremble and then the big bang.

It knocked me right off my feet. I lay on the damp, April cold earth that smelled of dank and humus and mold. Rain soaked my hair and ran in icy rivulets down my neck. Got in my nose and mouth until I painfully turned my head aside. Soaked my legs and my feet. I'd lost my shoes somewhere. I wanted to get up but all my wits and all the bones in my body seemed scattered and disassembled. I was supposed to call someone. Andre. Supposed to go somewhere. To Dom's. I went nowhere and called no one. No one called me, either. Infinity passed. A crowd grew down below, around my car. I would have called out to them but I had no voice. Crawled down to them, but I had no strength. The cold and damp seeped through my clothes, through my skin, through my bones. A warm, black cloud of oily smoke floated across my face. I reached for the warmth, fell into it, drifted.

CHAPTER 25

"YOU'RE WRONG." A firm, decisive voice, a little irritated. "When she tells you what happened, it will be so fantastic you'll think you've been transported to Never Land, and every word of it will be true. Right, princess?" A hand patted my shoulder. I moaned and swatted it away. It felt like someone had laid a red-hot branding iron across my shoulder and chest and another one around my abdomen. The rest of me had just been kicked with hobnailed boots.

"Ah," the voice came again, "the lady wakes."

I didn't bother to open my eyes. I already knew I'd be in a hospital and hospitals make me sick. Indeed, I'd vowed to stay out of them, but someone who hadn't signed on as a guarantor had foiled me once again. I also knew, from Florio's comments, that he wasn't alone. There was at least one eager beaver cop there salivating for the details of the accident. "Florio, can I just die and get it over with, or do I have to linger here and chat with asinine cops who won't believe a word I'm going to say?"

"See!" Dom's voice was positively gleeful. He loves it when I'm surly. It used to shock him, but he's gotten over it.

"Mrs. Kozak . . ." New voice. Precise, officious. I still didn't open my eyes. I didn't care to see him. He'd be just like all the others. I'd seen them before. Asking questions, assuming he knew the answers, and not listening when I told him what he didn't expect to hear. It wouldn't matter to him if I'd just lost both legs. He had forms to fill out. "I need to ask you a few questions. . . ."

"The Cabots speak only to the Lodges and I speak only to Florio," I said. "Dom. Am I alive?"

"Princess, as soon as you give Officer Crimmins here the answers to his questions, I'm going to take you home and Rosie will tuck you into bed."

It was the best news I'd had in years. "You mean I'm not broken? You mean they're not going to keep me here and poke and pinch and prod and stick me with needles until I go mad and have to be hospitalized?"

"At least your sense of humor isn't damaged."

"It's been a long day, Dom. A horrible long day. I had the worst fight with my mother and then my car . . . I want to go see Rosie." The thought of Rosie, beautiful, wise Rosie, waiting to tuck me in made me want to cry. "What does Crimmins want to know?"

"The details of the accident, ma'am," Crimmins began. "In your own words."

"As opposed to whose words?" I said. "The guy who tried to kill me?"

"Say what?" Crimmins said.

Dom took my hand in a firm grip and held on. My life line. I couldn't have continued without it. "Dom, do you know what's going on? What's been going on? So you can translate if this gets confusing. My mind is like a big soupy pudding right now. Don't expect me to think straight. . . ."

He squeezed my hand. "Just tell the story as it comes. We can worry about details later."

"I'm cold," I said.

"I'm not surprised. You were lying out there in the rain for quite a while before they found you. They thought you were in the car."

"Good thing I wasn't."

"Let's see if we can get another blanket," he said. "Oh, here's one now." He wrapped it around me and took my hand again. "Go ahead."

I organized my thoughts as well as I could and began. "Where Route 24 merges from the left. A car came along side. Banged into me. Andre told me to be careful but I'd just been at my parents' for a party and had a big fight with my mother, and while I thought I was looking in every direction, with the rain and all, I didn't see him coming. . . ."

"Was there drinking at this party, Mrs. Kozak?" Crimmins interrupted.

I opened my eyes and looked at him. Baby-faced and pink skinned, with pinkish scalp under his marine-short hair. His face was too wide and his forehead too high. He looked unlined, unformed, and uncaring. Just because I'd been put through the wringer and left out in the rain didn't mean I had to let myself be pushed around by a baby cop. "I had perhaps half a glass of wine over the course of two hours," I said, carefully and precisely. "Then I had a disagreement with my mother and left." I closed my eyes again.

I heard the scratch of pen on paper. "So you were upset when you got in your car? Angry?" Crimmins said.

"He wouldn't listen to you, would he, Dom?" I said. I tried to turn my back on him but nearly every part of my body protested in a chorus of pain. "Oh, ouch! I don't suppose you could rustle up some Darvon or Demerol or something? I have never hurt in so many places. I feel like I've been bouncing around inside a dryer."

"Well, you were pretty wet," Dom said.

"Florio. Please?" I got a lot of pleading into that please.

"I'll see what I can do," he said. "And don't bother her until I get back, Crimmins. She's got an awful temper."

I opened my eyes and watched Crimmins warily. The curtain hadn't stopped swinging behind Dom's departing back before Crimmins was asking questions. "So, you were upset when you got in the car, is that right?"

"Is that a new crime in this state, Officer? Driving under the influence of a temper? Because, as someone said to me recently, tonight I didn't lose my temper, I found it. Is it still tonight? After he blew the car up and I was knocked over, I was watching the sky and then I drifted away with the clouds. Warm clouds."

"Very poetic, ma'am," he said. "Now, could we get back to the facts? When you left the party after having a few drinks, you were very upset . . . angry . . . at your parents?"

Never sign anything the police give you without reading every word. Never agree with a statement by a cop without parsing every word. Never eat at a place called Mom's, never play poker with a man called Doc, and never sleep with anyone more unhappy than you are. Rules for life. "Officer Crimmins," I said, gathering as much self-control as I could muster, which, as I was weary beyond words, wasn't much, "don't put words in my mouth. I did not say a few drinks, I said half a glass of wine over the course of two hours. Maybe you could repeat that back to me so I know you've got it right this time?" I waited. Crimmins said nothing. He looked unhappy. People were supposed to cower before his authority.

"So when you got in your car, you were very angry. . . ."

Oh, please. I was too tired for this. I longed to bury my face in the pillow and weep. "I wish I had a court reporter here to read this all back, Officer. I believe, though with this headache and being in so much pain and it being so soon after an accident that I cannot be quite certain, that I said I left. Left. Not left suddenly or left rapidly or left in a huff. Just left. Isn't that what I said?"

The curtain parted to admit Dom and a nurse. I knew, from the look on Dom's face, that he'd been listening. The nurse popped some pills into my mouth and held the water so I could drink. I sank back on my pillows, depleted and discouraged. Infuriating as he was, I didn't have the strength to fight Crimmins through every line of my story. And I hadn't even gotten to the important part.

"Officer Crimmins," Dom said, "how long have you been in law enforcement?"

"Two years."

"Well, I've been in this business for twenty-eight, and I'd like to give you a little advice, if I may. . . ."

"Sir?"

"If someone tells you not to question a witness unless they are present—" He let his voice drop, paused, and then said harshly, "you damned well better not try to question the witness while they're out of the room. You understand?"

"This is not your case, sir," Crimmins said stiffly.

"Dominic," I wailed, holding out my arms. He hugged me. Very, very gently because he knew how it hurt. "Thanks. Now I'm going to tell you everything I remember. Once. Straight through. Then we're going home, right?'

"Right."

"I was right at the merge where Route 24 comes in from the left. Another vehicle—car, truck, van, I couldn't tell you which, was suddenly along side, bumping me. . . ." Crimmins cleared his throat, about to speak. "Don't interrupt," I said. "I'm only doing this once. Bumped. A hard, jarring bump . . . and you know how people drive . . . he didn't back off, he stayed there and kept pushing. I checked the next lane, it was clear, so I gave the wheel a hard jerk to the right . . . and the steering let go. . . ."

"The steering let go?" Crimmins said, disbelieving.

"Well, something went wrong, because when I went to straighten it out again, the wheel just turned in my hands and the car didn't respond, it just kept heading right, into the next lane of traffic." I cringed, remembering the noise, the lights, the bump when the car in that lane hit me, the jarring. "It hurts my bones, remembering. I thought I was dead." I closed my eyes, but the play of lights went on across the inside of my lids. Too painful. I opened them again.

"What did you do then?" Dom asked quietly.

"I hit the flashers and the horn and looked for a break in the traffic that might open if I could slow down. . . . It all felt like it was happening in altered time. That I was just drifting inexorably forward toward death and it was all out of my control. At least one car hit me. I heard an awful thud and it jarred the whole car. Spun me around so I was heading toward the guardrail driver's side first. . . ." I saw the railing coming at me, the window shattering. I closed my eyes.

Dom's hand was on mine again. Strong and comforting. "When you can," he said. "Take your time."

"I hit the rail and the car started to tip and then it rolled over and over down the hill and stopped in the ditch. The metal was groaning and creaking. All I could think of was fire and my door wouldn't open. Neither door would. I pushed out the glass, crawled through the window, and started up the slope. I wanted to get high enough so that if it exploded . . . I didn't know if cars explode often or rarely but I wasn't going to wait around and see. It was all I could think of. . . ."

"Not very—" was all Crimmins got out before Dom shushed him.

"I went up the slope on all fours. Not the one I'd rolled down. It was too steep. The other side. Partway up I was ready to lie down and take my chances but somehow I kept on. I got to the trees and when I looked back down, I saw him."

"Saw who?"

"I don't know. It was so dark. Raining heavily. A man. That's all I'm sure of. That it was a man. I thought he was coming to get me out of the car . . . I was going to call to him, but then he stopped, looked up toward the street, where people were, and instead of opening the door or looking in the car, he went to the front . . . and did something underneath. It was tipped sort of sideways in the ditch, lying on the passenger's side. There was a flash—a lighter, I think—he held it to see while he did something . . . then the light clicked off and I heard sounds, gurgling and splashing, like liquid being poured. He bent down. Clicked the lighter again and ran away. He never looked in the car. He set it on fire and never looked in the car." I squeezed Dom's hand. "He never looked in the car."

I was holding on so tightly I was probably hurting him, but he didn't complain. "There were people coming down the bank—to rescue me, I thought—I wasn't sure they could see the fire. I tried to call to them. I left the woods and went toward them. It flared up with a huge roar and then. . . ." I tried to remember. "A small pop, like a champagne cork . . . and a big roar as the fire took hold. My whole car was burning. Then an explosion. Knocked me down like a bowling pin. I couldn't get up. I didn't think they were going to find me. It was so cold. . . ."

My eyes closed. I'd given them what they wanted and now they'd let me rest. I could feel the drug beginning to work, feel the tangible spreading of relief and a delicious lethargy.

"How fast were you going?" Crimmins said.

"Around fifty-five. The rain had started and it was hard to see."

"What did you observe about the vehicle which allegedly bumped you?" Crimmins asked.

My eyes popped open. "It didn't allegedly do anything, Officer. It bumped me, hard, stayed there and kept on pushing. And if my car hadn't burned . . . or maybe even now, a shrewd detective who knew what he was looking for might find traces of paint there, if he bothered to look. Paint from the car that pushed me. And I suppose your next question will be about the man I allegedly saw, right? Well, there's no allegedly about him, either. I can't tell you who he was, but I can assure you he was there. Probably trying to destroy evidence that the car was tampered with." I thought about that. Realized what the other possibility was; the other very likely possibility. The man had never looked to see if I was in the car. The man Sonia's cousin had seen in the street, working on "his" car. "And to destroy me."

Crimmins kept looking at me like I'd offered him caviar and served him baloney and marshmallow fluff. I didn't know how to make him happy. There might be something more but my poor, weary brain couldn't cough it up. Not now. I needed R & R. Rest and Rosie. "Don't look at me like that, Officer. I wish I remembered more. Had noticed more. Maybe I did and I just can't recall it right now. It all happened so fast. In the dark. In the rain. Have you ever been in an accident, Officer Crimmins?"

He shook his head. "No, ma'am."

"Ever had someone deliberately try to kill you?"

"No, ma'am." He was staring at me like I'd gone loco. I hadn't, though. If I had nine lives, like a cat, then I've already used up several. It's not the sort of thing you can explain to disbelieving strangers.

"Maybe that's why you don't understand. Why you don't believe me. And I can't help you. Is there anything else?"

"Can you give me any sort of description of this man?"

I started to shake my head and thought better of it. My brains were scrambled enough already. "He was wearing a raincoat and a hat."

"Tall? Short? Old? Young?"

"It was dark. It was raining. I saw a man. That's all I can tell you." I plucked at the blue and white hospital gown I was wearing. It seemed to be all I was wearing, except panties. "I can't go out like this, Dom. Where are my clothes?"

Dom made a face. "You wouldn't want 'em right now. Blood, mud, grass stains, prickles. Soaking wet. I'll throw them in the washer when we get home and see if anything can be saved."

"But what am I . . . ?"

He held up a brown paper bag. "I've brought you my favorite sweats, fresh from the laundry."

"They'd better be, Florio, I've seen how they look when you're done with 'em."

"And there's this." He pulled a brownish-white item out of his pocket and let it dangle from his hand. It was a bra. Not very clean. Probably mine. "It's almost dry. I washed it out in the sink with my own two hands," he said proudly. "And I wouldn't do that for just anyone." Crimmins stared stupidly from the bra to me and back to Florio.

With his glasses on, in his conservative, detective attire, Florio looks like an aging, bearlike accountant. Take off the glasses so you can see his probing, intelligent eyes, and you can see the detective. Give him a basketball and dress him in sweats and you've got an aging jock. Put him with Rosie and you've got a romantic hero. My second favorite cop, Dom Florio, is a human chameleon.

"I love you, Dom," I said, holding out my hand for the bra. "How did you find me?"

"Meagher." Steve Meagher is Dom's partner. "He heard something on the radio, Red Saab. License number. Steve's a good detail man. He called me. I called here, got Crimmins and got the story, and jumped in my car. Steve says to tell you hello."

"A good man in a tight spot," I said. "Speaking of good men. Does Andre know?" Dom nodded. "What did you tell him?"

"Fender bender. Cut on your arm. A few stitches. I would bring you safely home and put you to bed."

"He was okay with that?"

"He knew I was lying. He told me so. He wanted to know how bad it was. I said you weren't even staying overnight in your least favorite accommodations—minimal blood loss, minimal stitches, no broken bones, and only a mild concussion—and I would keep you under police surveillance twenty-four hours a day." I let out the breath I'd been holding. "He just caught a nice, fresh murder and was on his way out the door. I promised you'd call him when we got home. They'll page him." He stroked my arm. "It's okay, Thea. He knows you were being careful. I think he's getting used to your ways. Now, if Rosie were to get herself in scrapes like this . . ."

"You would be awestruck," I interrupted. "You would stare at her in wonder and suggest that while you'd rather she didn't, you knew she was going to do what she was going to do and you'd ask her to please be careful . . . and not hurt the other guy too much."

"You're right. Impossible women hold a fatal attraction for me."

"We hope it's not fatal," I said. Crimmins's mouth was pinched up like a prune with disapproval.

Dom reached in the bag and pulled out a handful of gray fleece. He dumped it on the bed beside me. "You need some help with this?"

"Maybe you could send a nurse?"

He made a face. "I'm perfectly capable. . . ."

"I know you are, Florio, but what would Rosie think?"

My second favorite cop considered. "That I'm a crass opportunist?"

I nodded. "I'll find a nurse," he said.

"Take Crimmins with you?"

"With pleasure."

Even with assistance, getting dressed was no picnic. The medication helped, but I was sorer than sore and stiffer than a whalebone corset. Where the seat belt had held me in, there were livid strips of red as tender as a burn. It felt like the bruises went all the way to my bones and all the bones were shaken loose. My neck was so stiff I couldn't turn my head. A bulky bandage on my arm. Glass. Six stitches. The nurse gave me some prescriptions and helped me off the table. She'd given me an efficient and daunting rundown of things to look out for and worry about, so that at any minute I was expecting to be killed by an embolism or experience blinding headaches as my brain swelled. Most likely my insides would rupture and I'd discover several joints were dislocated. My body temperature would drop, I'd go into shock and be unable to stop shaking. And I should expect to have nightmares for a few weeks, and difficulty riding in cars.

I limped out, leaning on her arm. Crimmins was in deep conversation with a real mean-looking black trooper. Probably trying to persuade the guy to arrest me on a charge of being America's Most Wanted. Somebody wanted me, that was for sure. Wanted me dead. I wished I knew who.

CHAPTER 26

TRUE TO DOM'S promise, Rosie was waiting for me, her expressive face creased with worry. She hovered by the door, leaning on her cane, as I limped in with Dom at my heels like a sheepdog. She was wearing something long and green and flowing and looked like a Madonna in an old painting. She stared at me and shook her head. "In the bathtub. Now. You look like you've been plowing a field with your face." She turned to her husband. "Dominic, I can't believe this. At that hospital they didn't even wash her face. We need health care reform, all right. Back to good old-fashioned basic care."

I looked in the bathroom mirror and was even more outraged than she had been. I did look like I'd been plowing a field with my face, right after I finished a swim through a canal and a romp through a hayloft. No wonder Crimmins hadn't believed me. I looked like a lunatic. A coal miner. A fireman after a fire. I turned angrily toward Dom, the abrupt motion causing so much pain my frayed temper fizzled and snapped. "Why didn't you tell me I looked like this?"

"I didn't want to upset you."

"When I'm feeling a little better, I'm going to kill you for this."

"I just wanted to get you out of there as quickly as possible."

"Arms up," Rosie ordered, ignoring our squabbling. Like a cooperative kid, I stuck them up and she pulled off the sweatshirt, making a face at my filthy bra.

"Don't look at me. He washed it. Or he says he did."

Rosie stared at her husband's embarrassed face and started to giggle. "You never stop surprising me," she said. "Now get out so I can get this girl into the tub. . . ."

"Hey, no fair," he said. "I brought it home. I get to keep it."

"You get to go make everyone a drink and find the portable phone so Thea can make a phone call and set someone's mind at ease," she said. "Now shoo."

He shooed. I sat down on the toilet seat and rested my filthy head on Rosie's velour shoulder. "I had the worst fight with my mother tonight. She'll never get over it. And then someone tried to kill me. . . ."

"Let's get the rest of these things off and get you in the tub and then you can tell me all about it." As I struggled with track pants and underwear, she poured in a handful of lavender. "Very soothing," she said.

"It would take a whole field to do me any good."

"We'll see. I know you don't want to hear this, Thea, but you're awfully lucky, considering."

I didn't feel lucky and things wouldn't look better in the morning, when I'd hurt even more and face hours replacing credit cards and my license, as well as my car, while work piled up on my desk. I didn't want to think about it. I submerged completely except for my bandaged arm. Combing my hands through my hair, I found bits of grit and chaff and glass, moving cautiously over the tender spots where my head had banged into the seat and the window. When I popped up, Rosie handed me a washcloth. "Here. I'm going to go find you a nightgown."

A knock on the door. It opened a crack and a hand came in, holding a phone. Rosie took the phone. The hand disappeared and reappeared, holding a glass. She took the glass and set both it and the phone on the toilet seat within easy reach. "Wash your face and make that call," she said. "I'll be back."

I followed orders. The washcloth came away filthy. I rinsed it and rubbed again. Carefully. Under the dirt were a bunch of tiny nicks from the glass. Rinsed and rubbed again. Squeezed out some shampoo and washed my hair. Putting off the moment when I'd have to call Andre. The phone rang. Dom stuck his head around the door. "It's for you."

"Andre?"

"Are you all right?" A world of worry and tenderness packed into four words.

"Nothing broken. Fewer stitches than a baseball. But I feel like I've been through the wringer."

"Wish I was there. Are they taking good care of you?"

"The best. Well, maybe second best . . . I wish you were here."

"Should I come?"

"As often as possible and only with me."

"You are okay," he said, a sigh of relief in his voice.

"Dom says at least I haven't lost my sense of humor."

"What have you lost?" he asked, suspicious.

"Some skin. Some security. And my car."

"The next one better be a HumVee."

"A what? It sounds like a buzzing insect of the blood-sucking variety."

"Sort of a cross between a jeep and a tank."

"Does it come with bodyguards?"

"That could be arranged. I was thinking of Rapunzel's tower myself. I'd build it and put you up there and . . ."

"And I'd let my hair down and you'd climb up. . . ."

"And we'd make whoopee."

In the background, I could hear other voices, the crackling of radios, someone yelling. "Where are you?"

"Crime scene," he said. "Guy shot his ex-wife and her boyfriend. Killed the wife, the boyfriend may make it. It's touch and go right now. In front of their kid." His anger that this kept happening was heavy in his voice. And yet he had the time for me.

"Maybe I should be building that tower for you."

"How about a tower for two? As long as I know you're out there waiting for me, I can handle—" He stopped abruptly. "I should go. Bastard's out there somewhere with a whole arsenal. And his four-year-old kid."

"I had a terrible fight with my mother tonight. I walked out of Michael's engagement party. She'll probably never speak to me again."

"Don't worry. She'll speak to you. If she doesn't speak, she can't tell you how wrong you were and how badly you hurt her feelings." I could hear someone speaking in his ear. "Gotta go. I'll call you tomorrow. . . ." A pause. Someone shouting at him. "They think they've found him. I've got to—"

"Andre?"

"Yeah?" The response of someone who's already gone.

"Be careful."

"You know it," he said grimly. "You, too. You be careful, too."

I put the phone down and picked up my drink—bourbon— which, Dom knows, is like mother's milk to me. No. Not like mother's milk. Not from *my* mother. Why had I let myself lose my temper like that? It wouldn't do any good. She hadn't heard what I was saying. Now I had both of them mad at me, and probably Michael and Sonia, as well, and I'd gained nothing from it. She wouldn't see me any differently and she wouldn't treat me with any more respect, understanding, or consideration. I just hadn't been able to help myself.

Inwardly I sputtered and fumed and replayed the argument, alternating, like avant-garde cinema, with clips from the accident, while I softened the memories of both by inhaling the soothing aroma of lavender and the water grew lukewarm. Once I picked up the drink, even though I knew that strong spirits are strictly forbidden to drug-taking slightly concussed accident cases like me. I was lucky Rosie and Dom hadn't given me a lecture instead. But they're real practical folk. They were letting me make my own choice. For once, I decided in favor of prudence, letting the melting ice turn my abandoned drink a nice pale gold.

Finally, Rosie stuck her head around the door. "Are you all right?"

"No. I'm brooding and obsessing."

"Good words," she said, coming in and closing the door behind her. "Ready to come out?" She tested the water. "Ugh. Too cold. Come on." She held out a big towel and I heaved myself upright and got wrapped in it. She searched through the medicine cabinet and found me a brush. "You'd better come and help me with Dom. He's storming around out there like an enraged water buffalo. I guess he didn't care too much for the policeman who questioned you at the hospital?"

"That would be putting it mildly. He was remarkably restrained, though. You would have been proud of him."

"I often am." She stared from me to the rejected glass as if remembering something. "When was the last time you ate?"

"I had a loverly brunch with the man of my dreams."

"No dinner?"

"Well, I was going to have dinner. My brother's engagement dinner, but I never made it to dinner. I had a huge fight with my mother and left before . . ."

"Uh-oh." Rosie shook her head. "Two sources of turmoil in one evening? On an empty stomach? I think this calls for some serious pasta." Dom and Rosie believe that food is the answer to most of life's problems. Food, discipline, love, and compassion. She handed me a nightgown—luckily she's tall, like me—and pulled a pair of socks out of her pocket. "Put these on. I'll get you a robe and then come in the kitchen. Helping me cook will give the water buffalo something to do. Hold still." She picked up the washcloth and scrubbed at a spot I'd missed. "There. Now you're beautiful again." She said it the way a mother talks to her child. "You want me to brush your hair?"

"That's okay. I can do it." She put the brush in my hand and went out. Rosie moves faster with her cane than most people who don't use one. When I first met her, she was in a wheelchair and her doctors doubted that she'd ever walk after being the victim of a hit-and-run driver. A drunk driver. But Rosie has more guts, grit, and courage than an entire football team; she pushed herself through an arduous and discouraging rehabilitation and taught herself to walk again. Dom had gotten himself assigned to traffic duty and had been so relentless in stopping and arresting drunk drivers, including some of the town fathers, that they'd promoted him to detective.

I looked in the mirror. Beautiful only in a mother's eyes. I looked pale, spotty, bruised, and worn. The whites of my green eyes reddened with weariness. Dom brought the robe, helped me into it, and tied it for me like I was one of his children. He finished tying it, straightened up, and held out his arms. "Hard day, kid," he said. I walked into them and felt safe.

"Rosie says you've been storming around like a water buffalo."

"Does she? Well, I get upset when bad things happen to my friends and bad cops make it worse."

"Crimmins?"

"Oh, he's not such a bad cop," Dom said, "he's just young and thinks he knows it all. I was probably a little like that myself. But I like to think I knew better than to be so rude and suspicious with an accident victim."

"I've dealt with cops who thought I set my own house on fire, tried to commit suicide, and even hit myself over the head with a frying pan. I'm getting used to it."

"That's just the problem," he exploded. "People shouldn't have to get used to it. A shocked and injured person should be treated with compassion." He cast a nervous glance toward the kitchen. Rosie worries about Dom's blood pressure. She's always on his case about his temper. "Let's go help the chef. She's making something very special for us."

Something special was a pasta that looked like long ringlets served with a sauce of sun-dried tomatoes and smoked cheese and roasted eggplant and red peppers and olive oil. It was sensational. So were the bread and the salad.

"Here's to midnight dinners," Dom said, raising his glass. We drank. "Only next time, Thea, you don't have to take such extreme measures to get an invitation. Rosie is always happy to have someone to cook for."

"Besides the water buffalo," she said. "It's all old hat to him." I didn't think Rosie's cooking would become old hat, even to an undiscriminating beast like a water buffalo, and I said so.

"When did she start calling you a water buffalo?" I asked.

"It's a term of endearment," Rosie said. "Don't you think it fits him?"

I shook my head. "No horns. Old accountant is what comes to mind."

"Oh, he's horny enough," Rosie said. "I keep thinking as he gets older he'll slow down, but I'm seeing no signs of it." Now that their kids had left and Dom had stopped treating Rosie like an invalid, they were pretty frisky. I'd dropped by more than once and found them pink faced and in robes in the middle of the day.

Dom made a threatening gesture with his fork. "See if I come rescue you again."

"Oh please! Threaten me with no more of Rosie's cooking, or that you'll never loan me your sweats and wash out my undergarments again, but please don't say you'll never come and rescue me. It's one of the foundations of my existence." It was true, I realized. Dom and Rosie had become very important to me. The kind of parents I would have chosen if I could choose. Thinking about parents plunged me back into a welter of gloom.

"I keep hoping I'll never have to," he said.

"I don't deserve this from you. From anyone," I said, waving my hand at them, at our feast. "I keep trying to stay out of trouble but I just don't seem to be able to."

"It's not like you drove yourself off the road, Thea," Rosie said. "Isn't the real question would you stop helping people because it would make you safer?"

"That's what that cop at the hospital thought," I said, ignoring her question. "He thought I drank too much at a party, had a fight with my mother, and went out and caused an accident. He wasn't even listening when I told him about the car that bumped me."

"He was a jerk," Dom said, "instead of jumping to attention when you told him you thought the car had been tampered with, he . . . hey, wait a minute!" He stared at me, his detective's eyes gleaming. "What did you just say?"

"I said he wasn't even listening."

"I mean the rest of it. . . ."

I tried to remember. "He wasn't even listening when I told him about getting bumped."

He shook his head impatiently. "That's not exactly what you said."

"When I told him about the car that bumped me," Rosie said.

"Exactly!" Dom said, getting excited. "At the hospital, she said she didn't know if it was a car or a truck or a van. Now she says it was a car!"

"Calm yourself, Dom," Rosie said. "She probably didn't mean anything by it."

"Did you?" he demanded. "Was it a car?"

"Why does it matter?" Rosie asked.

"Because I was expecting to be bumped—that is, I was expecting I might have some trouble—from a guy who drives a van. And if it wasn't a van . . ." I closed my eyes and rubbed my temples, trying to bring back the memory. "It's no good," I said, after a minute. "I can't remember."

"Try harder," Dom said.

"Leave her alone," Rosie snapped.

"It might be important."

"It might be," she agreed. "But aren't you the guy who just a minute ago was criticizing cops who bully people when they've been in accidents and they're vulnerable and in pain?"

The water buffalo looked sheepish. He pointed at an empty chair. "It weren't me, Black Bart, it were him."

"Tell me another one," Rosie said. "Come on, Thea. Bedtime. I'll get you settled and then I'll send Dr. Florio in to apologize and give you your medicine." She steered me into the bedroom and tucked me in, just like I'd imagined she would. She didn't even make me brush my teeth. Dom came and brought me painkillers and a sort of an apology. But it was okay. Nice as it was to have Rosie protecting me, I knew he was right. If I'd seen a car, that might be significant. If only I could remember.

"I'm sorry about the car. About not remembering."

"You can't force it. It may come back to you, completely out of the blue. Or over the next few days as you get farther from the accident. Don't mind my impatience. I should know better. . . ."

"Someone tried to kill me tonight." The words had a hard, ugly reality when spoken aloud.

"It does appear that way," he agreed. He didn't suggest I had an overactive imagination or try to soften things. Andre wouldn't have asked him to take me in if the dangers hadn't been real.

"But I don't know why. Other than Duncan Donahue. And he doesn't have a reason. . . ."

"Since when have we expected killers to be reasonable?"

"I do. I believe people have to have reasons for . . . for the awful things they do. Maybe not logical ones, but reasons."

"So we're saying the same thing. And you're convinced that it wasn't just an accident?"

"You heard what I told Crimmins. A car bumping me . . . that could have been accidental. But the steering . . . that was no accident. And even if it had been, how would you explain the man who set the car on fire? Someone tried to kill me, Dominic." It must have been a delayed reaction. I'd told Crimmins about it and hadn't felt a thing. Now my skin crawled horribly as I thought about being burned. My throat tightened, choking me, as I imagined not being able to get out of the car. Supposed I'd been more seriously injured? I would have been a sitting duck. A roast duck.

An earthquake of emotion—the aftershocks of fear, frustration, and rage—shook me from head to toe, setting off a tsunami of tears. "You'd better get out of here," I warned. "It's going to blow." He sensibly left me alone to scream and cry and pound the stuffing out of my pillow. When it was finally over, I fell into an exhausted sleep. A sleep tormented by dreams in which I rolled down endless slopes, crawled through many broken windows, and chased a formless, faceless man through an unending rainy darkness.

CHAPTER 27

MORNING CAME, AS it always does, bringing with it the wretched agonies that are the aftermath of a bruising experience. Even my ears and the soles of my feet hurt. Outside the window, rain splattered steadily against the glass from a leaden gray sky. April showers may bring May flowers but today the weather too closely matched my mood and I didn't need any more gloom.

I could have slept all day. My body needed the rest but I've never mastered the art. Besides, the smell of bacon was enticing. I staggered to the breakfast table, stiff as a board and limping badly, to find bacon burning in the pan while Rosie and Dom stared riveted at the small kitchen television. They both turned with such alarm I wondered if they'd forgotten I was in the house. "Bacon's burning," I said. I dumped myself into a chair, put my head on my arms, and closed my eyes. I felt awful.

Dom and Rosie silently rescued the bacon. In the unnatural silence, the announcer's voice penetrated the fog of my brain, as he said, in that carefully modulated voice they install at the factory where they make newspeople, ". . . the standoff, which has now been going on for more than three hours. A police spokesman on the scene expressed concern for a state trooper who traded himself for two civilian hostages, a elderly man and a young child, earlier this morning. The trooper was later wounded by Moreau when police came too close to the house. Negotiators spoke with the gunman by phone minutes ago but were unable to persuade him to release the trooper, who has tentatively been identified as State Police Detective Andre Lemieux."

There was more but I didn't hear it. I'd gone cold all over with an icy, bone-chilling fear. Fear that I'd lived with on the edges of my consciousness as long as I'd known and loved him. The fear of losing him like I'd lost David that had held me back from commitment; that had made me hold loving in reserve until needing him and loving him and the pleasure and comfort of having him around had forced me to open the door, despite my fear of being left alone again. Now here I was with the door standing wide open and a cold wind pouring in.

The camera panned the scene, a jumble of police cars, fire trucks, vans, ambulances, and news vans. Men with rifles crouching behind cars. Men in helmets and protective vests. I jumped up. "I've got to go there. I've got to go now. . . ." I had no idea where "there" was. I had no car, no purse, no credit cards, clothes, or shoes. Nothing but a borrowed nightgown. They stood holding hands and watching me. Worried parents whose daughter was in trouble. They knew what I meant. Rosie had been a cop's wife almost as long as Dom had been a cop. She'd known those nights of waiting, when the phone finally rings and your heart stops beating; when your hello is as fragile and tentative as a baby's breath. And Dom knew. Dom had made those calls and gotten the call himself; heard the hushed pained voices, had almost lost Rosie.

Dom called in to take an emergency personal day while Rosie and I got me dressed. I'm taller; she's broader. I ended up in a pair of their son's baggy jeans, fashionably short and wide enough for a hippo, cinched at the waist with a belt, a stretched-out blue sweater that Rosie apologized for, and socks. We tried to find shoes but I felt like Cinderella's sisters, trying to find something that fit. Rosie's feet were just too small. "Forget it," she said, "Dom can stop somewhere and get you a pair." She dug in her purse and handed me a fistful of bills. "Take this. I know you don't have any money." I shoved them in my pocket, kissed her, and we were off.

"Where are we going?" I asked.

"Chelsea," he said. "Little town near Augusta. How far is that?"

"Three and a half, four, if you drive the speed limit."

"Cops don't drive the speed limit." He reached into the backseat and grabbed a blanket. "Wrap this around you."

"How did you . . . ?"

"Been there. Done that," he said.

"Of course."

"You won't be warm again until you see for yourself that he's all right."

"What if he's not?"

"We will cross that bridge when we come to it. For now, we assume things will turn out okay. It's the only way to function."

We didn't talk much on the way. The rain was hard and steady, with rotten visibility as cars and trucks threw up residual sand left from the winter. My mind kept going back to the what ifs. Things I should have said or done that I might never get to, now. The things Julie Bass and I had talked about last Monday.

Was it just last Monday? It seemed like several lifetimes ago that I'd gone home for Easter dinner, shaken Julie's delicate hand, and been drawn into the situation that had dominated my mind ever since. Would my discoveries over the weekend give her lawyer enough to persuade a judge to let her go free on bail?

I hoped so. A week without their mother was an eternity for Camilla and Emma. And, though no one had asked my opinion, I didn't think her brother Duncan was fit to care for a slug, despite his bull-headed loyalty.

Duncan Donahue. The terror of the north. Julie had said it with such affection. More proof, as if the world needed it, that love is blind. This morning we'd be traveling past the spot where he'd driven me off the road. He'd done it once. Had he done it again last night? Had I noticed anything about the person who bumped me? Could it have been Calvin Bass? He had good reason to hate me for coming in at the last minute and spoiling his neat little scheme for running away with the girl and the goods. Had it been a shiny green Lexus? Or perhaps it was Eliot Ramsay, figuring that if he couldn't get the mortgages, he could at least get me. None of it made any sense. There was no reason for any of them to run me off the road. The person who was most upset with me was my mother, and she'd been too busy giving a party.

I tried to remember what I'd seen but it was hopeless. As I'd said to Dom last night, where the accident was concerned, my mind was a great big pudding. Last night I'd said it was a car but I wasn't sure. For all that I could recall now, it could have been a car, a truck, or a buffalo. There's nothing like a few good knocks on the head to scramble a memory. The mind doesn't like to remember bad times. It's as protective as a doting mother, storing those bad memories away out of sight to keep us from getting upset.

I shifted restlessly, trying to find a comfortable position. There was no comfortable position. I was too beat up and I was so tired of hurting. "Dom, what's the matter with me? Why do I keep getting myself into these messes?"

"You don't mean like what's happening with Andre?"

"No. I mean with Julie Bass . . . this business that happened last night, all the stuff that's happened in the last week. Other people don't do this kind of thing. Ask the average Joe on the street when was the last time someone held a gun to his head and he'll just give you a funny look."

"Is this rhetorical or do you want an answer?"

"Answer."

"You care more than a lot of people about making the world right. Making it safe. You're the big kid—the big sister—who makes sure the littler kids are okay."

"Can I get over it?"

"You mean, like having a cold? Take some Vitamin C and stop caring?"

"Like with Julie Bass. Let her handle her own problems. Or my mother can do it. This was all her idea!"

"Let me ask you this," he said. "Why didn't you just say no when your mother asked you to help?"

I considered his question. "At first, I did it because Mom asked me to. And because Julie reminded me of Carrie. . . ."

"And you couldn't help her," he suggested.

"You think I'm going to spend my whole life taking care of lame ducks because I couldn't help Carrie?"

"I don't know if this really is about Carrie," he said. "But I know some of it is about your mother."

"We had the worst fight last night. I don't expect she'll ever speak to me again."

"How do you feel about that?"

"You sound like someone's shrink, Florio."

"Sometimes cops are a lot like shrinks. Are you avoiding the question?"

"Watch out!" He swerved to avoid a cardboard box in the center of our lane. It bounced onto the hood, off the windshield, and tumbled away over the roof.

"Hey! It's okay. It's okay," he said, stroking my shoulder gently. I realized I was cowering against the door with my hands

over my face. Like the nurse said. I might have a hard time riding in cars for a while.

I dropped my hands and sat up. "So," he said, "this fight you
had with your mother. You want to talk about it?"

"Maybe later. Right now I'm choking on my heart. It's stuck
in my throat. I feel like I'm about to take the hardest exam of
my life and I'm not ready for it."

"You are," he said. I didn't know if he meant taking a hard
exam or ready for it and he didn't explain.

I was so tense I'd shatter if anything touched me hard. "Tell
me a story, Dom," I said.

"Once upon a time . . ." he began.

"In Italian."

"*Cara mia*," he began, and told me a story. A long, expressive story with different voices and waving of hands, explosive
sounds, soft passages. It was very soothing. I don't understand
a word of Italian.

We were more than two hours into the trip and well over
the speed limit, with the situation reported as unchanged, when
a blue light loomed up behind us. Dom slowed down and pulled
over, muttering under his breath, still in Italian. I didn't need
to know the language to understand what he was saying.

The trooper who appeared at the window was tight-faced
and frowning, with a torrent of rain rolling off his wide-
brimmed hat. "Sir, do you have any idea how fast you were
going?"

"I know exactly how fast I was going, Officer," Dom said.
"I'm trying to get someplace in a hurry."

"And where would that be?"

"Chelsea. That trooper the gunman is holding hostage?
Andre Lemieux?" Dom pointed at me. "This lady is in love with
him. She says she's got to get there. Under the circumstances,
I had to agree."

His stiffness relaxed a trifle. "Your license, sir?" Dom handed over the folder with his police ID, badge, and driver's license. "Detective Florio?" Dom nodded. "And the lady's name?"

"Thea Kozak," I said. "You could ask Roland Proffit. Or just about anyone he works with. Only please hurry." It took all my self-control, which I had very little of today, to keep from jumping out the window, grabbing the man, and shaking him until his teeth rattled.

"Wait here," he said, and walked back to his car.

We sat in the rain, the motor idling, the wipers clicking, the clock running. Both staring straight ahead. Neither of us speaking. Time and its possibilities lay heavy on us. Not that there would be anything we could do when we got there, but at least we'd be there. Dom was right. I couldn't get warm. Not with my blanket. Not with the heat on. Not by drinking coffee from the Thermos Rosie had given us. I wouldn't be warm again until I saw Andre.

The trooper appeared at the window and rapped on it sharply. He handed Dom's identification back. "Follow me," he said. We did the rest of the trip with a police escort, blazing along first on high-speed roads, past the scene of my earlier encounter with Dunk Donahue, on into Gardiner, and crossed the Kennebec, until we came to a barrier across the road. The cruiser stopped. We stopped behind it. The trooper and Dom got out. Dom opened the back door, pulled out a yellow raincoat, and shrugged it on, handing a second one to me.

The three of us approached the barrier. "What's happening?" our escort asked.

"Heard a couple shots a minute ago. I don't know if anything—"

I ducked around them and started to run. Running not like the battered wreck I was but like the track star I'd once been, the cherry-red Converse hightops Dom had bought me flashing as I charged through puddles and crunched over sand. I didn't care if seven hundred people were chasing me. I ran past other police cars, past knots of civilians, past the ambulance, still standing ready. I would have run right through the cops and into the house but someone tackled me, grabbed me, and pinned me to the ground. What the hell. I was getting used to lying in the mud.

It was like mud wrestling, as he tried to restrain me and I tried to get away and we would have fought to the death but someone pulled him off, grabbed me, and pulled me roughly to my feet. "Just what the hell is going on here? What do you think you're doing, young lady? If you're another of those goddamned reporters, trying to get yourself killed to get a better story . . ."

I looked into the angry white face of Andre's boss, Jack Leonard, peering out from under his hat. "Is he alive, Jack?" I said.

"Thea?"

Oblivious to the mud, I gripped his arms and leaned right into his face, violating his personal space. "Is he alive? Do you know if he's alive?" I asked again. I was probably yelling.

He shook his head. "We don't know."

"What were the shots?"

He shrugged. "Moreau just came to the window and let off a few. He's got to be getting tired. It's been six hours. . . ."

Dom came up to us and I introduced them, explaining that Dom had driven me up, and how kind the trooper had been to give us an escort. He was panting and puffing. "I didn't know you could run like that," he said.

"I can't," I said. "Fear gave wings to my feet."

A small, dark man in heavy gear came up and whispered in Jack's ear. "Excuse me," he said, nodding toward the house, "phone call. Stay back behind the van, please. I'll be back as soon as I can." He followed the dark man forward to join a group of men in similar gear clustered behind a smaller van. Someone handed him a phone. His lips moved, stopped, and he listened.

I leaned against the van, pulling my hood back so I could see Dom's face. "This would be a good time to be a smoker." He nodded. "What's all this supposed to accomplish? Andre could be dying in there. He could be—" I couldn't say it.

"It's always better to try and talk them out than to get people killed."

Jack came back, looking grimmer than ever. "He wants something to eat. Gave us his order. Two Quarter Pounders, two supersize fries, and two coffees."

"Sounds like food for two," I said hopefully. "If Andre can eat, he must be okay. . . ."

"Could be a ploy. Could be the scumbag . . . uh . . . Moreau . . . is just very hungry. He's had a long night." He said something to a trooper who whirled around, raced to a cruiser, and roared away, siren blasting, and something to another trooper who went over to the ambulance. Then he pulled out a handkerchief and held it out to me. "You've . . . uh . . . got some mud . . . on your . . . uh . . . face." My presence was definitely making his job harder. It wasn't just a cop thing anymore. Now they had family—if I counted as family—looking over their shoulders. "You two want to go sit in a car or something? Get out of the rain? No sense in the two of you freezing. We'll call you the minute anything happens."

I shook my head. "Dom might. It is cold out here." Dom declined the offer, too. His job was to take care of me and he was going to do it if it killed him. Which, given the weather, it might. Dom suffers in the cold. After a few minutes of fruitless conversation, we lapsed back into silence. There wasn't anything to do but wait, and talking didn't make it any easier.

Defying Jack's instructions, I peeked around the front of the van for a look at the house. We were parked several hundred feet down the road, with a few vehicles sitting closer. The house the gunman had invaded and taken refuge in was plain, desolate, and ugly, a square little box without ornament, lapped with dull brown siding, sitting in a patch of brown lawn, behind a muddy brown driveway. A few sections of white fence, once added for decoration, tipped drunkenly toward the road, while a one-winged wooden butterfly, that once-ubiquitous decoration of rural Maine homes, perched forlornly beside the door. Strips of torn plastic that had once sealed the door off for winter snapped angrily in the wind.

It was worse than a dentist's waiting room, where you hear the agonizing sound of the drill and breathe the hot, bitter scent of pulverized teeth. Here there was only silence and waiting. Busy lights and busy, purposeful people, going nowhere and doing nothing. There was nothing to be done until Moreau made a move or the sharpshooters could see him. It was too dark, too dim, too rainy, for them to see much. Moreau didn't have any lights on.

We lounged against the truck, leaning against each other for comfort, watching the distant house, the empty yard. Rain dripped off my slicker and soaked the backs of my borrowed jeans. I was wading inside my shoes every time I shifted my feet. I thought about Andre lying in there. Maybe in pain. Maybe scared. All alone. Nothing I could do to help him. "I feel so useless," I said.

"So does everyone else out here," Dom said.

"I'm a terrible person," I said.

"How so? You think this is all your fault? That's something else everyone here thinks. That if they'd just gotten a shot at the scumbag or gone in themselves . . ."

"That's not what I meant. I mean that I always think I'm trying to bring order to the world and all I'm really doing is screwing things up. Everything I get near, I screw it up. I only end up hurting myself and I'm not doing a shred of good for anyone else. Like this business with Julie and then last night with my mother and I wrecked my car and nearly wrecked myself and now I'm just standing around and there's nothing I can do here, either. . . ."

"Thea, what the hell are you talking about?"

"I don't know. After last night, I don't think I've got any family. I used to think I had such a happy family. I had such a happy life. I loved David and I loved my work and I had Mom and Dad and Carrie . . . and now it's all gone. David's dead and Carrie's dead and Suzanne's talking about moving. It's all collapsing around me. Everything I used to think was fixed and secure. All I've really got left is you and Rosie and Andre . . . and if anything happens to him, I just don't know if I can—"

He grabbed me and squeezed so hard I screamed. "Dammit, Thea. Don't even think like that!"

I put a hand over his. It was like ice. "And I'm making you stand out here in the rain and be miserable, just because I'm so stubborn. . . ."

"So let's go sit in a car, like the boss suggested, and while we warm up you can confess to Father Florio all the ways in which you've failed in this world . . . okay?"

"Can I start with last night?" He nodded. "It was my brother Michael's engagement party. She only called to invite me at the last minute. . . ."

"Takes advantage of you, does she?"

"I didn't say that. Anyway, just before dinner, she called me into the kitchen and started in on me again about not doing enough for Julie. . . ."

"Did she know what you had done?"

"No."

"No? You didn't tell her?"

"Tried to. She wouldn't listen. And last night, I just lost it. I couldn't be polite any more. I told her everything I'd done. All the time I'd spent. All the danger I'd been through . . . all the hurt . . ."

"You wanted her to acknowledge your efforts, to be proud

of you. To appreciate you." I nodded. "And did she?"

"She didn't pay any attention. I got mad when she wouldn't listen, when she diminished what I'd done. When she accused me of going out to play instead of helping, I yelled at her. Then they both—she and my dad—yelled at me for choosing the wrong time and place to bring it up . . . and I walked out. Just gave up and walked out of my brother's engagement party. Listen to me, Dom. I sound just like a little kid saying that parents are unfair."

"Yes, you do," he said, "and, yes, they are. Don't you realize that you can't please them, no matter what you do?"

"But I—I just can't seem to get anything right." I confessed all my sins and Dom listened well, occasionally telling me they weren't sins, and if it didn't make me feel any better, at least it didn't make me feel worse, and it passed the time.

An approaching siren signaled the return of the eager cop who'd gone for take-out. He came charging down the road, too fast for the rain-slicked tar, braked, skidded, and slid with a jolt into us. I heard the metallic thud, felt the car shudder behind my head from the impact, felt the whiplash snap of my neck, and for a minute I was plunged back into the swerving, skidding, crashing nightmare of the accident.

CHAPTER 28

I WAS BACK in my car, sitting stiffly in the seat, clenching the wheel, trying to stay in a lane while the rain made the lane markers disappear, my windshield a glare of lights off the rain the wipers couldn't keep up with. The steady tunk of the wipers, the skin-pricking scrape of sandy rubber across the glass were the background din as I scanned the side mirrors for careless mergers, behind me for tailgaters, in front of me for cars cutting in too soon, for cars going slowly in the fast lane.

Suddenly, it was there beside me, a low, blue car, hovering for a minute just at the edge of vision and then swinging violently toward me. A crash, the car backing off, another swing, another crash. I checked the mirrors, swung sharply to the right, and plunged helplessly out of control, reliving the uncontrollable skid across the next lane, the thud as another car struck mine, sawing helplessly at the wheel as mine turned, crashed over the guardrail, and began that long rolling journey down the hillside. I put my hands over my face, trying to blot out a vision that was inside my head.

"Thea! Thea! Are you all right?" Dom asked, his hands on

my shoulders as he stared at me with a worried face.

I stared at him, confused, not quite sure where I was, what he was doing in the car with me. "Hey, hey, come on. Talk to me. Are you all right?" he repeated slowly.

My neck hurt and my head was filled with cement. "I . . . the crash. It was happening again. What just . . . ?"

Someone jerked the door open and leaned in, staring at us. "I'm sorry," a voice said. "I didn't know there was anyone in the car. Are you guys okay?" A hand reached toward me and I took it, let him help me out of the car. A burst of rain slapped my face, reviving me a little. Reminded me I wasn't at the crash scene. I looked around for Dom.

He was right beside me, glaring at the trooper who'd helped me out, who held McDonald's bags in his free hand. "Drive much?" he muttered. The trooper ducked his head apologetically and turned away without answering, carrying the food to Jack Leonard. "You don't look good," he told me.

"I was in the accident again. I remembered. It was a car," I said. "Last night. You can tell Crimmins. It was a car. A car. A blue car. A low, blue car." I touched my head, which was still swimming, and closed my eyes.

"Good girl!" he said, wrapping me in a bear hug. "I knew you could do it."

I pressed my cheek against the cold, wet rubber of his raincoat, happy to have finally done something right. I didn't feel like I'd done anything right. "But I was expecting a black van," I whispered. "I don't know who drives a blue car." I leaned against him, feeling useless. My brain might have been surgically removed. I simply couldn't think. "My father drives a blue car."

"It will come to you," he said gently. "And it wasn't your father."

I could see Jack, surrounded by a cluster of troopers, shaking his head, talking loudly, making angry gestures with his hands. In one hand he held the bag of food. "I wonder what's going on," I said. "I'm going to see." I took off before Dom could stop me, and approached the group. They were arguing about who would deliver the food.

Jack's searching eyes found me and locked on. "I told you to stay in the car," he said.

"It's not a safe place to be," I told him with something approaching a giggle. "Gets run into." I was bizarrely light-headed, as though the jolting and snapping of my neck had shaken all sensible thought out of my head and disconnected the synapses.

"Oh, Jesus, look," Dom said. We all looked. Moreau was standing in the door, holding an elderly woman before him. I heard the sharpshooter behind me suck in his breath as he searched for a shot that wouldn't hurt the woman. The old lady was screaming and struggling and begging to be freed.

"Shit!" Jack said. "Where'd she come from? That old man said there was no one else inside. No one else! She must have been his wife or his sister or something and the old fool just plain forgot she existed. Happy enough to get out of there and save his own hide and not a thought for anyone else. Not just him. His neighbors . . ."

The bags of food were still dangling from his waving hand. Without thinking what I was doing—I was too woozy to think clearly about anything—I dropped my hood, letting my hair blow free so Moreau could see I wasn't just another cop in a yellow raincoat, grabbed the food from Jack's hand, and took off across the field. I'd waited long enough. I was going to find out if Andre was alive.

"Thea, don't you dare!" Jack yelled. "I can't let you . . . you come back here . . . it's too dangerous. You don't understand." I never even looked back, just kept heading toward the old lady and the man with the gun.

The damp air brought Dom's voice, a fragment: ". . . have told you that she's a bit headstrong. . . ."

Headstrong. A nice solid word. Not pejorative. A bit complimentary, even. Not a bad sendoff for a journey from which I might not be returning. "Thank you, Dom," I whispered.

Determined or not, the distance to the door seemed eternal. Every step jolted my aching head, so that it was an act of will to keep going. I wanted to fall over, close my eyes, and sleep. I knew that at any second I might be shot, but I had been walking toward that gun—a gun that I knew was loaded—ever since I'd heard the news this morning. I was almost there.

I stopped about fifteen feet away and held out the bags. Dizzy. Disoriented. Scared stiff. "You ordered takeout?" The voice, I suppose it was mine, sounded perky and cheerful.

"Come here." His voice had the harsh grate of stone against stone. It sent a shiver singing down my spine. I took a few steps forward. Slowly now. Baby steps. That was all my trembling legs allowed. Trembling legs. Trembling arms. Trembling heart. I had to remind myself to breathe. "Stop!" he ordered. I stopped. "Take off the raincoat and drop it on the ground." Very slowly and carefully, with hands that were shaking violently, I took off the coat, one sleeve at time, and laid it on the ground. When I bent down, my head swam. "Good girl."

I peered at him through the rain, everything slightly blurry like an out-of-focus camera. Not a tall man, but broad, with massive arms and a big round head, balding on top, with curly tufts of gray-yellow hair. Eyes recessed under thick eyebrows like yellow caterpillars crawling on his forehead. I couldn't see their color, only an impression of wild paleness peering at me over the old lady's head. The woman's face was gray and I could hear the ugly rasp of her frightened breathing from where I stood.

"You've got to . . ." I searched for words but I was brain-dead. ". . . let her go," I said finally. "Listen . . . She'll die if you don't."

"Shut up! I give the orders around here," he yelled. He waved the gun at me. "Take off the rest of those clothes. Everything but the underwear." I didn't move. "Do it! Now! An' I better not be seein' no gun on you." A burst of gunfire kicked up the ground around my feet.

I held out the bags. "What shall I do with these?"

"Set 'em on the ground. And hurry up. You try an' run back, I'll shoot her an' then I'll shoot you."

The things we do for love, I thought giddily, fumbling with the heavy sweater, performing my first, and hopefully last, striptease before every major network and nearly every trooper in the state of Maine. I could sell my story to "COPS" and retire for life. I'd have to. I'd never be able to show my face, or anything else, anywhere again, except when I went on "Oprah" to talk about how it felt to strip at gunpoint. I pulled off Rosie's warm blue sweater and dropped it on the raincoat.

Cold, cold rain on my cold, cold skin. Once again, bending over made me dizzy. Ever since the car had run into us, there had been something very wrong with my head. I undid the belt—fumbling awkwardly, as if it were the first belt I'd ever undone. It seemed to take an age. I was very conscious of Moreau's gun pointing at me, of his watching eyes—and then suddenly the pants were down around my ankles and the cold rain falling on my legs. I lifted one distant, heavy foot, shook one leg free, then the other, and stood defiantly in my underwear and cherry-red sneakers.

I took a step toward the bags. Moreau said something but his words were lost in the roaring in my head. I thought I heard the word food. I took a step toward it, stumbled. Saw him jerk the gun up. A firecracker exploded behind me. The old woman was falling and I couldn't help her because the ground was rushing up to meet me. It smacked me, hard. I smelled earth and grass as I fell into a squirming darkness as noisy as the Fourth of July.

The flashes behind my lids were not fireworks. I opened them to find a reporter taking my picture. I'd been a reporter. I knew what bottom-dwelling scum they were. He'd get the most salacious picture he could and he'd use it. Close-ups of me in my muddy underwear on the front pages of every paper he could sell it to. Not if I could help it. I tried to push myself up, to get at him, to grab the camera, but it was hopeless. Whatever had made me topple over in the first place kept me down and dizzy now.

Beside me, a voice bellowed, "Hey!" followed by scuffling feet, a torrent of bad language, and something dropped on the ground near my head. I was Chicken Little and the sky was falling. I opened my eyes. A camera. Then a foot stomping on the camera. A furious voice yelled, "What the hell! You can't do that!"

Then a voice I recognized. Roland Proffit. "Sorry, sir. Accident. Now, if you could just step back. . . ."

I smiled. Despite the roaring confusion in my head, I understood this. I was among friends; he wasn't. Andre's colleagues understood that he wouldn't want these pictures printed. The camera was mauled by a horde of milling feet, reduced to a flattened mass of parts, the long spiral of film curled up like a piece of fallen fly tape.

Someone put an arm around me. Help me sit up. Draped a coat around my shoulders. I was drained and weary and inert, desperate to know what had happened, too confused to ask. Through the milling legs I caught a glimpse of a figure on the ground, a tuft of graying yellow hair. Moreau. No sign of Andre. I should get dressed. There were people around. It was what he would want me to do. Andre was a very private person. He might never forgive me for this. A wave of dizziness came, shook me, and passed, leaving me weak and confused. I wanted to find him. To see if he was still alive.

Something dropped into my lap. Soft and soggy. And cold. My clothes. I looked up, slowly and carefully, humoring my brain's tendency to slosh, and saw Jack Leonard glaring down at me. "Get dressed," he growled, and turned away.

"Jack. Wait! Andre . . . is . . . he . . . ?"

"Alive," he allowed. "On his way to the hospital. Get dressed, for heaven's sake. Aren't you embarrassed?" He hurried away.

Okay, okay. So I'd get dressed. Did the big lunk think I was enjoying this? It wasn't like I wanted to be undressed or anything in the middle of a cold wet field before dozens of people. If I'd planned on it, I would have worn something a bit more elegant. I had some navy-blue lace that would have been stunning with livid red bruises and pale blue skin. I giggled. Jack just didn't get it, did he? I would have done a heck of a lot more than this if I thought it would help save Andre. Maybe Jack had never loved someone. Maybe image was all that mattered.

I picked up the bundle of clothes and tried to sort them out. My hands couldn't have been more inept if I was wearing boxing gloves. I couldn't separate the top from the pants, couldn't find sleeves or legs. Remembered Moreau staring at me, the harsh voice and eerie eyes. I was suddenly light-headed and dizzy and sure I was going to be sick. And so cold. I wrapped my arms around myself and hugged, grateful for the coat. Was it Proffit's?

"You look like you could use a hand," Dom said, squatting down beside me.

"Some guardian angel you are," I said. "Where have you been?"

"Checking on Andre."

"And?"

"It ain't pretty, princess, but I've seen worse. And he's a tough guy."

"Come on," I said, grabbing his arm. "We've got to get to the hospital."

"Like that?"

"Like what?"

"Your clothes," he said. "They're a bit damp, but you might want to put 'em on."

"Please. If you'd help me. . . ."

"I am at your service." I stood up, took off Proffit's coat, and let Dom drop the sweater over my head. It smelled of Rosie's perfume. Then, with one hand on his shoulder, I stepped into the pants. From the knees down they were cold and wet; the rest was just damp. I rested against Dom's chest while I fastened the belt. I still felt sick and dizzy, but it would just have to wait. There were places to go and people to see.

"Well, shall we go, then?" Jack Leonard said, reappearing suddenly. Like me, his place was at the hospital. Jack and I weren't friends. Never would be. I wasn't his kind of woman and he wasn't my third favorite cop. But he was a good man, and fair, and right now just as worried about Andre as I was. "You want to bring your own car or ride with me?"

"I'll drive her," Dom said.

"Follow me, then," Jack said. "It'll be faster."

Dom helped me put Proffit's jacket back on and we followed Jack back down the road to the cars. It was still daylight, which surprised me. It had been a very long day. I wouldn't have been surprised to find weeks had passed.

Dom kept one arm firmly around me and I needed it. I was like a cartoon character with great long rubber legs. Jack waited impatiently by the cars for us to catch up, standing with arms folded while I stopped and threw up in the grass. I was surprised when he stepped forward and held out his handkerchief, an unexpected kindness that shook my tenuous hold on control.

"Thea," he said, "You're a brave girl. If anything happens to . . . if Andre . . . I just want you to know . . ."

"Please, Jack. Not now. Let's wait and see what happens. . . ."

"Right. See you at the hospital." He folded his lean frame into the car and took off. So much for following him.

Dom and I staggered down the road to his car, where he opened my door, tucked my blanket around me, and we set off.

"I'm sorry," I said. "I didn't mean to . . . I've put you through a lot today, Dom. Thanks for being here for me. I couldn't have done it without you."

Dom shook his head. "You sure don't make it easy on a guy, Thea. Leonard nearly died of apoplexy when you grabbed that food and took off. Earlier, you know, you were asking me what's wrong with you? Well, I think I've figured it out. You've never outgrown that adolescent belief that you're immortal. Everybody else, see, they reach a point where they're more concerned with saving their own skins. They don't want to take chances. You don't even stop to think about the danger."

"That bad, huh?"

"Not very sensible."

"So I'm immature as well as headstrong. If it had been Rosie in there?"

"Then everything I just said is bullshit. I would have taken the house down. . . ."

"Whatever you all may think, Dom, I didn't mean to do that. I wasn't trying to be heroic or anything. I was feeling awfully dizzy and confused and I couldn't stand their dithering. All the delay. Not with Andre in there. Something came over me. . . ."

"That's the point I was trying to make," he said. "Those things don't come over other people."

"Can you stop the car? I'm feeling sick again," I interrupted.

"We'll be at the hospital in a few—"

"It's your car, Florio." He stopped. Cops who are completely sanguine about people bleeding in their cars will stop on a dime if the person threatens to be sick. I'd be the same way myself, with my own car. When I was hollow all the way to my toes, I wiped my sweating face with Jack's handkerchief and got back in the car. "I forgot to call my insurance company about the accident," I said. "And my credit card companies. Got to get a new driver's license. . . ."

"You'll roast in hell for sure. Look, Thea . . . you said you've been feeling dizzy ever since we got rear-ended?"

"Uh-huh."

"And now you're sick to your stomach?"

"Very."

"Sometimes, when a person has a concussion, the effects are delayed. After what you've been through, it might be a good idea to get yourself checked out."

"Dominic, I was checked out last night. It's no big deal. Don't you start fussing over me, too. Turn at that light up there. Hospital's down the hill. Oh, cripes. I am so sick. I feel like I've been poisoned. What were all you guys thinking back there when . . . when I . . . when he made me take my clothes off?" I didn't want to ask but I had to know.

"The general consensus was that Andre Lemieux is a pretty lucky guy. And one idiot who thought you were too thin. Silly twit. Uncle Dom thinks you're just perfect."

One of the things I cherish about Dom is his ability to appreciate me as a woman without a touch of the salacious. He's seen me in my underwear more times than any man except Andre and David, and it's always the same. His face says I'm am attractive woman and he doesn't need to prove it somehow. When we were working on Helene Streeter's murder, people who saw us having coffee together made a point of calling Rosie to tell her about it. Rosie's response was priceless—she said she didn't care where he whetted his appetite as long as he took his meals at home. Dom Florio was a guy who would always go home for dinner.

"About the undressing," he said. "Don't feel bad. Gunman once did that to me. And I don't look half as good as you."

"Have I told you lately that I loved you?"

He shook his head. "Not for a few hours. You've been distracted." He pulled up behind Jack's car and stopped. "Here we are. Why don't you scoot in and I'll go park the car."

I got out. Doubled over. Threw up again, just barely missing my shoes, and staggered into the emergency room. I was trying to ask about Andre when someone collared me and dragged me into a curtained cubicle. Jack Leonard followed me in. "I heard you hit your head when the car got banged," he said.

"Maybe that accounts for my bizarre behavior," I suggested. There was a bed in the room and suddenly I was desperate to be lying down. I even let Jack help me. The mattress and pillow felt good. Now all I needed was a blanket. "Where's Andre?"

"They're taking him upstairs to surgery," he said. "It will be awhile before we know anything."

I sat up. "Upstairs where?" I asked, ready to jump off the table.

"Hold on," he said, grabbing my arm and pressing me back down. "You're not going anywhere until these guys have checked you out."

"I didn't think there was anyone left in the state who hadn't checked me out."

He rolled his eyes and sighed. "It was a sight," he said finally. "Please. . . ." It sounded like a word he didn't use very often. "Just let 'em take a look at you. I've got enough to worry about."

"You and me both," I said. His plea was so like Andre's "put a cork in it, Thea and try to cooperate," that I shut up and stayed put.

"Okay. I'll stay. But promise you'll let me know if anything . . ."

"Scout's honor," he said. There was a tremble in his voice. We both knew that any news that came at this point would be bad news. He squeezed my hand and left.

Dom came in, and assorted medical folks who poked and prodded and flashed lights in my eyes, clucked and fussed over all my livid bruises, and declared me genuinely concussed. So what was new? They gave me a vile elixir to settle my stomach and left me to rest.

Alone at last, weak and shaky as a newborn kitten, I thought about Andre. In a way, our relationship had begun with my being sick. Sick to my soul at the shocking pictures he showed me of my sister Carrie's body. Would it end the same way?

CHAPTER 29

IN A MINUTE, I would get up and find Andre. Attach myself to him like a limpet and never let go. First I had to rest. Had to let my stomach settle and my sloshing head, too. I closed my eyes and nestled into the soft pillow, the warmth of the blankets, relieved of the effort to stay upright, to be alert, to fend people off. I dozed and dreamed. I was on a racetrack, whizzing through the corners, Nick's cocky voice, half amused, half cynical, barking instructions in my ear.

Then, the way a projector that's been out of focus suddenly projects with startling clarity, I was looking at Tony Piretti and the pieces of the puzzle began to fall into place. My mind works like that. I'll be totally immersed in one thing and suddenly instead I'll be thinking with perfect clarity about another. I forced myself to relax and let the pictures come. I was having lunch at the racetrack, still flushed with the exhilaration of driving, pulling pictures out of my purse. Piretti sifting through them and holding out a picture of Dr. Durren. "Who's this?" he said.

"Doctor at the local hospital. Thomas Durren."

"Looks like a guy I used to race with years ago," he said. "But he was called Chuck Durren. A real wild man."

A click. The slide changes. I'm walking across the parking lot to meet Durren, sitting in his fancy *blue* car.

A click. In the emergency room. I'm thumbing through a copy of *Road and Track*, waiting for Dr. Durren. A copy of *Road and Track* with an address label reading: Dr. Thomas C. Durren. C for Charles? Chuck?

A click. Dr. Durren, holding the same magazine, staring after me, a strange look on his face.

Click. I'm back in the fancy blue car and we're talking. Durren says, "I disliked the man intensely. For what he did to her. I admit that. Still, it was a horrible way to die. To have something go wrong with the suspension and crash and burn like that. . . ."

And one last click. I'm talking with Andre. I ask him what he learned from the Connecticut police about the cause of the accident. "Nothing," he says. "They won't release any details. Not even to me." And there had been nothing in the papers. I took a sharp breath and sat up. Suddenly. My head swam but my thought was clear. "So how did he know it was the suspension?" I asked an empty room.

Click. I'm at the engagement party, trying to be polite, only half listening to Sonia's batty cousin and her comments about how odd it was to have some guy working on his car out in the street. In suit pants and shoes. She was wrong. What was odd was not that he was working on *his* car but that he was working on *my* car.

I'd had all the information and never seen it at all. But Durren thought I had because of that stupid magazine. And because he'd overheard the nurse telling me he wasn't at the hospital on Saturday evening. Something I'd paid no attention to at all because my mind had been on other things. And yet, if Durren had had his way, I'd be toast. An awful shudder went through me, thinking about what might have been.

Click as I picked up the phone. Click. Click. Click. The mellow tones as my long-distance carrier came on and processed the call. Click as the phone was answered, the directory assistance operator gave me the number and added that I could automatically dial it for just a little more money. I pressed a button, let the circuits whir, and got Julie's attorney on the phone. Told him where I was. Reminded him who I was. Told him what I knew. Everything. Told him to call the police. Listened impatiently to a few confused questions. Told him I didn't have time for Q and A, just do it. Make them find that car before Durren repaints it. Click. I hung up. I didn't even bother to say good-bye. I had to get to Andre.

But it wasn't enough. I had to tell the police myself. Julie's attorney wasn't going to be the most credible source, though he might be the most confused. Only I didn't know whom to tell. My father would know. I picked up the phone again. Dialed. Heard the resonant bong of the chimes. Punched in the number. Dom came in quietly, looked at my face, and knew enough not to speak to me. He sat down on the edge of the bed and waited, listening.

My stomach was dancing again, only this time not from a head injury but from a heart injury. I could still see Dad's furious face across the kitchen. I got through the formalities and his secretary put me through. His "Yes, Thea?" was surprised, icy, distant.

I almost hung up. The phone was shaking in my hand. But this was business. Something I had to do. I swallowed hard and forced myself to speak. "Dad, I know who did it. I know who killed Jon Bass. Who should I talk to . . . at the police station, I mean?" I spoke in a voice that was not my own.

"Are you all right, Thea?" he asked, still cold, slightly surprised.

"No."

"Where are you?"

"Kennebec Valley Medical Center."

"A hospital? What's happened?"

"I don't want to talk about it. Just give me the name. . . ."

"Do you want me to come there?"

"No. Don't come. I don't need you." I could be as cold as he could.

"Now then," he said brusquely, stung by my own coldness, "what's this about knowing who killed . . . uh . . . Jon Bass?"

"Just what I said. I know who did it. Look, I haven't got time to chat. Tell me the name of the cop, if you know it." I was losing control; wondering if I'd made a mistake calling him at all. After last night, I didn't feel I had anything to say to him. I certainly wasn't going to waste time on the phone with him while Andre might be dying.

"Thea, you aren't making any sense," he said. "Now calm down and tell me what you're doing there."

I took a deep breath, feeling like I might cry. Wanting to slam down the phone, needing him to listen instead of talk, to give me information instead of asking questions. Why the hell couldn't they ever just believe me? Why did I always have to jump through hoops just to get heard? Dom put an arm around me and sat me down on the bed, and he kept the arm there. I leaned back against him gratefully.

"I'm perfectly calm," I said. "And how do I know who killed Jon Bass?" The minute I started telling it, I wasn't perfectly calm. My nice coherent mind began to disintegrate again. "I'm . . . he tried to kill me . . . he . . . they . . . everyone's tried to kill me but I guess you just can't keep a good woman down, Dad. I'm okay. Not great, but okay. I'm sorry I can't chat but I've got to go see about Andre. Just tell me who to call. . . ."

"Larry Dixon. Lieutenant Larry Dixon. He's the local guy who's handling it. What's the matter with Andre?"

"He's been shot." I could barely say the words. I couldn't talk any more. I couldn't call Dixon. I was out of time. Andre might die while I was still trying to explain this. "Look, could you call Dixon? Tell him it was Thomas Durren. He used to race cars. Tell him that Durren drove me off the road last night on 128. There will be a report somewhere. The state police, I suppose. . . ." I couldn't remember who I'd talked to, or refused to talk to, at the hospital.

"You're not making any sense, Theadora," he repeated. "Slow down and take this step by step. What makes you think it was Durren?"

"I'm making perfect sense. You're not listening. And I don't think. I know. I saw him trying to set my car on fire." Dom's arm tightened around me, giving me the support I needed to spit out the last of my message. "Tell them to look for paint on my car. Blue Porsche paint. If they've got questions, they can call me here. Kennebec Valley Medical Center. That's right. In Maine. Augusta. Tell Mom I did my best. If this doesn't get Julie out, there's nothing more I can do."

"Thea, wait!" There was a softening in his voice, and regret. "We need to talk. You and I . . . your mother . . . I . . . she . . . we . . . didn't mean . . ."

"Not now." He was still talking when I dropped the phone and closed my eyes, seeing them both yesterday in the kitchen, so determined that manners and control would prevail over love and truth. Yes, in time we would talk. Of course we would talk. We all had a lot to say. But this was not the time. Not while my wounds were still so fresh and I had other, more urgent things on my mind. Like poor Julie Bass. And Andre.

"I'm going to go scout around for news and something to eat," Dom said. "You want anything?"

The idea of food was awful but I was thirsty. "Ginger ale?"

He leaned down and kissed me on the forehead like a beloved daughter. "Don't let the bastards wear you down, princess. You done good. Rosie sends her love and says to tell you she's fretting because she isn't here to look after us."

"I could use a little Rosie right now."

"Couldn't we all? Look, I know this is hard for you to believe right now, but I've got good cop's instincts, right?" I nodded. "And I think everything's gonna be okay."

"Thanks, Dom."

He turned to leave, paused, and turned back. "So you figured out who did it, eh? Was it because of the car?"

I nodded. "The bastard. How could he let her go to prison like that, for a crime he committed, if he loved her?"

Dom shrugged. "I hate to say it, but nothing surprises me anymore. Every time I think I've seen the basest form of human nature, something worse comes along. That's why I like to hang out with the good guys. Like you. Get some rest, Thea. I'll keep you informed."

I lay back in bed, seething. Thinking about Thomas Durren, about what kind of love—can it even be called love?—lets the loved one be wrenched from her children and sent to jail. His cooperation didn't make any sense, either. What had he been hoping I would discover? Was he hoping to be found out? Was it all just a smoke screen? Was he just keeping tabs on what I knew, so he'd know whether he should be worried? Or maybe Julie didn't matter and all that mattered was getting at Cal. Maybe it was a guy thing, a struggle for control. Two possessive control freaks with Julie in the middle.

Perhaps, to view it in a kinder light, he'd never considered the possibility of Julie being arrested and was left with no idea what to do. It's an odd fact about criminals, obscured by the glitz and pace of TV and movies, that they usually haven't thought things through. He hadn't struck me as the decisive type. But what did I know, I who had declared so decisively that he wasn't the murderer. I didn't understand. Maybe I never would.

At least I was pretty sure Julie wouldn't go back to Cal. As for the rest, I didn't care, as long as they caught Durren. It was up to the police to decide who else, in the whole nasty mess, they wanted to go after. I was pretty sure Eliot Ramsay had hired the thugs, though they'd probably never be able to prove it. Still, once the feds were done with Cal and Ramsay and the bank and the missing mortgage applications, their careers would both be destroyed. I might want to see them both publicly hung up and flayed, but our system, our snail's-pace, inadequate system of justice, doesn't allow for stocks, ducking stools, the lash, or other public displays of disapproval.

Then there was Duncan Donahue. I didn't know what to do about him. My earlier plea for clemency had been for Julie, to protect her from any further distress while she was locked up helplessly in jail. To provide a familiar refuge for her children. Once she was free, as I was sure she would be in a matter of hours, I didn't need to protect her any more. Andre and Roland Proffit were right. I wasn't doing anyone any favors by allowing someone so violent and unbalanced to be walking about. Maybe I'd rethink that one, if I still could.

I shook my head wearily. It was a sordid, complicated mess and I was glad to be done with it. Maybe tomorrow I'd feel differently. Right now I didn't care. It would have been easy to beat up on myself, second-guess all the decisions I'd made, and try to figure out if I could have known about Durren sooner. But, as always, I had to prioritize my tasks. It wasn't my problem anymore. I'd done what I could to help Julie. No one, not even my mother, could ask for more.

Now I had more pressing things to think about. Like my future with Andre. "Come live with me and be my love," he'd said. I'd said I'd think about it, but would I get the chance? Sighing at the state of the world, I got out of bed, ignoring my shaking limbs and uncertain head, and shuffled off to find him.

I knew I was in the right place when I found a room full of troopers sitting, standing, and milling about, strangely silent ex-

cept for occasional shoulder pats and murmurs. A couple reporters spotted me, surged forward, and were blocked by a wall
of troopers. Roland Proffit offered me his arm and I was not too
proud to take it. Andre's parents were there, holding hands, and
his sister, Aimee, hugely pregnant with her fifth child. Some
aunts, uncles, cousins. Andre's landlady, eyes and nose red, knit-
ting as if his life depended on it. A whole room full of people
holding their breath. All of their eyes were on the door through
which the doctor would come.

Jack was there, sitting with his long legs stretched halfway
across the room, staring at his shoes. He looked up when I came
in and shook his head. "No news," he said. "He's still in surgery.
They'll let us know as soon as they're done. . . . How are you?"

"I've felt worse."

He didn't look like he believed me. "You shouldn't be out
of bed," he said.

"I couldn't stay away," I said, and he didn't argue. The man
beside him got up to give me his seat. I shuffled over to it and
sat down, wishing I could have brought my bed with me. All the
rest had done was make me tired. I could barely remain upright
but I couldn't have stayed downstairs. "What do they think?"

Jack's face was grim. "I won't lie to you," he said. "It doesn't
look good." I stared down at my lap, the faded blue dissolving
in a mosaic of tears. I almost wished he had lied. I'd lived in fear
of this moment for so long. Used it as a shield to keep from loving. He patted my knee. "I'm sorry I don't have better news. Can
I get you a coffee or something . . . ?" He stopped abruptly, remembering how sick I'd been. "Guess that wouldn't be so good,
huh? Something else?"

"Soda?"

"You've got it." He sent a trooper to get it. "Where's that
guy Florio?"

"Getting something to eat, I think." We sat in silence for a
while. A long while. Whenever the door opened, we'd lean for-

ward, sinking back when it turned out to be nothing. In the harsh fluorescent light we looked like refugees, our faces etched with pain and anxiety and the weariness of waiting for uncertain news. Many of the people there had been out at the hostage site, and the room smelled of damp clothes and the sweat of old fear.

I thought about Andre. Times we'd spent together. Things we'd said. I thought about the rumble of his voice when I laid my head on his chest, the sound of his voice when he read aloud, the way he liked to tease. I thought of presents he'd given me, special one-of-a-kind things that were perfect, though I never would have picked them for myself. The meal he cooked for Valentine's Day, when I was so sick and miserable. Heard his voice again, in my mind. "I want you to live with me . . . I want to come to bed every night knowing I can have you beside me like this. Not just sometimes. All the time. I want to be able to throw a leg over you and feel your skin. I want to curl up like spoons when it's cold. It feels safe. It feels real. It feels good."

I didn't have a tissue. My sleeves were wet and muddy. I let the tears run down my face and drip onto my lap. I cursed my infernal caution, my defenses, my hesitation, my fear of commitment. Would I even get a chance to say yes?

"You know I didn't want you to do that," Jack said abruptly. "Delivering the food. It was no job for a civilian. . . ." There was a long pause while he debated what to say. "But if he lives—" He choked and pushed on. "—it's probably because of you. Because you distracted Moreau and we were able to get off those shots. He was running out of time."

I put my hand over his. It hadn't been an easy concession. "Thank you, Jack. I was never more scared in my life." I tapped my forehead gently. "My brain wasn't working, you see. All I could think of was that we had to do something. That it had gone on too long. Then I got out there and realized what a stupid thing I was doing, but there was no turning back. Not with him pointing that gun at me."

"It wasn't bright," he said, "but it was brave."

Dominic Florio, my second favorite cop and today my Rock of Gibraltar, came in carrying food for himself and a ginger ale for me. I grabbed it out of his hand and sucked greedily on the straw. "They're all in an uproar downstairs because you got out of bed," he reported. "They were planning to seize you bodily and carry you back. I think I've convinced them it's a waste of time. Oh, and you had a phone call from the Grantham police. I said you couldn't be disturbed. Durren's dead. Ran his car into a bridge, going about ninety. He left a note, saying he acted alone. Telling Julie he never dreamed they'd suspect her. He apologized to her . . ."

"Fat lot of good that'll do her," I muttered. "She sure could pick 'em, couldn't she?"

". . . and to you."

"I wonder why he did it. He was such a cold fish. He didn't seem like the type for drama, for emotional endings."

"Maybe he couldn't stand failure."

"Failure?"

"Humiliation? He was a complete bust as a murderer. He tried to kill Cal Bass, and failed, and then he tried to kill you and failed again." He started to unwrap a sandwich. "Sure you don't want some of this?"

I made a face. "Very sure. How could anyone eat at a time like this?"

"You learn," he said.

"I hope I never have to."

The door opened and a tired-looking man in surgical green came in, surveyed the room, and settled on me and Jack and Andre's parents. "Thea Kozak? Lieutenant Leonard? Mr. and Mrs. Lemieux?" Jack nodded. They nodded. A dozen pairs of eyes were fixed on the doctor's face. Well-trained eyes, trying to read his message before he spoke.

I took a deep breath. Held it. Rose slowly to my feet, my eyes glued to his face. Everyone else rose, too, as if we were in church. Dom reached out and took my hand.

"It's been touch and go in there," he said. No one breathed. No one moved. No one made a sound. The doctor's eyes were on Jack, on the ramrod-stiff posture, on the set and anxious face. "We'll know better in a few hours, sir, but I think your boy is going to make it."

Everyone exhaled. Dom, Jack, and I shared a tight, silent embrace, dried our tears, and settled in for the long wait ahead. Sometimes the good guys win. Our boy was going to make it.

Follow Thea to Hawaii
in Kate Flora's new novel,

DEATH IN PARADISE

I was in Hawaii. The double doors opening to a lanai, the sway-
ing palm trees, the inviting blue water all confirmed it. So did the
airy tropical décor. I knew for certain that I had gotten on a plane
in Boston, flown to Honolulu and changed for a plane in Maui.
So why the heck was I crawling around on my hands and knees
searching for a dropped earring when it wasn't yet six A.M.,
already late for my first meeting of the day? Why wasn't I walking on the beach? Because I was a grown-up, a working girl, and
a slave of duty.

Someone banged on the door. The banging increased. I limped
to the door and jerked it open. It wasn't Martina Pullman, conference director, head of the National Association of Girls' Schools
and wicked witch extraordinaire, but her pallid acolyte Rory
Altschuler. "Something's wrong. I was supposed to have a pre-
meeting meeting with Martina at 5:30. She didn't show."

"Maybe she overslept. She did have a lot to drink last night." I
stepped back into the room. "Come on in. We'll call her."

"I did that. Three times. She isn't answering. I have a bad feeling about this. Maybe her phone isn't working. I'm going to go
up and knock on her door." Rory marched to the door of my
room, where she hesitated. "Aren't you coming?"

We drew up outside Martina's door. I, having the bigger fist
and the elevated title, pounded vigorously, waited, and pounded
again. I considered the outrageous yet pleasing possibility that
the other Board members had had her kidnapped so we could
proceed with the conference in peace. Rory plucked my arm with
nervous fingers. "Something awful has happened...."

I rolled my eyes. "You've been watching too much television.
Come on. We'll go get the key." We went down to the front desk

and explained our dilemma. We were joined by the assistant manager, who needed the story repeated. He, in turn, summoned Security, and finally the four of us marched back to the elevator and rose skyward to Martina's room.

This time it was the assistant manager who raised his fist and knocked. When the expected result didn't occur, he and the security man consulted briefly and then unlocked the door. The manager gestured for me to enter. "Perhaps, as you're her colleague, it would be best…"

I stepped past him and into the room, calling, "Martina? It's Thea…" Martina, being the VIP, had a suite. A big, beautiful sitting room. A table set for two. Champagne in a bucket. Glasses. A plate of soggy caviar and toast. All untouched. I went into the bedroom, calling Martina's name again.

I stopped as suddenly as if I'd run into an invisible screen. I tried to block Rory's way but she wriggled past me, took one look, gave a blood-curdling scream, and then, still screaming, turned and ran from the room. I took another step into the room, drawn reluctantly toward the figure on the bed. Martina Pullman was one of those tall, handsome, fashionably thin women who loved elegant clothes and wore them well. The outfit she had on would, under other circumstances, have been laughable. Under these circumstances, it was jarring. Embarrassing. Horrible. She lay on her back across the bed in a scarlet lace bustier, red thong panties, and lacy red garter belt. Her long, unnaturally dark hair, hair that was usually confined in a severe chignon, spread out around her head, as though she awaited a lover. The garter belt still held up one sheer black stocking, that foot still sported a scarlet spike-heeled shoe. The other shoe was on the floor beside the bed; the other stocking was knotted tightly around her neck. Her eyes were open, protuberant and staring from a grotesquely purple face.

In my shock, the absurd, awful thought raced through my head that the advice our mothers gave us about clean underwear ought to be expanded to include not wearing anything we wouldn't want to be caught dead in….